blue
rider
press

HOW TO
SURVIVE
A SUMMER

∎

BLUE RIDER PRESS

NEW YORK

HOW TO
SURVIVE
A SUMMER

■

NICK WHITE

blue
rider
press

An imprint of Penguin Random House LLC
375 Hudson Street
New York, New York 10014

Library of Congress Cataloging-in-Publication Data

Names: White, Nick, [date-] author.
Title: How to survive a summer : a novel / Nick White.
Description: New York, New York : Blue Rider Press, 2017. | Includes
bibliographical references and index.
Identifiers: LCCN 2016058812 (print) | LCCN 2017017206 (ebook) |
ISBN 9780399573699 (epub) | ISBN 9780399573682 (hardback)
Subjects: LCSH: Graduate teaching assistants—Fiction. | Gay
teenagers—Fiction. | Camps—Fiction. | Psychic trauma—Fiction. |
Mississippi—Fiction. | Psychological fiction. | BISAC: FICTION /
Literary. | FICTION / Gay. | FICTION / Coming of Age.
Classification: LCC PS3623.H578726 (ebook) |
LCC PS3623.H578726 H69 2017 (print) | DDC 813/.6—dc23
LC record available at https://lccn.loc.gov/2016058812
p.   cm.

Printed in the United States of America
1   3   5   7   9   10   8   6   4   2

Book design by Gretchen Achilles

To my parents, for their love and support.

*Sometimes we wake not knowing
how we came to lie here,
or who has crowned us with these temporary,
precious stones.*

—MARK DOTY, "Tiara"

PART ONE

■

MISTER

MISSISSIPPI

■

A place that ever was
lived in is like a fire
that never goes out.

—EUDORA WELTY,
"Some Notes on River Country"

ONE

BASED ON
A TRUE STORY

A Saturday afternoon in late May, Bobby came into our office talking about a movie. I had never heard of it before now. Later, when I finally tell others about this moment, they simply cannot believe that *that* movie could have snuck up on me the way it did. At the time, however, it was not so unusual: I was a graduate student in film studies, yes, but my interest was in postwar melodramas of the 1950s. *Imitation of Life, Magnificent Obsession.* New releases rarely caught my attention. From what I gathered by the way Bobby carried on, this one was a scary movie, a real doozy—well outside the bounds of my expertise. "Creepy stuff," he was saying to Cheryl, another officemate of mine.

The three of us shared a windowless space on the third floor of the English Department at a midwestern university—one I'll refrain from naming because it hardly matters for my story. The office was barely big enough for our three desks. Each one was shoved against a different wall, mine beside the community filing cabinet. Normally, the office cleared out for the weekends. So this morning I had been surprised—and mildly annoyed—to find Cheryl at her desk, that carrot-colored hair of hers all bunched up behind her head in a scrunchie. She quietly paged through several books, making notes, never once turning around to bother me. Then Bobby showed up and ruined it.

Together they made a genuine commotion. Bobby wanted to pull up the movie trailer on YouTube to show her what he was talking about, his beefy fingers clicking along her laptop's keyboard. I fumed. I was going to ask them to use headphones to watch the trailer, but Bobby pressed play before I could speak, and a voice from across the room—not to mention from across space and time and even death—rang out from the laptop's speakers. Acoustic, bare: "Beulah Land," the voice sang. "I'm longing for you."

My skin prickled at the sound of her voice, with the memory of old sores long since healed. On the wall above my desk, several postcards were thumbtacked to a cork board by a grad student before my time. Rio, Tokyo, Amsterdam. A god's-eye view of the cities: their winding roads and closely packed buildings, each snapshot taunting me with elsewhere. The song continued on, infecting the air. Her voice, Mother Maude's, like a slap. The office, the camp—they collapsed into one. The stink of Lake John. The other boys shouting, louder than hell. *Lord*, they cried, *burn me anew!*

In the summer of 1999, when I was fifteen years old, I spent almost four weeks at a camp that was supposed to cure me of my homosexuality. Though I changed in many ways at Camp Levi, my desires—to the grief of everyone involved—did not. The camp-grounds were located in central Mississippi on a rural spit of hinterland called the Neck, two and half hours south of the Delta, where I grew up. Camp Levi wasn't affiliated with any particular Christian denomination. The founders, Mother Maude and Father Drake, had ties to churches of all kinds, each of them instrumental in helping raise the money to pilot the program, including the church where my father was once the pastor. Before she started the camp, Mother Maude enjoyed a short-lived career as a gospel singer that ran out of steam sometime before her twin brother (and former manager) contracted AIDS. After his death, she vowed to save other boys from a similar fate, and so the idea for the camp was born.

Her cover of "Beulah Land," popular on Christian radio in the mid-1980s, accompanied the movie trailer playing on Cheryl's lap-top. There was no voice-over. Only clips from the movie, which I couldn't stomach looking at, and Mother Maude's weepy voice, which I couldn't escape. Their bodies leaned into each other, the way lovers do, forming a kind of triangle. Their affair was a secret. I'd discovered it, without even trying, months ago simply by reading this kind of body language. I always forgot the reason it was such a scandal for them to be sleeping together. One or the other was married, but I couldn't remember who. Cheryl was the first to speak: "Wow," she said. "That was—just wow." Bobby followed by con-demning the South: "It's fucked up, all of it. Those people." His pronouncement was enough to settle the matter between them. They changed the subject, and he asked if she was hungry. "Always," Cheryl told him, her voice low and vaguely suggestive, while on the other side of the room, I was biting my lip to keep from screaming. They debated possible restaurants, agreeing on Mexican. "Is this the one with the good fried ice cream?" Bobby asked, as they brushed past my desk. They spoke to me then, briefly, a casual remark said in a hurry, over their shoulders almost, *How are you*, and I nodded. I smiled, though they weren't looking at me. Why would they? Their minds were on each other, on what was next. Once they were gone, I locked the door and killed the lights. In the dark, I slid under my desk. I was small enough to fold my body into the leg space down there and still have enough room left over to pull my rolling chair up to my chest and rest my face, cheek down, on the warm cushioned seat.

When I returned home from the camp, I had trouble with the details of what had happened to me. They were slippery things, made of water. Even when I testified at the trial, I struggled to answer definitively the lawyers' questions. "I can't recall," I'd say, until the judge interrupted me, and said, not unkindly, "Son, can't or won't?" Only later did particulars resurface. The first time occurred when I was moving from Vanderbilt to where I live now. I had driven for most of the day and stopped at a Comfort Inn. I lay in bed, the AC unit turned up as high as it would go, the curtains closed. As I drifted, I heard the chant we boys used to holler before jumping into the lake: "Lord, rend my flesh! Lord, burn me anew!" I sprang up from the mattress. I checked the closet, looked outside my window and down the hallway. Nothing. And that was the terrible part: the silence that followed. The silence that proved you were crazy all along. Sometimes there were only voices. I'd be reading, making dinner, bathing, and snippets of conversation from that summer would float by as if coming from a television set that was left on in another room. But sometimes it was worse. The voices grew into memory, and the memory gathered itself into muscle and bone. Into Father Drake's hands clasped around my neck, pushing me against the Sweat Shack. Into Mother Maude's terrible embrace, holding me still until the others had found me. I'd get the shakes then and break into a cold sweat. One time, in a graduate class, a professor saw me in the thrall of one of these spells and, thinking I was a diabetic, sent another classmate off to the vending machine to fetch me a pack of Skittles.

As I sat under my desk, I considered Mother Maude's song in this new and strange context. Her music never brought her any wide acclaim outside of the Bible Belt. The notion that her song would be part of the soundtrack for a movie was ridiculous—unless, that is, the movie had something to do with the camp. I gripped the chair and pressed my face harder into the seat cushion. In my front pocket, my cell vibrated with an incoming call. I turned it off. I breathed, clearing my brain of distractions. My breath became deeper, more precise. I don't know how long it was—thirty minutes? an hour?—before there came a knock. I reared back, slamming my head against the top of the desk. The doorknob jiggled. Someone was frantic, calling out my name, "Will? Will?" It was my friend Bevy, who had planned on meeting me at the library this very afternoon. I had forgotten.

"You just missed him," I called out. "Come back tomorrow."

She hit the door with what sounded like her fist. "I'm not playing," she said.

A graduate of law school and a tireless advocate for social justice, Bevy had what people called "direction." A thing my dissertation (and possibly my life) sorely lacked. My future in academia was in question, and she had agreed to help me sort out a plan for how to finish writing my dissertation and graduate on time. She excelled at strategy: locating the problem and determining the best solution for solving it. My dissertation was a queer analysis of Douglas Sirk films, but after finishing the first chapter on Dorothy Malone's campy performance in *Written on the Wind*, I lacked the intellectual stamina required to complete the project. At twenty-six, I had been in school for most of my life; I was tired. I wanted to turn my brain off from thinking about ideas that were specific and erudite and try something else. Something that tested the body and let the mind alone.

When I opened the office door, Bevy was awash in fluorescent light. Her voice was deep and unforgiving: "What are you doing?" She said she'd tried calling. "I mean, what the fuck, dude?" I pretended to yawn, and my mouth, liking the suggestion, stretched into a real one. "So imagine," I lied, "I fell asleep in my office." I stepped back, my eyes adjusting to the bright hallway. Bevy was in her lawyering outfit. Her black hair parted down the middle. Foundation blended into her moon-pale skin. Her suit tailored to the square angles of her body, slightly wrinkled from a full day at the firm where she worked. Just the sight of her, adorned in all this evidence of her full and busy life, racked me with guilt.

"Oh, Bevy," I said.

Her face relaxed, and she sighed. She wouldn't press me any further. I imagined she would treat her clients like this: hone in on the lies worth pursuing and wave away the ones that weren't. Our friendship was built on her mastery of this skill. We had met at a crowded gay bar downtown a few years before. Bevy was going from table to table handing out fliers encouraging queers to vote in the upcoming state elections, and I was waiting for a date, someone I had met online. She slapped a neon-green handbill on my table. "So what's your story?" she said, and I said, "Do what?" She laughed. "Do what? Did I stutter?" she asked, mocking my drawl. I had my canned answers. The vagaries I told boyfriends and fellow grad students and professors when they asked me to account for myself. But with Bevy and her straightforwardness, I froze. She must have recognized the bewildered expression on my face. A look that told her my story could not be summed up in a few words. So she changed tactics. She laughed again, more gently this time, and gave my arm a squeeze. She whispered, "No worries, hon," and moved along. Later in the night, after it was clear my date wasn't coming, she circled back and ordered us drinks— Long Island iced teas. We kept the conversation light, discussing our hatred of the second Bush, an easy point of reference back then.

From that night on, a friendship developed. Any time she needed a plus one and her girlfriend—a doctor in residency—was too busy, I was called. I joined her for protests, too, outside the offices of public officials who had attracted her ire. If she believed in a cause, she supported it tirelessly. (I flattered myself in believing I was one of them.) She did most the talking when we were together. Which I didn't mind, even encouraged. She told me about her hometown in Iowa; about her parents, both high school teachers and semisupportive of her interest in girls; about her goals—after practicing law for five years, she planned to go into public service and run for local office. The only hiccup was her inability to pass the bar. "Like most standardized tests," she once told me, "the bar is racist and sexist." She was currently studying for her third try. I asked her once how a test like that could be prejudiced, and her eyes squinted, and she said, "Isn't it obvious?" and I said, "Oh, right," like I had remembered the answer even though I had no clue. About me, she knew very little. She knew I was from the South but thought Tennessee since I had attended Vanderbilt. I didn't see any reason to correct her. She never asked about my parents. Perhaps she sensed a tender subject in how little I mentioned them.

She'd never seen me just after one of my spells, either. If she noticed anything peculiar about my behavior now, she had the grace to keep it to herself. She leaned against the puke-colored wall as I packed up, thumbing through e-mails on her smartphone. The picture of professionalism. I had no delusions: Bevy was more important than I was. Her time too valuable to be squandered. I told her so as I shoved my laptop and papers into my satchel, trying to be quick. When I was ready, she looked up from her phone and nodded for me to follow her out, not a trace of resentment in her face. She looped her arm through mine as we walked downstairs. A kindness like hers could break over you like a strong wave, nearly bringing you to your knees. As with other people in my life, a gulf of the unsaid lay between us. She was different, however, because she'd not let that stop her from cobbling together a relationship with me. I couldn't understand her persistence any more than she could probably understand my own strange ways. We didn't question it. Wasn't our style. Outside, she guided me through the empty campus, down a sidewalk edged with sprays of periwinkles, to the concrete parking garage near the library. There was no need for her to tell me she was taking me home. On this, at least, we understood each other perfectly.

I braved a question about the movie when we were close to my apartment.

"Oh, that shit." Bevy was surprised I hadn't heard of it. "Aren't you like, um, getting a PhD in film studies?"

"Not contemporary film."

The movie, she told me, was based on a memoir. "But just barely," she added. I knew about the book. Three years ago, a copy had appeared in my mailbox. I couldn't bring myself to read it, but I couldn't throw it out, either, so the book sat on my bookshelf in a kind of limbo. "Supposedly," Bevy said, "it happened down in your part of the country—one of those camps." She didn't linger on the memoir. The movie was the offense—which was only tangentially related to the original story. The script had undergone many rewrites, she said, before becoming a slasher flick in its final incarnation. "*Proud Flesh*." She turned down my street. "Think *Friday the 13th* meets *Sleepaway Camp* meets I don't know what."

"Sounds awful."

Her foot eased on the brake, and she looked at me. "More than awful, Will. A group of pretty straight people are terrorized by a damaged gay dude in the woods. It's not just awful—it's fucking incendiary."

My apartment was in the university district, one of the cheapest neighborhoods in the city. The area had that air of collapsed beauty found in most forgotten places. Weedy front lawns and wrecked sidewalks and sagging front porches. Old Victorians that were once the symbol of an aspirational middle class and now were an under-graduate dumping ground. I lived on the second floor of the house at the end of the street. Vines clung to the east wall, knotty and funguslike, blotting out the sun from coming through my bedroom window. A noisy elementary education major shared the first floor with her Great Dane, and as Bevy pulled up to the curb, I longed for them. I wanted to leap from Bevy's Volvo and race up the fire escape and plop down on my bed in the dark and lose myself in whatever electronic dance music my neighbor's stereo was thumping out.

Before we parted, Bevy asked a favor. "Funny you should men-tion the movie," she said. "QueerLive is actually meeting about it next week." Bevy had tried to coax me to attend these consciousness-raising meetings at the university ever since I'd known her. But I had had enough congregations for one lifetime and wanted none of it. When I placed my hand on the handle, Bevy locked me in. "I'm not asking," she said, half kidding. "Not really."

In the front yard, green buds studded the branches of a lone tree. When I was a boy, I knew all the species of trees around the parsonage—water oak, dogwood, pine. In the Delta, trees break up the flatness. Their names were easy to learn, fell on my tongue and never left, but here, in a city so far away, I couldn't even remember the name of this one I'd seen cycle through the seasons for nearly five years.

"Will?" Bevy was eyeballing me.

"I don't understand why you need me there, exactly."

"Exactly?" Her eyebrows, so thin she had to pencil most of them in, arched. "A little context is all." She shifted in her seat to face me. "I need you to explain to the group how this movie is the worst thing to happen to our community since Pacino turned tricks in *Cruising*."

"And why would they listen to me?"

"Because," she said, "they are tired of hearing me bitch and moan at them. Because you *are* an expert." She leaned forward. "And don't give me that line about how the movie isn't in your wheelhouse or whatnot, okay? I need the appearance of expertise more than anything. Someone to underline my words for me. These faggots, Will, have gotten too complacent in this . . . this"—she waved her arms—"this new acceptance. They've never known what it was like before gay was cool. Never known the struggle we did—and you are going to help me wake them up to their own marginalization. Woke, Will. I want them woke."

"Bevy," I said. "That sounds intense."

"Damn right." She sat back and scooped her hair into a ponytail. "Hand me a rubber band, will you?" She gestured toward the glove compartment at my knees; I popped the latch and riffled around old combs and plastic wrappers and gummy coins before I found her one that was reasonably clean. After twisting it into her hair, she loosened her tie and then tilted the rearview mirror toward her face. Using tissue paper and spit, she dabbed makeup from her skin. She was prepping, I recognized, for the gym. After long days at the office, she liked to take to the track and, as she put it, "outrun her nerves."

Then I remembered what I'd needed her for in the first place. "Oh, shit," I said. "My dissertation!"

She told me to relax, that we could reschedule. "You just be ready, mister, to help me next week."

I nodded and got out of the car. Above the rooftops across the street, the sky had warmed into hot pink with zero clouds to blemish its wide expanse. As I reached in the backseat for my satchel, Bevy said, "Oh, and there'll be someone there you should meet."

I pulled out my bag then stopped, blinked. "Wait—romancewise?"

"I'm not sure."

"Bevy, no."

She had never tried to set me up before. Plus, she knew it had been only two months since my last relationship had imploded. My long-distance boyfriend, a librarian in upstate New York, confessed to still being in love with his ex, someone who lived much closer to him. "Someone more open to something more real," he had written in an e-mail, and I didn't ask him to explain because, of course, I knew what he had meant. I'd heard it all before from the men who found themselves in my bed for longer than a night. "Tell me," they said, "tell me everything." And when I didn't, because I couldn't— how could I tell *everything*?—they spotted the trouble and sooner or later they were gone.

Bevy waved me away from the car, a bemused look on her face. "Just keep an open mind," she said. "And look smart."

I squatted down and gazed at her through the open passenger's window. "And how do I normally look, goddamnit?"

She drove away without saying.

The Victorian was dead silent.

Only the moaning of an old house long past its prime as I climbed the stairs to my apartment. Elementary Ed had most likely gone out, and the Great Dane was probably snoozing. While a Lean Cuisine nuked in the microwave, I cut on the TV. Twin brothers were explaining to a middle-aged hetero couple why they couldn't afford the house of their dreams but could afford a shabbier version the brothers would gladly help them renovate. But when they discovered more money was needed to repair shoddy plumbing, I turned the TV off.

After dinner, I stripped down to my underwear and combed the Internet for porn. I used an outdated desktop for these searches— Xtube, Pornhub—but nothing interested me tonight. The thrashing of naked bodies vaguely sickened my stomach. I switched over to my work laptop and netflixed *Written on the Wind*. Something familiar to counteract the funk I'd fallen into. But the movie was useless at

stopping the rocks turning over in my head. So I went into my bedroom and stared at my bookshelf. My fingers traced the spines of the
books, pausing over the one shoved-in spine first so I couldn't read
the title, though I knew it all the same: *The Summer I First Believed*.
I slid it from the shelf. The cover showed a shirtless boy, arms out-
stretched to affect the shape of a cross, wading into a pond of water.
The book felt insignificant in my hands, a slim thing, two hundred
pages at most. I flipped it open to the title page. A sloppy inscription
from the author to me read, "I hope this story finds you." The words
always mystified me. Now I read them differently. Now it sounded
like a warning.

I n the days before the QueerLive meeting, I gobbled up the book.
My dissertation lost priority. I gave myself up to old ghosts, old
ways of moving and thinking. I only had to set the book aside two
or three times—when the words became too much for me, when one
of my spells threatened to pull me under. The author of *The Summer I First Believed* was anonymous, but I recognized him because
he admitted he was a counselor, and Camp Levi, short on funds,
employed just two: both of them theology students from a New Orleans seminary. Rick was tall and thin. His beard covered most of
his face—from his cheeks to his Adam's apple. Larry was huskier, a
blue bandanna perpetually tied around his slick bald head. Of the
two, Larry interacted with us the most, always quick with a Bible
verse. Rick mostly hung back and observed. He had planned on
writing an article about the summer for *The Baptist Record*, a description of the camp's tactics—however extreme—and their effects
on curbing the devil's most insidious of sins.

According to *The Summer I First Believed*, Rick and Larry spent the summer battling their attraction to each other and didn't recognize the trouble until it was too late. Rick never mentioned our names or singled us out. He referred to us as "the boys." His version glossed over so much, including the "accident" that shut down the camp. The book didn't lie exactly; it told the truth poorly. Which maybe we all do a little in telling our own stories. Rick never experienced Lake John or the Sweat Shack firsthand. In his book, the focus was on his acceptance of himself as a gay man and his secret rendezvous with Larry at night while the rest of us slept.

After finishing *The Summer I First Believed*, I drank codeine-laced cough syrup left over from a bout with strep throat. Then, woozy, I composed an e-mail to Rick. I sent it to the publishing house with instructions for the message to be forwarded on to the author, wherever he was.

My dear Rick,

Just finished your book. At last! In time to see the movie. I hope our blood was enough to make your pockets fat, you bastard.

Sincerely,
Will

P.S. Totally knew you and Larry were homo for each other.

QueerLive was held on the second floor of the student union, a sprawling labyrinth of concrete and glass. I arrived late to the meeting, walking in just as Bevy was asking everyone to please take their seats. She wore a cream-colored pantsuit, and her hair was pulled back in an extravagant-looking French braid. When she saw me, she waved me forward. "There you are!" she called out.

The others in the conference room glanced my way. Chairs lined against three of the walls formed a semicircle big enough for twenty people. By my count, ten had shown, mostly the sort I always expected to find at one of these get-togethers. The pierced and purple haired. The sissy queen and the bull dyke. I even clocked a trans man in a Fleetwood Mac T-shirt, his neck studded with puka shells. Some unusual suspects, too: two young women, both wisp thin and hair sprayed, in matching hoodies emblazoned with the Greek lettering of the Delta Delta Delta sorority, as well as a muscly athlete in a backward baseball cap and flip-flops. He must have been nineteen, maybe twenty, and looked like so many straight-acting white males on campus did—all of them versions of the same masculine prototype, filling up space because it was theirs to fill. A birthright you never questioned. We locked eyes; he smiled. His teeth were big and impossibly white. I couldn't fathom what had led such a specimen so far away from his gang of bros and into this camp of dissatisfied queers. Unless he was questioning. In which case, for all I knew, he could have been the person Bevy wanted to introduce to me. If so, I was tempted.

Most of them didn't want to be there. I knew it the moment I ducked in. Such a feeling was often in my freshman writing courses, especially on the first day of class. A commingling of suspicion, woe, and resentment washing up to the front of the room where the poor teacher stood: *Astonish us*, the students said in all the ways they didn't speak, their silence an indictment.

If Bevy noticed this, she didn't let on. After I took a seat beside

the podium, she began her tirade against the movie without any pre-
amble or introduction. Hunched over the podium, she preached fire
and brimstone, listing off the many offenses of *Proud Flesh*. I
thought of my father. He proselytized to congregations not much
larger than this one. His means for reaching the unbeliever were le-
gion and probably inappropriate for the setting. No matter the occasion, he could be counted on for a sense of humor—something
Bevy, bless her, did not possess. Even the whimsy of a French braid
was lost on her hardness. As she spoke, I scanned the crowd. Flip-
flops and several of the queers slouched in their seats, their eyes ti-
tled upward to the ceiling. Only the Greek sisters convinced me, in
the peppy way they nodded their heads at Bevy's talking points,
that they had any interest in the meeting. Bevy powered through,
making a case that the movie was an egregious step backward in
how our community was represented on film. The film's release,
she argued, could lead to rises in gay bashings, suicides, and oppressive
laws. "You just wait," she told us.

I'd tried all week to figure out what to say, but nothing came. After finishing *The Summer I First Believed*, I googled the movie and
learned, to my surprise, the project had begun in earnest. The book
was a moderate best seller, attracting the attention of a production
company. They bought the rights to the story for a hefty sum and
kept Rick on—at least initially—as a story consultant, still protect-
ing his anonymity. Several prominent directors considered the
property; all passed. Officially, they claimed "scheduling conflicts."
Unofficially, it was reported, they feared the material was too dark
and, certainly, too gay. Not long after, and for mysterious reasons,
Rick left the production. After his departure, the screenplay went
through many more "treatments" before producers were happy with

it. A director was hired at last. He was an upstart with a background in prestige television. I'd never watched any of his credits, TV or otherwise, but the name Robert Dolittle kicked something loose in my brain. He tinkered even more with the script, according to reports, and in a year, *The Summer I First Believed* was transformed into *Proud Flesh*.

The new story erased most of what happened in 1999. Now the plot centered on a group of hipsters—all straight and mostly white—who traveled to the dilapidated campgrounds in Mississippi one summer with intentions to refurbish and rebrand it into a gay-affirming camp. Years before, the camp had functioned as a nightmarish retreat for boys afflicted by the homosexual lifestyle. In the world of the movie, not completely unlike the world it was based on, the camp closed after one of the campers went missing, presumed to have killed himself in the woods though a body was never found. Unbeknownst to the hipsters, the boy was not dead. He was now a man crazed by years of living alone in the wild. The appearance of the hipsters sent him into a chaotic killing spree. In one scene after another, would-be do-gooders meet their demise at the hands of the traumatized homosexual.

Bevy paused to sip water, then asked, "Did you watch the trailer I posted in our Facebook group?" No one answered, and she winced—showing her hand at last. "People, I—" She stopped herself and shuffled papers around on the podium, producing a manila folder. She opened it and flipped through the pages until she found the one she wanted. "Listen to this," she told us. "Just you listen: The tagline for the poster says, 'Someone is coming for them. An abomination they can scarcely imagine.'" She repeated the second sentence then added: "*Abomination*—you hear that?"

Her intention to rouse the audience from their stupor affected only me. I slumped in my seat. This time, my spell began with the memory of water. The burning in my nose and throat, the gagging. I shut my eyes. I told myself to remember my location, the facts of my current surroundings: I was in a gleaming student union. Miles away from the camp. Safe. As the hallucination faded, I opened my eyes to find everyone gawking at me. I shook my head as if I were trying to wake myself up. I had successfully forced the memory back down. A first. Turns out, my fear of making a spectacle of myself overpowered all others.

Bevy looked puzzled. So did everyone else. It dawned on me they were waiting for me to respond to a question I hadn't heard. I coughed, said, "Say again?" and Bevy did what I knew she hated most: She repeated herself, speaking slowly, every word labored over. "Explain to them," she said, "why this movie will hurt us." She glanced at the group. "Will here studies film and is gay, so . . ."

I stood up. Then I sat back down. Always best, my father once recommended, to focus on a single person when speaking to a group. Deciding on the person—that was the tricky part. Not Bevy. She still lorded over us from her perch behind the podium. Not the girl across from me, the one with pierced cheeks gnawing on a strand of multicolored hair. Her sharp eyes warned me away. Flip-flops was no help. He crossed his legs, then uncrossed them, then did it all over, reflecting my own nervous energy back at me. I settled on the trans guy. He was smiling and nodding. Now that I had the floor, the words seemed to evaporate before I could think of them. Normally, I excelled at speaking off the cuff in my classroom, where I pretended to be an intellectual. Here, in this room, I didn't know how to feign confidence.

As I considered the stiffness of the trans guy's overly gelled hair, a rogue idea fell into my skull. *Well, stupid, why not tell them the obvious.* The answer was there all along, and I had avoided it, as I do so many other things. Not even Bevy knew the bomb I could drop in this room. I'd begin by telling them all the ways the movie misrepresented what had happened. *There was a lake*, I would say, *that ravaged the skin. And a boy didn't go missing, no. He died. I know because I watched it happen.*

"So then," I said instead, "because thou art lukewarm, and neither cold nor hot, I will spur thee out of my mouth."

The Bible verse and my irony in using it went over everyone's head: more looks of confusion. Bevy said, "I'm sorry?" and the vibe in the room tilted precariously toward catastrophe. All my doing. I had failed to be of any help here. I hated groups. Queer groups especially. All those gaping wounds in one place. To save us from the abyss of awkwardness, I went for a joke. "So a gay serial killer, you guys." I paused a beat. "Think Jason Voorhees with more fitted coveralls."

No one laughed. Flip-flops raised an arm, and asked, with all sincerity, "So he kills gay people?"

"No, no, no," said one of the Tri Deltas. "A serial killer who just happens to be gay. Which I think is kind of progressive."

Pierced cheeks spoke up then and told her why she was wrong.

And with that, they were talking. A full-blown conversation. Eventually, the trans guy's voice clamored over the rest. "But I hear," he said. "I hear it's based on shit that really happened." A rhinestone sparkled in his left ear. "What about Jeffrey Dahmer?" he asked no one in particular. "Total gay, total killer. If it happened, it happened, right?"

"That doesn't matter," Bevy told him. "It's not about accuracy. Goddamnit!" She slapped the podium. "It's about representation."

Now everyone laughed.

After the meeting, Flip-flops sidled up to introduce himself. The minute after he said his name—something bland and suburban—I forgot it. I learned that, in addition to being a scholar athlete, he used the word "really" more than anyone ought to. "Really the best talk I've been to all semester," he told me, producing a form for me to sign. "Just to verify that I was, you know, really here and all." His attendance fulfilled a requirement for a gender and sexuality course he was taking. Several other students held similar-looking forms. Which explained their attendance despite their in-difference. A shame.

"I think you need her." I nodded toward Bevy. She was lurking in the entryway, shelling out fliers that promoted the upcoming protest of the movie. Tomorrow night, queer groups across the country were staging demonstrations at theaters before the movie premiered at midnight. Bevy was leading one at Cinema Station, the local movie house just off of campus. She had created a logjam of students, with the sorority sisters in the lead, telling them why they should be at the demonstration.

Flip-flops took in the scene. "Really?"

When I said yes, *really*, he snatched the bill of his baseball cap and twisted it forward. He ventured into the fray, the sound of his flip-flops clacking in his wake.

The trans guy sat down in the chair beside me and told me his name was Zeus. "You were about to say something else," he said.

"Right before you quoted the Bible—you stopped. What for?" He wasn't smiling anymore. His face had twisted into a look of curiosity. I told him I hated public speaking. "Doesn't everyone?" he asked. Tiny pockmarks speckled his cheeks, and there was a slight gap between his two front teeth. He gave off the impression of a used-car salesman. Someone who wanted to be liked, who was prepared to convince me he should be liked no matter what else I might want to think of him. I didn't mind. I liked to be courted for my affections. I said, "My father—he was good at it. He was a preacher." I normally told people my father drove a truck, the line of work he fell into after he left the church. My openness startled me. I didn't know why I had confided in Zeus more truth than I normally told most people over a long dinner.

"Cool." He stared right at me when he spoke. "So Bevy tells me you're coming to the thing tomorrow."

"Did she?" My attendance would be penance for my poor performance tonight. Our friendship, I realized, had entered a new phase where I constantly made up for disappointing her by agreeing to one commitment after another. Maybe this was her way of getting me out of the house more. "The fun never ends," I said. He slapped me on the knee and stood. "She says we got a lot in common." He barged through the clot of students to give Bevy a hug. Her eyes found mine over his shoulder, and she winked, confirming what I had begun to suspect: He was the person she wanted me to meet.

A day later, I stood in front of Cinema Station with Bevy and her girlfriend, Alix, and Zeus. A building made of glass walls and neon light, Cinema Station was nestled in the downtown area amid a slew of hetero bars and glitzy chain restaurants. A city ordinance required us to remain at least six feet from the premises during our demonstrations. The four of us gathered around a stone bench exactly six feet from the automatic doors. When the doors whisked open, we could smell the buttered popcorn and hear the chatter of excited movie-goers. As people passed us, we chanted slogans—"Homophobia is the real killer!"—and brandished handmade signs that echoed similar sentiments. Every half hour we tossed handfuls of glitter in the air while Bevy stood on the stone bench and hollered more slogans into a megaphone.

Still, we made little impression on the passersby. We were half-hearted, gloomy at the poor showing of supporters. Bevy most of all. During lulls in the crowds, she and Alix bickered. The gist of their argument was never clear, but both of them wore these ador-able tuxedo shirts, making their fighting somehow funny, verging on the adorable. Zeus and I were left to make conversation with each other. Once, during a lull, Zeus shook his sign at me, and said, "Revelations."

"What?"

"Revelations 3:16—last night, the verse you spit out."

"Lot of good it did."

"Maybe you should have said what you wanted to—before you edited yourself."

I shrugged. I told him I hadn't known what I wanted to say. "I sort of went blank," I said.

"That's a lie." He smiled, flashing his gap, and changed the subject. "Bevy says you're working on a book."

"A dissertation—it's academic."

"*It's academic*," he said. "What the fuck does that even mean?"

I admitted I didn't know. "Not really," I said, flinching as I remembered Flip-flops' poor verbal skills from last night. Zeus laughed loud enough that Bevy and Alix paused in their argument and looked our way. I added, "It's about the movies—well, I don't really know what it's about anymore."

"Is that why you're so wound up?" He tapped his sign against mine. "I get it. I write—Bevy thinks we can help each other." He told me he was writing a memoir about his transition from a lesbian woman from Puerto Rico to a gay man living in the great Middle West.

"Sounds complicated," I said.

A group of teenagers walked up, so we shouted, mimed anger and outrage as best we could, and after they entered the building, Zeus leaned over, and whispered, "Only to those who don't understand."

The abundance of streetlights washed out the stars and faded the sky purple. As the night wore on, my feet ached. I took regular breaks by sitting on the bench, but Zeus never sat down. He maintained the posture of a soldier at attention. During another lag, he lit a cigarette. American Spirit, no less. He held the cigarette to his lips as if he might flick it away at any second, the bud flaming on and off with every suck of air. I thought of Brando in *On the Waterfront*. Zeus's swagger wasn't stagey. I believed in his masculinity wholeheartedly, down to his dingy work boots and the way his eyebrows were left unkempt and fanned out from his face.

He held the pack of cigarettes between us, and said, "Want one?" When I shook my head no, he shoved the pack into the back pocket of his Levis. He took one last drag from the one in his mouth and, exhaling smoke, said, "Bevy says you're secretive, you know that? A big mystery man." He dropped the butt to the gum-splattered side-walk and stomped it out. "That you like to keep to yourself."

Throwing glitter had stained our hands, and his sparkled like magic as he moved them in the air while he spoke.

"I'm just busy and live in my head."

He mulled this over, and during the next break, he got closer, and said in a low voice, "You're just a tease—that's what I think." He tilted his head the way a dog might and put a booted foot on the patch of sidewalk between mine. He got in my face. Real close. His smoky breath made me dizzy, the smell of ovens and old men. Our conversation had taken such a swift and unexpected turn that I hadn't any time to question it. Maybe that was the point. My cock, pressed downward against my thigh, began to thicken and jerk to the beat of my heart. The pain a kind of pleasure, too. "Are you a tease?" he asked. People were chattering nearby. Getting closer.

"I don't know," I said.

He rolled his eyes. The look on his face—the look of a fox—stabbed me with longing. I wanted to say what he wanted me to, but I didn't know what that was. Across from us, Bevy had dropped her megaphone and was saying, "Oh, shit, oh, shit," into her cupped palms. When she removed her hands, strings of snot and blood leaked down her face. She was no stranger to these nosebleeds. They happened when she was agitated. Alix had come prepared, produc-ing a roll of toilet paper from her bag. She waved us away when we tried to help. "Watch our stuff," she said, and guided Bevy to the bathroom inside the theater to clean herself up. Not long after they were gone, an old couple walked by, stepping over the fallen signs, baffled by the glittered sidewalk. Once they were inside, Zeus said, "We'll get the next group." But we didn't. Instead, we gathered up our belongings and piled them up by the trash can, out of the way. "Well," I said. "This is the saddest Friday night I've had in a good long while."

He shook his head in such a way that I didn't know if he was agreeing with me or not. "I think I need a drink," he said. We sat on the bench with enough space between us for another person. The flirtation had cooled off as fast as it had begun, and we didn't speak until Alix and Bevy returned. They were calling it a night, they told us. Toilet paper balled up in her nostrils, Bevy looked pale and miserable. Alix was already holding her keys. "A fucking mess," Bevy said, and hugged me good-bye. They took the signs and the glitter and the megaphone with them when they left.

No longer a protestor, Zeus went inside Cinema Station and rode the escalator up to the bar. I followed.

The Lost Ticket was an open-concept oasis of cushioned stools and low lighting right before you reached a hallway of doors leading to the big screens. Zeus and I were the only two in the establishment tonight, the absurdly priced well drinks scaring off the college and middle-aged patrons in equal measure. The house gin loosened up Zeus's lips. He spoke openly about his failed love life— which I didn't mind hearing about as long as I didn't have to share mine.

"Gay men," he said, "are fickle beasts—once they learn I'm trans, it's no-go." He pulled his thumb across his neck in a slicing motion. "Then you get the ones who are just curious to take my pants off and see what's there." He thumbed away the lime on his glass, and asked, "Which one are you?" Blood rushed to my face, and he waved the question away, saying, "I kid—of course you are curious, yeah?" He placed a hand over mine, one of his fingers pressing gently into the groove of flesh between my knuckles. This is when he told me he had once been engaged to a woman. "Valeria, Valeria, Valeria," he said, in a singsong voice. "She never cared nothing for no one but herself because she believed you have to be selfish in order to be true."

When I asked him if this Valeria had been his fiancée, he gave me a puzzled look. "Don't be silly," he told me. "Valeria was me." His fiancée's name was Jaylene. They met at university in Río Piedras and had similar ambitions: Both wanted to be nurses and leave Puerto Rico once they had completed their degrees. "No jobs on the island," he said. "Much worse than the papers say." Once on the U.S. mainland, Valeria began taking testosterone injections; she knew a doctor who sold them to her on the sly. Jaylene did not approve of the treatments because she feared they would change Valeria from the person she'd fallen in love with. "And seeing how things turned out, you could probably argue they did," Zeus said. "But the hormones, you see, helped me become more of the person I knew I was all along." Jaylene stuck by him during the transition. They even continued to plan the wedding; Jaylene, a confirmed lesbian, resigned herself to marrying a man. But Valeria, in the process of becoming a man, came to a realization—one neither Valeria nor Jaylene could have predicted. After a year of treatment (and countless hours of therapy), Valeria understood that he was not only a man, but a gay man. The same day he came out to Jaylene, he moved out of their apartment. He thought a clean break would be the easiest. Jaylene never spoke to him again. "I'm sure she felt betrayed," he said. "And I don't blame her. The danger of becoming the person you are is you run the risk of hurting the people who love the person you were." He sipped on his drink, then added: "I took the name Zeus after I left her. It is a bold name, a strong name, yes? And you have to be both if you want to take the life that is yours." He raised a glass. *"Dios del río!"*

"Amen," I said.

The gin and tonic had pulled me underwater, my head tipped back and forth by a slow invisible current. Zeus glanced down at his drink, and drunk or not, I recognized the sadness on his face. The kind of low-level gloom that stays with you even when happy. I wanted to cheer him up. "You're a good storyteller," I said. "I can't wait to read your book." He said that we're all eloquent in the telling of our own stories. "A famous writer said that; I forget who." He removed his hand from mine. "You do sort of just let people go on, don't you?" he said. I told him I liked to listen. His eyes narrowed. "I think I just figured out why you don't like to talk about yourself."

"Oh?"

"Too cliché."

"Excuse me?"

Zeus proceeded to tell me his theory on queers and their life stories. "It's like this: The world allows us only so many narrative trajectories that don't end in tragedy. Our lives often conform around one or another of them." My story, he said, was probably your typical migration to a metropolitan area. "Let me guess. You left a small town for the promise of the big city, where your identity could be fully expressed." He'd used air quotes when he said "identity." I couldn't tell if he was being sincere or sarcastic, maybe a little of both, but I let him go on because we were drinking and my brain was beginning to misfire and he was partly right in what he said. At eighteen, I couldn't have articulated this sentiment so clearly, but the impulse to leave had been imprinted on me nonetheless. I knew (or thought I knew) that I must escape to the metropolis if I wanted any chance at happiness. Now, after living away from my home for so many years, I understood the result of leaving was perhaps more complicated than I had originally imagined.

Zeus left for the bathroom, and when he returned, he placed a pair of tickets on the bar, and I laughed when I read the movie title. "Now hear me out," he was saying. "I think it's wrong to dismiss a movie we've never seen."

I told him I needed to smoke before I saw the film. "And something stronger than those damn American Spirits." There was no time to smoke: *Proud Flesh* began in ten minutes. Zeus produced a tiny pillbox, and said, "But I have these." Valium. We downed two pills apiece with club soda. I said, "This is crazy." He took my hand and pulled me off the bar stool.

At first I couldn't focus on the screen, or on the previews for other movies, or on the long roll of opening credits that harkened back to an earlier era of filmmaking, or even on the eerie music—which was nothing like Mother Maude's singing, for which I was thankful, but it was still frightening. Most of my attention was on Zeus. The armrest between us remained pushed back out of our way. We kissed. And it was like burying my face into an overripe fruit: messy but sweet. We pawed at each other's bodies, too. Our hands brave in the dark. His cupped my crotch, pressed deep into me, digging his fingers into my denim jeans, lifting me off the seat.

Mine explored his body more carefully. He'd told of having his breasts removed four months ago, and I worried about his soreness. I traced his rib cage through his shirt, slowly working up to his nipples. They were as hard as pebbles. When I leaned forward to lick one through the fabric, he cried out. I pulled away, afraid I'd hurt him or that somebody had heard. But no. He put a hand on my chest and held me against my seat as his head sunk down to my lap.

There was a lush field on the screen. Hot air steamed up from the ground. Hollywood's version of vague countryside in Mississippi. (I'd read that the film was actually shot in Georgia for tax reasons.) Soon the camera centered on a solitary figure in the middle distance walking down a gravel road that wound into the trees. The figure was a woman—late thirties, white, wearing a pair of ratty jeans. She left the road and climbed up a hill into tall weeds. She was making her way to a watering hole. The camera showed her face in a close-up: She was searching for someone, her brows scrunched up with worry. She noticed a nearby hammock strung up between two pines. A flash of arms drew her closer, then the sound of moaning. The camera panned over a pile of clothes in the dirt, then flashed to the two bodies in the hammock, both teenage boys, nude. Though the camera revealed very little, the suggestion was the boys were doing to each other what Zeus was now doing to me.

His head popped up. "You okay?"

"What? Why?"

"You're shaking."

I tried to speak, but all that came out of my mouth was a sob. Zeus sat up and put his arms around me. *Shh*, I heard Father Drake say. *Just be still.* I pushed Zeus away so hard he fell off his seat. Embarrassed, I zipped up my jeans and stumbled into the lobby, my arms groping air. People gave me startled looks as I ran to the bathroom. I reached a toilet in time to empty out my stomach with several deep heaves. When Zeus appeared in the bathroom, I had relocated to the bank of electric hand dryers. I was patting my mouth with a wet paper towel. He said, "I didn't think I was *that* bad at giving head." He moved closer. "This was a bad idea. Jesus." I told him that I couldn't hold my liquor anymore. He put an arm on my shoulder, and I forced myself not to pull away. "You don't have to lie," he said. "Please don't."

Even though my apartment was within walking distance of Cinema Station, Zeus insisted on driving me home. Along the way, we listened to the Mountain Goats on his iPod and didn't speak. He parallel parked in front of the Victorian, killed the engine, and said, "Look."

"My apartment's a mess," I told him. "So I'll invite you up another time, okay?" He put both hands back on the steering wheel and jerked it right and left the way a child would when pretending to drive. "I don't have to know," he began, but paused when a large red truck cruised by, Kanye West's manic voice blaring out the windows. "I just want to say," he said, as the truck turned at the stop sign. "That it helps to talk about our bad days—I know, I know"— he held up his hands—"it sounds like cheese, but I got bad days, too, you know? Enough to fill up a whole fucking calendar, I got so many. But it's like lifting—the more you do it, the more you tell it, the stronger you get. Bevy thinks you're hurting. And just from the time I've spent with you, *I* think you're hurting. Understand?"

"No."

"Come on, man." Then he told me I wasn't alone. The pureness of his voice rankled me. I preferred him when he acted more aggressively. "Okay," I said. "Thank you." And I tried really hard not to sound like a bitch, but I knew I did anyhow. He got out of the car, intent on walking me to my door, the poor bastard. The night had turned brisk, so we kept our hands shoved in our pockets as we stepped over the broken pieces of concrete that hadn't passed as a sidewalk since before either of us were born. From inside the Victorian, the Great Dane barked madly at our approach. Elementary Ed screamed for him to shut up. At the stoop, Zeus went in for another kiss, and I gave him my cheek. He frowned. "I really fucked up, huh?"

"My breath—I smell like puke."

Walking back to his car, he yelled over his shoulder, "Bevy gave me your number! Expect a phone call."

I told him I expected nothing, which was true with everything, and went inside to brush my teeth in the dark.

The next morning, an e-mail appeared in my inbox.

Dear Will,

I'm so thankful your note found me. Let me begin by saying I understand. You've every right to be angry over the movie—over everything, really. I can't change it. Lord knows, I wish I could. But that's beside the point. Just know that Rick was upset about the movie, too. When he saw the direction they were going, he protested. He tried to buy back the rights. Of course they wouldn't sell and even barred him from the set. He became very ill afterward—depressed, mostly. We suffered through a dark time, but that story is too long and complicated to be repeated here. Suffice to say, I'm happy he passed before the movie was released. He was spared that last humiliation at least.

I suppose you are wondering why on earth I'm writing. Well, I have a request. I wouldn't bother you, I swear, if you weren't my last resort. As you probably know, the property in and around Camp Levi has been vacant for years now. It has come to my attention that the area is run-down, a refuge for transients and the like. I want to buy the land, Will. As you probably also know, it's where Rick and I fell in love, and I have sentimental attachments to the place no matter how dark and stormy its history may be. More than that, I have big plans for what to do with the area. Here's where you come in. My lawyers have written to your father, and so have I, pleading with him to sell me the deed. His silence is troubling but expected. I will gladly pay double what the land is worth, and since you reached out, I hope you may be open to a dialogue with me. I think your father would listen to you. I'd bet my life on it.

Please let me know.

Sincerely,
Lawrence

Not many people knew Mother Maude was my mother's younger sister. We kept this information from the others at camp. "So there is no question," Mother Maude had said, "of favoritism." I thought Larry knew because he was a counselor, but maybe he was as clueless as the campers. Anyhow, the truth was revealed during the trial, and he and Rick were in court the day I testified. They were the only people from Camp Levi I saw in the courtroom. Mother Maude had fled. We boys were kept apart so we wouldn't influence one another's story. And the prosecution had successfully petitioned for Father Drake to be removed to another room to view our testimonies by video. When my turn was over, I was escorted outside by my legal representative, where my father waited in his pickup. He never asked me about the camp, the trial—any of it. After I returned to him, he drove us to Dairy Queen. We ordered milk shakes and a large basket of curly fries. This combination was a favorite of my mother's. We didn't speak of her, either, but in dipping the salty fries in the ice cream, we grieved her absence all the same.

Larry's e-mail left me winded for several reasons—not the least of which was learning about Rick's death. All day long I wallowed in bed listening to the movements of Elementary Ed below me. She clanged around in the kitchen, first making coffee, then frying eggs. At ten o'clock, she watched *The View*. The Great Dane barked not long after, and grumbling, she took him for a walk. While they were gone, my cell rang. It was Zeus. I ignored the call and sent him to my voice mail. A few minutes later, Bevy tried, and this time I picked up. "Wow," she said. "I was thinking I would leave a message."

"Just leave your message after the beep," I said. "Beep." She wanted to have dinner with me. "Me and you and Alix and Zeus," she said. "Damn the movies! Let's go to a restaurant and chill—just the four of us." I wasn't surprised at the request, but I was surprised when I agreed. "But not tonight," I told her. "Let's shoot for tomorrow." We decided on a Chinese restaurant on the outskirts of town, one that served real Szechuan food. I told her I'd never been on a double date before, and before hanging up, she said, "You know I love you, right?"

My father and I never agreed on much of anything in this world, but we do share a love of driving. It's instinctual, the pull of the road. "It's where," my father always said, "I do my best thinking." My car was nothing special, a silver Honda Accord I called Doll. I took her to these lesbian mechanics in town who kept her oil changed and her tires rotated. She was good on gas, easy on the eyes, and had never given me any trouble. More proof of my affection for her: I didn't park her on the street. I paid fifty bucks a month to keep her in a hotel garage a few blocks from my place in a nicer area of town. On the day of my double date, I took her out early with every intention of meeting everyone at the restaurant.

May was ending with an unseasonable cold snap. Steely clouds traced across the sky, washing the color from the trees. Everything was pale. Wintry. I arrived at the restaurant an hour before I was supposed to be there and circled the parking lot. The China Blossom was in a strip mall between a Japanese karaoke bar and a store that sold used books. No one was around. The parking lot was rife with potholes, and not wanting to park, I took Doll back out onto the road. Traffic was light, and the driving soothed me.

My father and I had driven across many highways and interstates in Mississippi. Before he left the church, the span of his outreach had grown—from Olive Branch to Kosciusko, and all points in between. When I tagged along, I learned to manage a vehicle well enough, driving his pickup on back roads while he napped in the passenger's seat. I took Doll onto the interstate, hoping to outrun the overcast. Mississippi never had much of a spring and was probably sweltering now. Nothing like this, where you went hunting for sunlight. When I left home, I thought I'd never miss the summers. But after a few brutal winters, I came around to appreciating warmer climes, even longing for them.

Bevy once told me that we can't help loving the places we came from—no matter how broken or terrible they were. I wasn't sure I believed her. Sometimes people just like to talk, and she was no exception. I wasn't sure I believed Zeus, either, about that business of telling your story making you stronger. Like the more you chewed on the past, the easier it was to swallow. My story was the story of Camp Levi, which was the story of the Neck, which was also the story of my family. A circle of bad—one secret led into another and another and so on. Doll cruised at seventy now, humming along nicely, and I thought, *Fuck it. Why not?* So I turned off my cell phone and kept on driving, headlong into my past.

TWO

THE NECK

I learned about the Neck long before my summer at Camp Levi. My mother knew of its colorful lore and shared the stories with me on occasion—usually when my father was out of earshot. "East of a town called West," she'd begin, "and west of a town called Weir, there was the Neck." She often produced a drink koozie from the back of a kitchen cabinet with the same quote scrawled across it lest I disbelieve her. The Neck was in the Mississippi hill country and thick with trees. The geography was so different from the Delta that it might as well have been on another world. A nowhere land in between two counties, lousy for crops because of all the flooding from the Big Black River. "Bad for growing," my mother said, "but good for mischief."

She talked about the Neck without adding any varnish to what my father called "the rougher side of life." The women in the woods, the moonshiners, the lost mother—these were stories of the Neck I knew by heart. But she kept her own story, which included a girlhood at the Neck, mostly to herself.

One time or another, she said, "Most decent people stayed away from there."

And I said, "But you lived there."

"Yes, nugget, but I wasn't much decent myself—not before I met your daddy." She said she had no intention of ever becoming a preacher's wife. "No, sir. I was a bona fide wild woman." When I asked her what "bona fide" meant, she said, "The real deal. Down to my toes. I was bad." But that was as far as she'd ever go, and for a while, that was all I needed.

My full name is William Bruce Dillard, but my parents, the Reverend Dr. Frank and Debra Rose Dillard, sometimes called me Rooster. The nickname was inspired, so I was told, by the way my tuft of blond baby hair poked up in the mornings like a bantam rooster's comb. Then the name became, in my toddler years, a form of discipline. I'd hear, "Rooster, boy—I'd be ashamed," and was liable to glance over my shoulder for the boy my parents corrected. Certainly not me. I felt more like a Will Dillard, plain and simple. This Rooster person was somebody else. Another boy entirely. The older I got, the more I understood: The reason the name never stuck had something to do with how I misbehaved.

One Sunday, when I was seven, I was singing in the choir, and the week's offertory hymn was "In the Garden." I cut loose during the first chorus. I shook my hips back and forth, gyrating to Mrs. Audean's slightly off-tempo rendering of the old song on the piano.

He walked with me and he talked with me and told me that I was his own. I lowered my voice and swung my arms. The night before, while my father prepared his sermon at the church, my mother and I had watched *Written on the Wind* on TV. It was my first time seeing Dorothy Malone shimmy with Rock Hudson. My mother and I were mesmerized. "Look at her," she said. "Just beautiful." Later in the movie, as Malone frolicked by herself in her bedroom to a jazz record, her father was felled by a heart attack, tumbling down a long flight of stairs. We were riveted by the scene, my mother and I, and held each other close until the very end. In the choir, I copied Dorothy Malone's chaotic movements.

My carrying on amused some in the congregation, mostly the older ones up front—the widows and widowers who cut me more slack than they did the other children because I was the preacher's son. Every Sunday they filled my pockets with peppermints and denture-safe chewing gum, and told me what a fine boy I was. I'd done nothing, so far as I could tell, to earn such praise, but I was happy to have them say it, especially in front of my father. My mother, sitting in the very back pew, was hard to make out in the audience. I imagined the look of surprise on her face at how well I remembered the dance from the movie. Also watching me were the Woods, the Dickersons, and the Musclewhites—the three families who had founded Second Baptist. Various cousins and aunts and half brothers and distant relations connected by marriage. I paid them no mind. My mother said they were all stuck-up. "Those people," she remarked more than once, "think they are that white speck on chicken poop—and you know what, nugget? That's chicken poop, too." My father was hidden behind the pulpit, seated in his maple chair that looked more like a wooden throne. When the hymn was over, he rose to lead us in prayer. His face flushed, his ears the color of blood.

"You, sir, need to grow out of this curiousness," he told me later. He'd kept me behind after service and sent my mother on back to the parsonage to get dinner started. He and I sat facing each other in his small office, a large metal desk between us. The picture of Jesus—the blond, blue-eyed, pre-crucifixion Jesus—hung on the wall behind him, angled just above his head. The Son of Man's lips were arched in a slight smile and glitter dusted his white robe. I asked my father what he meant by "curiousness," and he sighed. He removed his rimless glasses and rubbed his eyes until they turned pink. A heavyset man, my father had a wide, moon-shaped face. "You can't see how you're acting?" he said. "How you embarrassed yourself?" He asked me what I had been thinking.

"I guess I was just doing my best, Daddy."

"Your best?"

"Yes, sir."

He told me to explain myself.

"Well." I swallowed and glanced about the room. His framed diploma from seminary hung beside Jesus on the wall. My father, it told me, was a doctor of divinity and entitled to all the rights and privileges pertaining to that degree. "I wasn't acting," I said. "I was just showing the Lord my best—my best self. Who I am." I decided in the moment not to tell him my inspiration for the dance. It seemed like tattling on my mother, though I wasn't sure why.

"Rooster, boy," my father said. "You've got no clue who you are. Not yet you don't." He rapped the top of the desk with his knuckles to punctuate the importance of his words. Normally a quiet man, my father never said five words when one or two would suffice.

Even in his sermons he spoke to the congregation in a volume just above a whisper and called them "Dearly beloved" like they were the sweetest children in the world. When I displeased him, like now, I wanted nothing more than for him to yell at me. Bring down Old Testament judgment upon my head. In the Bible people who transgressed were rebuked. Lot's wife was transformed into a pile of salt for looking the wrong way. Moses was kept out of Canaan for hitting his walking stick against some rock. Their sins baffled me as much as my own did. My father never punished me severely. He believed the quickest way to the heart was through the brain. When you know better, he told me, you do better. "Boys don't act that way," he said now. "You see what I'm saying, don't you?" I was silent. He whispered, "Rooster?" as if I had disappeared from his office. "Rooster?" As if he were searching desperately in a crowd of strangers for the boy who was his son.

First, the women of the Neck.
    They had skulked in those woods since time immemorial, my mother said, and would probably still be there, too, if the moonshiners hadn't showed up and ruined everything. "A commune before it was fashionable." A mix of blacks and Choctaws and poor white trash. "Tough women," she told me. "Hard women. The kind who carried knives. Knew how to hunt." They fashioned tents from whatever they could find: old tarps, hand-me-down quilts, clothes. They ate what they killed, mostly squirrel and deer, and traded wares with men who braved the woods to find them. Their company grew one at a time, mostly when a woman's unhappiness became too much for her. "Not just sad," my mother was always quick

to add, "but the deep-down blues that don't have a name." A woman would be hoeing the garden or sweeping off the back porch or hanging up bedsheets on the clothesline when she'd hear a voice. The gentlest voice, whispering, "Find me." Invariably, she'd look over her shoulder. Nothing. Maybe the wind. A child's voice from far away. But no, not either of those, and the voice persisted. At dinner, in bed, seeing her children off to school—*find me, find me.*

"Like a ghost?" I said.

"Not exactly," my mother said. "More like a feeling so strong it only *felt* like words."

A kind of rapturing when she left. One minute she was there, and the next she was gone. She went to the Neck with nothing more than the clothes on her body, drawn there by the rumor of these women, and if she ever found them, nestled in that sanctuary of trees, hidden from the busy world, she never left. My mother could only guess at what sort of agreement existed among them. The here and how never made it beyond them. But for a time, at least how my mother tells it, the Neck was theirs: a hundred or so acres of freedom.

"You ever feel that pull?" I said.

"Oh, honey." My mother smiled, dragging her fingers through my hair. "All the time."

Before returning home on that Sunday of my scolding, we drove to the First Baptist Cemetery across town. Hawshaw had several Christian denominations, and the church building for the First Baptist congregation was easily the most impressive. The church was built more like a cathedral: large walnut doors, maroon bricks, a steeple piercing the sky. A house of worship fitted with stained-glass windows depicting scenes from the New Testament. By comparison, father's church was a modest affair, big enough for ten rows of pews with an office tacked on to the side and a fellowship hall in the back. He preferred his church house to this other, grander one. The plainness of it, the smell of sawdust rising from the floor, the pure light blasting through the bare windows—the little church fed his notions of God as homegrown and personal, not highfalutin. "High-dollar worship," he called First Baptist, even though we were bound to the church for all the facilities we couldn't afford: its baptistery, its large fellowship hall, its several acres of land for the dead. We called on them when one of our members needed to be saved, married, or put to eternal rest. Which was often—our members were a lively bunch, always up to something. And he and I took frequent trips to the First Baptist Cemetery. We checked on the grave sites of our members, made sure they were kept neat, that the floral arrangements around their tombstones hadn't been knocked over or blown away.

On the drive over, both of us smarted from our conversation about my behavior in choir. In my father's old Chevy, we passed Hawshaw with the windows rolled down, the humid air slapping our wet faces. A paved side street took us through a neighborhood of houses with small lawns where the grass was yellow and dry. Two men stood beside a smoking grill, one of them wiping his shiny face with his shirttail. In another yard, a sprinkler spurted out streams of water that arced several feet into the air. Delirious children my age jumped into and around and through the steady pulse—boys, shirtless and bandy-legged, their joy a kind of mystery to me. They hooted and hollered, and I pictured myself among them, my laughter as loud as any of theirs. Myself, but different. I was rowdy and true, a boy who knew the things a boy was supposed to know in order to please his father even when doing wrong.

After we crossed a river bridge and turned down East Leflore Street, the First Baptist steeple appeared in the distance, a spear rising above the squat buildings constituting downtown Hawshaw. Long before I was born, the Woods, Dickersons, and Musclewhites left First Baptist over a dispute concerning the election of deacons. Supposedly, a Wood was denied the deaconship because he was divorced, and in protest, the families removed their letters of membership and formed Second Baptist. The Woods' construction company built the church out in the country, using Dickerson lumber and Musclewhite land. The Musclewhites donated a nearby house and grounds of a recently deceased relative to be used for the parsonage that eventually became my first home.

It irked the families that we were still so dependent on First Baptist. Not enough for any of them to fork over the money needed to add on to the church, of course. For his part, my father was more than friendly with the preacher of First Baptist. In his late twenties and single, Brother Mims came over to the parsonage at least once a month to eat my mother's cooking and talk God with my father. Brother Mims was a fiery little man who often yelled even when he was agreeing with you. Once, he brought over an inkblot the shape of Jesus's face. He said he liked to show the image to children my age and had me hold the paper up to the light and stare at it uninterrupted for thirty seconds. Then he directed me to close my eyes, which I did, and there, burned onto the backs of my eyelids, was the glowing face of the Savior. It was startling. Brother Mims explained the power of Jesus was such that he could see inside us, that he knew our hearts and our souls better than we did. We could hide nothing from him, even the darkest corners of our minds. He said, "Confession. It's the only way—for he already knows how filthy we are!" His voice rose so that it became almost funny, but I didn't laugh because he was a guest in our home and my parents were watching. After he left, my mother and father argued about the demonstration. My mother believed it was wrong to use fear to scare children into salvation. "Unseemly," she kept repeating. My father contended he didn't care a lick about the method so long as a soul was spared eternal damnation.

As my father and I canvassed the cemetery, I thought about that picture Brother Mims had burned into my brain and how the more I learned of God the more terrifying he seemed. Even after my mother showed me how the inkblot had been a trick. "A cheap one," she said. Even after she made me hold other black-and-white pictures up to the light to prove how ridiculous it had been, how anything could mark our vision in that way. Still, I knew the works of God, how stern and immovable he was. The cemetery was a stark reminder of where we all were headed. No matter what, I was destined to face him, one on one, without the shield of my parents' love to protect me.

Late June and the cicadas had already burrowed out of the earth, leaving the ground squishy. As if we were walking on a sponge. At the back of the cemetery, right before the grass turned wild with honeysuckle and cattails, we came upon a fresh grave. A member of First Baptist who'd died while giving birth. A plaque had been planted at the foot of her grave that gave the woman's name and age. It would remain there until the tombstone arrived a couple of weeks later.

"Poor thing," my father said. "She was fourteen."

Yards away, a man rode a lawnmower, his droopy straw hat ob-scuring his face. He'd already cut the grass where we stood, but he was headed back in our direction anyway. The wind caught his straw hat and blew back the brim, revealing the boyish face of Brother Mims. After he coasted up beside us, he killed the engine. "Lordy," he said. "I guess my ox was in a ditch today!" He took off the hat to fan himself like an old woman would.

"You picked a hot one, Mims." My father was older than Brother Mims and better educated, but he didn't make nearly as much as the young preacher. If this bothered him, he never said. He treated Brother Mims like a kid brother, someone to mentor. "A shame you had to put this one to rest." He nodded to the grave.

Brother Mims retrieved a thermos from the cup holder at his side. He squirted water on his face then opened his mouth and shot some inside. He looked like a teenager. He wore overalls and no shirt, and his pink shoulders bulged with damp muscle that I wanted to pat dry with my bare hands. I longed to touch the skin, feel the hardness in my hands. I knew it was wrong, that it was somehow connected to the "curiousness" my father had accused me of earlier that morning.

"A mess," Brother Mims was saying. "The whole business." When he spoke, my urge to touch him lessened. His voice always shouting. Like he was speaking to us over the din of a noisy room. *Maybe he'd find himself a wife*, I thought, *if he didn't talk so much*.

"So I hear," my father said.

"Half the church didn't want her put here if you can believe it."

"Oh, I can."

Even I knew of the scandal. The young girl had gotten herself pregnant by an older cousin. They had tried to run away to get mar-ried, but the family caught up with them in Arkansas—the girl was brought back home to have the baby while the cousin, a boy in his early twenties whom my father claimed was "soft in the head," was sent away to distant relations in El Paso.

"Mary-Beth was young," I said, and my father slapped me. Just barely. Hard enough to shut me up and prove something to Brother Mims, who'd looked startled when I spoke the girl's name. Brother Mims probably assumed the slap was a reminder for me as a child—a child of a preacher, no less—to be seen and not heard, but I knew even then that my father's slap was more significant. In part, it was a delayed response to our earlier conversation. Excess steam exploding through a relief valve of sudden violence.

"People do all sorts of things," my father said, "before they know how truly wrong they are."

No amount of Bible study or prayer could rid my mother of her bawdy laugh. The laugh of Ethel Merman in *There's No Business Like Show Business*, the laugh of Rosalind Russell in *Auntie Mame*. A laugh that glowed, that said, *Come in and take your shoes off.* Her laugh must have been the first thing my father noticed about her, a serious man of God like he was. Must have both repelled him and drawn him in. They met in 1982, two years before I was born. My father was leading a prayer service at a run-down Piggly Wiggly in the lonesome town of Weir, not ten miles from the Neck. He had yet to find a church home and was traveling the state ministering in abandoned storefronts, living on the meager collections he received.

Dr. Dillard—when he met my mother—still had all his hair. With a body more muscle than fat back then, he was an attractive man even if the pictures from that time show him in oversize cardigans and slacks. Clothes he would grow into as the years went by and my mother's cooking took ahold of him. His eyes were the color of slate, and once they locked on to you, you were done for. You couldn't look away. At the prayer service on the night my mother attended, he spoke in his usual quiet way. People probably leaned forward in their metal chairs to hear him, the stink of wet cardboard in the air. Baptists, as a rule, like their preachers to pronounce, to be bombastic, to be on fire with the Word—like Brother Mims. My father used other tactics; he wooed you to the Lord. His unlikely demeanor probably explained why it took him so long to find a church family. But I don't mean to suggest he wasn't effective. He'd get to speaking, his Texas drawl coming on strong, and you'd likely wonder what had taken you so long to accept the Good News. My mother was no exception, I'm sure.

She recounted their first encounter to me like this: On that night, he told of the Samaritan woman who met Jesus at Jacob's well. He often used the story for his sermons at Second Baptist. My father got a lot of mileage from the water metaphor. On his way back to Galilee, Jesus asked a woman if she would give him a drink of water from the well. The woman was taken aback. Jews didn't speak to Samaritans—such was the custom of the day. The woman questioned Jesus about this, and Jesus told the woman that if she knew whom she was speaking to then she would ask a different question, a better one: She would ask him, the Son of Man, if she could drink the living water. "Dearly beloved," my father likely said, standing on the cracked floor of the Piggly Wiggly. "Do you know that this selfsame water is offered to you tonight?" My father was a believer in baptisms. Not just the sprinkling on the forehead as performed by the liberal Methodists, but total immersions. "Dearly beloved," he continued. "Don't you know that this is a water to abate all your thirst?" At the benediction call, while the congregation sang "Open My Eyes That I May See," Debra Rose, who'd been sitting in the back, as was her custom, stood. They had enchanted her, my father's words. I never knew her to make a spectacle of herself in public, but this was different. A chance for salvation. Not only from her sins, but also from her past—a history on the Neck that she ran from at full tilt as she strode to the front where my father stood with open arms. When he hugged her, she laughed—that full-throated sound, reminding my father of all he'd ever known of heaven and hell. "Will you accept him into you?" he asked this husky woman, probably already a little in love with her, and she answered, "I will."

They embraced again, and this was when, she told me, she fell in love with him. A heavyset girl with a pretty face held by someone kind, someone steady. Her body shook with more laughter, both of my parents vibrated with her joy. As if a warm light had opened up between them. He pulled her away from his chest to get another look at this creature the Lord had sent his way. She was beautiful, yes, even if careworn around the eyes, and perhaps a little tacky with her plastic jewelry. He sensed sadness in her, too. A mystery. The words rolled out of his mouth, my mother told me, before he could stop himself. "Who are you?" he asked.

And maybe—who can say?—my mother gave him more of an answer than she ever gave me.

P eople often lost their way in the Neck," my mother said.
So many trees and hills. One pine looked like another, and not much sky could be seen from the ground, the trees packed as

tightly as they were. The stars were useless for navigation. Only the stupid and the brave crossed into the Neck, and only the stupidest and the bravest went looking for the women. Some men traded wares with them, but as time passed, the women learned an ugly truth about their dealings with the men: They got more when they traded their bodies for valuables. For a rut, they got guns, bowie knives, good fabric. "They weren't the best-looking sort," my mother said. "And I am sure they stank to high heaven, having only the river or the lake to bathe in." But that was all right with the men. In town they told of how the women's rough bodies felt in their hands, how they looked you in the eye the whole time you did your business, holding a blade to your neck in case you made a move she didn't agree with. The danger helped them gain notoriety, especially with those who liked a little spice with their lovemaking. A thrill, I guess, in never knowing if the woman who climbed on top of you would slice you open before you finished. Some of the men, it was known, wanted more than the women were willing to give. These men came back from the Neck wide-eyed and bleeding, missing an ear, or limping, or sporting a blade in their bellies. Occasionally, the law tried rooting the women out, but they always failed. The genius behind their business was mobility. They never stayed put in the same place longer than two nights, circling back to previous locations. The map of the Neck emblazoned on them like instinct. They hid their tracks so well some even claimed they weren't really women at all, but spirits. "Or witches," my mother said, frowning.

"But they were women, flesh and bone, right?" I said to my mother, when I thought I understood everything. "They were whores. Like in the Bible."

My mother winced. "That's an ugly word, nugget."

The back porch of the parsonage had fallen in and was home to knuckle-size dirt daubers. The roof had been patched and re-patched so many times neither my father nor my mother knew if there were any of the original shingles left. Most thunderstorms came and went without any fuss, but once or twice a year a heavy downpour would settle over us and leak through. Brown stains bled down the walls in the living room and the breezeway, obscuring the yellow wallpaper Agnes Musclewhite, the widow who'd lived there before us, had purchased from a store that must have specialized in religiously themed housewares: Little white crosses and black thorny crowns ran in alternating rows from the ceiling to the floor. The brown stains from the rain looked intentional almost. Nature's opinion of Agnes Musclewhite's questionable taste.

Because they didn't pay rent for the pleasure of living in the par-sonage, my parents met these discomforts with humor. When the window unit in the kitchen broke down, or the hot-water heater sprang a leak, or the lights flickered off when a strong wind blew past, they would look at each other and, almost always, shout in unison, "Oh, Agnes!" They knew nothing about the woman, so they could blame her for the troubles with the house. It was easier, I guess, than blaming the deacons, who were always slow to repair what had been broken, or themselves for landing in the Delta at a poor church that kept us in such paltry and dismal conditions.

A hundred steps separated Second Baptist from the parsonage. A hundred steps down a gravel road that snaked through cotton fields and under a crisscross of power lines, where turkey vultures gathered when animals lay dead in the ditch. Roadkill happened more frequently on Sundays when our dirt road saw most of its traffic as members of Second Baptist drove in from Hawshaw to worship. Inevitably, there'd be some possum or armadillo, too slow in crossing, popped open by a car wheel. Our closest neighbor was an old widower farmer named Mr. McBride, who chewed Red Man tobacco and still planted and picked a field or two all by himself. All his children lived up North and had nothing much to do with him anymore; he rented most of his property to dirt farmers who lived closer to town and didn't own enough land of their own to turn a profit. He had bought up most of Agnes Musclewhite's land when she died and vaguely resented us for living on the handful of acres the Musclewhite family had given for the parsonage and church. Mr. McBride wasn't a churchgoer. Sunday afternoons, my father and I would stop off at his place on our way back from the cemetery. I'd wait in the pickup as my father, his Bible tucked under his arm, climbed the front steps of Mr. McBride's house, a large two-story with a wraparound porch and a car-size satellite dish perched in the backyard. My father knocked and knocked on the screen door. And each time the silence that followed was excruciating to me because it was fake. I knew the old man was inside—so did my father. Mr. McBride, as silent as death, biding his time until we left.

We didn't visit Mr. McBride on the day I danced in the choir. Passing the old man's house, I asked my father if he thought our neighbor was going to hell. "Tough to say," my father said. "He might get lucky in the end. Come to his senses." In addition to total immersions, my father believed that once saved, always saved. No matter what you did, your acceptance into heaven was nonnegotiable once you asked Jesus into your heart. He had little patience for other denominations that believed otherwise. Like the Methodists, who kept to this notion of conditional salvation, where you could sin badly enough that your soul slipped out of fellowship with the Holy Spirit and you were in danger of damnation. "My God," my father said, and said often, "only had to die once for my sins." He especially hated Presbyterian salvation. They believed in predestination. And if he ever began to give his thoughts on the matter of predestination, his voice would rise to the volume of Brother Mims's. "I do not, do not, do not," he'd shout, if pushed, "believe in a God who punishes people before they are even born! It's not just cruel, it's undemocratic."

When we got home, my mother sat rocking on the front-porch swing, sipping on a pink can of Tab. After we parked, she hollered that supper was almost ready, and my father hollered back for the menu. "Well, let me see," my mother said, rising to her feet as we joined her under the shade of the porch. "I did up the rest of the squash and fried some cornbread and—" When she glanced at my face, she swallowed the rest of her sentence and put the cool soda can up to my cheek. "Get a bug bite, nugget?" I was fair skinned like her, my flesh always burning and peeling in the sun but never turning brown. Even the tiniest of licks, like the one my father had given me in the cemetery, would show up and linger for days. My father walked inside the house without comment. She removed the can from my face and took another swig, thinking, her own face flattening from a look of confusion to something else I couldn't read. We left her question unanswered and followed my father through the breezeway, then turned right to pass through the living room into the kitchen, where he was already seated at the card table, ready for her cooking.

No one in the Delta, least of all the residents of Hawshaw, knew of or cared about who my mother may or may not have been before joining them. Whatever happened in parts of the world beyond the Yazoo River was of little concern. If you were white and married to a man of semiprominence like my father, then you were welcomed. However, her reputation as a preacher's wife grew considerably more beloved when she established herself as a cook. My mother had *Bell's Best* memorized and never met a casserole she didn't like or try to reverse engineer if the person who'd cooked it had not been forthcoming with the recipe. Her work with the Crock-Pot—the stews and the briskets and the roast beefs—became the stuff of legend. It was her desserts, though, that cemented her in the hearts and minds of the Woods and the Dickersons and the Musclewhites. Pound cakes made with Crisco instead of butter. Spongy peach cobblers with caramel sauce. A three-layer red velvet cake slathered with icing so white the cake seemed to be lit from within. Her most favored dish—the one the three families requested most for fifth-Sunday meals—was the cream-cheese crescent squares, known affectionately as Sugar Dump, for obvious reasons. The few times she bought expensive name brands were when she fixed this dish. A layer of Pillsbury crescent rolls popped from the tube and rolled out onto a casserole dish. Then a layer of Philadelphia cream cheese mixed with a cup of sugar, followed by another layer of crescent rolls. She baked it at 350 for thirty minutes, and while it cooled, she drizzled the top with a thin glaze of powdered sugar and milk. A simple recipe with store-bought ingredients, but people loved it. I suspect my mother took great pleasure in feeding her husband's congregation. Perhaps a kind of communion: The more they ate her food, the less she felt like that old Debra Rose, the bona fide wild woman I wanted to meet, and more like the woman she had willed herself to be: Dr. Dillard's wife.

We ate meals in the kitchen, the coolest part of the house. For a time, the air conditioner had been wedged in a living-room window, but then one day my mother passed out cooking dinner, so it was moved to the window beside the fridge. At night the parsonage was bearable. A box fan in the attic was cut on so air was always moving through. But during the day, the same rooms settled into a swelter so dense it pushed me outside where shade was hard to come by. The only relief from the heat was the kitchen, and only, that is, when my mother wasn't cooking, which wasn't often. In addition to the cornbread and the squash, she had also made poppy-seed chicken and string beans that Sunday. The food sat in dishes shiny with fat while my father said grace. I stared at my hands during the prayer. After he finished, I dug in.

With eating, I was all boy, or so I had been told by my parents, who were always amazed by the amount of food I could put away, gobbling up whatever they put in front of me: pickled eggs, chitterlings, catfish tails. We'd grown into a plump threesome, my mother the biggest among us. The extra weight fit the frame of her body better than it did my father's. He was a man who had *put on* while she was a woman who had *filled out*. During the meal, she was silent and rueful, gazing at the air conditioner as it droned on and on. My father tried to make conversation, but she answered in *hmms*. I asked, finally, what we were having for dessert, and she said we had leftover crescent squares in the fridge.

"Sugar Dump!" I cried.

My father looked upset. He told me to think about skipping dessert. "You're getting to be a little big, ain't you?"

"Big?" My mother acted like she had never heard the word before. "Boys do better when they are husky, don't they?"

I asked what "husky" meant, but neither one said. I had always heard the word in reference to the brand of blue jeans I wore, but here, for the first time, I realized the word had another definition. Something that had less to do with the pants and more in common with the bodies that wore them. My mother shot up from the table and pulled out the tray of crescent rolls from the fridge. She cut out two squares with a spatula and set them on a saucer the size of my fist. When she set the dessert down in front of me, I looked at my father, who was furiously mashing up his cornbread with his fork, and said, "Am I fat, Daddy?"

He dropped his fork. "No, Rooster, you're not fat."

"See how you make him fret? See?" My mother was putting another square onto another saucer. She brought this one over to him, and his eyes widened when she set the plate on the table in front of him.

"Do I need to"—I searched for a word I'd heard on daytime television—"diet?"

My mother threw back her head and roared with laughter, and the serious look on my father's face broke into a smile. Soon he was laughing, too. I was more confused than ever. He stacked his square on top of mine, and said, "Boys don't diet," then after my mother had put her arms around his neck, he added, "Eat, son." I stared at the three flakey squares, gobs of cream cheese oozing out of their sides. I felt the seams of my own body expanding. The softness rolling over my pants and pressing against my shirt. "Eat, Rooster," my mother said. She reached over my father's shoulder and grabbed a square and held it up to my mouth.

M y mother freely admitted that most of her understanding of
the Neck came from hearsay and gossip. She reminded me of
this when she talked about the moonshiners. "The men," she said.
"Trouble always comes when you bring in the men." During Prohi-
bition, they began distilling hooch in the Neck. At first, the women
didn't mind. The men let them be for the most part. Sometimes
their paths crossed when a moonshiner needed an itch scratched,
which cost him, on average, two jars of shine. The women found
they liked the drink and wanted to make their own. But the moonshiners, seeing a conflict of interest, refused to share their knowledge. A spat broke out when the women camped too close to one of
the moonshiners' makeshift distilleries by the river. In the dark of
night, they crept into their camp and picked over the wares, trying
to learn the secret of how to make the product. When a couple of
the moonshiners stumbled upon them, they exchanged gunfire.
"No one hit nothing important," my mother said. "Just arms and
legs, but everyone was okay." The skirmish, however, attracted the
attention of the law. Police from Weir and West raided the Neck,
rounding up only the men, for the women had disappeared into the
trees and, as usual, escaped capture. The men were impounded in
the Holmes County Jail in Durant. When they were brought before
the court, the judge asked where these boys were from, and the
prosecutor answered, "The Neck," an important moment for the
history of this area, seeing how it was the first time the place had
been labeled as such in official documents. The trial ended with
acquittals all around after a nasty dispute between the officials of
Attala and Holmes Counties over jurisdiction hijacked the court

proceedings. Neither county wanted to take responsibility for the mess, so no one did.

"Most of the moonshiners moved on, not wanting to fool with the women, but one stayed behind," my mother said. This one had taken a liking to one of the women, a redhead who claimed to hail from the Great Smoky Mountains. He had often bought her affections and now, free and clear with the law, wanted something more. Not just from her, but also from the Neck at large. Soon after his release, he drew up papers to purchase the Neck and made agreements—unofficial, of course—with the two counties the Neck bordered. The deal was simple: If they (the counties) left him alone to do whatever businesses he wanted out there, he'd get control of the Neck and make sure none of the skirmishes or lawbreaking ever made it into their towns. Amazingly, the counties agreed, but most people doubted he could exert any control over the women.

He found them by moonlight, the deed to the Neck tucked in his back pocket even though he was skeptical the paper would mean much to the women. He offered, in essence, a merger. He would show them how to moonshine, and they would share the profits of their business with him. He had it all planned out. He had enough money left over from his moonshining to build them a large house. "He wanted to give them a roof," my mother said, "not knowing that a roof was exactly what some of them were opposed to." In the end, half agreed to his plan. "I was told the others went on to New Orleans," she told me. "But maybe they stayed—just got better at disappearing in the trees. A person can find enough spots in the Neck to get lost in if she's smart."

"Were the women and the moonshiner still there when you lived at the Neck?" I asked.

"No," she said. "Nothing left but the stories."

I asked who told the stories to her.

Her mouth pursed. "My mother did."

"My grandmother?"

"Yes."

"What was she like?"

"Lonely," she said.

That night, in a dream, I went searching the parsonage for my mother. My subconscious made the house cavernous, adding rooms that didn't exist in the real world. Secret rooms through doorways hidden behind furniture. Rooms that mirrored those I half remembered from my waking life: from school or church or restaurants we went to during the week when my mother didn't want to fool with cooking supper. I somehow found my way inside her closet: a hallway of sorts that went on and on, a wall of clothes on either side of me. I pushed through the dresses and the blouses and the slacks, kept going forward, and was eventually emptied onto the back porch. The hole in the porch, the place where the plywood had collapsed into nothingness, wasn't teeming with insects like in real life, but was quiet and deep, a circle of night sky in the ground. The outside was another room, a larger one that held the whole world within its walls. My father sat cross-legged on the good part of the porch, his body facing the hole that separated us. He held my mother's oversize nightshirt to his face, the one she always wore to bed that had Minnie Mouse appliquéd on the front. As I approached, he tossed the shirt into the hole and it was sucked in as if by a vacuum. He had a crazed smile, the looniest he'd ever looked.

His face screwed into a laugh, but no sound came from his mouth. His lips were stretched over his teeth; his eyes were squinting—and he was totally mute. I asked him, *Where is she?* And my voice, like his, was sucked from my mouth unheard.

I woke up.

My left shoulder and arm were numb from lying on my side. I rolled onto my back. Unlike in the dream, the parsonage had just one bedroom, where my parents slept. My room was not a room at all, but a portion of the breezeway segmented off by a wicker divider we'd inherited from Agnes Musclewhite. The headboard of my twin bed was pushed against the wall beside the bathroom. A light above the medicine cabinet had been left on, and it pooled into the breeze-way, bisecting the mattress. So I saw the wet before I felt it. A deeper shade of blue than the rest of the duvet, blooming from my midsec-tion. When I pulled back the covers, I smelled it. Sickly sweet and familiar. I slid out of bed, dizzy with the stink, and peeled away my underwear then my shirt. I tiptoed into the bathroom and shut the door behind me, carefully turning the knob to make as little sound as possible. The mirror showed that the mark on my cheek had shrunk to the size of a dime and faded from red to green. I shoved my damp clothes in the hamper beneath my father's under-shirts and his coarse work jeans. Once awake, I always had trouble getting back to sleep, so there was nothing left to do but sit on the cold linoleum floor and listen to the familiar night sounds of the parsonage: my father's deep snoring, the box fan's hum. The bath-room had a large old-timey sink and an even larger tub, both of them porcelain and cool to the touch, the nicest fixtures in the house.

In my parents' bedroom, the mattress creaked as someone turned over and got up. Footsteps, light and quick, padded into the breezeway. A pause to take in the wet mattress. Then a voice at the door: "Rooster, boy?" my mother called. There wasn't any lock to keep her out, but she didn't come in. And when I didn't say anything, the footsteps trailed away. A minute later, I went back out to the breezeway and put on a fresh pair of underwear and an extra-large shirt belonging to my father, the hem falling well below my kneecaps.

My mother was reclining on the couch when I came into the living room, her thick legs propped on an armrest. Most of the furniture was bought at Hawshaw's Salvation Army store, and my mother prized the couch above the rest because, she claimed, it looked the most expensive, with its deep-set cushions and multitextured patterns. The shapes and colors muted in pastels reminded her of the Gulf Coast. My father argued that the couch looked nothing like a beach. "More like the inside of a sweater," he said. We usually didn't sit on the couch unless we had company over. If we did sit on it, the cushions were turned over to protect the whimsical fabric from wear and tear. Tonight my mother lay sprawled across the unturned cushions, one arm tossed across her face.

"You okay?" I said.

She sat up and patted the seat beside her. I sat on my knees, worried my sour crotch would pollute her sofa cushions.

"I had a bad dream," she said. "Then couldn't get back to sleep— must be getting old, nugget." She wore her Minnie Mouse nightshirt, the same one I had seen in the dream, and her toenails matched the hue of red in the big bow between Minnie's ears. "You reminded me of my baby brother," she was saying, "when you was up there in the choir. Guess it's what was cause for me dreaming about him."

My parents never spoke much about their families. My father's people lived in Dallas, and according to him, they found it difficult to maintain a close relationship with him because he was too Holy Rolly for their tastes. "Occupational hazard," he said. My mother's people were even more mysterious. My parents spoke of her family in coded ways, peppered with indefinite pronouns and references to events I wouldn't fully understand until years later. Her parents were dead—this much I knew—but I'd never been given the cause, and for the longest time, I'd assumed it was old age, which most of our members at Second Baptist had died from. I also knew my mother had a younger brother and sister, whom she didn't speak to. After their parents died, they went to live with people in Nashville since my mother, who was eighteen at the time, had been too young to care for them. I had guessed this caused the rupture between them. My father and I sometimes heard her sister, Maude, on Christian radio when we were out driving. He'd turn up the volume and we would listen to the whole song before he'd grin, and say, "That one is a strange bird," and sometimes he'd add, "She's got a pretty voice, though, don't she?" But nothing more was said about my mother's family until tonight.

She told me her brother's name was John, and I asked her why a dream about John was bad. She said, "John was different."

"Was he curious?" My stomach flipped over itself like it did when my father went over hills too fast in the pickup.

"Yes," she said. "I mean—no." She glanced down at her hands. Each fingernail curved a quarter inch from its finger and was French tipped. "I mean, I don't know." She said we looked alike, her brother and I. "Same blond hair, same nose and eyes. But I'd not recognized him in you until today, nugget."

I asked her why.

"The dancing. It was something he would've done." She laughed. "The boy was crazy—wore taps on the bottoms of his shoes so if the mood struck him he could do a little number for me and Maudie-girl. Drove Mama and Daddy to distraction with his click-clacking. And, Lord, you might as well hang it up if the boy's feet ever hit on a slab of concrete." Her face seized with sadness as she remembered something else, something I knew she wouldn't share with me. Even when she was at her most open, there were limits to how far she would go. "I feel guilty, I guess," she said. Her eyes were light blue with a ring of yellow around the pupils. Sunflowers, I called them. "When he passed, I didn't go to the funeral. You was still very young, but I could've gone if I had wanted." In the dream, she told me, she was at the funeral. "How I imagined it was anyhow. Maudie-girl was singing and I was just so happy to be at a funeral that I didn't know what to do with myself, you know?"

I didn't.

Extended family was strange to me. I didn't have brothers and sisters or aunts and uncles. No grandparents active in my life, either, save for the random birthday cards from my father's parents with five-dollar bills tucked inside. My parents were all I had to help me make sense of the world. I sat on the couch beside this beautiful woman, my mother, who was as bighearted and loving as she was strange and secretive. Now I understand that two women made up my mother: the woman she was and the woman she wanted to be. Oftentimes these women were one and the same. But when they weren't, the jolliness left her cheeks, and her eyes dimmed. After she told me about her brother, I saw the hardness gripping her face, and I thought about the women of the Neck. The deep-down sadness. I told her about my own dream then. Even though I felt it would be a mistake to share it.

I had this notion that speaking the dream aloud was dangerous. Tempted fate to make it come true. And if she left my father and me, we'd crumble from the inside out like the back porch had. Our abiding love for her, though different, was a rare piece of common ground between us on which we could stand and find a way to love each other. Even at seven I knew this. She listened patiently to me as I told her about my dream: "You left," I said, "and I couldn't find you. You had joined those women, I think, or fallen in a hole, or just disappeared."

"Oh, nugget." She wrapped me in her arms, enveloping me in the warm pillow of her body. She wore Clinique Aromatics Elixir, and it stayed on her even after she showered, becoming for me *her* smell. With me safe in her arms like this, she began to tell me of the lost mother.

"Long after the women and the moonshiners left," she said, "there lived a family in the Neck."

After having her third child, the mother had a case of the deep-down blues. During the afternoon, while her children napped and her husband ran the gas station, she took long walks in the Neck. Long walks, by themselves, did nothing to abate the unnamable grieving in her heart, but she found the Neck reviving. "From maps," my mother said, "the place doesn't look very big—it wasn't the bigness she was attracted to, but the emptiness." So empty, in fact, that the Neck could hold all the sadness, all the evil, inside you and still have room left over for more. The mother always returned home in time to make supper for her family, but the father didn't approve of her leaving. He didn't understand her need to be alone, to go off gallivanting through the woods like some half-cocked boy explorer. The children didn't mind so much. When their mother returned, she came back with these amazing stories of the tribe of women who had lived there. "The children's father," my mother added, "was not an easy man to live with. He ran a convenience store in the Neck, the only sign of life for miles, that barely broke even in the good months, which made the father even harder to bear. Her stories were good distractions, nugget, cubes of sugar in the brandy." When the children asked the mother how she came to know the stories, she told them the land kept a better record of events than humans and paper ever did. "The children were too young," my mother said, "to ask her what the hell that meant."

One evening the mother didn't return at the end of the day. The children ran when the father came home to find her gone. His mood turned violent, his arm striking anything close enough to reach. The children didn't try to find their mother in the Neck during night-time, the woods too dark and spooky for them. They spent the night under the porch, listening to their father rage above them like a tornado, knocking over chairs, kicking in walls, screaming. "He was mad at the world," my mother said, "for giving him the bad business and the crazy wife." The next morning the children went looking for the mother and found her sleeping by the pond in a hammock she had fashioned for herself out of potato sacks. The mother was surprised when they woke her. Claimed she was dozing by the pond and had no intention of staying there the full night. But the sleep had been peaceful. She felt renewed. She returned home a new woman, keeping up with the chores, never straying too far from the house. The father assumed it had been a phase, the disappearing. A month passed. Then another. But little by little, the dreamy look in the mother's eyes returned. One afternoon, when the children napped, the mother went back into the Neck. By evening, she had still not returned, but the children weren't worried. They had come to understand their mother needed these excursions. "She was like a battery," my mother said. "And the Neck—it recharged her." The father was devastated to have this happen again. In a rage he doused his convenience store in gasoline from one of the pumps and then threw a lit box of matches through the front door. As the store burned, he made his children pack up as much as they could fit in their suitcases. They loaded into his truck, and he drove them far, far away—so far that the mother would never be able to find them. "And so the next day, or whenever it was, the mother returned to find, what? Ashes. Her whole life gone."

Hot tears leaked down my face. "It doesn't make sense," I said. "How could the mother not find them? How far could they go?"

I pushed away from my mother, clawing at her terrible fat breasts, but she wouldn't let go. She held me tighter. I wanted to shake myself loose—from her, from her stories. I wanted something true but didn't yet know how to ask for it. "Please, just listen, just listen," she was saying. She was crying now, too, her face drenching my shoulder. Suddenly, we were falling, the full weight of her body pushing me into the couch. Across the breezeway, my father had stopped snoring, and I wondered if he was awake. If he could hear his family sobbing and what he would possibly make of this scene we were making on the couch.

"*Shh*," I said. "Mama, please."

She leaned up, and I was able to breathe again. Her face was swollen and wet. "I'm sorry," she said, pushing her hair back from her face. We sat on the couch and stared at the doorway as if we expected my father to come walking through it and admonish us. But he was snoring again, and she took my hand and led me into the kitchen. "Sit," she told me, and riffled around in the fridge. We had eaten all the Sugar Dump earlier, but that didn't matter—my mother's fridge was full of many delights. When she reappeared from behind the fridge door, she toted a half gallon of chocolate milk. She sat the jug down on the table and went to the cabinet above the sink, where she found a large plastic cup. She filled the cup to the brim and then plunked two straws inside. "On three," she said, and sat down beside me. I knew this game. She and my father had played it before. They'd sip through their straws as fast as they could and use the kitchen timer on the microwave to see how long it took them to drain the cup. We didn't bother with the timer tonight, but I pulled on my straw as fast as I could anyway. I imagined my body infected with the deep-down blues, which maybe it was, and the chocolate milk was the antidote.

We slurped till there was nothing left but bubbles at the bottom of the cup. My mother tilted back her head and sighed. "Dear Lord," she said, "I hope heaven has chocolate milk."

"Do you think your brother is in heaven?"

My mother took the cup and rinsed it out with water and left it upside down on the sink counter. The kitchen had more cabinets than we had silverware, so she filled the empty ones with other stuff. My father's baby pictures, his thick books from his days in seminary. It never occurred to me that she would keep relics from her own past in there, too. I had thought I knew all the secrets in the parsonage. But she surprised me. She stood on her tiptoes and reached for something on the top shelf of the cabinet beside the window unit. This shelf held, I knew, a fedora that collected loose change, a calculator my mother used when paying the bills, and the koozie with the kitschy expression scrawled across it. Her arm snaked around and through these known things for something unknown: a wooden box. She placed it on the table where she had set the milk jug.

"Go ahead," she said. "Open it."

The hinges cracked as I flipped the lid back. Like an old book spine. The inside was lined with this red fabric that felt like how I imagined velvet would feel: soft and rough at the same time. A sash was inside the box, folded into a rectangle with the same sort of tight precision I'd seen with flags, and beside it, a tiara. Some of the rhinestones were missing in it, but the crown still caught what little light there was in the kitchen and twinkled.

"Your daddy says that when we go to heaven, we get crowns to lay at the throne of Jesus." My mother took out the sash and unfolded it, revealing glittery letters sewn into the fabric: HOMECOMING QUEEN 1968. "But some of us get crowns here on earth, too."

I picked up the tiara. At both ends of the band were these little combed teeth that secured it into your hair. My mother didn't tell me to put the crown back or to be careful with it. In fact, she wasn't saying anything I would have expected of her in this moment. She said, "Johnny had a flair, nugget. Like you do." And this was as far as she would ever come to giving me permission to do what I did next. When I placed the tiara on my head, she laughed—that warm and lusty laugh of hers—and reached over. At first I thought she was going to take the tiara off. But she only straightened it, pushing the combs deeper into my scalp. Then her fingers moved down my face, lightly touching the place on my cheek that had bruised.

"There he is"—my mother tried to sing, her voice nothing like her sister's—"Mister Mississippi."

THREE

•

THE NEW FAMILY

I recognized the recklessness of leaving my life with no warning to anyone, no preparation for the trip, and no goal, really, except seeing my father, a man I'd actively avoided for nearly half a decade. The first night on the road, I arrived in Cincinnati when most of the stars had already faded back into the navy fabric of the sky. Doll cruised along at sixty, five miles under the limit, the high beams illuminating slices of road in increments of six feet or less at a time. The interstate took me straight into the heart of the city through a tightly packed tangle of narrow roads and bridges free from any sort of traffic at so late an hour. I checked into a motel on the outskirts of everything important. It was a single-floor block of rooms facing Big Tally's 24-Hour Truck Stop, the convenience store's checkout counter also serving as the motel's front desk. I used my credit card to pay for the room since the available cash in my checking account was dwindling and a long summer of unemployment lay ahead of me once school let out later in the month. The room smelled of bleach and cigarette smoke. But the two twin beds were neatly made with bedsheets in neutral colors, and the carpet appeared clean enough to walk on barefoot. I had no luggage to unpack. No toothbrush to use. Not that I would have done either of those things if I could have. Soon after walking in, I crashed on top of the mattress closest to the window and passed out.

I slept hard. Though I hadn't spoken to Bevy or Zeus since the day before, when I awoke the next morning, I first called Cheryl, my adulterous officemate. Her voice was high-pitched when she answered, her cell phone probably not recognizing my number. "Oh, Will," she said, after I told her my name. "We share an office," I added, and she laughed. "Of course, of course!" Still unsure if she knew who I was, I cut to the chase. I asked her to take over my class, the freshman composition course I taught three days a week as part of my assistantship for the university. "Just until Wednesday," I said. Wednesday was six days away. I had no way of knowing if that was enough time, but it was better than asking her to teach the class until the end of the semester two weeks from now. The university could fire me for that—or I thought they could. I wasn't exactly up-to-date on departmental policy regarding the absences of teaching assistants, but I knew enough to know the optics of my not finishing out the semester in person looked bad. "They'll submit their final papers online to me, and I'll send you all my lesson plans," I said. "All you will have to do is stand and deliver." I also promised to deplete my checking account even further, adding a hundred dollars to whatever the university forked over for her filling in for me. Turns out, I was gilding the lily. Cheryl needed the extra cash, which

I should have known—what grad student didn't? Before saying good-bye, she mentioned how she hoped everything was okay back home—no sick family members or the like. "Oh, nothing like that," I said, and when I didn't elaborate, she said, "We should get coffee when you're back in town." I told her that sounded nice. And it did, it really did, though I was sure it wasn't likely to come to pass. My friends were people I disappointed on a regular basis nowadays, and I'd feel guilty adding another name to the list.

Case in point: Bevy. For this conversation, I sat down and took a breath. I selected her name on my cell-phone screen and hit call. "Before you say anything to me," Bevy said, after answering on the second ring, "just tell me one thing: Are you hurt?" I was fine, I said, and then she went off. Calling me everything but a child of God. "You motherfucker, you son of a bitch, do you know that I was this close to calling the police? And I hate the police!" When I reminded her she couldn't report a person missing until twenty-four hours had passed, she said, "Well, by God, we were just going to lie." She proceeded to tell me what had happened after I didn't show up at the restaurant, as if the story were a punishment in itself. When thirty minutes went by with no word from me, they tried calling. When their calls went straight to voice mail, they panicked. "I've told you about turning your phone off, Will!" Her voice sounded like she had been crying or had just woken up. I preferred to think the latter. "We drove to your place," Bevy continued, telling how she kept knocking until Elementary Ed came to the door. "And her dog was going ape shit—you know how Alix is afraid of most animals, so she nearly collapsed with fear right there on your goddamn doorstep." Elementary Ed claimed to have seen me leaving the apartment earlier in the afternoon. "A real jewel that one. She wanted to know if we'd like to come inside and partake of a fresh batch of pot cookies while we waited for your return." At this point I wanted to jump in to add my neighbor had not once asked me inside to sample her potent edibles, but Bevy kept on at such a feverish pace of chatter that there was no room in the conversation for my voice. "I remembered how you didn't park your car on the street," she said, so they walked over to the garage. There, they discovered Doll wasn't in her usual parking spot. Seeing this, Zeus made a prediction. "He said you'd most likely gone back home and I said, 'Gone back where?' and he said, 'Wherever the trouble happened,' and I said, 'How do you know so damn much?' and he said, 'He had that look,' and I said, 'What look, Zeus? And please stop speaking in riddles,' and he said, 'The look of someone with loose ends.' You know, sometimes I think Zeus likes the sounds of words more than their meanings."

She paused, finally, and I asked if Zeus was upset. "He doesn't really get upset—that one knows how to keep his temperature cool. Listen to this: I asked him if we should call the police, and he just sort of shrugged." I wanted to know what kind of shrug. "Like shrugging because he doesn't know or shrugging because he doesn't care?" I asked, and Bevy snorted. "Knowing Zeus," she said, "probably a little of both—why do *you* care which one?" I ignored the question and answered one she hadn't asked yet, telling her I was headed back to Mississippi to take care of some things. "Wait—I thought you were from Tennessee?" she said, and I said, "Yeah, well," and she clicked her tongue. "I know that's about as much of an explanation as I can expect." When she figured out I wasn't speaking because she was correct, Bevy continued, "I don't have to know. But if you are going into enemy territory, then I expect you to check in twice a day." I told her that was too much to require of me, so she lowered the bar. "Okay, hotshot, once a day." I agreed. "But voice calls only," she said. "None of this texting bullshit. I like to hear the other person's voice when I talk to them."

Both conversations had drained me. I walked over to Big Tally's for a cup of coffee and, while there, perused for toiletries in the travel aisle, picking up a toothbrush and a stick of deodorant. The other aisles were stacked with all the delicious foods I avoided in my day-to-day life: powdered doughnuts, cookies, and potato chips, kettle cooked or otherwise, seasoned to taste like everything but a potato. In the end I purchased a greasy sausage from the rotating metal spit by the register, convincing myself it was meat and therefore low in carbs and practically harmless. The heavyset woman behind the register had a name tag that said PEGGY pinned to her chest. She asked me if I'd like anything else. I did. Or, I guess, it's what I didn't want. I didn't want to check out. If I hit the road now, I'd be in Mississippi by evening. That seemed too soon. I asked Peggy if I could extend my stay for an additional night, and she said that would be just fine. She even seemed pleased. Walking back to my room, I ate the sausage in four bites and found I was pleased, too. It was close to noon, and I planned on spending the rest of the day in bed, napping, listening to podcasts, watching free HBO on the room's outdated TV set. But first, I wanted to call Zeus. Which was surprising. I rarely *wanted* to call anyone.

He didn't answer. Then he shot me a text message: "At movies," it said.

"Which movie?" I replied, already knowing.

"THE movie," he wrote back.

"WTF."

"I know, I know."

"Explain."

"Can't."

"Try."

He didn't respond anymore. And I didn't know how to feel about that or if I had any right to be offended. His silence stretched the minutes like taffy. They eked by as I checked, and rechecked, my phone for some acknowledgment from him. Last night I'd slept on top of the covers, my body wallowing in the same clothes I'd been in all day. Now they stank. I filled the sink with warm water and soaked my polo shirt and khaki shorts, then hung them over the shower rod in the bathroom to dry. I did the same for my underwear and socks. In my nakedness, I stood over the air conditioner, the cold air whipping at my balls.

I checked my phone again: nothing. I rolled down the covers and slid into bed, flicking off the switch to the table lamp. My body, even after years of living in it, was still a mystery to me. I lay in the dark, aroused, my dick so hard it ached to cover it with a thin bed-sheet. Zeus's silence worked on my skin as potently as a caress. I pictured where he was at this exact moment: in a theater, perhaps back at Cinema Station, watching a butchered version of my story unfold. The deep planes of his face made more lovely by the projector's silvery light blasting from the wall behind him. He slouched in his seat. His faded shirt was hiked back, showing a belly covered in hair, the product of almost two years on testosterone.

My erotic life existed primarily in the subjunctive. Past encounters filled with disappointment, the fumbling and embarrassment due, in part, to my own clumsiness. The future didn't promise any change—I was what I was no matter the expertise of the person in bed with me. But when alone, I found great pleasure in thinking about what might have been. Now I lay in my motel room bed revising that night at the movies with Zeus. I didn't have one of my spells. In this version I didn't leave my seat to throw up in the bathroom, either, and Zeus kept his mouth ringed around my dick, his eyes wide open and looking directly into mine. The movie playing on the screen was not *the* movie, but just a movie, something forgettable and routine. It had been a while since I had come, so when I was finished, I felt light-headed, my muscles twitchy and sore as if I'd been swimming laps. I looked at my phone. Still nothing.

I moved my clothes from the bathroom and draped them over the air-conditioner vent so they'd dry faster, then I stepped into the shower. The hot water pelting my skin made me pink and tender. After drying off, I slipped on my still-damp underwear. The soap had left a sticky residue on my chest. I didn't feel any cleaner, only layered in perfume. When my phone still had no messages for me, I broke down and sent him another text: "???" I was sure Bevy had filled him in on my whereabouts, so he knew I was safe. I didn't understand his silence now when before he had been so eager to talk. I only knew I wanted to be busy when he did reach out to me. Nothing seemed more pathetic than waiting for his call like some heartsick teenager. I looked up zoos and museums nearby. All of them were downtown, an area I wanted to avoid because parking was a hassle and nothing made the lonely lonelier than close proximity to small groups of friends laughing and carrying on. An idea came to me, a bolder one: I'd go to the damn movies myself. At least it's dark enough in a theater to pretend the others seated around you are alone, too.

I used my phone to find a theater nearby. One was a mile away, near a Walmart Supercenter. The next showing for *Proud Flesh* was in an hour. Enough time for me to dress. My clothes were dry but carried on them a faint sourness like rot. Before leaving, I pulled Doll up to a gas pump at Big Tally's and filled her up. Eschewing the card machine attached to the pump, I went inside the store to pay. I wanted to see Peggy again, maybe tell her I was going to the movies. "Not just any movie," I'd tell her, "but the movie Hollywood based on something that happened in my life. Can you believe that, Peggy?"

This conversation would never come to pass. Her shift, I discovered, had ended some time ago. A man named Tom stood behind the register. Pimply and sullen, he removed his earbuds and gave me a stretched-out smile, showing too many teeth. When I handed over my card, he informed me I could've paid outside. "You know that, right?" he said, and I acted like I'd forgotten. "Oh, yeah," I said. He ran my card then asked if I wanted a receipt. I said, "I sure would, Tom!" startling even myself with the enthusiastic sarcasm in my voice.

I was the only person in the movie theater. The first ten minutes, the part of the picture I'd already seen with Zeus, went by without incident. The roll of credits, the woman finding the two boys in the hammock, her horrified scream at the sight of them naked and embracing. This time was easier to watch. For a couple of reasons: one, my bloodstream wasn't laced with booze and antidepressants and, two, my psyche was prepared for what I saw. I was heartened by my resolve, if that's what it was. After the boys were discovered, the screen faded to black and flashed forward fifteen years. A group of twentysomethings was arriving at the campgrounds in their swanky

Land Rovers. The men had beards and tattoos and wore skinny-jean cutoffs, the fraying denim whirling about their knees in yellow wisps. They bounded out of the vehicles, hooting and hollering. Clad in ironic shirts, the women—two brunettes and a blonde—complained of the humidity's effect on their hair as they unloaded camping supplies from the trunks and called for the men to come back and help. They spoke in naturalistic dialogue, all of them talking over one another, harkening back to Altman's style of filmmaking. The camerawork was shaky—a technique to give the scenes not only an indie vibe but also the quality of found footage from a documentary, or maybe the director had no clue what he was doing.

The group built a bonfire, the flames licking up sticks and twigs and clots of brown leaves. Greg rolled out a cooler of beer and the others applauded. They cracked open cans and gathered about the fire to tell stories, a ritual as old as man. "The boys at the camp," Greg told his friends, starting them off, "were forced to do these cleansing activities." His hairy arm was slung around a woman, one of the two brunettes, who had an image of Supergirl on her too-tight shirt. She spoke next. "They did more than pray the gay away," she said. "They took weekly swims in the lake behind us." Another man, a blond guy, said that swimming didn't sound so bad. He reminded me of Fred from the Scooby-Doo cartoons. The others had faded behind the flames, and these three took priority in the storytelling. Greg explained how the water was polluted, how it burned the skin. "Too much chlorine," he said. "Made it harder for them to jerk off—themselves or one another." Everyone agreed that sounded nuts, but Blond Fred was skeptical. "How much chlorine would you need to pull something like that off?" Nobody knew, but Greg said one of the boys had a particularly bad reaction to the water. "People say his skin," Supergirl said, "was so badly blistered he could barely walk." Before one of the swims, the boy had resisted, and the others turned against him. "They threw him in," Greg said. "And the water took him and didn't give him back." The counselors went wading into the lake after him. The police were called. "They dragged the lake," Supergirl said. "And nothing—he wasn't there. Gone. Poof!" When Supergirl clapped suddenly, everyone jolted back, and she squealed. "Jumpy?" she asked. "They believed he'd dragged himself out and got lost in the woods trying to escape." The other brunette woman said, "What was his name?" She was the only one who wore glasses, which typically meant she was smart and virginal and, in the logic of horror movies, marked as the person destined to survive. Greg told her he didn't remember the boy's real name. "Only what they called him," he said. "Rooster."

At hearing my old nickname, I remained calm. Rooster. The producers must have consulted the other campers or my father. Maybe they traveled to his home in Mississippi for an interview. I imagined the conversation would've been stilted, tense. My father would not appreciate someone asking about his old life, especially now that he had a new one. No longer a preacher, he lived in Bucksnort, a neighboring town to Hawshaw. Last I heard, he had himself a double-wide trailer and a new wife to go with it. An invitation to their wedding had shown up in my campus mailbox at Vanderbilt. When I didn't RSVP, a barrage of phone calls from him followed. I never answered. By then, my father and I were not on speaking terms, and I didn't see any reason to change course. No matter what he said, I doubted he wanted me at the ceremony. Plus, my anger toward him was still ripe. I wouldn't have made for a good guest. The best I could've done for him was not go.

In the movie, when the campfire talk ended, Blond Fred ventured to the lake by himself while the others went to their cabins to sleep. Toting nothing but a flashlight, he trampled over brush and through trees to an area that was once Lake John. His flashlight revealed it was no longer a lake. The water had been drained, or had evaporated, and all that was left was this mushy oval of ground sucking at his feet as he stepped in. Here, the camerawork subtly changed—became smoother. I was no longer watching the character; I was stalking him. The point of view was now firmly aligned with that of the killer's. This was a technique employed by older slasher flicks—perhaps most famously in the original *Friday the 13th* where, before the murders, potential victims were viewed through the eyes of the vengeful Mrs. Voorhees, the mother of the dead Jason. Blond Fred knelt and placed a hand to the ground, then to his nose, smelling for chlorine. A noise, something like footsteps, got his attention. He glanced toward the camera. He pointed the flashlight, momentarily blinding the shot, filling the screen with light. "Hello?" he called, moving the flashlight away, coming closer. His face took up most of the thirteen-foot screen, a giant peeking into the real world. "You okay?" he asked, and I said, despite myself, "No, I'm not." Then it happened: the squish of a sharp object pushing into soft flesh. The camera stayed on Blond Fred's face, capturing the realization in his eyes as they widen in surprise, then shock, at being stabbed.

The movie theater wobbled under my feet. The sticky floor tilted forward, rolling me out of my seat. I tried to stand but fell again, my knees not properly working. The voices returned. The boys screamed. "Now," they cried. "Do it now!" I yelled back, "No!" so long and so loud that an usher ran in. She carried one of those LED batons that ground crews use at airports. She looked all of fourteen years old, even in her uniform, a tuxedo with shiny cuff links. She offered me a hand, and I took it and stood. My legs worked again. The movie screen had gone black, and as she helped me down the stairs toward the lobby, the lights were cut on, revealing row after row of empty seats. I was thankful. The usher spoke to me when we were in the hallway by the restrooms. "You need a water?" she asked, and I said that would be nice, and she said, "Wait here." But I left before she returned, ducking through the side exit that emptied directly into a parking lot full of gleaming cars. The place had filled up. Parents waddled around on the baking asphalt wearing sandals and weary expressions, their children pulling them toward the theater. When I got to the car, the inside was almost unbearable—air slick with heat. As the vents pumped cool gusts onto my face, I called Zeus. I didn't expect him to answer, and he didn't. Calling him had become, in this short time, routine. Something to hold on to. Lord knows what I'd have said to him. The more of the movie I saw, the more bizarre my connection to it seemed. I wasn't sure anyone would believe it. I had trouble believing it myself.

The first time I saw the killer's mask I laughed out loud: a princess face, one of those plastic husks with hollowed-out eyes and nostrils. Pink cheeks framed in chunky brown curls. A yellow crown topping the forehead to indicate royalty.

The movie revealed the mask midway through. During the same night the blond guy got murdered, the girl with glasses woke up in the

cabin she shared with the other girls to what she thought was screaming. Like your typical dimwitted character in a horror movie, she left
the cabin to investigate. At first, she set out toward the lake carrying
a flashlight similar to the one the blond guy had with him. As soon as
she was outside, we were back in the killer's perspective, following
her at a distance. His footsteps were loud through the brush, and
when she turned, he dipped behind a tree in time to avoid notice. When
he looked again, she had stopped in front of the shed, the metal lock
unhooked from a chain looped through a hole in the door. Of course,
she went inside. Instead of following, the killer went around the shed
and peeked through a window. There was someone else in the shed.
Greg came forward, smiling. They embraced. Their conversation was
muffled, but the gist was basically this: He had thought she would
have been there sooner, and she explained how she'd fallen asleep waiting for Greg's girlfriend to fall asleep first. She asked, "Did you hear
any screams?" and he smiled again. "Not yet," he said, and I understood then that neither of them was long for this world.

The killer moved back around to the door and slipped inside.
The girl had removed her glasses and held her arms above her head
as Greg took off her shirt. The light in the shed came from a fluorescent bulb above the door, giving the workroom a blue tint. As they
made love, the killer examined the tools on the wall. The scythe, the
machete, the double-sided ax. A gloved hand reached out to touch
them as if they were old friends, familiar in their rust. The couple
didn't notice him, so he took his time. On the table by the door,
there were more options—a hatchet, a lawnmower blade—but he
settled on the garden shears, using both hands to open and close the
long blades. When they cracked shut, the girl told Greg to stop. "I
hear something," she said. And that's when he rushed them.

I shut my eyes during what happened then. The screaming, the sound of flesh being torn apart. When silence returned, I looked. Still in the killer's point of view, we were gazing at the window in the shed, the same one we had peered through while outside, but from this side there was a glare. I blinked and leaned forward. The mask reflected back.

I was probably more shocked by my laughter than anyone else in the theater had been. The mask wasn't particularly funny, but the drive to Nashville had exhausted me and I was loopy. That morning I had left Cincinnati and made good time, rolling up to Music City a little before noon. This theater had more patrons in the seats than the one in Cincinnati had, and I disturbed several of them with my giggles. Bodies in the dark turned in my direction. When voices shushed me, I doubled over, my chest shaking with a sort of mad glee. I sat in the middle row of the theater, and someone from behind pelted me with popcorn. Other people were laughing now, but before it could become a trend, a man in the front stood and told us to shut the hell up. My stomach aching from the laughter, I stood and excused myself from my aisle, people gladly pushing in their knees so I could pass, ready to be rid of me. I held on to the railing as I climbed down the stairs to the entranceway, avoiding the glare of the man who had risen to hush me. He was still on his feet, arms crossed, when I passed by his row. He wore a wifebeater and sported a fascist undercut. Feeling ridiculous, I gave him a little wave, and a hand grabbed his wrist. The hand belonged to another man, still seated, who wore a matching undercut. This guy pulled on his boyfriend's arm until he nodded and sat back down.

———————

My hotel in Nashville was fancier than the motel beside Big Tally's. Most of the cheaper places were booked up in the city, I had been told, because of two events coinciding on the same weekend: an SEC softball tournament and a music festival celebrating the life and times of a recent country music singer who had died. Only the expensive rooms at the higher-end places were available, and I could have kept going, found something outside the city, but I was tired, and the movie was on my mind. I wanted to see it again, interested in how my life was being twisted and curious if I could endure watching it. My credit card all but smoked when the woman at the front desk ran it through the machine. Later that afternoon, after being run out of the movie for laughing, I walked up to a nearby Target to buy some extra clothes. All of them cheap and loose fitting, the shorts braided with elastic bands. I put on a pair and was on my way down to relax in the Jacuzzi when Zeus called. I let my cell ring four times before answering it.

All he could talk about was the movie, which depressed me. When I told him about my experiences trying to see it, he said, "So you haven't seen the ending yet?" And I said no. The ending was the most controversial part, he told me. "Radical," he kept saying, and I didn't know how he could sit through it. "All that killing," I said. "What's the point?" I sat on the large bed in my room looking at my reflection in the mirrored wall. In the oversize shirt, I looked small. Like a grown-up who had shrunk. Zeus asked if he needed to let me go, and I said, "Sorry."

"What for?"

"You know."

He did, but he had no intention of talking about my standing him up. "How are the gays in Nashville?"

"What?"

"The gays—maybe you can get a little strange." There was meanness in the way he said it. I understood then that I had hurt him far worse than I imagined by not showing up at the restaurant. His question was a way of testing the parameters. Friend or lover—neither of us was sure yet about the shape of the relationship. "Maybe it would be good if you fucked something on your excursion home," he said, his breathing heavier. He was losing his temper and, what's more, was pushing me to lose mine.

"Can I call you tomorrow—on the drive?" I wanted to end the conversation before he could say any more.

"I'll be around," he said. "And, by the way, I found it exhilarating."

"Huh?"

"The killings—it's like a dark gay revenge fantasy. When the blonde was offed, I almost stood up and fucking applauded."

I didn't know what to say about that so I didn't say anything at all.

The next day I drove through Tennessee at a diagonal, cutting through limestone cliffs and gradually moving into flatter land, into more fields and trees. A familiar geography, and with it came a tingling in my chest. And I knew why, of course. I was getting closer and closer to my father in Bucksnort, to the parts of myself I'd not considered in a long, long while. I didn't call Zeus. Or Bevy. I listened to public radio instead, zoning out to bigger crises in the world, the interstate pulling me south toward Memphis. I knew one of the boys from camp lived in the city. Someplace downtown near Beale Street. I flirted with the idea of stopping. The two of us had reconnected over social media during my years at Vanderbilt. We never spoke of the camp, and we never offered to drive the three hours to see each other, but our messaging had been pleasant enough, focusing on the now. He told me how he owned a popular chain of snow-cone booths throughout the city, and I told him about my majoring in film studies, my slow accumulation of useless degrees. A year ago he had sent me a message asking if I was still hiding in academia. Embarrassed, I didn't answer him, eventually pulling back from all of my social media accounts.

Sixty miles from the Memphis exit, Bevy called. She wanted an update as to my whereabouts, and when I told her, she said, "Taking your time, I see." I told her about the strained conversation with Zeus the day before. "He sounded different," I said. "Not like before." I passed a slow-moving eighteen-wheeler then set Doll's cruise control on seventy. Bevy said, "He thinks you may not be good for him." Then she breathed in and continued, telling me something she didn't want to tell: "He has his own problems—and he's worried about getting involved with yours." I told her that I didn't want anyone's involvement, that I had left to figure shit out by myself for this very reason. "I don't even talk about it," I said, and she told me that this was inaccurate. "You talk about it," she said, "in every other way but words. The way you act, the way you move through spaces. We aren't stupid, Will. It doesn't take a genius to figure out something is going on—something with you and that goddamned movie." I had unwittingly tapped the brakes and slowed down to forty-five miles an hour. A car behind me honked then passed. I put on my emergency lights and pulled onto the shoulder. All the while, Bevy kept talking: "I don't know what happened to you—but Zeus can't be burdened with it right now." I said I wasn't asking him to, and Bevy said, "You don't get it—all you can see right now is your own story—you're blinded by it—which is fine, and understandable. But other people have their own shit and . . ." I said, "I don't know what to do about that," and she said, "Just let him come to you—give him time." I remembered what he'd told me the night we saw the movie together. How he said he'd had bad days, too. I wanted to ask Bevy what he had been talking about, but what right did I have to know when I wouldn't share mine? Instead, I said the only thing I knew to say, an apology. "We don't need your sorries," she said. "We need you to get better; I need you to come back." I said I would, and I believed I was telling the truth.

Later a midday call-in talk show on public radio devoted a brief segment to the hubbub surrounding *Proud Flesh*. The host, a man with a thick Chicago accent, reported how the response to the movie from the queer community had been split. While a portion of us saw the movie as offensive, many others who watched it had a more nuanced and thoughtful critique, very similar to what Zeus's had been. "Some critics argue the movie is a defense of queerness as difference," one commentator—a professor of gender and sexuality studies from UCLA—told the host, "and contend that the killings are more symbolic than anything else." The host pressed the commentator on the particulars of this, and she said, "Well, there has long been a faction in the community who have resisted the push of mainstream queers to assimilate in heteronormative culture. Usually, the fight has centered on the question of marriage. Many militant queers contend that by marrying we bend our identities to shapes that don't fit us." The host asked, "Yes, but can a scary movie really do all that?" The professor urged him to consider the response of the director. When asked about the political dimensions of his film, he said the movie spoke for itself. "If it confuses you," he was quoted to have said, "then by all means, see it again." The professor said that was a clear invitation to look at the movie as something more than a gritty low-budget horror flick, but the host didn't see how. "But let's see what our listeners think," he said, and the show was opened up to calls. The first caller—a man named Dave—asked about the movie's relationship to *The Silence of the Lambs* and, more broadly, to *Psycho*. "Oh, there are clear connections to these films," the commentator said. "With one clear exception, of course— and that is the ending." When the host asked what she meant, the commentator refrained from further comment. "No spoilers from me," she said, and gave a little laugh. Then a woman named Cathy phoned in to say: "I read that book it was based on, and if you ask me, it all sounds completely different." The commentator agreed. "Yes," she said. "The production took many liberties—but like with most adaptations, there is a level of interpretation that we must take into account." Cathy said, "Uh-huh," and the host asked if she had another question, and she did. "Does the director hate gay people?" she asked. "Or does he just not care one way or the other?" The commentator laughed, more loudly this time, and said that neither was really true. "Robert Dolittle is actually gay himself," she said.

Robert Dolittle. The name caused another dust-up in my memory as it had when I had researched the film before the QueerLive meeting. Still, I couldn't place him. The ache of almost knowing more potent than pure ignorance. I turned off the radio and drove in silence, not taking the exit to Memphis. Not long after, the Mississippi state sign greeted me, its galvanized blue metal warped in the middle. Dapples of sunlight gleamed across it, a magnolia bloom sitting atop the second set of *S*s.

The town's name did little to recommend it. Bucksnort wasn't somewhere you went to; you passed through it. After my mother's death, my father and I drove up and down the highway that went through the middle of the town. Bucksnort had been predominately black, and we had gone into the area with hopes of attracting new members to Second Baptist. My father had been convinced that churches in the South—his church in particular—needed to be integrated. The greatest sin, he believed, was the lack of inclusion on Sundays when fellowshipping with the Lord. His liberal thinking only went so far. He was immovable in other respects, namely concerning sexual immorality, and firmly believed that those like me, the sodomites, fell short of God's holy plan for human relationships.

Early afternoon, I crossed the railroad tracks and entered Bucksnort proper. A cluster of dough-colored buildings, old but well maintained, constituted the downtown area, which was complete with a library, a Ward's restaurant, and a gas station advertising its wine and spirits in purple neon. Farther down the road, a neighborhood of single-story houses cropped up. Few people were outside, the heat keeping most of them indoors, dependent on their rattling air conditioners. Trembling and overworked, the units created waves of white noise, beautiful in its own way, a kind of music for summer. Those who had braved the humidity wore large hats and little else. Damp rags draped across their shoulders, they lumbered to and fro, going nowhere in particular, it seemed. Like other parts of the Delta, Bucksnort had few trees big enough for shade. In a little clearing beyond the houses, a herd of cows congregated on the west side of a blue-black shed, jostling one another for purchase under the sliver of shadow the structure provided.

The next turn was my father's. Canaan Road was paved with red gravel, and I drove slowly, Doll's wheels crunching over the loose rock. I remembered the name of the road from the wedding invitation. At the time, I'd thought it was just like him, my father, to live on a road called Canaan. It almost seemed as if he were bragging, but that wasn't his way. Trailers appeared on either side of the road. Single-wides, mostly: long tubular shapes of tin covered in vinyl siding nestled back from the ditches on little hills to protect the occupants from flash flooding. I knew he lived in a double-wide and that these, with their butane tanks and satellite dishes and freestanding swing sets and aboveground pools, were not his. It occurred to me that he and his new family could have moved since last I heard from him, but I wagered he'd have tried to get word to me somehow first. I began to worry that maybe this was a foolish notion to have about a man I no longer spoke to, and then on my right, there appeared a double-wide nicer than the others. One of those fancy models with glossy black shutters and a shingled roof. Red bricks trimmed the bottom of it, giving the impression that it was, in fact, a real house about three feet off the ground. In the side yard was a Chevy resting on cinder blocks. The blue paint, chipped and scarred, was the same shade of sky I remembered, and the sight of it caused an involuntary cry to gurgle from my throat.

I braked. Taken by surprise, Doll skidded in the gravel, doing a one-eighty in the road and nearly careening down into a ditch. A dust cloud was whipped up, coating the windshield with a skein of red powder as it settled back. I watched the yard and waited. No one was home, or if they were, they'd not been disturbed by Doll's crazy fishtailing. The lawn sloped upward from the ditch. A flagpole sprouted from a flowerbed in the middle of the yard, the American flag limp in the absence of wind, shuttered like an injured wing. Sticker bushes bristled below the windows, and a stone fountain, discolored and mildewed, stood by the side door. The grass was recently cut, no more than half an inch high. Each of these details a clue to my father's life now, to the man he had become. But my eyes kept returning, inevitably, to the truck.

What remained was simple enough: the parking and the getting out and the walking to the front door. The knocking and the waiting for someone to hear and come. Listing off the movements in my head, I realized how impossible they were. I no longer knew what I was hoping to find here. Doll was easy enough to turn around, and soon I was back on the highway headed toward Hawshaw, toward the familiar. My father was still my father, kind but wrongheaded. Who else was I expecting to find? After all, he'd hung on to that truck longer than he ever had to me.

An hour later, I was at my childhood home. The parsonage had been torn down years ago. Only a slab of concrete remained of Agnes Musclewhite's house. I stood on the foundation tracing the parts of the floor with my sneakers, cornering off my hallway bedroom, then my parents' bedroom, then finally the kitchen, easily the happiest room of the house when we lived there. I half hoped for there to be leftovers, pieces of the inside that hadn't made it to the landfill—a stray bit of religious wallpaper tangled in the monkey grass, chunks of hardwood floor left in piles. There was nothing; it had been wiped clean. I walked on, following the road to Second Baptist, counting to see if it took me the same amount of steps that it had when I was a boy. The windows of the church were boarded up and the doors locked. A part of the ceiling had caved in, and a wasp's nest had formed in the eave above the front door. Behind the church was a mound of dirt the size of my car. I climbed it, and at the top, I saw the Delta, flat and brown, go on and on in all directions. To my right, Hawshaw was blinking like a reflector mirror on a bicycle.

A four-wheeler motored up the road while I was walking back to Doll. I figured it was some kids mud riding. But the rider was a woman around my age, and she pulled right up beside me and got off, swinging one leg over the seat and jumping down as if she were dismounting from a horse. "We've had an outbreak of vandals in the past year," she said. She stood six feet tall in her knee-high muck boots and carried on her hip a pistol she didn't bother to hide. "I used to live here," I said, but this information seemed beside the point for her. "Teenagers mostly," she was saying. "Coming up here to screw and then get curious. Want to break into the church. See what's inside." She wore a purple shirt two sizes too big, pink cursive scrawled across it: SOUTHERN GIRLS LIKE THEIR TEA SWEET AND THEIR MEN SWEETER. I asked her if Mr. McBride was still living. "That fool," she said, not elaborating any more on the man, and adjusted the pistol holster at her side. Then she got back on the four-wheeler, a Yamaha Grizzly, the bear's snarling maw painted on the gas tank.

"You be careful leaving." Her voice almost lost to the small engine revving up when she cranked.

I drove to First Baptist across town. The church filled up a whole block now, thanks to the new addition of an elementary school, a long, squat building attached to the sanctuary. Evening had taken hold, and the dying sunlight shot slantwise through the stained-glass windows. Geometric patterns of red and blue and green imprinted the sidewalk winding around to the cemetery in back. The temperature had cooled off enough that I wasn't surprised to find a young boy cutting grass. He rode one of those zero-turn mowers, zooming in between and around tombstones with sudden and jerky turns. My mother's grave was in the back in one of the newer lots. Her tombstone was polished granite my father had bought on time, a double slab so he could be buried beside her. A fern of some kind had been set at the foot of her grave, its tendrils exploding in all directions, slick and green. On the left side of the tombstone, my father's name and birthdate had been engraved. I imagined he regretted binding himself to this final resting place, to a woman who'd not been his wife for almost fourteen years. Behind me, an ugly noise: the dull plunk of rock pulling loose from the ground. The boy had erred in a turn, knocking over one of the older tombstones. The mower had stopped at an angle, one of the back tires propped on the fallen stone. The boy hurried to fix it. He was off the mower and pushing it off the stone when a man shuffled out from the sanctuary, waving his arms and shouting.

The loud voice of Brother Mims had not aged, unlike the rest of him. His red hair had thinned and yellowed. His frame held fifty extra pounds of paunch around his middle. The boy Brother Mims harangued towered over the little preacher. Curls of red hair flamed above the boy's ears, the rest hidden by a green Delta State baseball cap. When Brother Mims glanced in my direction, I waved, and he stopped speaking. He shaded his eyes with a hand to get a better look at the stranger in his cemetery. "Will Dillard!" His voice rang clearly across the field of graves separating us. When I was close enough to reach, he grabbed my hand and shook it. "Look at you!" he said. Standing behind him, the boy clasped his hands behind his head, pushing the cap farther down. He was a baby when I knew him. As if reading my mind, Brother Mims said, "You remember my son, Toby?" He gave the boy a look, and the boy was obliged to nod. I said to him, "You've grown up," and Brother Mims piped in to say, "So have you!" He told Toby how I used to be heavy. "A husky thing as a boy—waddling everywhere, but then"—here he turned back to look at me—"you lost it all, didn't you?" I nodded. "It was not long after Mama died," I said. "Didn't have her cooking and it just fell off." For about a year after we buried her, I had tried to make some of her recipes—the casseroles, the Sugar Dump—but they always made my father and me sad, so I stopped.

Mentioning her caused Brother Mims to glance down at his feet. We stood by an ant bed, a little mound of red dirt the preacher kicked. An army of black ants, like crawling semicolons, swarmed out. Toby jumped back as the ants appeared to move in his general direction. "I thought I told you to pour them beds with gasoline," Brother Mims said to him, but before Toby could give an excuse, his father waved him away and asked me where I lived nowadays. When I told him, he whistled. "Lordy Lord! I bet it gets cold up there, don't it?" I said you get used to it, and he added, "If you say so, sonny boy!" We all moved away from the teeming ant bed toward the lawn-mower. Brother Mims told Toby to go on inside the church and cool off. "We'll worry about this mess later," he shouted to the back of the boy's head as he loped away. When it was just the two of us, Brother Mims asked what had brought me back to these parts. I told him a small truth: "In the neighborhood and thought I would visit Mama's grave." Brother Mims laughed and said she always had the freshest flowers. "I keep thinking I'm gonna run into your daddy one of these days," he said, "but he must come and go at early morning or dead of night." I said that sounded like him, not wanting to make a fuss. Brother Mims's voice turned serious when he said, "You know, I don't agree with how they treated him, son. Second Baptist was never the same."

I agreed. I didn't tell him how I could more easily forgive evangelicals for what they did to me than for how they abandoned my father, the truest believer I'd ever known. After he was voted out by the deacons of Second Baptist, he never ventured behind a pulpit to deliver another message, and I suspect the Christian faith was lesser because of it. I often thought his giving up on the ministry had, in part, to do with me, too. That he didn't think himself worthy to preach again because of how poorly I turned out. When I started attending the Mississippi School for Science and Mathematics in Jackson, I saw him only on major holidays and one month during the summers. While I perfected my ACT score and GPA, he moved around the state, following odd jobs. He spent my senior year on the coast, working offshore two weeks at a time. But the beach didn't suit him, so he returned to the Delta, finally settling in Bucksnort. In the meantime, we grew into separate lives. While in college, I discovered the longer we stayed apart from each other, the easier it became. By the time he married again, it was second nature to pretend he was as dead as my mother was.

Brother Mims's voice continued as loud as ever. "They never could find anybody like your daddy—so the church just shut its doors." He had his hands on his hips and was smiling. I wasn't sure what he knew about Camp Levi. The events never made the newspapers, as it wasn't something people were ready to talk about back then, and my father kept his distance from Brother Mims after he left the clergy. But I wouldn't be surprised if some gossip had reached him—such was the way with small towns: Information could travel from one mouth to another faster than most would believe possible. "All those Woods came on back to First Baptist," he was saying now. "And most of the Dickersons and Musclewhites, too." He laughed again. "I'm still not sure it was such a good idea to accept their letters of membership—they do like to meddle." He pulled a rag from his back pocket and wiped his face, a glimmer of the young man I had known still in the eyes when he wasn't grinning like a fool. "Their money sure is nice, though. Built that there schoolhouse by the road." He gestured behind me, and I turned to acknowledge the building I had passed walking over. When I wasn't facing him, he got brave and whispered, "You know, the people here was sure shocked by all that happened."

My head snapped back around. Old feelings of shame and embarrassment returned, the blood rushing to my cheeks. I was angry with myself for caring what this man thought of me. He kept on speaking in uncharacteristically hushed tones as if someone might overhear us. "There's nothing biblically wrong with it," he said, "with what your daddy did, but it sure bucked the sensibilities of his former congregation, let me tell you. They saw it as more of the same with that fuss he stirred up years before, when all he talked about was bringing the blacks into the church house to worship alongside the whites." The look on my face must have shown my confusion. He said, "What's the matter?"

"I don't know what you're talking about."

"What else?" His eyes widened. "Your daddy marrying that colored woman."

I almost laughed at the absurd words coming out of his mouth. I wanted to hug him and punch him, opting for a third choice instead: I backed away. But he grabbed my shoulder, holding me there while he continued to speak. "Please tell him to come see me—when he brings the flowers for your mama. I just, I just miss him." I shook myself free from his grasp. "I have to go now," I said, and he hollered after me as I scurried away, "You tell your daddy for me, son, that I still love him! The good Lord loves him, too! No matter who he chooses to love!"

At night Canaan Street was pitch-black. Not a single streetlight to guide me to my father's front yard. I'd parked a quarter mile down the road from his house and used my cell phone to light the rest of the way, stepping over the ditch and sidling up the steep lawn past the flagpole to the windows. I looked in several at the front of the house, the closed blinds shutting out everything but the glow of lamplight. The sticker bushes prevented me from getting too close. Around back, the blinds had been left open. In one of them, the living room: a ceiling fan, a U-shaped sectional couch, a flat-screen attached to the right wall. With her back to me, a little girl sat at a keyboard in the middle of the carpeted room, wildly slapping her hands against the keys. The keyboard must have been turned off since no sound came out of it. Eventually, a woman padded into the room from the left. Her hair was wrapped in a towel, and her nightshirt trailed down to her shins. She spoke to the girl, the well-insulated trailer blunting most of her words. The woman tapped the girl on the shoulder, punctuating some command she'd just made, and the girl got up. The mother—for who else could she be?—sat down on the folding chair in the girl's place. She flicked a switch at the corner of the keyboard, turning it on, and began to play. Now I heard music vibrating through the walls, and it was something familiar. A show tune—no, Gershwin. She played "Stairway to Paradise," and when she rounded to the chorus, a man charged into the room, the words belting from his mouth: *"I got the blues! And up above it's so fair!"* When they finished, the girl leaped onto the couch and applauded my father, who, like me, was much thinner, having lived so long without my mother's casseroles and cakes. He stooped to kiss the woman on her forehead. She was his wife, and jumping onto his back, this girl was his daughter. My sister. I pressed my face closer, my breath steaming up the glass. How lovely it was to watch them. Like a movie you never wanted to end.

FOUR

DO THIS IN
REMEMBRANCE OF ME

A year after my mother died, on a balmy night in 1996, my father drove us to an old county coliseum in Clarksdale to watch the Holy Warriors, a troupe of bodybuilders, perform feats of strength in the name of Christ Jesus. It was the middle of October, and neither of us especially wanted to go. Already that month we'd volunteered at the First Baptist Harvest Festival, manned the cakewalk, and sung in the choir at a religious play put on by the Baptist Student Union from a nearby community college. We were tired. But then there we were anyway, an hour from home, because we'd felt compelled to attend by Brother Mims. He claimed a portion of our ticket price went to missionaries in South America. "Well, that's something good at least," my father told me on the way. "Even if the rest is foolishness." My father had little patience for this type of ministry that combined the gleam of show business with religion.

My friend Suzette and I had researched the Holy Warriors online and found they traveled the South during revival season, from
Texas to North Carolina, spreading the Gospel with—according to
their website—a "unique blend of physical strength and prayer."
Suzette had wanted me to go with her to the movies instead. We
shared a love of classic film, and *The Postman Always Rings Twice*
was playing at the dollar theater in Greenwood. When I told her I
couldn't, she poked her lips out. Like me, Suzette had few friends,
and she took it hard when I bailed on her. "But, Willy," she said.
"It's Lana fucking Turner!" I was firm. "I *have* to," I told her, and
here Suzette dropped her head, knowing my next words, my new
excuse whenever I needed to be with my father and not with her.
"Because my mother would have wanted it." Sometimes she even
mouthed the line along with me, but never did she try to further her
case once I had mentioned the dead parent.

After we parked the Chevy in the empty gravel lot beside the
coliseum, my father looked around, and said, "Let's stay put a minute." He tilted his head against the window and shut his eyes. He
dozed. We were the first to arrive, and I was happy he'd found some
time now to rest. In the past months, the man had been unflagging.
The Harvest Festival, the BSU play, and his true mission, the one he
filled his days with in between preaching on Sundays at Second
Baptist: He proselytized in every corner of the Delta, expanding his
reach into the black neighborhoods and towns, encouraging residents to attend his church no matter the color of their skin, even
offering to drive them if they needed the ride. It'd become more
than a pet project for him. Since my mother had left us, he was ob-
sessed with integrating Second Baptist. When he told the congregation of his plan, couching it as something "the Lord has put on my

heart," the deacons threw a fit. They held an emergency business meeting after service, and a Dickerson man called for my father's immediate resignation. It was voted down, my mother's passing still fresh on everybody's minds. My father told them he needed to pray more about the matter before speaking on it again, and they thought, I was sure, that that was the end of it. Only I, sitting in the back pew during this meeting and listening to the men carry on, knew that my father had no intention of stopping. If anything, their resistance strengthened his resolve that he was doing the right thing. After this close call with dismissal, however, he kept quiet about the outreach, doing it in secret, with me riding shotgun in the Chevy with him.

As he slept in the truck, more vehicles pulled into the lot and filled the empty spaces around us. Some were these fancy church buses from the bigger churches in the Delta, filled with members who wore matching T-shirts. My father had wanted Second Baptist to make a strong showing, but none in the congregation had purchased tickets. This did not, however, deter my father from going. "Two is better than none," he'd said, and now he was snoring and I didn't have the heart to wake him.

At six thirty, two burly men in purple tanks and bicycle shorts pushed open the side doors of the coliseum. They remained by the entrance to collect tickets as people started to file in. Even from my perspective in the truck, a good hundred yards away, the definition was clear on their plump and hairless muscles. When Suzette had seen some of their pictures on the website, she admitted to being tempted to go herself. "But then," she added, "I bet they'd talk all about Jesus and it wouldn't be worth it." Thanks to her, I had seen several shirtless men before tonight. Her parents, Mr. and Mrs. Jin, kept a desktop computer with a dial-up Internet connection in the back room of their restaurant, The China Belle, and allowed Suzette and me to use it for homework. I was homeschooled and had already finished my homework when I saw Suzette in the afternoons after the bus dropped her off from the junior high. We mostly went on-line for dirty pictures. She had a talent for finding fake photographs of nude celebrities, the ones with the faces of famous people cropped onto anonymous bodies. She was partial to the Denzel Washingtons and the Chris O'Donnells. I claimed to like the Dolly Partons, making Suzette laugh hysterically every time I defended my choice. "Oh, you wouldn't know what to do with Dolly," she said, "if the old girl pissed on you first to give you a clue."

The coliseum was a spacious metal building normally rented out by the county to gun shows and beauty pageants. Tonight was something very different, and by seven, most everyone had gone inside except for my father and me. With the show about to start, the two Holy Warriors shuffled in last, but not before giving each other enthusiastic high fives. They left the doors open. It was a warm night, and the coliseum likely had no air-conditioning to speak of. Strobe lights suddenly flashed from somewhere inside and spilled into the parking lot from the open doorways—green to yellow to purple—set to an electronic dance mix, the kind of music Suzette listened to. After the lights and music were finished, a voice came on the sound system, welcoming everyone, so loud I understood every word from my perch outside beside my father. When the crowd went wild with applause, he finally woke.

He jumped, blinked, looked around. "All right," he said, sniffing. "All right now." He rubbed his nose, then nodded and said he was ready to get out. We entered the coliseum out of breath from the heat just as the announcer was saying, "Strength, Lord. We ask thee for strength. For your mightiest mighty." The inside looked like a gymnasium. There were bleachers and a stage and a concrete floor the size of two basketball courts. The Holy Warriors had forgone the bleachers and stage, and gathered everyone in the center of the floor around a platform festooned with strobe lights and half-hidden by fog from a fog machine. My father held an arm out in front of me to stop me from going any farther inside. I understood why: The audience, nearly two hundred souls, was standing in front of their rows of metal folding chairs with their heads bowed. The announcer, a Holy Warrior himself, was leading them in prayer. He stood on the platform, wearing the same uniform of purple tank and bicycle shorts as the rest. The strobe lights dimmed. He was both thinner and hairier than the two at the front door had been. He also had a microphone headset like Madonna's to amplify his deep voice. As he spoke, he sounded like thunder itself making words. We waited for him to finish, and then my father found one of the Holy War-riors idling by the bathrooms and gave him our tickets. This one was bald, with tattoos of the cross on one arm and a crown of thorns circling the bicep on the other. He led us to our seats, smiling the whole way, his wrecked teeth the only flaw on an otherwise perfect form.

"Here you are." The bald man pointed at the numbers taped to the backs of the chairs that matched the numbers on our tickets as if we might not believe him. Before going, he winked. "Y'all en-joy now."

As a series of demonstrations unfolded before us, each one more bizarre than the last, my father slumped lower and lower in his seat. He'd nod off only to be jerked awake, time and again, by another loud noise created by one of the performers crushing something or by a sudden flash of lights. He seemed to take this in stride, even grinning at some of the more ridiculous acts. The Holy Warriors were agile and fast. Their flesh looked stretched over pure rock, not over meat and bone like the rest of us. I wondered how long it took a person to get that big and that tough. Since my mother's funeral, I'd lost about thirty pounds. Our diet had drastically changed in her absence, and at twelve, I'd also hit my growth spurt, adding another five inches to my frame, compounding the weight loss and prompting my father to joke about putting a brick on my head to slow me down. I was thin but weak. These bodybuilders could easily break a nothing boy like me, a thrilling thought in itself. Onstage now was a black Holy Warrior who was screaming, "All for Jesus!" and toting several concrete blocks he then proceeded to pulverize with his bare feet. After him, twin Holy Warriors trotted out, both of them with thick handlebar mustaches. Their talent was breaking planks of wood with their faces. "I pray the prayer of Jabez," one said to the other. "Do you?" In answer, the other twin cracked several two-by-fours in half at once, using his forehead as a kind of battering ram. This went on and on between them, each brother adding another piece of wood to the pile they demolished until I thought one or the other would knock himself unconscious. Now my father was wide awake. He wasn't paying much attention to the twins; he was turning around and counting the number of people in attendance.

Onstage, behind the performers, sat a large blue tub covered in a tarp. I remembered this from their website. To the untrained eye, it resembled a large Jacuzzi minus all the jets and filtration pipes. Actually, it was the latest in evangelical outreach, a portable baptistery. Designed for Baptist missionaries in jungles where the water was too dangerous, the portable baptistery was used by the Holy Warriors to expedite the process of salvation. The idea was to get sinners to confess their sins publicly, accept Jesus into their hearts, and then baptize them—all in one night. Even Suzette had admired the efficiency. When she questioned me about baptisms, she was shocked to learn I hadn't been baptized. "Not yet," I said. "I think my dad's forgotten about it." While my mother was still here, all he talked about was the fate of my eternal soul. In his worried and quiet way, he'd explained to me the age of accountability, which I was quickly approaching. As soon as I reached puberty, I would be an adult in the eyes of the Lord and, therefore, needed to make some decisions. "This is not to scare you," he told me. "Just to prepare you." My mother told me in private that he wanted to baptize me himself, but he never said so to me. And lately he was too busy with other people's souls out there in the hinterland to worry much about mine.

"You see that?" I whispered to him. I meant the baptistery, and he said, "I sure do, son," referring to something else entirely. "Twenty-seven," he said, and I realized he was talking about the number of nonwhites in the audience. He was so gleeful that I didn't point out how they all seemed to be sitting in segregated groups away from the whites. He was goofy with happiness. The same kind of goofiness he carried with him on our visits into the black communities. A goofiness that made people who came to their doors suspicious and weary. Sometimes they never opened their doors but yelled through the walls for us to leave, to get the hell off their property. And we did—but not before my father yelled back that we weren't Jehovah's Witnesses and were, in fact, "good clean Baptists!"

His reputation grew in these neighborhoods until nothing greeted us at the doors but silence, that same sort we'd experienced at Old Man McBride's house. Still, we persisted. Then something strange happened back in August while we were eating lunch at a restaurant in Itta Bena.

A black woman approached our table. She wore this red coat with thick shoulder pads and a skirt of the same color. Her hair was tied up in a knot behind her head, not a strand of it out of place. She looked how I imagined a high school principal would look, and I could see on her face right away that we were in trouble. She asked my father politely if he was the man going around door-to-door, asking families to his church. He smiled big and said that was him. Without asking, she slid into the booth next to me, her face hardened for battle. "Now listen," she said, "I am the lead deaconess at my own church, and I don't appreciate you going off and meddling with a flock that don't belong to you." My father reached over the table to touch her hand; she flinched. "Don't touch me, sir." My father, taken aback, explained—in that same earnest way he tried to explain to his white churchgoers at Second Baptist—that he was doing the Lord's work. "You go faster alone," he told the woman, quoting a favorite Hebrew proverb of his. "But you go farther together." The woman laughed. "Cut the crap, honey," she said. "If you cared about these people, you wouldn't meddle with them like this. Most of them you are talking to can barely make ends meet— why don't you drop them off a food basket next time instead of an invitation to some white church that don't want them to begin with." My father tried to say something, but she wouldn't allow him to interrupt her. "And another thing: If I hear of anybody crazy enough to go to your piddly church and then get themselves embarrassed, or hurt, or worse—well, then, I am holding you"—she pointed her finger at him—"responsible for it." She then looked at me and her face was soft again. She patted me on the arm. "You talk to your daddy now and you tell him I'm right." She got up to leave, my father too stunned to say anything. Later we found out she had paid for our meal, a gesture that turned his cheeks red and inspired him to leave the waiter a larger-than-normal tip. In the Chevy, on the way home, he told me not to worry about that woman. People like her would come around. "It's scary," he said, "to do the new." As for me, I thought the deaconess made plenty of sense. My mother would have, too, if she'd been alive to hear it.

The last Holy Warrior decimated a phone book with his mouth, then the one who'd led the prayer in the beginning returned wearing only the bicycle shorts. He jogged onto the platform as the fog machine was cranked back up and the strobe lights flickered to life. As the music got louder and louder, he used all his strength, which was considerable, to pull the portable baptistery to the center of the platform. Sweating, he tossed aside the tarp, and the audience, sensing what was coming next, applauded. The announcer's body was similar to the swimmers' bodies I'd seen on TV at the Summer Olympics in Atlanta. Fooling with the baptistery had tired him out, and he panted, leaning against the blue tub, as the clapping died down. Then he asked, "Who will join me?" and while we contemplated his request, he did a limber backflip into the water, splashing the people in the front rows. The other Holy Warriors came back to the stage, as did a woman with a bowl cut who wore a floor-length robe that must have been suffocating for her to wear. She held a cordless microphone, and as the announcer resurfaced, she began to sing the praise song, "I Adore You."

Because he was hidden from the waist down, the announcer looked naked in the tub. The hair on his chest was matted from the water. "Come to me," he said. "For he says those who accept me on earth shall not be turned away in the hereafter." I imagined the celebrity face that would have been pasted onto the announcer's body. Suzette would most likely say Joey, that guy from *Friends*. I decided no face, famous or otherwise, should be on his. It was nice enough—a strong nose, dark black eyes, and a full thick beard. He held out his arms, and several people in the audience took this as their cue. They rose. The robed woman lowered her voice, singing the chorus of the praise song over and over in a hushed chant. When I stood, I half imagined my father would stop me. He didn't. He wasn't even paying attention to me; he was glancing at all the others who were standing.

My father often spoke of receiving a direct message from the Lord. He referred to it as a "call." He'd received a call to preach and another, he told me, to marry my mother. And yet another to desegregate Second Baptist. He believed everybody got at least one—the one being *the* call to salvation, this one being the most important. "When you hear him," he said, "all you have to do is follow." When I was younger, I had asked what God's voice sounded like, and my father explained it wasn't exactly a voice. "But a feeling," he said, "that gets stronger and stronger until you can no longer ignore it." I kept waiting for this feeling to find me, but it never did—or, at least, not *that* feeling. Several others came and went inside me, though, ones I wanted desperately to ignore: embarrassing longings for the same naked male celebrities that Suzette wanted, wild urges with nowhere to go and no language to express them. I hoped the call from the Lord would put these to rest once and for all. As I stood watching the shirtless Holy Warrior reach out for sinners, it occurred to me that maybe my case was special. Maybe I had to make the first move to show the Lord I was serious, willing. God, after all, had brought both of my most potent desires in tandem tonight: my want to be held by a man, to feel his body pushed against mine, to feel loved and sheltered in a stronger set of arms than my own, and my longing for true salvation, the peace that surpasses all understanding.

I was the first to walk down the aisle. Passing the rows, I heard murmurs of approval from the audience. When I reached the edge of the platform, the man-made fog had coated most of the raised floor so that the tub appeared to be floating on a cloud. Looking down at me, the announcer said, "This little one has come to the Father, and the Father turns none away." He beckoned for me to join him in the water. First I undid my shoes and then peeled off my shirt, revealing my scrawny chest, a cage of ribs protruding through the skin. I eased into the water one leg at a time. The coliseum had warmed it, so I wasn't cold as I sank into the little pool, the water reaching my collarbone. Like dew, droplets clung to the announcer's hairy nipples. I was close enough to lean in and lick them dry. He was no longer wearing his headset, so he shouted for all to hear when he asked, "Do you accept Jesus, my son?" I nodded. In that moment I would have likely accepted anything this man had offered. As if knowing this, he made his move, covering my face in his large hands. He plunged me down, down, down. The seconds I was under I prayed. I wanted to resurface into someone new, the old me, the strange boy I was, to be shed like dead skin. Rising back up, I heard the applause. A line of people had formed in the aisle. I waded over to the lip of the tub, winded and gasping. The announcer grabbed my toothpick arm and lifted it in the air to more applause. "Who's next?" he cried, and then he released me. He turned to beckon to someone else, and another Holy Warrior standing nearby onstage was telling me to hurry. "More souls!" he said. I monkey-climbed out, my body wet and heavy in the humid coliseum.

The bald Holy Warrior, the one who'd led my father and me to our seats, handed me a towel and ushered me back to my seat. When I glanced back at the tub, the announcer was helping an older lady in. She'd removed only her shoes, and the skirt she wore made the climbing over more precarious and awkward than mine had been. The bald Holy Warrior asked me how I felt. "Any different?" he said, and I lied. "I feel great," I told him. He smiled, showing off his crooked yellow teeth. "Now you have to be the light and spread it to other people so they can feel great, too." I was shaking the water out of my ears when he came in for a hug. The sour smell of his body sent shivers through mine, and I was immediately heartsick by how loathsome and hungry for touch I was. Nothing had changed. My father was no longer at his seat but standing by the entrance. I was crying when I reached him. I wanted to tell him how I hadn't done it right. Something was wrong with me. But before I could speak, he was embracing me. "I know," he said. "I know, I know." But he didn't, and so I cried harder.

I had first met Suzette Jin because of Henry Musclewhite, the ne'er-do-well son of one of my father's deacons.

In the spring of my mother's last year on this planet, the Musclewhite boy announced his engagement to Ginger Jin, Suzette's older sister. The news shocked the Musclewhite clan, and Henry's parents, Jim and Patricia, took it the hardest, claiming to anybody who'd listen, mostly to the people at Second Baptist sitting near their pew, that no son of theirs would marry some Chinese girl. My father opposed the match, too, but for different reasons. Because my mother had taken ill and couldn't cook anymore, we ate out with more frequency, spending at least one night a week at the China Belle. Ginger was often our server. We knew she was studying chemistry at Delta State University and wanted to go to medical school, and my father thought Henry Musclewhite jeopardized her future. Henry never held down a job for long, was dull-witted, and had recently been expelled from Ole Miss for driving his Silverado through the Kappa Alpha Order fraternity house after drinking too much tequila. "If anybody in that relationship is taking a step down," my father told my mother, "it's not the boy."

My parents took great pleasure in discussing the gossip surrounding Henry's engagement. It provided a necessary distraction from my mother's lingering infections. Every day my father came home with new bits of information to rouse her from the naps and the misery: The Musclewhites were threatening to take Henry to court and make him change his last name, or Henry was seen at the car dealership trading in his big truck for a midsize sedan, or Ginger had registered their wedding at Walmart. My father liked the idea of the Musclewhites having to reckon with a different sort of people. "It'll do them good," he said. "Maybe will do the whole church good—if we can get the Jins to come." (This was before he set his eyes on the African-American population; that would come later.) When Brother Mims came to the parsonage, he'd share his thoughts on the impending matrimony. He claimed his objections had nothing to do with the girl being Chinese. "Absolutely not," he maintained. "Everybody knows Asians are the model minority." Brother Mims took issue with her faith. "Buddhists!" he cried, his loud talk filling the house, making all of us participants in his conversation. "Bowing down to little idols and burning that foul-smelling incense and mumbling tommyrot!" My father contended that this was exactly why he hoped the Musclewhites were more open to the marriage. "We can change their hearts," he said. "But first we have to change our own, don't we?" Brother Mims said how that sounded fine and good in theory, but he pointed out that the Jins kept a Buddha in the China Belle, front and center for all to see. "They seem pretty settled to me. That little fat man is made of pure jade!" And here my mother piped in, saying, "Oh, it's the prettiest green, too, like something right out of *The Wizard of Oz!*" Neither of the men knew what to say about that, so she went on to speculate about Buddhists. "Where do you suppose they get married?" she asked. "Tents? Gazebos?"

The matter of Henry's engagement soon resolved itself when Ginger revealed she was pregnant. Henry Musclewhite—a heavy-lidded boy who always reminded me of the three-toed sloth I'd once seen at the Memphis Zoo—surprised absolutely no one with his failure to use birth control. But it was a wonder that Ginger hadn't. With the prospect of a new grandchild, Henry's parents relented, and it was decided that the wedding should happen as soon as possible. The Jins offered their backyard, and the Musclewhites roped in my father to officiate. He agreed to do it only after privately meeting with the couple for a consultation and deciding that the best thing he could do for them, and the new baby, was to ask God to bless the nuptials. "I'll do my best to give them a good start because I feel they are going to need it," he told my mother, who would be too sick to attend. She would send me along in her place, with instructions to report back everything I saw.

Only a handful of Musclewhites attended: Henry's parents, his older brother and sister, and their spouses and children. But on Ginger's side, several people came into town, mostly cousins from Memphis and Atlanta. The Jins' backyard was minimally decorated for the event: a latticed archway where the couple delivered their vows, ribbons of gossamer laced through the dogwoods and mimosas, and a couple of rows of metal chairs anchoring a dozen or so silver and white balloons. My father led the couple in a simple ceremony, reading some verses from Psalms before asking God to share his wisdom to guide them along the rocky road of matrimony. Afterward, we were invited to a small reception at the China Belle. The Jins' was the first Chinese restaurant in Hawshaw and, for many years, the best in all of the Delta, known for its large buffet. The restaurant was in an old VFW building remodeled to look something like Grauman's Chinese Theatre in Hollywood. My father and I were partial to their homemade wontons and the cherry sauce, and on the drive over, we wondered how exotic the menu would be for the reception. He worried the Musclewhites would react poorly to the food. "This could," he said, "be tense if not handled properly." I asked him what he meant, and he replied, "Oh, the Musclewhites will probably think they are being served cat and won't touch a bite of the food, and I can imagine hard feelings all around." But we found the buffet had been cleared of food, and the deep-red curtains had been pulled back, exposing the room to natural light. Everything gleamed like the inside of a jewelry box: the cushioned booths, the gold dragons spiriting across the red walls, the glass chandelier hanging from the middle of the ceiling. In the corner of the room, beside a potted Ficus plant, sat the fat Buddha. The little man's face was depicted in mid-laugh, his chubby features the perfect expression of contentment. When my father saw it, he whispered to me, "You know, I think Mims doesn't like that thing because it looks like him."

The Musclewhites and the Jins had kept their distance during the wedding, and now the Musclewhites were making an effort to mix, sitting at different tables amid the Jins. My father and I followed suit and sat apart from each other. I ended up next to Suzette Jin, who had not spoken a word to anyone the whole day. She mildly frightened me. She was a sulky girl, her bridesmaid dress a pink boll of cotton that she wore, whether meaning to or not, ironically. During the ceremony, her hair had been pushed in her face, but now it was kept behind her ears as she stared plaintively at the tablecloth. She looked like a younger version of her sister, but where Ginger had a smile, Suzette wore a snarl. To make conversation, I asked Suzette if she was hungry. She glared at me, and I blurted out that I thought Buddhism was cool, prompting her snarl to evolve into a smirk. I interpreted this as progress. Then I told her that Tina Turner was a Buddhist and she was my favorite singer in the whole world. A waiter appeared and filled our glasses with water, and Mr. and Mrs. Jin hurried off to the kitchen. They returned balancing steaming plates of steaks on their slender arms, looking like acrobats. Delicately, they placed the dishes in front of each of the guests, several of the waiters following their lead. We were served a lean cut of meat, a cloud of mashed potatoes, and a bundle of green beans. They were making an effort, too, so it seemed to me, to meet the Musclewhites more than halfway and not frighten them with their cuisine. After everyone was served, Mr. Jin—a serious-looking man in a gray suit—asked us to stand and hold hands. When Suzette tucked hers into mine, she dug her neon-green fingernails into the meat of my palm. She gripped tighter when I tried to struggle free. "Now," Mr. Jin was saying, "I will ask Mr. Musclewhite to bless the food." Mr. Musclewhite appeared surprised. He told everyone to bow their heads and proceeded to thank God for the Jins and for those who had prepared the meal that would, he said, "nourish the body, so that you may nourish the soul." Then I heard sobbing and looked up. At their table, Mrs. Musclewhite had lost her composure and was weeping into a napkin, trying to be quiet as her husband finished the prayer. Suzette whispered something.

I leaned toward her. "What?"

"Retards," she said. "You people are retards."

Once they began, the giggles were hard to suppress. I bit my bottom lip, asking God that Mr. Musclewhite—who went on and on thanking everybody he'd ever met, it seemed, since birth—would hurry up before I ruined the solemn moment. Every head in the dining hall was bowed except for three: mine, Suzette's, and—strangely enough—my father's. Later I would learn that this was the moment he felt the Lord speak to him. It was here, as the Musclewhites held hands with the Jins in prayer, that my father first envisioned the possibilities of an integrated church service, where all comers came together to worship as one. And it was here, too, that Suzette was exploring possibilities of her own. She was sizing me up—for what exactly I wasn't sure until afterward. I told my mother about all I had seen and done at the Jin-Musclewhite wedding. When I got to Suzette, my mother rose up from the bed and took my hand. "Oh, honey," she said. "You've made a friend!"

The day after the Holy Warrior baptized me, I walked over to the China Belle. Hawshaw was small enough to travel anywhere on foot. The problem was the humidity. The walk from the parsonage to the restaurant might as well have been underwater. I was drenched in sweat by the time I reached the China Belle's parking lot, the heat like a wet tongue licking me clean. A clot of gray clouds blotted out the sun, and lined along the front door, several grim jack-o'-lanterns grinned at me as I passed, their craggy smiles wilting in the heat.

The restaurant did the bulk of their business on weekends, so most of the tables were empty tonight. Henry Musclewhite sat at the table closest to the cash register, gutting a pumpkin. He looked up when I walked in and asked, "Raining yet?" and when I told him no, he went back to scooping out the pumpkin's stringy insides with a metal ladle. He knew I was there, like always, for Suzette. According to her, he had been a godsend at the restaurant. He did whatever they asked of him, waiting on tables and bussing them and sweeping the floors and answering the phone. He was also put in charge of seasonal decor, expressing a creative spirit no one knew he had, least of all me. In addition to carving pumpkins, he'd already hung orange and black streamers from the ceilings, and on the wall behind the cash register, he'd stapled a cardboard cutout of a witch riding her broomstick with a black cat perched on the broom straw, hissing.

I found Suzette in her usual booth: the one in the back, behind the buffets and beside the kitchen doors. She was staring at an open textbook, her face cupped in her hands. I slid into the empty seat across from her, and without looking up, she said, "Well?" I didn't know if I would tell her about the baptism. Suzette was weary of organized religion—she claimed to be agnostic. When I admitted the show hadn't been terrible, she glanced up from the book: "You can't be serious," she said. I told her I was and added how she would have had fun had she tagged along with me. She dropped her face to the table and pretended to bash her skull into the book. "This day, man," she said, "has been hell." Without her having to elaborate, I knew it was about her ex-boyfriend. The dreamy Derrick Wood.

Suzette was three years older and in tenth grade at the academy in Hawshaw. My father wouldn't send me there because he claimed it was a racist institution. Established not long after the public school system was finally integrated in the early 1970s, the academy had a predominantly white student body. After Ginger graduated, Suzette became the only nonwhite person enrolled there. I'd asked my father why the Jins were allowed to skate through admissions without any prejudice, and he said racism explained that, too. "Just a different kind," he told me. "The board of trustees probably believed the stereotype about the Chinese being all geniuses and good at math." Suzette *was* a good student, but she hated the school and struggled to fit in. The girls in her class, to hear her tell it, didn't quite know what to make of her. She swore, wore makeup, and didn't care a lick about cheerleading or football. And she was a little weird. If not for the school uniform—a pleated khaki skirt and collared kelly-green blouse—she probably would go to school dressed like some femme fatale from one of the film noir movies we liked to watch together. (She already did her eyeliner to match Barbara Stanwyck's in *Double Indemnity*.) Before she started dating Derrick, she begged her parents to send her to a prep school in Memphis. She had an aunt and uncle who would take her in, she said, and the city was like this promise to a better world and more opportunity. "Just think, Willy," she'd tell me. "When you'd visit, we could drink old-fashioneds at the Peabody and watch the march of ducks." But I didn't give a damn about the ducks and told her so. I wanted her to stay put. I knew enough to know that once you left Hawshaw you rarely came back. When she and Derrick Wood started going out, she stopped all her talk of leaving, and for that I was thankful. Friends were hard to come by when you didn't attend a proper school and your father was a well-known preacher—most of the kids who attended my father's church treated me like I was an extension of him, fearing I might report back to him all their sins if I saw any.

Derrick and Suzette's courtship began in secret after Derrick's family ate at the China Belle. She had been their waitress, and before leaving, he passed her a note. She showed it to me the day after, not knowing what to make of it. He'd written his number on a napkin. "You think I should call?" she asked me, and I told her if she wanted to call then she should. So she did, and then, just like that, they were dating. From his yearbook photo, he looked nice enough. He was her age and had brown floppy hair and wore braces to fix an overbite. I never met him personally—Suzette feared he might get jealous if he found out she was such good friends with a boy—but I probably knew more about his relationship with her than he did. When I dropped by the restaurant on days after one of their dates, she always filled me in on what had happened. The first kiss, the first grope. I even went with her to Eckerd to buy a pregnancy test when she let him screw her without a condom. "It just happened," she said. "He put it in me and then he was squirting." Neither of us mentioned Ginger and Henry, but I thought about them and I was sure she had, too, as we waited for the lines on the pee strip to turn a color and tell us her future. Luckily, her fate would not be that of Ginger's. A week after her scare, Derrick's parents found out about the relationship and made him put a stop to it.

The breakup had caused awkwardness between them at school. Their grade wasn't large, only twenty or so students, so they were bound to see each other every day whether they wanted to or not. Suzette decided to be an adult about it, she had initially told me, but today, during computer science, she had discovered that he'd asked another girl to the Fall Formal. "Becky Dickerson," she said, spitting the name out of her mouth as if she didn't think much of it. I told Suzette I knew her. Becky and her family went to Second Baptist, and she was a large athletic girl, with busy blond hair and a pretty face. Her father was the deacon who'd asked for my father's resignation. "One's a Wood and one's a Dickerson," I said, as if that explained it. Those families liked to stick together, and when I told her this, I added, "And I bet they are related somehow and their babies will be waterheads." She kept her face pressed to the book, too forlorn to laugh. It was Thursday, and I knew there was a seven o'clock showing of *Postman* we could catch if we hurried. But Suzette said she didn't feel like driving all the way to Greenwood. "What if I see him?" she said. "I'd totally puke."

So we spent the rest of the night in the back office on the computer. Waiting for the dial-up connection to work on her parents' Hewlett-Packard, we sat on the sofa Suzette's mother sometimes napped on when she was too tired to go home. Mrs. Jin prepared most of the major dishes for the buffet herself and was rarely seen outside these walls. Suzette told me she worked all the time because of guilt. Guilt because she had it so good here and so many of her family back home didn't. Surrounding us, on the walls of the office, were pictures of Suzette's grandparents and aunts and uncles and cousins who still lived in Hong Kong or thereabouts, people she knew only through stories from her mother. (Her father never spoke of home—he was a man, she said, who lived in the moment.) And when she spoke of her mother's people, it was clear to me that Suzette thought of them the same way I thought of my own mother's stories of the Neck—with wonder and suspicion that they had even existed at all. My father once said that the past always looked funny to us because we were appraising it from a backward glance with the heft of everything that came after to distort it. When I'd told Suzette this, she made a face and remarked how my father thought more deeply about shit than any other Baptist preacher she'd ever known.

Now she had her legs on my lap and was telling me she had decided on a Halloween costume. "Marilyn Monroe," she said. "From *The Seven Year Itch*." I had no idea she still went trick-or-treating; I'd never gone for religious reasons. She said all the employees at the China Belle were dressing up this year. "Henry suggested it—and we are going to hand out fortune cookies instead of candy." I told her that Henry seemed full of ideas since marrying Ginger, and she said, "He's good at being told what to do. So was Derrick. That's the trick— getting one you can boss around." I didn't say that Derrick didn't do *everything* she had wanted. Otherwise, they'd still be dating.

The Internet finally connected. Once online, Suzette checked her Hotmail account, and then we visited this New Agey website based in California and took several personality quizzes. We discovered through a series of multiple-choice questions that if I were a movie from the 1980s, I'd be *Dirty Dancing*; Suzette would be *Working Girl*. If I were a color, I'd be blue, and she would be yellow, which she claimed was racist. I asked how, since the quiz never asked about race, but she said they must have known anyhow and clicked off the page. Then she got that smirk on her face, the same one she'd had at Ginger's wedding reception and would always get right before she showed me a new collection of celebrity nudes. She made sure the volume was off and typed in a URL. At first I didn't know what I was looking at, but once I realized, I jumped back from the computer screen. Suzette cackled. Eventually, the camera pulled back to show a couple having sex on a barber's chair, the woman sitting atop the man, her large breasts shaking back and forth.

"She has big ones," Suzette said. The movie had paused because it was only thirty seconds long. The couple was frozen midfuck. "Like Dolly, jackass," Suzette added. The woman's hair was peroxided and big, but the comparisons to Dolly ended there. The man had a ponytail and a smooth torso, his penis shiny and fat. The website claimed to show full-length videos for a monthly fee. "Oh, yeah," I said, and she hit the replay button. For thirty seconds more, we watched the man bury himself again inside the woman, and this time Suzette turned up the volume. I had expected the cheesy music, the exaggerated moans—but not the sound of flesh on flesh, the squishy slap of two bodies being thrown together. "Are you sure this feels good?" I asked. Instead of answering me, Suzette leaned in to put her mouth on mine. And at first it was nice. The warm taste of another's tongue on my tongue exploring my mouth. I closed my eyes and let the kiss do its magic on me. I half hoped it would be enough to change me, this kiss, to wake up some inner boy inside me who had been asleep all along and waiting for this moment to come alive. The Rooster my father wanted so badly for me to be, the one who liked girls the way Derrick and Henry liked them. But the kiss only stirred up the old lust of mine, and I imagined not Suzette's mouth but the Holy Warrior's, his hairy face pressed to mine.

Eventually I pushed her off and went over to the couch. Through the walls came sounds from the kitchen, the clanging of pans and the loud erratic yells of Mrs. Jin to the employees. Suzette sat in the rolling chair, eyeing me, her hair all mussed about her face. Then she got up and rummaged through the little closet until she found a wig. "I bought this for my Marilyn," she said, and put it on. "Can I kiss you again?" She moved closer. Her face had lost its smirk. Her face showed me something more personal, something more dangerous: the look of desire. I had this idea that she wasn't even seeing me anymore—to her, I'd become just a body she could pretend was Derrick, the same way I'd done with her when we'd kissed. I said, "Suzette, please—we're friends."

She took off her blouse, then her undershirt. Her bra was the same warm beige as her skin. "Is it because I'm too small?" she said, cupping her chest and coming forward. "No—please." I put my knees to my chest, but she kept coming. It was like we were playing a game, a very adult version of Simon Says or Red Light/Green Light, only I didn't know any of the rules. "Is it because I'm Chinese?" She stood over me, her legs pressing into the couch cushion. She took off the wig and leaned in as if she were about to kiss me again. "Is it because I'm a girl?" Her eyes were dark and wet.

"No," I said. "I'm saved now." I went into this long spiel about last night. My baptism, the call—everything. At some point she sank to the floor, and there was only my voice, and then not even that because I had run out of things to say. We sat in silence, not looking at each other, the smell of grease and fried meat wafting into the little office.

"Oh, God," she said, almost like a prayer. "Oh, God, oh, God." She dragged her fingers across her scalp, then said, "I hate this place so much." I slid to the floor and tried to hug her, but she shook me off. "You will hate it, too—when you get older, when people start to figure out what you are." Her voice had turned hard again—something like Gene Tierney's in *Leave Her to Heaven*. She stood and tossed the wig back in the closet. "Most people probably already know a little bit. I did. Probably even dumb Henry knows." She pulled her undershirt and blouse back on. She fixed her hair. "Did your mother know?" She was smirking again. Only I knew her now. This ice-bitch routine was just bluster. A defense. She only acted this way when she was truly hurt. Still, my stomach felt like a foot was kicking it from the inside, and I wanted to hurt her more.

"Suzette," I said. "I'm worried about your soul."

She breathed in. "Get out."

"I think we should pray." I was talking crazy. We both knew it, but I kept going. "It's not too late for you."

"Get out!" She threw a couch pillow at me, and I was crawling on the floor toward the door. I was crying and crawling, and she was screaming and throwing. I wasn't fast enough for her. She rushed me, grabbing me by my shirt's collar, and pushed me out, slamming the door behind me, locking it. I tried knocking, but nothing. Not a sound. Like she'd ceased to exist once I no longer saw her. "Suzette, I'll pray for you," I said, my voice so small I doubted if she heard it. Up front, Henry had finished carving the pumpkin, and it sat on the counter by the cash register. He'd gone traditional with the nose and eyes, making them triangular, but the mouth had been sawed into a sneer, not a smile, with jagged teeth. He'd placed a candle inside, and the thing flickered with light. Henry still sat at the same table, but this time he was joined by Ginger and the baby. Ginger smiled when I came through. "How's your daddy doing?" she asked, and I told her he was fine. I knew she was enrolled in night classes and hoped to start nursing school in the spring. But I didn't ask about any of that. I was ready for home, for silence. As I pushed the door open to leave, Henry asked what I thought of the pumpkin. I told him it looked like something the devil made. "Like from hell itself," I said. Thinking that this was a compliment, he smiled big. "Cool," he told me as I barged into the night.

Not long after Halloween, my father called a special meeting with the deacons. He wouldn't let me sit in the sanctuary to listen to them—he expected fireworks—but the walls of Second Baptist were so thin that if I pressed my ear against the back wall of his office I could hear most everything the men were saying. Once he had them all together, he got right to the point: He proposed a plan for building a baptistery. "I've been inspired," he told them, "from an event I went to the other night." He didn't go into detail— maybe the Holy Warriors embarrassed him—he only said that it was something the church needed. "We should grow," he said, "if we are going to survive." It was voted down, naturally. The deacons thought the idea extravagant. "Especially," said Hubert Dickerson, Becky's father, "since First Baptist has a perfectly good one we can use."

At the next Sunday service, my father surprised the congregation by carrying a sledgehammer into the sanctuary. He stood behind the pulpit, clutching it, and said, "Dearly beloved, we need a new start." He lifted the hammer above his head and swung it into the drywall behind him. Flecks of wood and plaster flew out into the pews, and several deacons stood up. I was sitting in the back, and almost screeched, "No, Daddy!" when he swung again, heaving the hammer into the wall another time, then another, until a hole had been knocked clean through it. An old widower sitting up front was so excited by the commotion that he passed out, slumping and sliding out of his pew, only to be revived later and claim it was the best service he'd ever been to.

The deacons, however, were unimpressed. They convened again in another special meeting with my father in the sanctuary after church—this time no one seemed to notice my presence in back, listening to them harangue my father. The large hole in the wall loomed over the men like an angry mouth. They were divided on how to handle this latest incident. Hubert Dickerson, as he had before, wanted my father's immediate resignation. "The church house," he said, "is no place for stunts." But Jim Musclewhite, the father of Henry Musclewhite, came to my father's defense. He claimed my father should be allowed to shepherd them however he saw fit. "And," he added, "the congregation seemed to really respond to it." Perhaps wanting to repay my father for his officiating his son's marriage to Ginger, Mr. Musclewhite moved that they go ahead and build the baptistery, and I couldn't tell who was more shocked by the motion passing—my father or Hubert Dickerson.

————

All through Halloween and on into rainy November, Suzette and I didn't speak. I never got up the nerve to call her or even walk by the China Belle to chance running into her. Her talk of my being gay had frightened me off. I worried that what she had said was not only true, but settled. That I had made a choice about who I was without really knowing I was choosing. Meanwhile, my father had expanded his ministry, pushing beyond the Delta, spending all day out on the road, leaving me behind occasionally to do my schoolwork and chores. When home, he was at the church checking on the construction of the baptistery, which was going slowly. And so I was often left alone—really alone—for the first time since the passing of my mother, and I noticed her absence more than ever. After the funeral, we'd held on to most of her belongings, and now I returned to them, rooting out the tiara from the kitchen cabinet and her half-empty bottle of Clinique from her drawer in the bathroom. I sprayed the air with the perfume then capered through the mist, the tiara clutched to my head. I felt close to her again like this, her smell all around me, her voice ringing through my head, telling me about the Neck. I spent whole mornings writing down passages of what I remembered from those stories: the women and the bootleggers and the lost mother. Then I moved on to writing about my mother: all I remembered about how she looked and the way she said things and the meals she fixed. I got behind in my lessons and sometimes was so focused on writing about her that I'd forget I was wearing the tiara and only just remember when I heard my father's Chevy pulling into the driveway.

When not writing, I fantasized about the Holy Warrior in the baptistery: his dark eyes like little pools of black ink, the scrape of his hands on my skin. A week after my baptism, I was paging through my childhood picture Bible (something I'd begun to do to refocus my thoughts away from the untoward) when I stopped on a familiar drawing of John the Baptist. Wearing a lambskin thong, he was leading Jesus into the River Jordan. The sketch included the sinewy curves of his muscles, highlighting the result of a life lived in the wild. His eyes were not on Jesus but looking off the page, looking directly at me. I shut the book and threw it across the room.

Sometimes my thoughts were like a fever that never broke. Even in dreams, I wasn't safe. A dark figure haunted them—the amalgamation of the Holy Warrior and the John the Baptist picture. He slipped from the shadows at the foot of my bed and slid under my covers. His body pressed into mine, dead crickets falling from his hair, his mouth whispering nonsense. I grabbed at his face, his neck, pushing him off, but invariably pulling him closer. He put his hands under my back and—it always led to this, the dream—he flipped me onto my stomach. He fell onto me again and again, and I always feared I'd shatter into a million pieces before waking up, like always, with my penis throbbing into the mattress.

Masturbation provided only temporary relief. Six hours later, and I'd catch myself eyeing the picture Bible again, or remembering the couple fucking on Suzette's computer, or the sound of the Holy Warrior calling out my name. Guilt came and went, always waning as the desire grew. As fall turned into winter, and my loneliness persisted, my body began to change, and with this new body came a new geography of sensation. In the long, empty days I was alone, I touched myself all over. My chest, my arms, my belly, my balls. I couldn't help it. Once, I alighted by accident onto the tender knot of my anus, pushing one finger, then another, into the puckered lip until I went far enough inside to make contact with the deepest part of myself. Racked with pleasure so sharp and sudden, I blacked out. Later I'd wonder if other people—grown-ups who had jobs and lived in the world—knew such a thing on the body existed. If they did, how were they able to do anything else but this? When I did it again, and again, I began to believe I was touching something more ephemeral than an organ, the very essence of my existence, that part of a person you call a soul.

By Easter, construction on the baptistery hit a delay. The builders discovered they couldn't run a water line into that part of the sanctuary because of an outdated building code. My father was livid and spent many mornings down at the courthouse poring over old documents with a town councilman to find a solution. Spring had come, as it always had, with the white flowers on the dogwoods beside the church popping open, and one morning, while he was at the courthouse, I walked down to Second Baptist. The church seemed holier when no one else was around. After picking a few of the dogwood blooms, I went inside the sanctuary to see the progress of the baptistery for myself. The door was left unlocked because of all the traffic from the construction workers, and the inside smelled warm and soapy, like Pine-Sol and clean laundry. Every week a woman from Hawshaw polished the pews and vacuumed the carpet, and it appeared she had just been there. Everything shined. I sat on the back pew for several minutes twisting the flowers in my hand. Dogwood blossoms are white, with the edges tipped with dark red, the color of dried blood. Many Baptists believe Christ was crucified on wood made from this tree, and afterward, it flowered these bloody crosses as a kind of memorial to him. I used to take this as proof of God, these trees, and then I learned it wasn't in the Bible, that it was just a story somebody made up. To which my mother said, "Just because it's a story don't mean it ain't true." I wondered whether or not she would have thought the baptistery was a good idea. It had divided the church, with many believing, like Hubert Dickerson, that it was foolishness. "Throwing money in the wind," he had said after the vote to build it had passed. And now the hole my father had made in the wall was a window. The window looked into the baptistery: a blue-tinted tub about four feet deep, much smaller than the one that had been at the coliseum, and on the wall above it, facing the congregation, was a mural of rolling hills and blue sky. The baptistery only lacked the water line being finished. My father had joked if he couldn't install a drain and faucet soon, then he would just use a bucket and hose.

At Mrs. Audean's upright piano, I played some notes, banging out "Heart and Soul" and then what little I knew of "In the Garden." I removed my sneakers and slid my socked feet across the carpeting that ran between the pews to the front door, my fingers crackling with static. Next I sprawled out on the sweet-smelling floor and did snow angels, trying to make my body into one ball of electricity, and in all that movement, my pants slid down, and the carpet cupped my naked ass like a warm paw. From somewhere far away, the air-conditioning kicked on with its reassuring hum. On the wall, beside the front doors, was a painting of Jesus similar to the one in my father's office except in this one he was holding a lamb in his arms, a cone of light circling his head. To the left of the picture was the offertory table. Etched into the side of the wood were the words we repeated when we drank of the body and ate of the flesh: DO THIS IN REMEMBRANCE OF ME. Instead of the bread and juice, today there was a row of white candles on the table, stubby things no bigger than my fingers. I waddled over to them, my shorts tangled about my knees.

The drone of the air conditioner blunted any noise my father might have made in returning to Second Baptist. His movements are easy to trace. He entered through the side door that led into his office and went down the hallway and climbed into the baptistery from the back entrance. I'm not sure how long he was standing there before he noticed me. The image of his son prone on the church floor, nudging a candle in and out of himself, must have taken more than a few seconds to fully process.

When I saw him, it was already too late. I struggled to stand, to pull up my shorts. If I had been faster about it, I would have bolted out of the church, put as much space between my father and me as I could. But I was not fast, and he reached me in no time at all. He was not a violent man, but this—*this*—had been on the docket for a long time. Ever since I'd first embarrassed him in the choir with my sissified dancing. When his fist first landed against the side of my face, I almost sighed. *Finally,* I thought. *Let it come. Let it all fall down.* A rage had broken loose from inside him. He beat me until there was no cry left in either of our throats, and then he fell to floor, red faced and exhausted.

"Goddamn," he said. "Goddamn."

I grabbed a pew and got to my feet before he had fully recovered.

The door to the outside had never seemed so far away as I stumbled toward it.

"Rooster," my father called, but he wasn't coming after me. He was still too winded.

My back had taken the worst of it, but nothing serious enough to keep me from walking. If anything, the walking helped loosen the soreness in my joints. I rambled through Hawshaw not knowing where to go but ending up at the only place I knew to go: the China Belle. I had this notion that Suzette would see me like this, all bruised and beaten up, and instantly take pity. She would lead me into the back office and clean me off, touching me tenderly. We would never speak of what had happened between us that awful night six months before, and by the end of the evening, we'd have it all worked out. She'd tell me I could stay with her, with the Jins. I knew it was fantasy. That didn't stop me, however, from going into the restaurant with this ridiculous hope that seeing her would make everything better.

It was Tuesday, and the place was almost empty save for the table by the cash register. Henry sat there holding his baby in his lap and blowing raspberries on her cheeks and neck. The baby's name was Stacey, and she had enough hair to wear pigtails now. Ginger sat beside them, her daughter's pudgy hand gripping her finger, but when Ginger saw me, she stood. "You fall, Will?" You never know how bad you look until you see yourself in the eyes of other people. I nodded and told them how I wasn't watching where I was going and tripped into a ditch. "Just kept rolling," I said. The lie came so easily to me it was a wonder I didn't tell more of them. She grabbed some napkins from the metal dispenser on the table. "Sit," she instructed, waving me to their table. Still holding the baby, Henry had managed to produce, as if from nowhere, a glass of water and crushed ice. Ginger dipped the edge of a napkin into the glass. "Looks like you caught the wrong end of a fist," Henry was saying as Ginger touched the cool wet to places on my forehead where the skin had broken open. After wiping my face, which had more blood on it than I'd realized, Ginger used cotton balls to dab the cuts with hydrogen peroxide, causing them to froth and bubble. "You need us to call somebody?" she asked. "Your dad?"

I shook my head. "Suzette around?"

"Not until May—unless Mama lets her stay in Memphis for the summer, too." She smiled. "Next time you fall, honey, I might be a nurse and have to charge you for the cleanup." Baby Stacey squealed as if she understood her mother's joke and approved. It had been almost six months since I'd set foot in the restaurant. I wanted to say, "Well, of course," because I wasn't surprised at all, really, by Suzette's hightailing it to Memphis, though it stung she hadn't said good-bye. Maybe it had been easier not to face me again, or maybe she hadn't cared enough one way or the other. I never could tell how much or how little she felt about something until it was too late. Mrs. Jin came out from the kitchen and spoke to her daughter in Chinese. Ginger said something back and then tossed the used cotton balls into the trash bin. "My mother says you should stay for supper." I tried to say thank you to Mrs. Jin, but she had already disappeared back through the swinging kitchen doors. Thirty minutes later, she brought out steamed buns stuffed with pork and sliced cucumbers. Mr. Jin was out of town, and Henry and Ginger sat at one end of the table tending to their daughter, leaving Mrs. Jin and me to make conversation. She had never spoken to me directly. Now we sat across from each other in silence while her daughter and son-in-law cooed with baby Stacey, who they'd squeezed into a wooden high chair. Henry was feeding her banana-flavored baby food, the yellow mush finding its way onto the baby's clothes more than in her mouth. Mrs. Jin and I locked eyes several times, and once she gave me one of Suzette's smirks. I asked her how her daughter was doing in Memphis, and she gestured vaguely. "Away," she said, and shrugged. I wondered if she would have said the same thing had I asked her about the people who were in the pictures on the wall in the back office. *Away.* As in *better off*? Or, simply, *not here*? Outside, it was dark now: The streetlight in the parking lot had flickered on, and I dreaded the trek back to the parsonage. Most likely, my father would already be in bed, not wanting to face me. At some point during the meal, Mrs. Jin sat back in her chair, closed her eyes, and began to snore lightly. Ginger heard it, and said, "Don't mind her—she lives tired."

"No," I said. "It's beautiful."

And this made Henry stop feeding his daughter and grin—first at Ginger, then at me. His grin turned into a chuckle. "You, Will, say the strangest things," he said. "You almost make me look normal." Ginger cocked her head at him. She laughed now, too, the sound jerking Mrs. Jin awake, which tickled all of us, even baby Stacey.

A toe. A leg. Then all of her. My mother left this world a little at a time.

When I was nine, a spider—we never found out what kind—made a home in the warmth of one of her slippers cast under her bed. She claimed to have felt nothing when she put them on in the morning and went about her day and wouldn't have noticed anything out of order if the blood hadn't begun to leak through her cloth shoe, leaving a trail of red behind her. By then she was already a diabetic, and a poorly managed one, too, often missing her insulin injections and failing to check her glucose levels. When she had first been diagnosed, the doctor told her to change her habits, and she'd thought that meant eating less instead of eating differently. The same starchy casseroles and breaded desserts appeared on our dinner table. My father complained, but it did no good. She said she did the best she could with the small budget we lived on. The bite never completely healed, and she began to limp and then, the pain too much for her, rarely stood at all. She became bedridden not long after that. The toe was removed the December before Henry and Ginger's wedding. Then the whole leg came off, and she stopped leaving the house for good. The infection persisted—coming back in bedsores that festered on her back end. The doctors were amazed at how fast she went. "Usually," one of them said to my father, "a person just hangs on suffering, but it's like she made up her mind about it and that's all she wrote." At my mother's request, the casket was closed. "I don't want people gawking at me," my father had remembered her saying. Surrounding the casket were peace lilies, gerbera daisies, violets. It was springtime and people were generous. All of Hawshaw came to the funeral home to pay their respects. My father and I stood at the foot of her casket to receive them, both of us too dazed to be sad, not quite believing she wouldn't be there lumbering around the kitchen when we got home. My father didn't give the eulogy, he claimed he was too emotional, and so the task fell to Brother Mims, who screamed the whole way through it, which was comforting in that it was, at least, expected. After we'd put her in the ground, my father went to his bedroom, and I went to the kitchen. In the refrigerator and the cabinets were all the ingredients I needed: milk, crescent rolls, sugar. It took an hour or so to make, and I didn't wait for the squares to cool before I began to eat them. I shoveled them into my face, chewing and swallowing all that flakey sweetness, the very food that had a hand, I knew, in killing my mother. I ate every single square of the Sugar Dump. Later that night, I vomited them all back up, making it outside in time to do it quietly in the monkey grass so as not to wake up my father.

Since our confrontation in the sanctuary, my father and I had spoken only a handful of words to each other, and the Sunday the baptistery had been completed was no different. He rose before the sun and was already in his office at Second Baptist before I finally woke up around nine. My mother had taught me how to iron my dress shirts and slacks and how to fix my necktie into a double Windsor. Today I wore a blue coat and a red tie—clothes I had inherited from a cousin in the Musclewhite family who had outgrown them. I sat in the back row, arriving just before service began so I wouldn't have to speak to anybody. My mother liked to sit there, so she told me, because it allowed her to read the crowd. She judged how my father's message landed with them. If she ever saw the congregation slumping in their seats or fidgeting or doing anything that made them appear restless, she would signal my father to hurry up and get on to the important part of the message already because he was losing them.

On this Sunday, with the baptistery behind him, my father opened the service by calling on Becky Dickerson's father to lead us in prayer. Hubert Dickerson thanked the Lord for giving us the funds and the patience to complete the project and then he asked that the baptistery might be used "to save souls, far and wide." At this, my father cried "Amen," and mumblings of agreement drifted through the pews. During announcements, one of the Woods reminded everyone that after service a lunch had been prepared in the fellowship hall for everyone. The lunches and the dinners at Second Baptist were always the hardest because my mother had played such a vital role in them. I dreaded the casseroles and the desserts that awaited me. Some of the women had taken to cooking my mother's dishes, but their variations on them were never good enough, always off in some way. Often I left resentful for their attempts and guilty for not trying hard enough to like them.

We had finished with the offertory hymn, and it was a quarter past twelve. After the song leader took his seat, my father returned to the pulpit and was reading from scripture in his quiet, melodic way, the words becoming almost a song in his mouth. One of the double front doors clicked open, and I turned around. A family of four shuffled in: a mother and father, followed by their two sons. They paused in the back by my pew and surveyed the scene before them. The mother pointed to the middle pews, to one that was empty. The father nodded, and then they walked down the big aisle in single file. The congregation didn't pay them much mind at first. But slowly and surely, I noted the turn of heads. The whispers came next. An old Musclewhite woman sitting up front turned all the way around shaking her head in her seat to glare at the family before turning back around.

As for me, I was flooded with the insane giddiness that comes from watching the slow-motion buildup to a disaster. My father hadn't noticed them yet. He had his eyes trained on the verses he was reading aloud from his ratty leather Bible. His sermon centered on some words from the Apostle Paul to the Corinthians about spiritual growth. When the song leader returned to lead the congregation in "Count Your Blessings," my father stepped aside and glanced out to his flock—his head jerking in a double take when he saw the family for himself. I tried so hard not to hate him in this moment. Not to hate the way his eyes widened or how his mouth curled into a big goofy smile. When the song was over, he said, "Can I hear an amen?" and nobody spoke for the longest time. He was forced to repeat the question, his smile never wavering. Jim Musclewhite— perhaps my father's lone ally in the church—gave a weak amen and dipped his head.

Anger bubbled up from the pews like heat. Only a fool could have missed it, but maybe my father was such a fool. The family kept their eyes straight ahead, as if they had rehearsed it, studying the pulpit, my father, the baptistery. My mother would have given him a signal to hurry the sermon along before there was an outburst. But I was not my mother. The wave of anger moving through the church-goers and washing over me was more satisfying than I expected. I wanted my father to feel the full wrath of his congregation, his bigoted worshipers he'd wasted his life on trying to enlighten. Oblivious, he preached. The joy on his face was so pure I wanted to claw my eyes out. A black family had wandered into his church at long last, and my father had no idea that this would be, in fact, his last sermon at Second Baptist—but I did, and I took no pleasure in, for once, knowing more than he did.

———

Mother Maude and Father Drake entered our lives two years later, in the winter of 1998. Neither had come to my mother's funeral. To be honest, I didn't even think of the possibility. If my father had notified Mother Maude of her sister's passing, he didn't share the information with me. Which was nothing new, since he rarely shared anything with me. Now their arrival in town was a surprise. I was walking home from the library and had taken the long way, going up the main road that curved beside First Baptist and my mother's grave. My father never included me in his decisions for the flowers he put out on her tombstone, so I liked to go by every now and then, and appraise his choices. He kept daisies on there in summers and poinsettias for wintertime. The poinsettia for this year had already gone green and was too heavy for its plastic pot. It was constantly tipping over only to be righted again when I came by. It was a stormy day, and I should have gone the shorter route home. I'd brought a raincoat, but the rain fell slantwise, blurring my vision as I trudged on through puddles and mud.

My father and I had moved out of the parsonage after he was voted out of Second Baptist, and we now lived in a one-bedroom apartment above a barbecue restaurant called Missy's. The place would have been too cramped for us if my father wasn't gone most of the time. All his driving to proselytize to neighboring communities had prepared him for a profession in truck driving. He carried galvanized metalwork in the back of an eighteen-wheeler for a company out of Memphis. He spent two weeks at a time out on the road, but when he was home, he might as well have been gone. Our silence had persisted after he left the church. Now it felt almost ridiculous for us to carry on a conversation with each other beyond the pleas-antries you would offer a stranger. *How are you? Fine. Good.*

The best part about moving was the apartment's proximity to the library. I was still homeschooled and did most of my studying there. I had befriended a young woman named Erin, the children's librarian, and she served as proctor for when I had to be tested. The Jins had sold their restaurant and moved to a suburb of Memphis by then, so Erin was the closest thing I had to a friend now that Suzette was permanently out of the picture. Erin checked off many firsts for me: She was the first adult to insist I call her by her first name, the first person I knew who had a tattoo (a four-leaf clover on her wrist), and the first to tell me about the charter school in Jackson. She taught a class in publishing there every summer, she said. She had noticed my reading habits, and knew my test scores, and said I should be in a school that challenged me. "You keep reading Trol-lope," she told me. "And everybody who reads Trollope is a genius in my book." But I did more than read at the library. There was a bank of desktop computers near the entrance, and because I was older than twelve, I could use them for as long as I wanted, all by my lonesome. Erin said the rules stipulated that since I was under eigh-teen I would need a parent to sign for me, but she waived the re-quirement since she knew my father was a busy man and usually out of town. The computers were closely monitored by the other librar-ians and by a strict website blocker, so I never ventured to any of those sites Suzette had shown me. There were other avenues, how-ever. I frequently visited the fine art websites, always finding my way to the nude male form. Caravaggio's *John the Baptist in the Wilderness* was a particular favorite—I'd stare and stare at the shirt-less torso and the way the lit skin shimmered. Then, when I got home, I would shut my eyes and there the portrait would be, burned into my brain like Brother Mims's Jesus portrait had been all those years ago. My lust, an old nagging friend of mine, was just as feverish and cloying as the night I was baptized by the Holy Warrior, and I'd spend whole nights rubbing myself raw in service to it.

Before leaving for home that rainy day, I had been working through one of the SAT-prep books out of the reference section. After going over the entrance exam for the charter school, Erin had decided that boning up on my vocabulary and basic algebra was my surest way of doing well. I was set to take the test in April, and if I was admitted into the school, I would let my father know then, though I was hopeful he wouldn't mind since he barely noticed me when he was home and probably wouldn't mind my absence. At five o'clock, I put the SAT-prep book on the returned-books shelf and told Erin good-bye. She was on the phone—engaged in some dispute over a lost book—and rolled her eyes as I drifted by the front desk. Once I was outside, I had to hold the front of the hood of my raincoat to keep it from blowing back in the wind.

Entering the cemetery lawn, I noticed a figure by my mother's grave. Most days the cemetery was empty of the living, and at first I thought I was hallucinating. I blinked. I wiped the water from my face—and, still, there *she* was, for it was a she. I saw that now. I circled around and was taken aback. This woman was clearly not my mother—she was fifty pounds lighter, wore heavy makeup and a sparkly jumpsuit—but there was a slight resemblance nonetheless to Debra Rose around the edges. She looked up from the tombstone and appeared stricken by the sight of me.

"My God," she said. "You do look just like him, don't you?"

"Who?"

She ignored my question and crossed the space between us to embrace me. Her voice sounded like my mother's—deep but feminine. I'd never seen any pictures of my mother's sister, and the times I'd heard her on the radio, I hadn't cared enough to visualize what she might look like. "I'm Maudie," she said, still holding me close, as if I might try to run away if she released me. She told me the Lord had brought her to Hawshaw. "When I called your daddy last week," she said, "to ask for a donation and he told me of all your troubles—I had no idea." The ground got muddier as she spoke, and our feet were sinking into the wet suck of earth. "When I told the good Dr. Dillard about the camp, he couldn't believe it—he started to weep right there on the line, honey. And you know why?" She squeezed me hard and didn't give me enough time to answer. "Because the Lord had a plan to bring us together." I noticed that her hair was synthetic—the kind you see on dolls. A wig. "Oh, the plans," she was saying now. "The plans I have for you!"

I asked her what she was talking about, but instead of answering, she gave a command: "Come on. We'll give you a ride home." I remained silent as we walked out of the cemetery. She seemed too cartoonish to be a real adult. More like a child's conception of a what an adult woman should look like. Curls of hair were piled on top of her head, every strand of it teased and stiffened by hair spray, immovable even in the stormy wind. Once we were on the sidewalk, I scraped my sneakers along the concrete to get rid of the mud on them. She wore rubber boots—nice ones that were as shiny and black as a seal's skin—and her stride was wide and fast, making it a challenge for me to keep up with her. I followed her to the parking lot, to a beige RV with a blue line running down the side. The door on the driver's side was popped open, and a man with a crooked face climbed down to greet us. And when we got closer, I realized his face only looked crooked because he kept a wad of tobacco in the side of his mouth. He spat on the ground. He was built like the Holy Warrior who had baptized me: wiry and muscled but with a face that was meaner and more suspicious.

"Look at this boy," Mother Maude said to him, as he came closer to inspect me, the first camper for their new camp, though I didn't know it yet. "Ain't he Johnny made over?"

The man I would come to know as Father Drake spat again, and said, "That is exactly what I'm afraid of."

FIVE

•

QUICKSILVER

When I was thirty or so miles from Memphis, Bevy called. She hadn't heard from me in the requisite twelve hours and was mildly panicked. "Have you been watching the news?" were the first words out of her mouth. No, I told her, I had not. I'd stopped listening to NPR, and my iPod was hooked into the speakers instead. She took it upon herself to fill me in on the latest with *Proud Flesh*. Thanks to social media, she told me, during the two weeks of its release, the movie had garnered a cult following. No longer protesting the movie, queer groups flocked to it. "Can you believe this shit?" Bevy said, and the truth was that maybe I could. I asked her if she had gone to see it for herself, and she was quick to answer. "Not a fucking chance, dear heart." She told me how the studio had just released a digital copy of the movie online two days ago. Now several gay clubs in U.S. cities were throwing viewing parties. "They all wear the killer's mask,"

Bevy said. "And act crazy and dance. All very tacky." She was relieved to hear I hadn't been to one while I'd been home. "Zeus went, and he had a time. Almost got himself killed."

The interstate branched into four lanes, each one packed bumper to bumper with vehicles. I was entering the industrial park on the city's outer perimeter. My father must know this route well. He had probably thundered through this traffic in his massive semi countless times.

Last night I had watched them for about an hour or so. The singing had been the highlight of the evening. Soon after, the mother and daughter shuffled off to their bedrooms. My father sprawled on the couch, watching late-night TV alone. I got sleepy watching him yawn and went back to my own room at the Days Inn in Hawshaw. When I woke up this morning, I hit the road. I was ready to return to academia and the great Middle West. Ready to pretend this wild notion of mine to go home hadn't been a waste of time.

"Are you even listening?" Bevy said. "Zeus was at that club downtown watching the movie and the event turned wild and . . ." She searched for the best way to describe what happened next. "He got jostled and then got into a fight with some queen who called him a tranny." One thing led to another, she told me, fists were thrown, and the police were called. Zeus got arrested and was sent to a female jail. "All very humiliating."

"Is he okay?"

Bevy scoffed. "Are any of us?"

Doll was inching along as Bevy continued the story of Zeus's trouble. He was home now, she said. Shaken up but physically unharmed. "But it brought up all this shit that happened to him a couple of years ago," she added. "Back when he started the transition, and a group of bastards caught him out one night in the park and turned his ears to cauliflower." She told me how during the beating they kept calling him a tranny. Ever since, the word has been a match to his fuse, she said. "I probably shouldn't have told you so much. But, dammit, you just let me go on." I assured her I would act every bit surprised should he ever tell me the story himself. "If we ever talk again, that is," I said.

The comment pissed her off. "I do not like," she said, emphasizing each of her words, "being some go-between for you boys." She had her own life, with her own problems. And she would appreciate it if I would ask her about them every now and then. I said I understood, and in the sincerest way I knew, I said, "And how *are* you, Bevy?" and she, in equally sincere tones, said, "Fuck you, Will. I am not good." She explained how she spent most of her days studying for a test she no longer believed in. "And Alix is worried I'm not taking care of myself and eating too much processed food in my diet, but does she ever offer to cook? No—no, she doesn't. It always falls to me." The bar exam was in another month. She felt "totally" unprepared for it. I told her I was sorry because that's what you say to other people about their problems when you can't fix them. I was sure she would have given a similar response to mine had I the courage to share them.

Traffic was moving again. I zoomed Doll into the exit lane. Soon, I was going down a residential street, passing large houses with deep front porches, the windows caged with iron bars. Bevy asked when I was coming back. "Don't we need to talk about your dissertation?" and I told her I was stopping off in Memphis first to see an old friend. At this, she feigned shock. "You?" She gasped. "Friends?"

But before hanging up, she said, more seriously, "Hey, I'm glad you're headed back—I was, I don't know, worried that I wouldn't see you again. That you'd go off to Mississippi and disappear."

Peering in on my father's new life had been surprising. I wondered how he could have the emotional stamina to redo fatherhood and marriage. He had thrown himself into a new relationship at a time in life when most men his age were thinking about retirement and receiving AARP catalogs in the mail. Widowed, ousted from his church home, estranged from his queer son, my father had fashioned this whole other life for himself. What's more, he seemed happy. Hence my other surprise—not at his happiness, but at my own response to it. I felt no jealousy, only this vague sense of pride that he'd possessed the gumption to carry on. Our familial bond had been all but extinguished in our years of silence, and yet enough of it still existed for me to feel sympathy for him. *Didn't at least one of us,* I thought, *deserve to be happy? Didn't he deserve the peace of a normal life?* The only way I knew how to not destroy what he had made was by turning around and leaving. Which was exactly what I did.

When I got back to the motel, I e-mailed that survivor from camp I knew who still lived in Memphis. His name was Rumil. I told him that I would be in the area and wondered if he would like to meet up. Minutes later, Rumil replied, saying he would like that "very much." He owned several snow-cone booths in the city and told me to meet him at the one off of Beale Street. "The flagship," he had called it in the e-mail. Once I got downtown, I parked Doll in a garage a few blocks from the address he'd given me. We were to meet at noon. I was twenty minutes early, and I wandered down Beale, the neon signs dimmed in daylight and showing their age. I went by the statue of W. C. Handy then crossed into a little courtyard. A man in tight jeans and matching denim vest was playing a pedal steel guitar for a small crowd of onlookers. The case for the steel guitar was tossed open, inviting donations. The way he bent sound into music, that unmistakable twang of country, kept me in the courtyard listening for longer than I'd intended. He didn't sing, but the songs were familiar country ballads—"Someday Soon" and "Aces." Many of the people around me knew them by heart and hummed along.

This Rainbow Ice location was a shotgun shack wedged between two boarded-up houses and painted in loud greens and purples and pinks. A large sign was perched atop the roof that boasted of more than a hundred different flavors, which were listed in alphabetical order. The line of customers curved from the service window half-hidden under the awning and spilled onto the sidewalk. I got behind the last person in line and looked around for Rumil. I wasn't sure I'd even recognize him. He'd been fourteen last I knew him: a Filipino boy adopted by well-meaning white Christian parents.

The line moved slowly. Customers stepped up to the window, stooped under the awning, and spoke to the person behind the glass. While waiting, I learned what separated Rumil's operation from the ones I remembered from childhood: In the evenings, when Beale Street turned on its neon, customers could add liquor to their flavored ice. MUST SHOW ID FOR SHOTS was clearly displayed in a cursive font below the list of flavors on the sign. Over in the alleyway between Rainbow Ice and one of the boarded-up houses, a dingy picnic table stood in the grass. Two boys sat across from each other, slurping down their red and blue concoctions, their teeth tinted to match their flavors.

I never heard him approach—only his voice, when he said, "I think I know a guy who can get us to the front of the line." He had changed little. A foot shorter than I was, he wore a fauxhawk. His ears and nose had several piercings. Otherwise, he was still the boy I had met at Camp Levi: compactly made and beautiful. "God," he said, looking me over. "You look just like a preacher!" He grabbed my shirt and pulled me into a hug. Pressing his face against my collarbone, he spoke into my chest. "These are crazy times, sweetie, crazy times—suddenly that summer is news?" He glanced up at me with water in his eyes. We had not mentioned the movie over e-mail. I tried to say something now about it but couldn't, a sudden surge of emotion clogging my throat. He intertwined his arm in mine and escorted me around to the backyard of Rainbow Ice. "I keep thinking about going and seeing it," he said, "and then turn scaredy-cat at the last minute."

Around back, Rumil opened the screen door and knocked on the wooden one until a husky trans woman opened up. She scowled at us. "What the fuck, Rummy!" she said. She had a shock of white hair and affected the stance and demeanor of a tired cafeteria lady, complete with a dishrag tossed over her shoulder. Rumil said that when she was finished with the cone she was making she should make us two medium coconuts with cream. She pursed her lips. "Or," he said, "get out of the way and I'll do it." She gave him a smile then. "By all means, sugar." Her voice dripped with sarcasm, and she stepped aside for us to enter. When he shuffled by her, she smacked him on the ass, and said to me, "You watch this little bottom—it'll get you into trouble every time."

The contraption that shaved the ice looked like the offspring of an old-timey icebox and a meat slicer. Rumil opened a trapdoor on top and saw that the machine needed ice. So he hunched down to the minifreezer under the counter and hauled out a large block the size of my head. He dropped in the ice, then fitted the lid back over, and hit some buttons. "Here we go," he said. "The only way to make snow in Memphis!" From a little chute on the side of the machine, a fine powder dusted into the Styrofoam cup Rumil had placed underneath to catch it. "When my partner and I ended things," he told me, over the crunching of ice, "he got the house and the parrot; I got the dog, who soon after died, and this business, which took off." He asked me if I was seeing anybody.

"It's complicated," I said.

He stared at the shaved ice collecting in the cup. "It always is."

Rumil selected a glass bottle of flavored syrup labeled coconut and gave healthy pours over each newly formed cone of ice. Then he went to the cabinet beneath the register and retrieved a bottle of Four Roses. "Let's make the adult version," he said. One splash for me and another for him. We decided to eat them outside on the plastic table in the alleyway. The pair of boys was still sitting there when we came out. Rumil said, "Shoo on home—grown-ups coming." One of the boys tried to give him some attitude, something about how Rumil didn't own the alleyway. "Ray Boy, I will call your mother right now," Rumil said. "Gladly will I call her! Please give me a reason to watch her beat that ass." Ray Boy gave a little nod, and off they went. Once we were alone, Rumil told me how he was not having kids unless he could get them sometime in their late teens. "After two years, send them to college—then have them take care of me when I am old and worn down." Because of the heat, my snow cone had already melted down into a slush. I sipped it, the coconut flavoring mixing with the bourbon to form a poor man's piña colada. "I have to believe that kids are worthwhile and that people have them for reasons other than selfishness." Rumil's eyes looked up from his snow cone. "Jesus, where am I going with this talk? Sorry."

A plane soared overhead, cutting the sky with sound. After we finished eating, he led me down Beale past all the specialty shops, and we eventually found our way to the river. Birds wheeled in the air. They might have been pelicans, but I wasn't sure and was too shy around Rumil to ask. The river was churning, as brown as chocolate milk, its little waves capping and falling, capping and falling. "This is beautiful, isn't it?" I yelled into the wind. He took my hand and held it as we tarried down the sidewalk overlooking the water. People milled about all around us. "You don't worry about being public here?" I said. He looked surprised. "Why?" he asked. "Why would I ever?" He didn't say anything else. He didn't have to. His hand went limp and let mine go.

We kept walking. He led me away from the water toward an area of the city full of abandoned warehouses and old factories. The brand names of companies long out of business were still tattooed into the dirty brick. We were to have dinner at a funky restaurant he had said was off the beaten track. I wondered if this was where he had meant, someplace new in someplace old and forgotten, full of hipsters. I didn't mind. The snow cone had been my only food today, and I was getting hungry. When my stomach growled, he said, "I want to show you this before we get a bite to eat—a surprise." He took me to one of the warehouses, and we stopped before the big sliding door. He snatched its handle and yanked it open, the door rumbling like a train sidling down the track. We stepped into the poorly lit room, a cavernous space thick with chemical smells. It was a workroom of sorts, filled with glass and wood and an assortment of tools. Only the glass, I realized, wasn't really glass—it was mirrors. All shapes and sizes of them: on the walls, piled in the corner, propped up on pedestals. Rumil draped his arm around my shoulder.

"You're trembling," he said. I asked him what this place was used for, and he said his boyfriend had a thing for mirrors. "A thing?" I told him I wasn't being dense on purpose, and he smiled. "He silvers them," he said. "That's the technical term anyway." We stood in front of a big oval one, the kind you might hang above a fireplace or in a dining room. Rumil's arm was still across my shoulder when, without warning, another face appeared between ours in the reflection. The suddenness of it alarmed me, and I jumped, shaking loose from Rumil and nearly knocking the mirror off its stand. Shiny and round, the new face was babyish, familiar. Both of them were laughing.

"You still got crazy-ass hair," the new face said, and his voice— sort of girlish *and* deep at the same time—triggered his name from my mouth on reflex.

"Christopher," I said. "Dear Lord in heaven."

Both of them laughed. Rumil said, "Thought he just *looked* like a preacher and now he's *talking* like one, too!"

At Camp Levi there had been five campers—the inaugural class. Here in this warehouse, surrounded by mirrors, three of us shared the same space again. The mirrors multiplied our bodies: A dozen Christophers and Rumils bemusedly stared at a dozen of me. They made a handsome couple. Their physical incongruity worked for them—Christopher, with his tall and soft body, towering over the small Rumil. I had so many questions for how this union came about. As if anticipating them, Christopher began to explain their coupledom, tucking a hand in the back pocket of Rumil's skinny jeans and pulling him close. Their relationship—the romantic part of it, anyway—came about years after camp, he told me. Around the time Rumil and I were chatting online, he was also reaching out to the others from Camp Levi. Christopher turned out to be the most eager at reestablishing a friendship. "I was living in Baton Rouge," Christopher said. "Fresh out of rehab and looking for healthy friends." He didn't mention the reason for his treatment, and I didn't ask. At the time, both had boyfriends and weren't looking. "I think we just needed each other to listen," Rumil added. Like me, they had been withholding the events of that summer from the people in their adult lives. When Christopher drove up to Memphis to have dinner with Rumil, the conversation proved to be—according to them both—like a balm they never knew they needed for wounds they assumed had already healed. "It wasn't like talking with him," Rumil said. "Talking makes it sound too simple a thing for what happened. More like plugging my head into his head, and our thoughts sort of commingling and making one complete thought."

I asked Christopher if I could sit down. But he didn't keep chairs in the warehouse. "Sitting," he said, "is the new smoking, and I'm pre-diabetic." He said the floor was reasonably clean and that I was welcome to it. I plopped down and crossed my legs, waiting for the great swirl of thoughts and feelings to settle down inside me. Lower to the ground, the chemical smell thickened. I breathed through my mouth, the air tangy on my tongue. Rumil and Christopher followed me to the floor, sitting on either side. "You okay?" Rumil touched my leg, and I nodded, saying I thought so. The three of us formed a circle on the hard, cool ground, our knees barely touching. Rumil told us how his maternal grandfather had often warned of sitting on hard concrete: "Claimed it caused hemorrhoids," and Christopher said, "Well, honey, if you haven't got them already." We laughed, the sound echoing in the high-ceilinged warehouse.

The temperature in the building stayed somewhere between ninety and hundred degrees during the summertime. Christopher claimed that the place was perfect for silvering mirrors and, consequently, lousy for small talk. He charged ahead anyway with the conversation, defending the heat. Told me it allowed the reflective coating on the glass to set or, in his words, "precipitate." I nodded along as he described the various ingredients he needed for mirror making—silver nitrate, Rochelle salt, distilled water. "It's much easier to repair one," he said, "than it is to make one wholesale."

As he spoke, Christopher gave me the impression he wasn't all that pleased to see me. Nothing overt in his behavior. Just his state of being. The aggressive way he steered the conversation. The suspicious glances he threw my way as he talked and talked, never once letting me or Rumil add a word in. Mother Maude had used mirrors in our treatment at the camp. His obsession with them seemed to me to be obviously connected to our shared history. But I didn't offer this opinion. If Christopher *was* nursing a grudge against me—and considering how I'd behaved at Camp Levi, I didn't necessarily blame him—then rehashing the camp would only lead us into trouble. So I avoided it altogether. When he finally finished talking about mirrors, I put a very simple question to him: "When did you start this"—I was seconds away from saying "hobby" and only in the last breath nixed it for a more respectable word—"job?" Perhaps

I would have offended him no matter what word I'd chosen to use. At any rate, he sighed. "Not a job," he said. "It's my *art*." He was a graduate student at the University of Memphis, he made sure to mention. This collection of mirrors was part of a larger project.

"How nice," I said.

Rumil said, "You'll have to come back when it's all finished—for his art show in the fall." He nodded at Christopher to second the invitation. Instead, Christopher said, "You'll see more tonight at the house—basically we have mirrors in every room. Like a fun house minus all the distortions."

My stomach was upset. Either from the fumes, the heat, or the hunger. I couldn't tell which. Rumil must have read the discomfort on my face. He fished out his cell phone from his jeans pocket. "I can have a pizza here in ten minutes," and he called a place supposedly just up the street and ordered us an extra-large pepperoni with jalapeño cheddar baked into the crust. "You eat meat, yeah?" he asked me, before he gave the person on the phone his credit card number. I told him I would eat just about anything at this point. From underneath the folds of his apron, Christopher produced a joint. "Smoke?" There was never a moment I least wanted to smoke than this one right now. I was woozy and hungry, and weed promised to aggravate both conditions. But I didn't want to give Christopher more ammunition for disliking me. "Sure," I said. He lit the joint with a Zippo. After puffing to get the cherry started, he offered it to me.

This much became clear to me: The process of becoming adults had made them interesting people. Rumil, the entrepreneur of hooch-drenched snow cones, and Christopher, the quicksilver artist. By comparison, I was so completely uninteresting. So unchanged, really, since I was fifteen. Academia had provided me with a hole to hide in, to burrow away from life and hibernate, while everyone else—Rumil, Christopher, and even my father—had moved on. To prove I had nothing to prove, I partook of his weed. I sucked the sickly sweet taste into my lungs. When Rumil was finished with our order, I passed the joint to him.

In a haze of smoke, our conversation turned to the movie. Neither of them had seen it Yet. I admitted to trying three times to watch it. Rumil wanted to know why I kept going back to see it. "I don't know," I said. "Maybe to prove I could."

"It's always there," Rumil said. "The camp. Even when you forget about it."

Christopher said, "I just can't believe Dolittle was the one who got to direct it—of all people in this world."

The name again—*Dolittle*—tumbling around in my head. I asked them what was so wrong with this Dolittle person. "Dolittle, Dolittle," I repeated the name, rolled its syllables around on my tongue, half tweaking on Christopher's stash already. "How do I know him?"

A look passed from Christopher to Rumil, this look said, *See here, this imbecile you have brought home?* Rumil answered first: "Robert Dolittle—think about it for a second." I wasn't thinking fast enough for Christopher, who blurted, "Sparse, you bastard. Sparse." The nickname worked on me like a splash of cold water.

"You're fucking kidding me." I couldn't believe it was him, the ultrathin black boy from Camp Levi. If I wasn't so high, the news would have wrecked me. Sent me crawling under the worktable. Besides the three of us here, Sparse was the other camper who had survived the summer. In speaking his name, Christopher had inadvertently invoked the name of the one who hadn't made it. His name we *didn't* say. None of us could be fucked up enough to mention him, I didn't think—and yet the memory of him invaded our circle anyway, bullying away every other thought in our smoke-addled heads.

Rumil's cell phone vibrated. He looked at the screen and said the pizza had arrived. He went outside to meet the delivery guy. I leaned back on my hands and tried to act casual. Like the information they'd just shared wasn't overloading my puny brainpan. Christopher gazed down at his crotch and mumbled something. I said, "Huh?" but he didn't repeat himself.

My gaze traveled to Christopher's worktable, where a medium-size mirror sat propped up at an angle, reflecting the complicated metalwork bracing the ceiling. A crack split down the middle of the glass, one Christopher would repair in the days to come. Apropos of nothing, I said, "'Repair' doesn't seem like the right word when you fix a mirror, does it?"

Christopher looked amused. "Oh? What word would you use, professor?"

Rumil came back, balancing the oversize pizza box in one hand, clutching his phone in the other. "I hope y'all are hungry," he said.

Christopher slapped my knee. "What word then?" and I said, "I don't know. Forget it." But he said he didn't want to forget it. Rumil set the pizza box down on the floor between us. The smell of grease and cheese broke over my face, reminding me of my hunger.

"What are you two talking about?" Rumil said, and I felt my cheeks redden. I wanted to change the subject. I felt silly. But Christopher wouldn't change the subject. He told Rumil how I had come up with another term for him to use when he resilvered mirrors.

"He doesn't like the word 'repair.'" Christopher placed a hand over the lid of the pizza box. Clearly, no one could eat unless I finished my thought.

"Okay, okay," I said. "I was thinking that it's more like you heal them instead of repair them."

Rumil said he thought that sounded kind of poetic. "Heal," he said, marveling at the word.

Christopher wasn't so generous. He said we were high. "Fucking high," he repeated. "*Heal* is something you do for the wounds of the living. Or *heel* is a command you give a dog."

Our bellies full of pizza, our brains all cottony from medium-quality cannabis, we decided to cap off the night by seeing *Proud Flesh*. The idea came to us slowly, a plan formalizing when I told them what Bevy had told me about the gay clubs hosting these viewing parties. I said, "They seem to be making a to-do."

Christopher frowned. "They?" He went on to say how he doubted seriously the fervor had reached Memphis. Interested, Rumil searched for information on his phone. "Oh, wow!" he said, and turned the phone sideways and scrolled down. Sure enough, he told us, a club in Midtown had shown the film last night and was planning on a repeat this very evening. "You know the place, too." Rumil flashed Christopher the screen of his phone. "The Joan Crawford," he said for my benefit. "A dingy bear den—should we go, you think?"

I told them Zeus's experience at one of these parties. "And the film! It's low-grade horror at best, a B movie." I was shaking my head and using my hands to be convincing. In essence, I tried out my best Bevy impersonation, channeling all her disgust for the picture.

It didn't work. Christopher's sleepy eyes flashed open for a second, the weed maybe wearing off. He said it would be an *experience* for us to venture into the masses while they were watching *our* movie. "Moving among them," he said dreamily, "like celebrities incognito." Later I would think he was only being contrarian, choosing the opposite to whatever opinion I had formed. Ultimately, the deciding vote went to Rumil, and he admitted to wanting to see the movie, too. "Of course, I'm curious," he said to me, as if he were apologizing. "And I'd like it if we all saw it together, too. If we go, we can't go as ourselves, though. We need to go as other people." Christopher and I agreed even though I hadn't a clue what he meant exactly until I was at their house twenty minutes later.

Their home was a pale-brick two-story in the historic Central Gardens area. Ferns dangled like ear bobs from the eaves of their wide front porch. "My, my," I said, "the snow-cone business must be booming." Both of them remained silent as we climbed the steps to the porch. Rumil, his keys tinkling like bells, struggled to unlock the door. He was nervous, provoking Christopher to sigh and tap his foot. Neither of them could look at me or at each other. *All my fault*, I thought. I had forgotten how southerners didn't like to talk money. If Christopher was keeping a mental list of all the ways I had fucked up tonight, he'd just gotten himself another prime example: "First he makes a jab about my art," he would probably later say to Rumil, "and then he tries to make us feel guilty for our house—like he knows property values in Memphis."

At last Rumil got the door open. He scurried ahead of us, going from room to room, turning on lights. Each time he hit a switch, there I was, materializing from the dark. My reflection appeared from several vantage points. They'd hung mirrors on the walls like most people hung artwork—to Christopher, I guess, they were. Determined to be nice, I said, "These are really great," and I meant it, because they were, these wood-and-brass-framed mirrors. The rooms were mostly furnished with antiques. Claw-footed fainting couches, armoires, earthenware pottery. And not that crap suburban moms buy at those fancy import stores, either, all done up to look old. These pieces had been lived with and lived on by people, it seemed, for ages before finding their way into Rumil and Christopher's home.

I followed them to the kitchen (fully decked out with a space-age dishwasher, double sink, and a steel oven worth more than what I made in a year on my assistantship) and then on downstairs to the basement. In this subterranean room, there was a washer and dryer and a scattering of old furniture. They immediately seemed more comfortable down here, as if this were the room where they really lived and the ones upstairs were only for show when company came over.

"These old biddies," Rumil said, and kicked a burnt-orange couch. "I've been meaning to cart them off to Goodwill—I've owned that chair over there since junior year of college, if you can believe it." He nodded to a La-Z-Boy, tattered and careworn. Clothes were piled on the seat—castoffs for both men and women, many of them vintage garments you'd wear as costumes. Rumil picked through the fabric and pulled out a leather vest. "For you, professor," he said, and tossed it over. Rummaging through another mound of clothes on the coffee table, Christopher explained how they dabbled in drag. He found a pair of bedazzled blue jeans and held them to his waist. "Hey, I bet I can squeeze into these," and Rumil, in a rare moment of sass, said, "Darling, the Crisco's in the pantry."

The scheme was simple: We were to dress in clothes we wouldn't dare wear in our everyday lives. Basically, we'd pretend to be other people. More for ourselves than for anybody else. An advanced game of playacting to psych ourselves up for the movie, Rumil had said. "To give us courage to watch the whole thing."

Rumil decided to go butch. He removed his earrings and combed out his hair gel, flattening his fauxhawk. He put on a big flannel button-down, sawdust-colored Carhartts, and a trucker's cap that had once belonged to Christopher's father eons ago and had been—until Rumil spotted it for his outfit—perched atop the dryer collecting loose change. Christopher and I were more flamboyant in our attire. He had to stretch out on the couch to zip up the sparkly jeans. They fit—if only barely. A thick ribbon of fat protruded above the waistband, which he hid under an oversize fuzzy top that resembled a Koosh ball. I tossed off my polo and slid on the leather vest. The thin hide stuck on my flesh like a second layer of skin. Then I stepped into a pair of Daisy Dukes. The hemline was cut so short the white cotton pockets flopped out on the sides of my legs like dog ears. For final touches, Rumil insisted on smearing Christopher's mouth with lipstick. For me, he said I needed a little fairy dust and sprinkled silver glitter into my five-day-old scruff. When he was finished with us, we clomped back upstairs and gathered in front of the large mirror above the sofa in the living room. "I can't tell," Christopher said, "if we look really good or really bad."

Rumil squared his shoulders and took out his phone. The lens flashed, capturing us in our new outfits for time immemorial. In a deep voice, he said, "Why can't it be both?"

———

We arrived at the Joan Crawford later than expected. We had trouble finding parking, eventually going back to their house and calling a taxi. The bar was in the heart of Midtown, a pink stucco building with blacked-out windows attached to a Mexican restaurant. By the entrance, a drag queen told us it was a fifteen-dollar cover and then asked if we'd like to donate any more to the cause. "What cause?" Christopher asked. She sat on a plastic chair with her legs crossed, the metal cash box on her lap. She was an undercooked Joan Crawford, circa *Mildred Pierce*, wearing pleated slacks, shoulders stacked with padding. "All of them," she said, smiling, and when Christopher didn't laugh, she told him he had lipstick on his teeth. After we forked over the cash, she seized a garbage bag from under the chair and doled out three plastic masks. All of them were the same princess design the killer wore in the movie.

Rumil unfolded his mask and held it up to the light. "What the fuck?"

"You wear it, sweetmeat." The drag queen had grown tired of us, her manicured fingernails clicking along the metal cash box. "In or out," she said. "No time for sissies."

Inside, the Joan Crawford had two rooms separated by a plaster wall chinked with holes. The entrance led us into the first one, the bar. Dingy and dimly lit, the room was disappointing in its plainness. I was expecting murals of the legendary film actress, posters of her most famous movies—*Grand Hotel*, *The Women*—cheeky references to her daughter's sleazy tell-all. There was none of that, however. The only suggestion of the club's namesake—besides the sassy drag queen at the door—was taped to the cash register: an autographed picture of Faye Dunaway from the late 1990s when she traveled to the South to shoot a movie based on a John Grisham novel.

Proud Flesh had already started in the other room. I could hear the sounds of the first kill. Poor Blond Fred and the extreme close-up of his face. I told Christopher and Rumil to go on ahead without me. "I need a drink," I said, "and I've already seen that part." Rumil came close, and said, "Just come find us, okay?" I nodded. "Of course," I said. His eyes were big, and butch clothing or no, he looked frightened. Christopher put out his hand, and Rumil took it. They eased through the doorway and disappeared into the shadowy other room. I waited around for the bartender, but nobody came. It finally occurred to me that I was the only person on this side of the Joan Crawford. I considered going behind the counter to help myself to the booze. But my own outlandish clothes had not made me very brave, so I followed my fellow campers into the other room and tried to spot them in the crowd.

Finding them was complicated by the fact that everyone wore the princess masks. On most nights, this second room looked like it served as the dance floor. Tonight, people stood motionless, as if in a trance, and faced the wall at the far side of the room where the movie was being projected. Numbering about forty, the audience was quiet, almost reverent, like a congregation gobsmacked by the Holy Spirit. I stood in the back beside someone who kept turning toward me. As if he recognized me. Or like I didn't belong. Finally, I said, "What?" causing several more princess faces to turn my way. The one beside me pointed to his face and then to the mask in my hand. "Okay, okay." I slid the mask on. A layer of wet immediately formed on my forehead and the bridge of my nose. "Happy?" I said to him. He didn't say. Once my face was covered, he lost interest and was reabsorbed by the story unfolding on the wall before us.

For me, the danger of studying film was losing the magic that had first lured me into the dark theater. I've known many professors who no longer take any joy from movies, who have seen a film too many times, scrutinizing every second, to ever really "see" it anymore. During my time in academe, I had critiqued shots, analyzed performances, broken down the choices of the director. I considered movies in terms of the historical contexts that produced them. I wrote, and rewrote, papers on scene development. All this, and still I loved them. Bette Davis's arch and embattled Margo in *All About Eve,* the pillowy face of Rock Hudson in *Giant.* These gave me two hours—sometimes more—of peace. A total absorption in a story that overwhelmed my own with the spectacle of beautiful people and their beautiful problems. And perhaps it's too simple and wrongheaded to suggest that film allowed me to forget that summer, but deep down I believed it did. That's why *Proud Flesh* was such a violation. I had found a world—in study and practice— separate from the one I had been born into. Now my past was polluting it. Mutated, my story had cornered me. "Here!" it cried. "Look at me!"

In truth, the popularity of *Proud Flesh* mystified me—as both a critic and a regular everyday cinephile. Here was a movie telling a story we had seen done several times before with much more sophistication and panache. I was stunned by the turnout at the Joan

Crawford tonight. Surely these queers had better things to do. Better dance clubs to spirit through, to wag their bodies in. Better drugs to swallow with vats of liquor. Around me, the masks were neither terrifying nor campy nor even ironic. I would have preferred the violence that Zeus had experienced. Some ruckus to put life back into these stiff bodies, these queer lives made small by a story that had no right to captivate them. Sparse's involvement was a puzzle I was still processing. I hadn't determined if it was an act of betrayal or poor judgment. Maybe a bit of both.

I was ready for the movie to be over. And as soon as the mask was revealed for the first time in the movie, the screen complied with my wish and went blank for intermission. The lights brightened. Our drag queen, the living homage to Joan Crawford, took to the platform, a microphone in hand. She introduced herself as Dixie Cups, inspiring mild applause from the audience. She asked everyone if that was the best they could do. Evidently it was, since no one responded with any more animation. She rolled her eyes. "Time for drinks," she announced. "And time for the bathroom and time for"—she paused to glare—"dancing!" Dance music filled the room, and nobody gave a shit. Many of them funneled into the smaller bar area for drinks to fortify themselves, I suspected, for the rest of the movie to come.

The masks were removed. I spotted Christopher and Rumil near the front by the platform. The two of them were huddled close and appeared to be speaking to Dixie Cups. The drag queen rubbed Rumil's earlobe and eased through the press of people, her body more liquid than not. When she passed me, her hand gracefully tipped back my mask—I'd forgotten to take it off like everyone else had—and then she kept on moving to the bar, never glancing behind her to see the face she had uncovered. My skin felt raw. I imagined my greasy face sparkling like a melted Christmas ornament. I could think of nothing more awkward than standing here, like I was, in the middle of the dance floor, when no one was dancing and everyone was rushing around me for drinks. I trudged to the side of the room and tried to get Christopher and Rumil's attention by waving. But it was no use. They were having one of those intense conversations couples have, the kind where all distractions were pushed into the background. Christopher's long arms were wrapped around Rumil's chest, holding Rumil as if his little body would float off should he let him go. I slid the mask back over my wrecked face. Like this, I watched them comfort each other until the movie started up again.

In the second half, Greg's girlfriend awoke. She was the next character to willfully leave her cabin to investigate. Once outside, using her cell phone to light her way, she called out her now-dead cabinmate's name. Her curiosity eventually led her to the shed, where her adulterous boyfriend and her cabinmate had been slaughtered. But the bodies had been moved. The only evidence of wrongdoing was the smear of blood on the ground. A path of red—too neat, too obvious—trailed out of the shed into the woods. Seeing this, she was unsettled. The woman, rather intelligently, then tried to use her cell: first, to call her boyfriend (no answer) and then the authorities (no service now). Panicked, she rushed back to the cabins and woke the others. Her pounding on their doors and her screaming confused them (two guys, both of whom I'd never be able to differentiate in a lineup, and a heavyset girl born to die in situations like these). It took a while for them to understand her ravings.

They followed her to the shed. Filmed from faraway angles, the movie seemed to be suggesting the characters were no more important than their surroundings, than the trees or the mud or the weeds. The movie had paid very little attention, in fact, to these people until this moment. After discovering the blood, no one suggested they get in the cars and drive away—no, instead, one of the guys came up with the idea of following the carnage. "Someone must be hurt," he said, and no one rolled their eyes at his announcing the obvious. The heavyset girl seconded the plan. Traipsing into the woods, they were as loud as possible, screaming the names of the missing into the dark. It became easy to hate them. *Dear God,* I thought, *I* want *them to die.* Usually, audiences rooted for the killer in an especially bad scary movie because, among other things, the characters were so poorly developed and behaved stupidly in moments of crisis. You begrudged them their lives. Here, though, the movie seemed intentionally pitting us against them.

The trail of blood ended at the edge of the dried-out lake bed. "This is *it*," one of them said. "Where they took the boys." And it was too dark to tell who was speaking to whom. A dull moaning came from the spot where Blond Fred had been taken down. Someone flashed cell-phone light in the general direction, revealing a pale hand exposed in the dirt, clawing. What happened next came fast: All of them tumbled into the lake bed to dig, using their hands to unbury the person from underneath the muddy silt. Once again, the camera shifted to the killer's point of view, and we watched the clamor from the edge of the lake bed, shrouded in the darkness. After they'd finished retrieving Blond Fred from the ground, the killer blasted on a high-powered spotlight, blinding them. After this, the killing was almost too easy. The two men who were toting

Blond Fred out of the lake bed stepped into a pit and fell several feet to (we assumed) their deaths. The two women spread out, running for their lives in opposite directions. The heavyset one went back the way she'd come, and her leg was snagged by a spring-loaded bear trap. The other one—Greg's girlfriend—climbed out the other side of the lake bed in one piece.

The point of view switched, once more, to focus on her, the last one, the final girl. Shots from above tracked her erratic movement through the trees. The night sky was softening as morning approached; her figure became more and more visible in the hazy light. In her random scurrying, she found her way—somehow, someway—to a clearing in a little valley. Amid the brush, there's a door in the ground. A metal door with a handle. She opened it to find a staircase leading down, deep under the earth. Preferring hiding to running, she went inside and fumbled with the latch to lock herself in. She pulled on a string dangling in her face, cutting on a low-wattage lightbulb. Yellow light spilled over the steps to reveal a small underground room. A tornado shelter repurposed into a bedroom complete with an army cot. A scattering of trash on the floor. Obviously, the killer's hideout. A place to shut out the whole awful world. Lying on the mattress was a hand mirror. She picked it up, glared at her own reflection. Remembering something, she dropped it and fingered her phone: still no service. She threw the phone against the wall. It shattered like glass. She screamed.

From above, a rustling—like footsteps. The door shook. A pause. Then it shook again. "Rooster," the woman cried, and sank to the floor. She rested her face on the cool concrete ground. "Oh, Rooster." Under the bed, she spied something that looked like another cell phone, but no. *What is it?* A square box with buttons and what appeared to be a speaker. She inspected it, fumbling with the switches. *A walkie-talkie?* She hit the tabs on the side, and there was static. She put her mouth up close to the speaker, and whispered, "Hello?" The rattling at the door continued, the kicking and hitting. The slender lock wouldn't, she knew, hold long. "Hello?" she said again, into the device. *CB radio?* She clicked more buttons. As if answering her, music played from it: symphonic beats, then the husky voice of a woman: "I'm a new pair of eyes, every time I am born." She dropped the device, a cassette tape player, and backed away from it as if it had turned radioactive, as if it were more dangerous than the anger raging outside the door behind her. For the last time, the movie returned to the killer's point of view just as he popped open the door. (I almost cried out but was able to stifle myself in time.) The woman turned to face Rooster, her mouth a perfect O as he fell upon her.

Once the movie had faded to black, and it was clear the thing was over, I heard someone ask, "That it?" Then another, his voice muffled by the princess mask, said, "What the fine fuck." The murmuring grew. Words flattened into boos. Into long, ugly sounds. Another drag queen, clad in a silver bodysuit, took to the stage to entertain us—a postmovie cabaret performance. Her appearance only inspired more shouts and moans of derision from those around me. Undeterred, she began to lip-sync Gloria Estefan's cover of "Turn the Beat Around." But the crowd proved too loud. She had trouble keeping time with the lyrics, her lips moving a millisecond slower than Estefan's speedy delivery. A few queers up front took off their masks and threw them at the performer. Now I saw how

Zeus's altercation might have happened. All this anger throbbing in one place. The crowd was upset over a bad movie and needed someone to blame. Instead of turning on one another, causing a mild riot in the Joan Crawford, they were focusing their hate on the poor creature miming disco in front of us. And yet the drag queen persevered, her show becoming too painful to witness. The club was emptying, and I gratefully followed the wave of people outside onto the street. I searched around for Christopher and Rumil. When I didn't find them, I fought the current of moving bodies to get back inside.

I reached the front door and bumped into Rumil coming out. He carried a wad of paper towels and a small bottle of water. "Rumil! Hey!" I said, and he paused, not recognizing me at first. "Christopher—he . . ." Rumil waved for me to follow. We slipped around people, going sideways, and went behind the Joan Crawford to a little alleyway. It was semidark and grassy. Christopher was crouched on his knees, heaving, and Rumil rushed over to him. After he unscrewed the water bottle and dampened the paper towels, he used them to pat his boyfriend's neck. The alleyway was about five feet wide, separating the Joan Crawford from another building that looked more residential, with deep-red brick and dormer windows. A row of boxy central-air units crowded that side of the alleyway. Dixie Cups sat on the one closest to the Dumpster. She was smoking. She flicked ashes into her palm, and said, to the vomiting Christopher, "Let it out, honey. I told you it was gonna be a show, didn't I?"

Back on the street, a large crowd had formed. People from the Joan Crawford were mixing with other rowdy clubgoers just beginning their night of revelry. They were singing and shouting and cursing. A mix of joy and rage. Cars honked at them as they passed.

Dixie told us the night before had been quieter. "Still got mad at the end, though." She sighed. "Always the end."

I said I didn't mind the ending, but nobody paid attention.

Christopher managed to make it to his feet. When Rumil tried to wipe his boyfriend's mouth, he swatted him away. "I'm all right now—it's over." He took a step and stumbled, then clutched the side of the Dumpster to steady himself. "If people hate it," he said to Dixie, swallowing hard between each word, "then why do you show it?"

Dixie laughed. "Why do you think, honey?" She rubbed her fingers together. "Money—you try getting a gaggle of queers out on the weekend when most of them would probably have preferred to stay in and watch the movie on their computer." She flicked her cigarette into the Dumpster and stood. "It's an *event*. And events that draw people out have become few and far between. Terrorism, premium cable—people have more than enough excuses to stay home and make a country inside their four walls." She patted the shoulder of Christopher's gaudy shirt. "You all look like hell, by the way, and no movie did that." When Christopher slapped her hand away, Dixie Cups laughed again, more gleefully this time. "Did you become gay last week or something? Don't you know to never insult the host?" She would have probably said more, but blue lights flashed from the street, followed by the short wail of a police siren. Her eyes were diverted to the goings-on in the front of her club. A cop car was nosing into the crowd. Before leaving us, she sauntered over to me. She said I needed to learn when to wear the party masks—"You look spooky just standing there," she said—and jerked the princess face (which I had forgotten I was wearing) from my own face, the plastic band popping behind my ears. She shoved the mask into the top of my Daisy Dukes. "Now you bitches play nice, hear?"

On the cab ride back to their place, I learned that Christopher was a Tina Turner fan and hearing one of her songs in the movie had been too much for him. "I'm surprised you don't remember him talking about her at camp," Rumil said. He and I were sitting in the backseat while Christopher sat up front with the driver, a wall of Plexiglas separating us. Rumil spoke candidly. "It upset him that Sparse used parts of us in the movie—little things. His love of Tina Turner. Your nickname." He kept his eyes trained on the back of Christopher's head as if he expected him to turn around and shush us. So I doubted he noticed my own mild shock at his remembering what my father used to call me. But then I supposed it shouldn't have. Mother Maude had forced us to reveal so much about ourselves to one another. We talked and talked and talked until words were reduced to incoherent sounds we made with our mouths. I was impressed that, years later, Rumil was handy with the details.

"How do you remember those things?" I asked him.

He gave me the same surprised look he'd given me earlier in the day by the river. "How can you *not*?"

I changed the subject and asked what Sparse had used about him. He pointed to the mask hanging out of my jeans. I pulled it out and flattened the face over my knee. "Of course," I said, the memory flooding back once I went looking for it. As a boy, Rumil had stolen a similar one from a Fred's Pharmacy during Halloween and was caught by the store manager. When his parents asked him why, he said he wanted to be a white girl like his sisters. "And that's when the therapy started," Rumil reminded me now. "Camp Levi was the end of a series of failed programs—I was a teenager and they said if the treatment didn't stick this time, they'd send me away to a military school."

I asked Rumil why he thought Sparse had been so keen to include little bits of us in the movie, and he said that he'd not spoken to Sparse in nearly five years: "Like you, he was hard to keep up with." Then he speculated that maybe Sparse had put our shit in there as an homage. "It's not very subtle: the killer possessing some part of each of us, but then I guess Sparse wasn't interested in subtlety, was he? Or art." He glanced out the window.

The cab pulled up to the curb in front of their large home with its pitched roof and expansive front porch. An uneasiness came over me, something undefinable in the pit of my stomach. About the way they lived. I had this notion that their newfound money was connected to the camp, but I didn't know how it all worked. I had suspicions. Every now and then, a lawyer—having stumbled across our story somehow—would e-mail me about pursuing a civil rights lawsuit. It never came to anything because, I always suspected, there was no money to be had. But I didn't know much about legal matters and so maybe Christopher and Rumil had found another way. While Christopher fumbled with his wallet to pay the driver, I asked Rumil if he'd spoken to anyone else from that summer.

"Like who?"

And suddenly I didn't want to know—let them have their secrets—so I shrugged and slid out.

In the kitchen, Christopher handed out Zoloft, and we downed the pills with sparkling water. He said it would help us sleep. His skin was still pale from puking. The lipstick had faded from his lips, the ghost of it still staining his teeth pink, as Dixie Cups had pointed out in the alleyway. While they got ready for bed, I went downstairs to fetch my clothes. All my toiletries were in Doll, which was still parked in the garage by Rainbow Ice, but Rumil had said they had extra toothbrushes and not to worry about it, so I didn't, only now I did. When I went back upstairs, they were arguing in the living room. Rumil had rolled out an old record player—a wooden piece of furniture I'd mistaken for an armoire—and wanted to put on Tina Turner's *Private Dancer*. As a result, Christopher was throwing a fit. "I don't want to hear it," Christopher was saying. "You've lost your fucking mind."

Rumil shook the record sleeve at him. "She still belongs to you, baby—don't be ridiculous."

If my face hadn't been smattered in grit and glitter, I wouldn't have bothered them. I would have found the guest room on my own and quietly gone to sleep. "I think I need to take a shower," I announced, and Christopher rolled his eyes. "And?" Rumil, in a tone not much kinder than Christopher's, said, "The bathroom's upstairs—you can find everything in the cabinet under the sink." They stared at each other, a stalemate, waiting until I left. When I didn't move right away, Rumil added, "Second door on the left," to send me off. It worked; I left. They continued the squabble by whispering. Christopher must have won because I didn't hear any music.

The shower had strong water pressure. I stuck my face directly under the stream to wash off the grime. When I finished, I changed back into my own shirt and shorts, and padded down the hallway, my bare feet leaving steam prints on the tongue-and-groove hardwood floor. I counted two guest bedrooms. When I tried the doors, they were locked. Like the forbidden rooms in the mansions of gothic novels. Downstairs in the living room, the record player was still pushed out, but the couple had retreated elsewhere. The record sleeve was left on the sofa, 1980s Tina Turner in a deep-cut top staring up at me, her legs kicked out below her in a kind of half squat. I removed the record from the turntable and slid it back inside the sleeve. I put it on the coffee table next to a miniature gong. The trinkets in the room astonished me. Rumil and Christopher had lived the same number of years on this planet as I had, and in that time somehow, the two had accrued more belongings, more knickknacks from foreign countries, and more antiques from flea markets. I didn't know if these were evidence of their having become more grown-up or simply more affluent. Either way, it bothered me. The same way the nice neighborhood and the art studio and the big house and the successful snow-cone business and the locked doors all bothered me. I was jealous, sure, but also suspicious, and I couldn't quite put my finger on why.

From the other side of the house, I heard a thump. Then another. "I was just going to bed," I called out. No one answered. The house had gone quiet except for more thuds. "The rooms upstairs are locked," I said, over the sound of furniture moving. I walked into the dining room, the walls papered scarlet, and then moved into the little hall where light from the room at the end bisected a green throw rug. They had left the door ajar. Like most of the others in the house, the walls inside the master bedroom were crammed with mirrors. But there were no mirrors on the one wall that the pencil-post bed frame thwacked against. I was not surprised to find what I did: Christopher pinning Rumil against the mattress. Nevertheless, I felt like a child walking in on his parents, confused by what he saw the adults doing. Maybe that was the Zoloft. A slate-colored duvet had been tossed to the floor along with their clothes. Christopher held both of Rumil's hands over his head by the wrists. And he pressed his forehead into Rumil's cheekbone and was swearing quietly: "You fuck, you fuck, you fuck," he said, as if he were speaking a secret language only the two of them understood. When Christopher lifted his face, Rumil spat in it. Christopher popped him across the mouth with an open hand. Almost immediately afterward, they were laughing and looked over at me.

I had moved to the far corner of the room opposite the door. I was watching their reflections, not them. Christopher untangled his body from Rumil's and rolled off the bed. "You have a good shower?" he asked, and I said yes, I had, in the calmest voice I could muster. He motioned for me to come closer. His nakedness wasn't alarming. Nothing I hadn't seen before. His low-hanging chest and his doughy love handles were comforting, almost motherly. It was his reflections, all gathered behind him in numerous iterations, that unnerved me. The magic of quicksilver making more of him than there was. "You wanna sleep here tonight?" Christopher hadn't sounded this nice to me all day, and that, too, was cause for alarm.

"Of course he does!" Rumil said. He was rolling on the bed, excited. "Look at the tent he's pitched."

And it was true. I was hard, my erection clearly visible through my shorts. If Christopher had taken one step in my direction, the tension would have been too much. I would have buckled and run. He must have known this because he remained at the foot of the bed, flaunting his imperfect, beautiful body like some prize, and he let me come to him. Once I was close enough, he grabbed ahold of my shirt and stabbed me in the gut with his cock. "You know what you are, Will Dillard," he said. "You're a lurker. You've been lurking around us all day. And I'm dog tired of you doing nothing but watching." He pushed his mouth onto mine. His teeth tore into my bottom lip, chewing it like a piece of jerky. The taste of copper leaked into my mouth. I wasn't sure if I was being kissed or bitten, or if it mattered much which it was. Love, hate—both were different shades of the same impulse anyhow. Christopher slung me onto the bed, and Rumil pounced. He helped me out of my clothes, his hands scraping across my skin. "Look at you," he kept on saying. "Just look at you."

I was never any good at sharing a bed. Boyfriends often complained of my restlessness, how I tossed and turned in my sleep. The one from upstate New York even joked, during one of his last visits, about tying my hands and feet to the bed frame. Once I got to sleep I became the problem, but before sleep took ahold of me, the presence of another body set *me* on edge. The stress of finding the right position—On my back? My stomach? The side?—frequently prevented me from drifting off right away and, arguably, contributed to my rambunctiousness once I went dormant. Sharing the bed with two bodies doubled the quandary. Christopher and Rumil slept on a California king. The mattress took up more square footage than my whole bedroom did in my apartment. But three still seemed too many for it.

After we had finished, I assumed one or the other would want to bathe. Perhaps we could take a shower together, continuing our play. I was game. I didn't mind the rewashing. They'd left me sore and sticky. The sour smell of sweat had returned to my skin. After coming—first Christopher, then Rumil, followed by me—we wallowed in the mess we'd made, our bodies tangled in one another and the cotton sheets. Then they, with no warning, fell asleep. When Christopher started snoring, I lifted my head. Rumil was wedged in between us, his head resting on my arm, his mouth slightly agape. I said, "Rumil." He didn't move.

I remained in this position for several hours. When Rumil turned over and off of my arm, I was suddenly free, so I took my chance. Slowly, I got up. I gathered my clothes and eased out of the bedroom. It was sometime before sunrise. The venetian blinds hanging over the windows in the living room lacked the blue glow of morning, but soon enough light would eke through them and ruin everything. Here, at last, I slept.

My hosts let me sleep well into morning. I'd wanted to hit the road early, but I'd forgotten to set the alarm on my phone. I didn't open my eyes until a quarter after ten, to the sound of Christopher clanging around in the kitchen. I wandered in, still loopy from sleep, to find him looming over the stove top, flipping pancakes. He told me Rumil was in the shower. By the look of his damp hair and pink skin, he had just finished his. "There's coffee," he said, and nodded to the brewed pot on the island between us. He had already made a stack of pancakes and told me I could help myself. I asked him why he wasn't having any, and he said, "Prediabetic, remember?"

He focused on the circle of dough sizzling in the frying pan. The marble counter by the stove was littered with all the ingredients he'd yet to put away—the egg crate, a plastic jug of milk, a bag of flour. Portions from each had been dumped and mixed in a shiny metal bowl, which now rested on the back stove-top eyes he wasn't using. He cooked with the same kind of intensity that he'd fucked with. It made me wonder if he enjoyed either, or if he did them because he felt it was the thing to do in the moment: At night you had sex, and in the morning you made pancakes. And whatever grudge he had put aside to fuck me last night had obviously returned in full force this morning. But I was too hungry to care. I found myself a plate in one of the glass-fronted cabinets and used my hands to shovel three pancakes on it from the platter. From the fridge, I retrieved the butter and syrup, and lathered my pancakes with each. "These are delicious," I said, after I took the first bite. I straddled one of the bar stools at the island and dug in. Still with his back to me, Christopher asked what my plans were after I left them. "Plans?" I spoke with my mouth full. I swallowed and told him about how I needed to finish my dissertation. Using a spatula, he slid the last pancake from the skillet, a sloppy amorphous one, and placed it on the platter. Then he shoved the pan into the sink and doused it in water, causing steam to pillow up in his face.

"So what brought you back?" he said, waving away the cloud.

"Seeing my dad."

"How'd that go?"

I swallowed more pancake. "Bad."

Rumil walked in, the floral scent of shampoo and body wash wafting in with him. "Glad you're finally up," he said. "We thought you'd decided to hibernate." He and Christopher wore nice clothes today—athletic-cut collared shirts, trouser shorts, loafers. Rumil hadn't returned the piercings to his face, either. I had this idea suddenly that what we'd done last night, dressing in other kinds of clothing, was something they did on a regular basis. Not drag, exactly. But a kind of escape. They never settled on one look or way of being so they'd never have to face who they really were.

Rumil and I finished off the pancakes while Christopher drank some kind of protein shake for diabetics. "Christopher is a master chef," Rumil said, "for all the foods he can't have." But conversation fizzled out when I told them my mother had been diabetic. "Oh?" Christopher looked interested, so I said, "She died—got an infection," causing Rumil and Christopher to make shocked faces. When we were done, Rumil insisted I take a shower before they take me back to my car even though—as I tried to explain to them—I would just need another one by the time I made it back home. I was planning on driving straight through, all the way home. By the time I'd make it back, I'd just be swampy and road ugly. He was persistent, however, so I showered again and dressed in the same worn clothes I'd arrived in.

On the way to the garage, Rumil mentioned he needed to stop off by Rainbow Ice first to pick up something. Their boat-size SUV—a silver Ford Expedition with an engine that hummed like a toy remote-controlled car—took us out of their quiet neighborhood into downtown. It was close to noon on a Sunday, and Memphis appeared to be taking a nap. Most of the stores were closed, and few people were out and about. Christopher and Rumil weren't offering much for conversation, so I told them about my friend Suzette from long ago. "This was before the camp," I said. "She moved here to go to some private school and I never heard from her again." Christopher drove, and Rumil gnawed on his cuticles. I wondered if their silence had anything to do with last night. I leaned up between the seats, and said, "I had a great time, you guys, you know that, right?" Rumil grimaced. I said, "You're acting like we're going to a funeral." While Christopher was parking on the street, I spotted the reason for their odd behavior through the tinted backseat window. My eyes lit on him immediately. He sat at the picnic table beside Rainbow

Ice. His hands neatly folded on the scuffed tabletop. He had on a linen suit and a beige straw fedora. He'd put on weight since I first knew him, especially in his face, but I recognized him anyway. "Larry," I said. Christopher and Rumil were already getting out of the car. And Larry was standing to greet us. Everybody was smiling.

Ambush. There was really no other word for what this was.

I know what you're thinking," Larry said. He slung words at me before I could say anything. "You're thinking I'm the last person in the world you want to hear from, but I hope you'll hear me out, Will, because I think we can help each other. I really do."

While he spoke, I pieced together the story of Christopher and Rumil, the one I had ignored during my visit so far. The clues had shown themselves to me: the quaint neighborhood, the nice house, the expensive antiques, the way they had little concern for money. Why would they? Larry had enough to go around. He had intimated as much in his e-mail to me. I saw it clearly: Christopher and Rumil must treat this man like an endowment—seed money for Rainbow Ice, then a small grant to indulge Christopher's obsession with mirrors. It made sense, their weirdness over my remarks about their lifestyle. They were embarrassed.

Last night, when I had asked Rumil in the taxi if he'd kept up with anybody else from camp, I had suspected Larry. Who else? Mother Maude was dead. Rick was dead. I'd not seen hide nor hair of Father Drake since he was shipped off to Parchman. Besides Sparse, there wasn't anybody left. It had to be Larry.

"I want to lay it all out for you," Larry was saying now. "So you

can see what I'm aiming to do." Larry and his guilt. Larry, the widower of Rick the memoirist. The counselors. The finagling it must
have taken to get him to Memphis. Probably Rumil and Christopher
told him of my visit as soon as I e-mailed Rumil about stopping by.
And then, as plans coalesced, Larry needed them to stall me until he
could get here. They were only too happy to oblige. He had done so
much for them, after all. It was the least they could do. So they let me
sleep in and then plied me with breakfast until they were sure—
checking their phones surreptitiously—that Larry had arrived. Hell,
that was probably why Rumil wanted me to take a shower. To buy
them more time. The red-eye from wherever he lived now had probably cost a fortune. I hoped it had. I wanted it to inconvenience him.
A part of me wanted him to account for himself. Screw this other
business about the camp. What I wanted were the details of his trip:
every little slight he had encountered while he journeyed to this surprise tête-à-tête. I wanted high-priced tickets, delayed flights, long
layovers. Some aggressive pat-down when going through security. I
wanted him to be roughed up by a guard. I wanted him to be dishev-
eled and a little crazed by all the travel. I wanted him to be at the end
of his rope.

He, however, demonstrated the calmness of a businessman used
to getting his way. His voice was level. His suit tailored. At camp he
had been a lackey to Mother Maude and Father Drake. One who
followed orders. He was cheerful but couldn't be trusted to keep us
safe from the Sweat Shack or Lake John. He had no right to me or
my time, and yet, here he was, talking.

"I just know we can work something out," he said. The four of
us had moved to the picnic table in the grass. Larry sat in front of me
and took off his fedora to fan himself. "I've forgotten the summer

comes sooner down here." He said he lived in Massachusetts nowadays, right outside of Cambridge in Somerville. "The Northeast has spoiled me," he said. Rumil and Christopher were nodding, silently agreeing with everything the man said. Both of them kept shooting me nervous glances. Like they expected an outburst. A scene. But I kept calm. Surprised even myself with how cordial I could be. I smiled and looked interested. I let Larry have his say. I did this, in part, to confound Christopher. He sat with his arms crossed, smirking. He was, I suspected, spoiling for a fight and only getting angrier the longer I denied him one.

Rumil told us he could open up Rainbow Ice and fix us snow cones. Larry nodded. "Do, hon," he said, and when Rumil asked if he was hankering for any particular flavor, Larry said, "Surprise us, why don't you?"

"Imagine it," Larry was saying once Rumil had gone inside the booth, "a camp in the South for gay teens, one that told them they were exactly who God had intended them to be, that they were already perfect." I almost laughed. I wondered if he'd gotten the idea from *Proud Flesh*. These camps weren't such a novel idea. I knew of several gay-affirming camps long before the movie came along. They existed mostly on the coasts. "We could remake the place into something better than it was—into something that could last, and give gay boys and girls a refuge. Built at the place where so much tragedy transpired—think about it."

"I have," I said. I told him that it didn't work out so well for the people in the movie who had similar ambitions. Larry waved my comment away. He said that he didn't want to talk about the movie.

"Why not?" I said. "Sparse gave us a hell of an ending."

Christopher said, "You can't be serious."

"I think I finally understand where he's coming from," I replied.

"Oh?" Christopher gave a weak laugh. "Do tell, professor."

"A place of inconsolable rage."

Larry fanned himself harder with the fedora. He said I should look to the future. "The camp," he told me. "It all goes back to the camp—and I have the money to change the narrative. We can rehabilitate that place." He seemed to think he needed to prove his wealth to me, so he explained how the money Rick had gotten from the memoir—"a pittance, really"—was put into other investments. Turns out, Larry had a knack for making money grow, and he wasn't at all shy about spreading some of it around.

"Rick," I said. "Why'd he kill himself?"

Again Christopher injected. "This is a good deal he's offering, Will. You and your dad would get well worth the price for the land."

One of the boys from yesterday walked by on the sidewalk. It was Ray Boy, the one Rumil had threatened with calling his mother. Seeing us, he said, "Y'all open?" When nobody at the table answered, the boy said, "You think I can't see you?" He sallied up to the service window under the awning and knocked on the glass. "Hey, Mister Rumil," he hollered. "Let me get a medium peach with cream!"

Back at the table, Larry narrowed his eyes. "Yes, Rick killed himself. It was ugly, Will. A damn sight. When he was kicked off the movie, he acted—I don't know—lost. I thought it might turn around when Robert got the movie, but he didn't want anything to do with us. Rick wrote him over and over—sent e-mails, handwritten letters, you name it. Finally got word from his agent. He said something about how Rick had had his chance to tell the story and now it was Robert's turn."

Rumil stuck his head out the service window and told Ray Boy that Rainbow Ice was closed. "That there is a business meeting," he said, pointing over at us, "and you need to run on." The boy said he had business of his own and put down some wadded-up bills on the window ledge. Rumil gave a groan. He took the money and ducked back inside.

Larry said, "I thought you would be more apt to help us with your daddy if you had a better sense of what I wanted to do with the place."

"The Neck," I said. "That's what the place is called."

We were silent while the boy waited for his snow cone. The sun at this time of day was directly overhead and left no shade for us at the picnic table. My nose and neck were blistering. Larry returned the fedora to his bald head. Over at the booth, Rumil was fast with the boy's order and returned to the window with one medium peach snow cone topped with sweetened condensed milk. The boy raised it to us as if he were giving a toast. "Y'all have fun with your business." He retraced his steps on the sidewalk.

"What makes you think that I—or anybody, for that matter— would want to entrust you with kids again?" The words were easier to say than I had imagined them to be.

But Christopher had had enough debate. He slapped the table with his hands. "That's not fair," he said, "and you know it."

I looked at him. "Do I now?"

"Yeah, you do." His voice was loud enough that Rumil heard him and came rushing outside. "You owe us this camp."

I wished Larry well and I got up from the table. "I don't think I can help you," I said. "And I am done."

Christopher wasn't. "You know you had just as much to do with Dale dying as anybody."

I should have kept on going. Doll was two blocks away on the third floor of the garage. I could be there in five minutes and on the road in fifteen. But Christopher had said his name. *Dale.* I said, "What did you say?" Which was ridiculous, because I had heard him clearly. I had never understood until this moment why people (usually in the movies) asked this question in anger. Now I knew the question was a dare. A taunt. I didn't think he had the balls to repeat himself.

Fuck him, he did. "You killed him," he said. "Same as if you put the knife in him yourself."

Larry stood now, too. And Rumil had drawn closer to Christopher. Gently, he slid his arms around Christopher's waist from behind, forming a belt around his thick middle. His touch was all it took. Christopher's mouth screwed up into a scowl. He made the sound an animal does when it's been injured—high-pitched and terrible.

"Goddamn," I said, and Christopher—all six feet of him—turned around and crumpled in Rumil's arms. "I'm leaving now," I whispered. I wasn't sure any of them had heard me. But it didn't matter. I took off in the direction of the parking garage, down the same piece of sidewalk the boy had used. A block away, Larry appeared, jogging up beside me.

"Please, Will," he said. "Think about all the good we can do. I've changed—we all have. Can you honestly tell me that you are the same person you were at Camp Levi?"

"Probably more than I'd like to admit."

"Please—I'll pay. Whatever you want. I've got my checkbook on me."

We reached Beale Street, and he kept following me as I crossed over to the other side. I was looking for landmarks to guide me back to the garage: the W. C. Handy statue, the little courtyard where the man had played the steel guitar. Nothing was familiar, and Larry wouldn't shut up and let me think long enough to get my bearings. "It's no use," I blurted out. I told him how I hadn't spoken to my father in almost five years. "And I chickened out the day before yesterday, okay? I walked right up to his door and just looked in—that's how fucked up I am, Larry. If you want the Neck so bad, go to his house yourself and *ask* for it. I'll give you the address. But as for me and my life, I am through." I walked farther down a side street. I thought I had found the way, but I hadn't, so I turned around and came back up to where Larry still stood, acting dumbstruck, like what I had told him was news. "My God. It's like I can never leave it, Larry." I waved my arms at him. And then he was walking away, so I called after him. "Like I will always be stuck at camp, praying and hoping and striving for God to take away my abiding love to suck cock!"

I was pacing in front of the park bench Ray Boy had picked to finish his peach-flavored snow cone. "You fags," he said, laughing. "Lord, God. Y'all fucking nuts."

I drove.

I'd paid an exorbitant amount for parking Doll in the garage for more than twenty-four hours, and once on the road, I looked for the fastest way out of the city. That meant driving south, then east, then south some more. I got tired of the interstate and decided to hit the Natchez Trace Parkway in Tupelo, traveling an hour and a half out of my way. The Trace snaked through historic portions of Mississippi and Tennessee and promised more scenery than the concrete embankments and gas stations of the interstate.

As I put some distance between myself and that mess in Memphis, a peculiar notion crept up on me. I imagined I'd died. The highway spread out, a ribbon of asphalt unfurling before and behind me. A cloudless sky, the color of the ocean, expanding on and on. An empty planet. Only it wasn't the emptiness but the distance that made me feel dead. I was so far from everyone who mattered. The people I knew were still going on without me, still living: By now, Christopher and Rumil were probably taking Larry out to a late lunch to discuss what to do about the camp since I had refused to help them; Bevy would be in a library studying for the bar; my father would be lazing in the backyard with his family; and Zeus would be—well, I imagined sunlight wherever Zeus was, the kind of light that gleamed but gave off no heat whatsoever. I had gone too far to return to any of them, and not a damn thing in this world seemed real to me but the feel of the steering wheel in my hand.

Somewhere along the way, Doll's air-conditioning went kaput. I rolled down the windows. The flurry of air caused a stir inside my car. Loose papers and empty soda bottles flew about, rattling and fluttering, as if gravity were losing its grip on smaller objects. Time shrank: A whole hour collapsed, and before I knew it, I was at the Natchez Trace Parkway. I parked at the rest stop and used the bathroom without ever seeing a single fellow traveler. And still the sense of my own death lingered. You had to be an optimist to believe in ghosts or any version of an afterlife. To persist in the notion that connection with others was possible after death. I had never been one to think seriously of suicide. Rick chose it, and bully for him. I hadn't asked Larry how, either, but I had wondered. I suppose it's natural to be curious about the mechanics. Pills, a gun, a blade. As if the means gave some final clue to the person. For years, I'd wanted God to work his magic on me and transform my spirit—a kind of self-obliteration in itself—and when that didn't work, I had wanted him to stop time and hit reverse. He's the Almighty, after all, so why couldn't he? I wanted him to go to the point in the world's timeline just before my father's sperm met my mother's egg and use his holy finger to block the fertilization. That had been a foolish, self-pitying notion to indulge, I know. But no more foolish than, say, my years after camp: sleepwalking my days away, pretending that summer didn't happen, going further and further into myself until I no longer knew my way out.

The Natchez Trace was 444 miles of two-lane highway that stretched from Nashville to Natchez, and somewhere in between, not thirty miles from the Trace, there was the Neck. And in the Neck there was the camp, slowly dilapidating and forgotten by everyone except for those of us who couldn't forget. A little piece of nowhere, and nowhere sounded good to me.

Sunlight bored through the windshield, hitting me right in the face. I rolled down all the windows again, and the debris once more came alive, dancing. I was passing the exit for Pontotoc, headed southward, when I felt my cell phone vibrate in my pants. It was Zeus calling, as if he knew I was going the wrong way and wanted to stop me. With one hand steady on the wheel, I used my free one to hold the phone out the window. The wind rushed by, pulling my arm backward. It took less than a second; then the cell phone was gone.

■

PART TWO

THE SONS
OF LEVI

■

And see how the flesh grows back
across a wound, with a great vehemence,
more strong
than the simple, untested surface before.
There's a name for it on horses,
when it comes back darker and raised: proud flesh,
as all flesh,
is proud of its wounds, wears them
as honors given out after battle,
small triumphs pinned to the chest—

—JANE HIRSHFIELD,
"For What Binds Us"

SIX

.

ORIENTATION

At dusk we followed Mother Maude to Lake John.

Behind the two cabins, a footpath cut across a clearing, running by the Sweat Shack and then eventually beside an abandoned house. I had never set eyes on it until that very moment—my mother's childhood home. I didn't react. Shingles and Sheetrock lay in dusty piles around the front porch like dead skin sloughed off; its windows were busted out. *Just a house.* A few yards more and we angled past the lime-green husk of a refrigerator and a warped metal bed frame half-sunk in red clay. Relics from another decade, from my mother's time at the Neck. I denied these objects their history, their traceable connection to me. I was just another camper, no one in particular, and *that* was just a house and these were *just things.* Soon we entered the woods. Skinny scrub pines arcing out of thickets of weeds and piss-colored honeysuckle. Daylight was seeping away. Shadows abounded all around us. Insects hummed and wheezed in the growing darkness, a thousand baby rattles in tandem. "They're just saying hello!" Mother Maude called over her shoulder. "Thisaway!"

The counselors, Rick and Larry, had encouraged us to be orderly, to walk single file, but our line had turned sloppy. Christopher led the charge, and Dale tarried far behind. In between them, Rumil and Sparse and I shuffled along in a cluster, side by side, speculating about the nighttime activity by the lake. No one had told us what to expect, and we were left to wonder about it like a trio of old men pondering this season's prospects of our favorite baseball team. Rumil guessed a baptism. Which, Sparse and I admitted, made the most sense. Water was involved, and Father Drake and Mother Maude claimed to be an offshoot of Baptists, advocates of total immersion. But if we were getting rebaptized—for all three of us had admitted to being, as Sparse put it, "already dunked"—then certain other details didn't make much sense. For one, the large mirror Mother Maude toted. For another, the way Rick and Larry were outfitted in coveralls, rain boots, and work gloves. The sort of clothing you wore to do yardwork maybe, not lead five teenage boys down to the waters to wash their sins away. Sparse wagered a commitment ceremony. "You know," he was saying, as we sidestepped a large bed of fire ants. "You admit what a mighty fortress is our God and kaboom! You *is* saved, son. Go and lust no more."

Whatever it was, I warned them, would likely be brutal. Hadn't they looked over the brochures? "My God," I said, not telling them how my father had helped Mother Maude and Father Drake with the wording of the camp's literature. Nor did I tell them how I'd been privy to the release forms their parents were required to sign. I felt like an interloper. A mole. But, above all, I was—I told myself—a true believer who wanted more than anything for these four weeks to work on me and them. I worried any slip of the tongue would ruin the rehabilitation for everyone. "A delicate process," Mother Maude had told me on the rainy afternoon she and Father Drake had shown up in my life out of nowhere: "It must happen just so, especially at the beginning." They were so careful around me during the months they'd stayed in Hawshaw preparing for the summer. I knew some details, but not enough to know what specifically to expect. Once at dinner, I'd overheard Father Drake brag to my father that they had discovered the water's "attributes" by accident before Mother Maude hushed him. She reminded him, as she often reminded me when I asked too many questions, that it would be a great disservice to my "healing" if I knew more than the other boys did. Father Drake glanced over in my direction, which always seemed to pain him, and said he suspected I knew too much for my own good already.

I wanted to impress on Rumil and Sparse that the camp was serious without showing my hand. So I repeated my father's sentences from the brochure. This was the only way I knew how to warn them and keep my relationship to the camp a secret: harp on what we all knew. The baby-blue brochures utilized clip art Mother Maude had cut and pasted from the word-processing program on a public-access computer in the library at Hawshaw: the sketch of a cross, a stock photo of some boy around my age with wavy brown hair staring pensively into the camera as if he were thinking really hard about not being gay anymore. Cheaply done but effective. In addition to asking for donations, the brochures quoted the infamous verse in Leviticus about homosexuals and explained—in vague details—how the camp worked, how it was different from other therapies that treated this "unnatural affliction." I had helped Mother Maude trifold these brochures and shove them in envelopes to be mailed out to various churches in her address book. While I was doing this with her, two sentences from those pages were burned into my brain. Surely the other boys had read them, too. "At Camp Levi," I recited to Rumil and Sparse, "we use extreme practices and revolutionary tactics to treat the body and the soul. Your son must be broken before he can be healed."

Sparse tittered. "Oh, baby," he said. "Don't you know they just say that shit? This my third time at one of these places and they just want to fuck with you a little at first."

Christopher jerked around. He nodded toward Mother Maude in front of him and mouthed, *Shut. Up.*

Earlier that day, after Dale's spectacular meltdown, Larry had warned us about our behavior. They were watching us closely, he said, to make sure our conduct was acceptable. Our words were just as important as our actions and even our thoughts. All would be scrutinized. If ever we were found lacking—and sooner or later we all would be because, well, that was the point—they'd send us to the Sweat Shack, a little hovel of concrete blocks that once served as a pump house and was now a thorny nest for dirt daubers and wasps. As with the activity down by the lake, he didn't go into particulars about the punishment. He finished by telling us Dale would not be sent there *this time*, and we should use this little dustup as a warning. "You're on notice," Larry said, smiling. "From now until July." Luckily for Sparse, Mother Maude hadn't heard him say "shit" and "fuck" just now as we were huffing it to the lake or if she had, she ignored it. She never stopped moving at her breakneck pace. Now she was yards ahead, seemingly determined to have us lakeside by sundown. And Rick and Larry weren't paying much mind to us, either. They had their hands full with Dale. He was lagging even farther behind than when I last checked. We couldn't see him anymore because of the trees; we could only hear his high-pitched wailing. Like the keening of some exotic bird.

Our rehabilitation began on Sunday, June 13, and was supposed to end on Sunday, July 4. Mother Maude and Father Drake had planned on milking the holiday for all it was worth. On our last day, we were to celebrate not only our nation's independence but also our own freedom from the tyranny of homosexuality in a ceremony that included the handing out of certificates, the delivering of testimonials in front of our parents, the singing of patriotic tunes, and the shooting off of fireworks. Our families were encouraged to arrive no earlier than sundown. During great explosions in the sky, Mother Maude was set to perform a rousing rendition of Lee Greenwood's "God Bless the USA." But we, of course, never made it to the Fourth. Camp was cut short three days before the scheduled festivities because of what happened to Dale.

My first day at Camp Levi stands out as the longest. A trick of memory, since it was barely half a day. Though much of my experience at camp has returned to me, the days leading up to it and the days right after remain shrouded in fog. I don't remember my father driving me to camp, for instance, though he must have. We probably left that Sunday morning of the first day and took I-55 in his Chevy. (He would have had no patience for the Natchez Trace and its strictly enforced speed limit of fifty-five miles per hour.) We probably didn't talk, as was our custom. Our agreement had been struck months before, while Mother Maude and Father Drake were still in town. The deal was simple. I had been accepted to the Mississippi School for Science and Mathematics in Jackson, and he would sign off on my attending the magnet school if I gave my aunt and uncle's camp a fair shot and came back rehabilitated. My father's words were something like this: "You have to come back, Rooster," he said, "as the person you were meant to be." His voice quavered. He had not used my nickname since our confrontation in the sanctuary. The idea of the camp must have quickened the flame of hope inside him because he suddenly seemed to believe again that I was a person worth saving. What my father didn't realize was that I didn't need a bargain to get me to attend. I *wanted* the camp as much as he did. Maybe more. Mother Maude's promises that I could be changed had awakened a little hope in me, too. Hope that I could be my father's Rooster after all.

After camp, the rest of July and most of August are as much a mystery to me as the three-hour drive into the Neck. Not a blur precisely. More like a great blank that lasts until August 23, when I started attending tenth grade at the magnet school in Jackson. The reason for my father fulfilling his end of the bargain was never made clear to me. Or if it was, I have forgotten. By all accounts, the camp had been a dismal failure. For many years after, I believed he sent me away because he had, in essence, washed his hands of fatherhood. My memory, however, sharpens for the remaining years of high school when he was no longer in my life that much. I can remember with great clarity the smell of wax on the shiny polished hallway floors that led me from one class to another. The squeak of sneakers and the hoots and ballyhoos from my classmates as we dashed between bells, a great mass of adolescents who had all tested in the ninetieth percentile on standardized academic achievement tests and were hungry, almost desperate, for knowledge. I lived in the dorms with boys who didn't know one whit about me. I could tell them anything about myself and they would buy it. This newfound anonymity gave me the courage to come out during my second semester, and I joined a roving pack of like-minded queers. We studied and bickered and fucked with wild abandon. All the while, our teachers, our academic counselors, our administrators spoke exclusively of the future: the people we would become, the fantastic lives we would lead in the metropolis. *Away.* Like Suzette. Like anybody who wanted to make something of himself. I learned there was no good reason to look back. Why bother? I never questioned this until the movie came along. Then I learned the past is not *the past,* a lump of time you can quarantine and forget about, but a reel of film in your brain that keeps on rolling, spooling and unspooling itself regardless of whether or not you are watching it.

I'd thought I would have been relieved to get away from my father—he had been acting nervous around Mother Maude and Father Drake, uncomfortable in pretending he didn't know them, and he was making *me* nervous with his stilted behavior, with the way he shook their hands for too long and how he couldn't seem to meet anyone's eyes, even mine. He was a man whose body didn't know how to hold a secret. The other campers said their good-byes to their families with hugs and solemn looks and tearful whispers. There was no sadness in our farewell. I gave him a wave, and he returned it with a funny little salute that was almost whimsical and completely out of character for him.

As our parents spoke to Father Drake and Mother Maude about any lingering questions they might have had about the program, the counselors took us behind the Chapel Cabin to a pair of wooden picnic tables. The tables appeared to be designed for children, much smaller than regular-size ones, and looked rickety, as if assembled by the wind. Dale sat by himself, his bulk barely able to fit in the space provided. The rest of us squeezed into the benches around the other one. Rick and Larry doled out paper plates crammed with hot dogs and salt-and-vinegar potato chips, followed by—as if it were the Lord's supper—Dixie cups filled with lukewarm grape soda. While they darted about us, Larry, the talkative one, took the opportunity to introduce themselves to us. He said they were seminary students from New Orleans. Mother Maude and Father Drake had never mentioned them in front of me, so their presence at the camp was certainly news. They had been here, Larry told us, for nearly a month already, getting everything in order. "But there is still much to do," he said, and Rick nodded in agreement. We were going to help them finish getting the place ready for the years to come, for the boys who would follow us on this journey, Larry added. "Oh, the plans," he said, beaming, "we have for you!"

Rick finally spoke when he blessed the food. His voice was much deeper than Larry's, and like my father's in that you had to listen closely to hear him.

After the prayer, they went inside the Chapel Cabin to prepare for our first activity down by the lake. From the front yard came the whisk of car doors shutting, engines fluttering to life, and very soon afterward, tires were crunching down the gravel road. I hadn't paid very much attention to the other parents, but in their leaving, I briefly wondered about their lives, about the conversations they would have on their drives back home. My father had no one to keep his counsel, and maybe that was for the best. When I heard his truck's growling over the rest of the vehicles, my heart dropped into my stomach. I was split. Part of me longed to be in the Chevy with him headed back to the Delta. Another part of me believed it was for my own good that I wasn't. And I understood which impulse had to be destroyed.

The hot dog and potato chips in front of me looked about as appetizing as the mildewed wood of the picnic table. I picked at the food, pushing it around the plate, my hunger overshadowed by other feelings, mostly sadness.

For the first time at camp, the five of us were alone. We kept silent for most of the meal until, at last, Sparse spoke, keeping his voice low so only we at the table heard him. "In prison," he said, "they say you can always pick which one of the newbies won't make it the first night." Our eyes followed his over to Dale. He was sitting all by his lonesome, his food, like mine, untouched. Homeschooling had shielded me from boys like Dale: a stout teenager with an impervious jawline and a head the size of a ripe cantaloupe. Still, I knew he was the type to make trouble for boys like me. I knew this about him the way a rabbit knows the danger of the owl perched in the tree limb overhead. Perhaps the other boys were picturing all the Dales they'd encountered before: übermasculine and proud, cavorting to their lockers without fear of anything in this world. Boys like Dale were talented, I suspected, at sniffing out the sissies among their classmates and zeroing in unmercifully. We stared at Dale, four pairs of unblinking eyes, until he broke under the scrutiny. He jerked his mulish head in our direction and scowled. Actually *scowled*. Then he brought down his fist onto the table as if he were squashing a bug. We jumped and looked away.

After a pause, Sparse changed the subject. "What bothers me is the woman," he said. "Too smiley all the time."

"Oh, she reminds me of somebody," Christopher said. He was overweight and sported an unfortunate bowl cut. He reminded me of how I might have looked had I still been heavy. He licked the chip crumbs from his fingers and then washed them down with the final swallows of his soda. "Somebody," he said again. "On the tip of my tongue."

"It's the wig," Sparse continued. He was as skinny as Christopher was fat, a stick man come to life. "All that makeup, too. Tammy Faye?"

Christopher shut his eyes to consider the person Mother Maude had conjured up in his mind. "Dottie West," he said finally.

Sparse and I shared the same bench, and he leaned over to me to whisper, "Who?"

"The country singer," I told him. "Died in a plane crash."

"Oh," he said, nodding. "White-people shit."

Christopher shook his head. He said Dottie West wasn't a plane crash. "You're thinking of Patsy Cline, ain't you? Dottie West was a car wreck."

"That's right!" Sparse held up his arms—he was, as my father would say, "acting." "Miss West was a drunkard. Left this world in a heap of carburetor and asphalt." His arms remained extended a beat longer. "Bless her!"

"Thought you didn't know who she was?" I said.

"Lucky guess—don't all those old lady crooners die tragically?"

"Them and us," Rumil said, and all four of us laughed. It was almost pleasant, considering the circumstances.

"Fags."

The word was like a fist thrown in our faces. After he'd spat it out, Dale's head dipped forward as if that neck of his had collapsed from the weight of his skull. Then his head sank down even more to rest on the table. Beside his face, flies swarmed the plate and around the lip of his Dixie cup. When two of them ventured over to his exposed cheek, dotting his flesh like animated punctuation marks, he swatted them away, but they kept returning. Finally, he gave up and burrowed his head under his arms.

As if on cue, the back door of the Chapel Cabin swung open and out sailed Mother Maude. A robust woman of early middle age, she wore knee-length khaki shorts and hiking boots and an oversize yellow T-shirt matching Rick and Larry's, except hers had MOTHER written across the back in bold typeface. She circled our table first and cooed as if she were warming up her voice for a song. Her acrylic nails raked across the tops of our heads as she hummed our names, making a little rhyme of it. "I see Christopher and Rumil. I see Robert and I see Will." Sparse started when she called him by his real name, but I was thankful she had used mine.

Mother Maude sidled over to Dale's table, his head still hidden behind his arms. "My lamb?" she said, and there didn't come any answer. She placed a hand on his shoulder. "Why you all by yourself, hmm?" After a pause, he gave a muffled "Dunno."

"You don't know?"

"No," he said, this time much louder.

"I see." She sat down across from him. "I think I may know," she said. "I think you think you are better than them over there."

From the woods, a bobwhite called, trilling its own name several times before it was satisfied and went silent.

"Oh, son." Mother Maude gestured in our general direction. "Those boys are no different from you. No less children of God. Why, my own brother was like you. My sweet John."

"Amen," Larry said. He and Rick had appeared soundlessly from the Chapel Cabin, newly fitted in their coveralls and gloves, already glistening with sweat.

Dale lifted his head.

"Fuck you," he hollered. He leaped to his feet and tottered back from the picnic table, taking a step to the side to steady himself. His eyes were wide and searching, the eyes of an animal cornered, hunting for the direction he might try to make his escape.

Rick and Larry kept their distance, perhaps not wanting to spook him any more than was necessary. Mother Maude crossed her legs and gazed up at him, the blandest of smiles curving across her face.

The sky was melting into one feverish shade of violet. Slowly, Dale's hectic breathing returned to normal. The simple fact of our situation must have finally settled over him: There was nowhere to go, at least not on foot. The gravel road in front of the cabins went for two miles before it ran into a highway, and even then it was another five miles before you hit a town. A minute passed. Then another. Finally, he slunk back to his table, to the side where Mother Maude sat, and shoved in beside her. She put an arm around him and whispered something in his ear. I strained to hear what it was. The only word I picked out was "sister." When she finished mumbling to him, Dale began to sob.

Larry came forward then to give his bit about our behavior. "We are your stewards," he said. "We will hold you accountable and love you through your darkest moments."

This time Mother Maude said, "Amen," and then she mentioned Rick and Larry's summer project. They were studying us, she said. "And they are going to write about us, too—write about us and shock the world holy."

On our long walk to the lake, Dale's crying continued. "He's acting like such a little bitch," Sparse said. "Like we're going off to war or something." No matter how much Larry encouraged him to hurry, Dale kept at his own wandering pace. His stubbornness irked me more than the tears did. By the time we reached Lake John, we were all seething because of him. Which was, I think, exactly what Mother Maude had been counting on.

The day I first met them in Hawshaw, Mother Maude and Father Drake took me home in their RV. Father Drake drove us down a residential street near First Baptist, heading in the wrong direction. When I told them as much, he pretended not to hear. I was sitting in the back on a little fold-out seat, the metal clasp of the seat belt broken and dangling around my ankles. The inside of the RV stunk of fast food, the greasy scent that clung to paper wrappers and then to your fingers long after the meal. In the far, far back of the RV, an unmade bed blocked access to the toilet. The tattered carpet matched the beige color of the walls. These details told me the story of their lives: They lived on the edge of things. Like gypsies.

Mother Maude was riding shotgun. After a couple of blocks, she squeezed her husband's arm, and said, "We ought to turn around, shouldn't we?" Father Drake grunted, apparently his signal for consent, and took a left at the first stop sign we came to, then another at the next one, putting us on Lee Street, headed eastward toward home more or less.

The sky had a terrible overcast, a gray murk writhing above us, spitting out rain and sleet in sudden spurts. Father Drake refrained from using the windshield wipers, causing the buildings and homes we passed to warp and slide and swim. Once we crossed the railroad tracks, I knew we were close and suggested they take a right at the county co-op onto the main drag in town. To my surprise, Father Drake listened. "There we are," I said, and pointed. A neon sign blinked MISSY's, incongruous with the rest of the house it was attached to. The restaurant was an old home with a screened-in front porch wrapping around the property. Our apartment was on the second floor. Brother Mims had helped my father find the place after we could no longer live in Agnes Musclewhite's old house rent-free. On the porch, under the thwacking of ceiling fans, customers came from all around Mississippi to eat the greasy barbecue. Living above the establishment had several challenges, not the least of which was the smell of smoked meat wafting up through our floor that coated our clothes and our furniture and even our bodies in the sour reek of pork. "My Lord," Mother Maude said, when she saw the place. We had stopped at a red light, and she leaned forward to get a better look at where we lived. I told them how we used to live in a parsonage, and truth was, it wasn't very nice, I said, but it was bigger, so maybe that made it only seem nicer. She wasn't paying much attention to me, however. As soon as Father Drake parked at the curb, Mother Maude was rushing us inside, hurrying me up the backyard stairs and through the door that led into the apartment's tiny living room. As she alluded to in the graveyard, my father had been talking to her for some months, discussing with them the merits of their summer plans. I hadn't been expecting him home for another two days and didn't notice his Chevy out back on the way up, so it was a surprise to find him sitting on the couch when we entered.

"Oh," I said. "These are—"

"I know who they are," he said.

For dinner, he had picked up pulled-pork sandwiches from downstairs for everyone, and as we ate, nobody was willing to carry on much conversation. It was a meal punctuated by skittish glances. Mother Maude would look at me, and I would look at my father, and my father would look out the street-facing window over my shoulder at the dimming sky. Father Drake stared at his food. He chewed, he swallowed, he frowned. His face was shaved clean, and his white hair clipped close to the scalp. He was handsome, I admitted, his stalwart masculinity exuding from his general state of being: from the way he sat (straight backed, both feet firmly set on the floor) to the way he chomped down his food (mechanically, methodically) with an expression of begrudging delight, as if he found delicious tastes such as this a frivolity that must be endured. In our silence, muffled conversations from the restaurant below filtered up to the apartment.

Mother Maude finally broke the silence by repeating a remark she had made to me at the cemetery. "I was telling Drake," she said, "how much your boy looks like my Johnny did." My father smiled and told her Debra Rose had often made the same observation. "The curly blond hair," Mother Maude said, "and the eyes—it's a remarkable resemblance. Don't you think so, Drake?" Father Drake shrugged, and she returned her gaze to me. "Did your mama ever tell you about Johnny?" I went to say she had but burped instead. Father Drake chuckled mirthlessly, and Mother Maude's eyes widened. (I couldn't tell if she was more surprised by my poor manners or by her husband's laughter.) "Pardon me," I said, and told her how my mother had told me a little about her brother but mostly about the Neck. "All those stories about the women and the moonshiners," I said, remembering the Sunday I had embarrassed my father in the choir and my mother confiding in me, later that night, about how I reminded her of her brother.

Mother Maude was laughing now. "Oh, yes—she and Mama liked to spin yarns, mixing the truth in with lies, all willy-nilly." She laughed again, remembering something. "I said to her once, 'DR—that's what we called her, you know—you should just sit down and write all that out and sell a book.'" I admitted suddenly, my mouth outrunning my brain, to having written many of those stories down in a notebook.

My father leaned forward, and said, "I didn't know that." I told him I would show him the notebook, and he blushed and sat back. A knowing look was shared between him and Mother Maude. Our talking about my mother's stories had opened up this warm feeling inside me—not a fire, exactly, but more like the kind of heat you get from filling up your belly with warm vegetable soup on a cold day. I told Mother Maude my favorite one was about the lost mother.

She squinted. "The who?" she said.

I told her the story as best I remembered it: the mother who liked to wander off, the father who moved the children away so she could never find them. The story was fantastical and stupid. As I spoke,

Mother Maude got very still, and her smile faded. When I finished, everybody at the table had gone silent. Downstairs was alive with loud talk and clinking silverware. She stared at the remains of her coleslaw, and said, "That's a pretty story, and I bet your mama meant well in telling it. She had a habit of pretending things weren't how they really were." My father said he would clear the table, and Father Drake said he would help. They took our dirty paper plates into the kitchen.

"I don't care that she didn't dwell on me, but I do wish your mama would've told you more about Johnny," Mother Maude said. "Back when I was trying to make it as a singer, you see, he helped me book churches and found the right people to let me cut a record." Her voice was a kind of music in itself, a mix of hum and accent. "He was meek, my Johnny. Gentle and loving. We supported each other—our parents had died and your mother, bless her heart, made it clear she didn't want anything to do with us. So it was just us, me and him, and he's the one who said I deserved to be on the radio, he's the one I prayed with before every performance. But he was also weak in matters of the flesh. A sodomite—you know what that means?" I told her I thought so. "Well, your daddy seems to think you know what that word means, too. If what he's told me about you is true, then you're halfway to hell already, my lamb." When the two men didn't return right away, I understood the reason. They wanted to give Mother Maude some time alone with me. She continued. "Let me tell you, Johnny would always be sorrowful afterward. Confessing his sins and promising to repent and doing good for about six months, maybe a whole year. Then he'd make a fool of himself with somebody or another. A miserable life in general, but especially miserable for a man like him who loved the Lord. And he did love the Lord. Do you love the Lord? Well, I think you do." She told me when she married Father Drake and cut back on her singing, her brother Johnny got mad and ran off. "I should have stopped him," she said. "Should have chained him to my leg, but there was no hitting pause on him, not my Johnny. When he made his mind up to do something, he did it." First, Johnny went to Charleston, only to eventually wind up in New York City. "That's where he was when the sickness was killing his kind off left and right." She didn't see him for two years, and then he called, finally, to tell her he was ill. "Imagine it: My beautiful and blond brother, the picture of health, like you are now, wasted down to nothing." He died before Mother Maude and Father Drake could move him back home, but they buried his body out at the Neck near the lake. "Because that was our place—where we would go when things got bad at home and we needed a place to get away. I'll show you when you come this summer. And I can tell you this, honey: He died a saved man, I made sure of it." After they buried him, she and Father Drake went back to the city with a new mission. "The city was filled with sinners about to meet their Maker without the Spirit in their heart. So we spent"—here, she yelled at Father Drake, who was still piddling in the kitchen with my father, "Oh, how many years was it, Drake, two, three?—going round the hospices and hospitals and shelters spreading the good news. It was the best of times and the worst of times. Saving so many people, only to have them wink out like a candle not long after." She said it was a race against the clock. "The hand of God is mighty and swift when his vengeance is being carried out. I said to Drake—after about the thirtieth funeral—I said, Drake, there must be a better way. A way to reach these boys before they get to this point of destruction."

Father Drake spoke up from the kitchen, saying, "I told Maudie we needed to get them early—get them before they have a chance to do so much damage to themselves."

Mother Maude interrupted him. "Get the afflicted off somewhere, like a camp or something. Be firm and strict and ruthless." Her husband and my father moved back into the living room and sat on the edge of the couch. Both of them were eyeing me at the table with great interest. I knew that they were waiting for Mother Maude to ask the question. She had been leading up to it the whole evening: *Will you come?*

"That sounds," I said, before she had a chance to say any more, "just wonderful." I would be the first confirmed camper. After me, they would begin the search for others. Everyone smiled at my reaction, even Father Drake, and I wondered if they had expected me to be so agreeable. A tingling had spread throughout my body— fear, excitement, I couldn't tell which. There's no doubt in my mind that I would have gone right then had the camp been ready. When Mother Maude and Father Drake left us that night, my father told me that sometimes the Lord put the perfect message in an imperfect vessel. I thought he was talking about Mother Maude, with her gaudiness, and the aggressive Father Drake—they were not my father's kind of evangelicals. Only later, when in bed, did it occur to me that he probably meant me. *I* was the imperfect vessel.

Lake John smelled like putrid flowers. Yards away, we stood in a circle of citronella tiki torches with Rick and Larry, and waited on Mother Maude to finish praying. She was kneeling in the dirt at the water's edge, her wig mobbed by mosquitos. The sky had drained of color, and darkness was settling over the trees. Mother Maude rose to rejoin the circle of light. Larry handed her the mirror and she held it lengthwise. The two-foot rectangle of glass scooped up the flickering flames and held them, glimmering, within its baby-blue frame. "Periodically," she explained to us, "you will come to the lake and commune with the Spirit." Her voice, like always, captivated. She said, "You are more than flesh. More than muscle and bone—you are souls trapped in a body that has betrayed you." She tilted the mirror to catch our reflections. "Each of you are products of sin multiplied by sin. Each of you can be broken to his will if only the soul is willing." Rick and Larry left the circle and stood beyond the rim of visibility. Mother Maude clutched the mirror close to her chest, and said in a quiet voice, "Which one of my lambs is ready?"

Dale moved backward, tipping into one of the torches, almost knocking it over.

"We've got all night," Mother Maude said.

Christopher was first. He stepped toward Mother Maude and the mirror. She held the glass up and instructed him to get closer and closer until he was nose to nose with his own reflection. "You want to be healed, yes?" she asked, and Christopher nodded. "More than anything," he said. She drew the mirror away from him and put her face inches from his. "But you can't," she told him. "You, my lamb, can do nothing. Not a thing." Her mouth stretched into a wide smile and she let her words sink in, then continued. "Your body will always be what's before me now: unmanly, soft." She shifted the mirror in front of her, giving Christopher a picture of what she meant. "Yes, *you* are not what's important. Because it is not about you. No, sir." She pointed heavenward. "It's about him. He who made the waters and the sky. Only he can illumine his might through your inadequacy. Only he can separate you from yourself, as he did the light from the dark on that first day of creation." She asked Christopher if he understood.

"I think I do."

"You *think*?"

"I mean—"

"You mean nothing, baby." She shook the mirror in his searching face. "What do you see here? Tell me fast."

"Um, me?"

"Exactly! And I want you to see the self behind the self. The other Christopher. The boy filled to the brim with the Son of Man!"

I heard it then, echoing across the lake. We all did. Clear and sharp: the sound of someone screaming. A deep yawl from the guts of Father Drake somewhere in the darkness beyond our circle of tiki lights. As his scream faded, Mother Maude went on as if she'd heard nothing, telling Christopher to repeat after her. "I am no one," she said. "I am nothing. Lord, rend my flesh. Burn me anew."

Dale began rocking back and forth, and mumbled, "Shouldn't be, shouldn't be, shouldn't be here."

Christopher turned. "Dale," he said. "You, Dale—*hush*." Amazingly enough, Dale did, putting his hand over his mouth and turning away from what happened next. Christopher looked at himself in the mirror and repeated the words, slowly at first, as if contemplating each syllable: "I am no one. I am nothing. Lord, rend my flesh. Burn me anew." Mother Maude told him to say it again, and Christopher obeyed. "Again," she said, when he finished a second time, and he shouted the words, screamed them at the image of himself. After he finished, his face was red, and sweat poured from his hairline, his bangs stringy and pushed back. Satisfied with his performance, Mother Maude brought two fingers to her lips and then placed those same fingers on his cheek. "Get undressed," she said. He recoiled. "Do what?" he said, and she told him that he must disrobe, go to Lake John, and bathe. "You must cleanse yourself from the outside in." She gestured toward the row of us standing behind him. "You all do. The flesh is weak and must be made compliant."

Christopher looked confused. "Here? Now?"

The humidity had taken its toll on Mother Maude's makeup. Dark rivers of mascara traced down her cheeks. "There's no shame in the here and now."

Dale made a noise between a cry and a gurgle. Rumil and Sparse locked eyes, then glanced at me, their faces saying: *This will be over soon, won't it?* The torches only seemed to make it hotter, the heat like a warm blanket being wound tighter and tighter around my chest. Mosquitos ventured across the flames, drawn to our stink. Christopher removed his sweat-soaked shirt first, his pale love handles as luminous as slices of moon. Then he kicked off his shoes, unpeeled his socks. Mosquitos the size of quarters swarmed him, but he seemed oblivious and let them feed on him in peace. At last he undid the button of his shorts and shimmied free of them. He stood now in front of the mirror, in front of us, in nothing but a pair of white cotton briefs wedged into the crack of his saggy, misshapen ass. He went to push them down, but Mother Maude's hand shot to his shoulder. "Leave those," she said, then: "I'm so proud of you. So very proud." In the song of her voice, I heard how truly pleased she was, and in me there arose this impulse to please her like this, a desperate need for her approval, to have her say to me what she had said to Christopher. From the lake came another voice: Larry's. "This way, Chris!" he yelled. "We're here! Come on!" Before he could go to them, Mother Maude held on to him a moment longer. "Keep your eyes shut in the water," she said. "Nice and tight."

He nodded from the circle. Moments later, we heard a splash. A flailing of arms, some coughing. "I can't swim, y'all!" he was screaming. "Oh, God!" Mother Maude yelled back for him to stand up. It got quiet then. The torches created a pool of light for us to stand in, but beyond them a curtain of darkness hung between us and the lake. When Christopher traipsed back into the circle, he was different. His feet and legs and arms were coated in mud. His hair was slicked back from the swim. "I feel tingly," he said to no one, to himself, as he touched his neck and face with a kind of wonder. He also wore a yellow T-shirt and khaki shorts, the word CAMPER etched across his back.

Rumil went next, and the sight of his nakedness snared my full attention. His body, buttery in the torchlight, looked liquid and smooth. A mole sat at the center of his back, and I imagined reaching out, stroking it. I stopped myself. No—*the words*. Listen to the words. The words seeped into me, pushing away all the clutter in my skull until they were flashing across my brain, bright as neon: *I am nothing I am no one God rend my flesh burn me anew.* When Rumil finished and left the circle, Sparse volunteered before I could.

Dale had gone silent and was still facing the direction we had come from. I wanted to tell him to turn back around. Didn't he understand? He was missing an important part of the evening—maybe *the* most important part. My father's dismay at me welled up in my chest and I focused it on Dale. I grabbed his arm—rock hard and immovable—but released him soon thereafter. Sparse was finished, had already taken off his clothes, and now, at last, it was my turn.

———

I heard Mother Maude sing live only once, and it was at First Baptist. My father and I had gone to Brother Mims's church the Sunday after our first dinner with my aunt and uncle. They were going to be asking for donations from the congregation and my father wanted us to show our support. Brother Mims greeted us at the front door with shyness, hugging my father when he got within arm's reach. Mother Maude and Father Drake had been there all morning talking with church members during Sunday school, answering questions about their summer camp, making sure not to mention their connection to us lest anyone refused to donate due to hard feelings toward my father.

For church, Mother Maude had chosen a different wig, one that fanned out over her shoulders like a cape caught in the wind. She wore a loose-fitting jumpsuit, green and spangled about the shoulders in glittery explosions. Even from the back row, I could see the heavy makeup. She looked like an oversize girl who had been meddling in her mother's vanity. When Brother Mims introduced her, he said how proud he was to have her and her husband visiting them and reiterated the importance of their ministry. He told everyone how lucky they were, because he had convinced her to sing that song from a few years back that had made her famous. After Brother Mims sat down, she clasped her hands together, closed her eyes, tilted back her head, and let her voice do the rest. "I'm kind of homesick," she told us, "for a country." Nothing about her appearance mattered now. The filigree of her look was in direct contrast to the pureness of the sound warbling out of her mouth. *This*, I thought. This *is the sound of God.*

W hat does my lamb see?" Mother Maude held up the mirror. A pale blond boy gazed back at me, hair a mess of curls, the bones of his face sharp and feminine. "Nothing," I said to her. "I see no one." Then I repeated the words as if I were casting a spell. As the others did, I spoke them several times until she lifted a hand to hush me. I was already tearing off my clothes before she asked. I added them to the pile forming in the middle of the circle and stepped between a gap of torches into the surrounding dark. The ground writhed under my feet with what I imagined were unseen pests: ticks, fire ants, wolf spiders. I made my way to the water in near blindness, slamming into Rumil and Sparse as they were coming back. We tumbled. My knee thwacked against the exposed root of a pine. Someone's foot slapped my chest. There was a confusion of bodies as we grabbed at one another, pulling and pushing, eventually making it to our feet again. Both Sparse and Rumil wore the new T-shirts and shorts, the skin on their arms and legs dripping with muck. "For fuck's sake," Sparse said to me. "I thought you was the boogeyman." Rumil's arm touched my head and removed something from my hair. "I was right," he said. "Well, sort of. All they want is for you to go completely under then they'll let you get out."

"Good," I said. "I'm ready."

They lumbered on back to the circle. I took another step then stopped and waited for my eyesight to adjust. I had lost my bearings. The lake hadn't seemed this far away in daylight. A few yards at most. Darkness had stretched the distance. A person could wander from tree to tree in this blackness, never finding his way out. I thought of my mother's bootleggers and her gang of women. All her stories were marauding through this dense clot of woods, and now I was a part of them, another character staking his claim in the Neck, wanting more from this land than it was prepared to give.

Slowly, the world took on more definition; the dark between the trees mellowed into deep blue. Not long after, Larry called out my name from somewhere to my left. I moved toward the sound of his voice. My vision was clearing. I saw the ground, my bare feet slushing through pinecones and leaves and sticks. Close to the lake, the earth turned muddy and soft, pockmarked by the others' footprints. Lake John was about the size of a football field. Rick and Larry stood about three feet out, coffee-colored water lapping against their knees. They waved me onward. "Come on," Larry said. "Hurry."

I eased in. A sludge of algae and particulates swam around me in a kind of stew that stunk of raw sewage. When I waded past Rick and Larry, Rick was the one to speak. "Go until you can't," he said, and so I kept going until the water came to my neck. The lake bottom felt waxy and sharp; I dug in my toes and let the current drift over my body, tugging me toward the center. The stars spun like fireflies fleeing capture. On the opposite side of the lake, headlights flickered on. Mother Maude and Father Drake had parked the RV on that side while Rick and Larry remained in a tent near the Sleeping Cabin to watch over us. In the middle distance, between the headlights and me, a figure stood in the water. Father Drake lifted an arm, and I did the same. As his arm remained in the air, I gathered he wasn't waving but likely praying. Embarrassed, I covered my eyes and nose and dove under. Beneath the lake's surface, I flapped my arms like wings to push myself deeper into the murk. The water obliged. My body became suspended down there, the lake a kind of womb holding me in place.

Mother Maude and Father Drake remained in Hawshaw for four months, leaving for the Neck at the beginning of April. During their stay, they lived in their RV, keeping the vehicle parked at the Piggly Wiggly across town in two spaces they rented from the store manager. For the most part, they kept to themselves. I presumed they were busy preparing for the camp. I imagined this entailed making phone calls and traveling through the Delta, as my father once had, ginning up interest in their unconventional ministry and, of course, collecting donations. They joined us for dinner on most nights when my father was home. Mother Maude could not cook like her older sister did, so we oftentimes ate from McDonald's or Ward's. But when my father wasn't around, only Mother Maude came over, claiming Father Drake was "too busy," but I understood that I made him uncomfortable. When my aunt and I were alone in the apartment, I learned she was like my mother in one crucial way: They were both great talkers. Especially when the men weren't around.

"Now listen," she told me on more than one occasion. "Here's how you became the sinner you are." She believed my "inversion," as she called it, had nothing to do with hormones, or having an emasculated father, or even some rogue gene in my DNA. "No, sir," she said. "Don't believe that nonsense for a second. Your sin's the culmination of sins committed before you were born. A whole history of wrongdoing for which you are the natural unnatural outcome." According to her, the trouble took root in the Neck after World War Two when my grandfather, Horace Dodd, bought up fifty acres of squalor from Attala and Holmes counties. "Lord knows how he got the money," she said. "Daddy never owned two pennies to rub together when I was growing up." She characterized the Neck as a place people went to kill or be killed. "That part your mama got right in her stories!" And she claimed to have been informed by reliable sources, though she never told me who, that he was able to purchase the land cheaply because he had worked out a deal with the county officials. As the moonshiner had in my mother's story, Horace Dodd gave them the impression he was the man to clean up the Neck, make it respectable. He wasn't from around there, and nobody knew much about him, but he looked like the sort of man for the job. "He was always wearing dark-rimmed hoot-owl glasses and white-collared shirts. He kept his hair greased back—oh, I'd love nothing better than to show you a picture of your grandparents, but my Johnny stole the one of them I used to keep in my purse." Any time she brought up her brother, she would become distracted and need a minute or two to find her way back to the original point. "My Johnny thought I was abandoning him by taking a husband. He never said as much, but I knew his heart as well as I knew my own, and he felt like I was leaving him to fend for himself just like our parents and your mama did when we were kids. Right before he left me, he got ahold of my purse and took the picture with him." Eventually, she recovered the original thread: "You'll just have to take my word for it—Daddy didn't have the appearance of a rascal. No, sir. He looked more like the kind of man who'd figure up your taxes, not open the doors to a juke joint and run a cathouse on the side." She paused at this part to take a sip of her large plastic cup of Diet Coke. "Which was exactly what Daddy did soon after the purchase of the property was finalized."

Mother Maude said the juke joint was easy to find. "A squat little building perched on the side of a gravel road right after you turned off the blacktop highway." My grandfather made sure to set it on the Holmes County side of the Neck because Attala was dry. In the beginning, the establishment was little more than a roof and four walls where men gathered to wet their whistles. "Didn't have electricity, so I doubt there was even a jukebox, but people called it a juke joint all the same. Don't ask me why." And if Mother Maude ever got to talking about the juke joint, then sooner or later she would get around to talking about the cathouse, too. It was unavoidable. "Now that was the stuff of legend and myth. I don't rightly know what to believe about it." From what she'd learned over the years, the cathouse was tucked so deep in the Neck you wouldn't be able to find it unless the whores wanted you to find it. Mother Maude admitted she'd never set eyes on her father's "little palace of iniquity" herself. "No, sir. He was done with all that by the time we kids came along." She'd heard a rumor, nothing she could say for sure, that once her father quit the whoring business, he burned the cathouse down. "Makes sense to me," she said, "considering what happened later."

Mother Maude would claim my grandfather, though wicked, did give order to the Neck. For this, the law from either county often let him alone to do his evil as he pleased. "And drunkards, poachers, gamblers, thieves—they all respected him enough to get his permission first before they started any trouble in his woods." Everybody called him the Boogeyman for how he slunk about his land, appearing and disappearing like a ghost. "Daddy was said to have known the Neck so well he could hide bodies no bloodhound could ever sniff out. Gives me chills just to ponder the man he was." Back when he kept a roster of women on the payroll, one in particular, a woman named Cheryl, was his personal favorite whenever he, as Mother

Maude put it, "dallied in matters of the flesh." "I know Mama and Daddy were bad people, but it's hard for me to see them as that even now. Daddy never seemed like a boogeyman to me. Far from it. Imagine this homely little man who stood guard behind a cash register all day." She'd claim the only time he ever lost his cool was at the end when he fought with her mother about her peculiar ways. "And Mama—for all I know she may well have been another Miss Kitty from *Gunsmoke*, but to me she was just Mama. Lord, I wish I still had that picture of them to show you what I mean." Once she got going, Mother Maude could dally on the theft of the picture. After Johnny died, she told me, she and Father Drake had riffled through his apartment in New York looking for the picture but never finding it. "Knowing him," she said, "he probably threw it away when he got tired of looking at it. Like your mama, he never dwelled much on where we had come from." She described the picture as a small black-and-white snapshot taken by the justice of the peace soon after he had pronounced her parents husband and wife. "In it, Mama's leaning against a door, her head cocked back, grinning. Daddy's right there beside her, looking all pleased with himself, his arm sort of shoved around her shoulder." From the look of her mother in the picture, Mother Maude suspected the menfolk came to Cheryl for more than her beauty. "Oh, she was pretty," Mother Maude said. "Imagine your mama without all the heft. And Lord, them eyes, narrow and green. They seemed to say in that picture, *I know what you've done, and I don't care because, baby, I've done worse.*"

Eventually, Mother Maude would get around to the thesis of her talks with me, the proof of her theory for my affliction. "Now I'm no theologian like your daddy, but in the Old Testament, scripture tells us plainly about sin. Deuteronomy, chapter five, verse nine:

'Thou shalt not bow down thyself unto them, nor serve them'—here it means heathen idols, but it may as well be referring to sin in general—'for I, the Lord thy God, am a jealous God, visiting the iniquity of the fathers upon the children unto the third and fourth generation of them that hate me.'" She believed my grandparents' history of whoring and drinking and probably worse tainted their offspring—the most noticeable stain showing up in Johnny's life and now mine. We have to acknowledge the sins of our forefathers and ask forgiveness—this was to be my first step toward healing, and so it was important, she explained, that she reveal our dark and stormy past to me.

Mother Maude told me how my grandparents attempted to turn from their sinning but did so in a roundabout, worldly way that ultimately didn't work. "It happened like this," she said. "When Mama found out she was pregnant, she decided to leave the Neck. A cathouse was no place to have a baby, and she was determined to keep this one after years of getting rid of them." When my grandfather discovered her plan, he threw a fit. Surprised all the whores within earshot, including my grandmother Cheryl, by his sudden surge of anger. The real shocker, however, happened in what came next. He told my grandmother he agreed: The Neck was not suitable for a family. Still, he wanted one with her, so he supposed the Neck must change. After she agreed to marry him, he turned out the whores and redid the inside of the juke joint. Mother Maude said, "He transformed it into the kind of place you'd buy fishing tackle and pickled eggs and unleaded gasoline. No small feat. Nearly sent him to the poorhouse, too." When he was finished with the remodeling, he called it the Filling Station—"though," Mother Maude was always quick to add, "one or two smart alecks would mispronounce it as the *Feeling* Station on account of Daddy once being in the business of whores." Needless to say, the rebranding had a rocky start. Problem was, nobody wanted to stop at a store in the Neck for long enough to fill up his tank even if his vehicle was running on fumes. "Daddy did his best to draw in customers. He ran spots on local radio stations and bought those large wooden signs advertising the store and had them hung on a number of fences that lined the outfields of Little League baseball diamonds." Nothing worked. "Folks weren't so quick to forget who he had been, and the Boogeyman is a hard moniker for a man to overcome." After several years of striving, my grandfather gave up trying to rehabilitate the Neck's image (and his own) and decided to lean into it. "Did your mama ever tell you their slogan for the Neck? East of West and West of Weir." She said my grandmother took credit for that gem and many others, such as "The Filling Station—supplying fuel to the fire since 1950." "They put these slogans on T-shirts and coasters and ashtrays," Mother Maude said. "They weren't proud." The merchandise attracted enough curiosity from locals and lost motorists alike to keep the business afloat during most of Mother Maude's childhood. "Mama helped it along with her cooking. She taught your mama how to deep-fry everything in corn oil—from potato logs to chicken livers. Mama wanted me to learn to cook, too, but the kitchen never made much sense to me. Oh, I can scramble an egg, but I have to put my mind to it."

She would speak of my mother's birth with equal parts envy and awe. When Debra Rose was born, Mother Maude said, she did much to improve my grandparents' reputation. In part, because of where they chose to send her for her education: the private school in West, the Christian academy. "Much like the one you have here in

Hawshaw," she said. "I imagine the students and faculty alike didn't know quite what to make of her at first. She was, after all, the child of a whore and the Boogeyman." But my mother had a way about her, even back then. "She had many friends, and all everybody ever talked about when Johnny and me were kids was DR this and DR that. She was the best thing since peanut butter and jelly. People said she had a big future. She was the one to watch out for. I got so tired of hearing about it. One time I asked Daddy about my future, and he looked sort of startled, and said, 'Well, Maudie-girl, what about it?' Like he'd not once considered I might grow up and make something of myself." Another sip of Diet Coke was required before she could continue. "Which, you remember, I did. You tell me how many of your kinfolk ended up on the radio besides this one here talking at you."

Unlike Debra Rose, Mother Maude argued that she and her brother were unwanted. "We were what people called oops-a-babies, meaning we were accidents. I can't say what kept Mama from taking the hanger to us, and that's the plain truth." My grandparents made it clear from the start to my aunt and uncle not to expect to be sent to the private school like my mother was. They could barely afford tuition for one child, let alone three. So the twins had to get up before sunrise each morning and catch the yellow bus to Ethel, all the way on the other side of the county. "Looking back, I'm glad we went to public school with the blacks. Your daddy is right about segregation—it's pure evil. Lord, I have enough on my conscience already. But I was happy to go to school with them. They didn't bother me one bit. They left us alone, and we left them alone, and everybody got along just fine, thank you very much."

When my aunt and uncle started school, the trouble with my

grandmother started. "I guess the reason your mama made up that business about the lost mother was to spare you the truth. Well, sparing the truth is what got you in your predicament, and I aim to tell you everything." My grandmother did not fare well at home on the Neck all by herself with her husband, too broke to hire any help, spending long hours at the Filling Station. He came back in the evenings so worn down he seemed to be sleepwalking. My mother was never home, either. The way Mother Maude told it, she was always over in West with her "glut of friends." "She was a cheerleader, and they always seemed to be throwing pep rallies. So many of them you would think they'd get tired of trying to get everybody revved up for the least little old thing." Mother Maude and her brother didn't make it back home from their long journey to the county school until late in the afternoon. My grandmother had so little to occupy her mind. They didn't own a TV set, and she didn't like housework or reading. "The walking must have begun with small distances. Little jaunts here and there—to the pasture and back before anybody was the wiser. Each day she must have ventured out a little farther. Circled the lake until her feet were numb with exhaustion." Then, Mother Maude said, my grandmother stayed gone for longer amounts of time. They would get home from school and she would still be away. The afternoon absences persisted, and she and Johnny didn't know enough to question it. One evening my grandmother stayed out until my mother "pranced in." Mother Maude said Debra Rose acted as if it were their fault their mother was gone. "What'd you yard apes do with her?" she wanted to know. When my grandfather got home, my grandmother's disappearance became a crisis. "He got so upset he hyperventilated. DR made him sit down and press a warm bath cloth against his eyes. The man, I tell you, was calm and steely except when it came to Mama." My grand-mother eventually returned. Each time one of them put the question to her about her whereabouts, she behaved as if she no longer under-stood the English language. She'd squint, as if something from far off had caught her attention, and say, "Oh, just out." At this point in the story, Mother Maude would imitate her mother by squinting and saying "out" in some highfalutin accent. "Can you imagine that?" she would often ask me, and I would tell her I couldn't. "Well, I got mad on Daddy's behalf when she'd get to talking like some English poetess who'd just come in from the moors."

Each time he came home to find her out, my grandfather flew into a rage. "Where you been?" he would ask her when she came drifting in the back door. "Who you been with?" He told her she was stuck in the Neck with him. That she was "plumb crazy" if she thought he'd let her leave him in this "godforsaken backcountry" with three mouths to feed. "Their fighting could last all night long. Lord, the noise they made. Their voices so loud the words slurred in their mouths. Some-times words weren't enough, either, and Daddy used his hands." The violence had a domino effect. "He'd beat on her, and then she would beat on him, and if Johnny and me were nearby, they'd pull us into the fray and beat on us." Before I could ask, Mother Maude said they never laid a finger on my mother. "She was hardly around, took to staying overnight with friends in West more and more."

The summertime came, and nobody stayed much at the house in The Neck except for the twins. "We were left to ourselves for hours at a time. We became so close that summer I believed we began to read each other's thoughts." She told me how all she had to do was shut her eyes to see what was running through her brother's head. They would remain this close, she said, until the day he left her. "He and I were thirty, and I was singing in a revival in Kentucky." Before she went on to perform, she hugged her brother close, and whispered, "Your sister's going to be a wife," and he said, "With who?" and she said, "That man who's been following us around to hear me sing." Her brother smiled and said that was fine—*just fine.* But Mother Maude knew different. "And he knew I knew—I know it." By the time she was finished with her song, he had already removed all his clothes from their RV—"plus, he took the liberty of pilfering Mama and Daddy's picture out from under me. Didn't say good-bye or go to hell." Either, she assured me, would have been preferable to the awful silence he left behind.

It was no great surprise to me when Mother Maude told me my grandparents weren't churchgoers. "Neither was DR," she would add, "which makes it all the more surprising she ended up with someone like your father, a true man of God if there ever was." She and her brother began attending church by accident. "Here's the thing about living in a place as empty as the Neck: like sin, sound travels." One afternoon they were alone in the front yard and heard singing echoing off the Big Black River. Having nothing better to do, they followed the song. "We walked and walked—a full two miles away—to a small country church." The choir director had taken his assembly outside to practice. About twelve of them, they were singing hymns to the trees and the birds. "When we came wandering up, all shy and confused, the leader stopped his choir, and said, 'Look here, y'all. We've done summoned a couple of changelings.'" My aunt and uncle were seven. "A full year before Daddy set the Filling Station on fire," she said, "and both Johnny and me were as towheaded as you are now."

The church took them in. In addition to attending regular

service on Sundays and prayer meetings on Wednesdays, they also attended choir rehearsal on Friday nights. "We had to practice with the choir for several months before the choir leader would even consider letting us sing with them. Johnny wasn't any good, but the choir leader said I had promise." He taught her scales and how to harmonize. "This will tell you just the kind of heathen I was: I don't remember the preacher of that little church or a sermon he ever delivered, but I do remember the breathing exercises the choir leader showed me, how to hold the air in my lungs and let it out a little at a time." Her brother tagged along for the practices, she said, because he was "getting sweet" on the choir director—"already his affliction was rearing its ugly head and we weren't even in our double digits." They were encouraged to invite their parents and sister to service, but they never did. "The church was ours," Mother Maude said. "A place where people told us we were special and not because DR was our sister."

While she and her brother found religion, their parents' bickering worsened. Mother Maude thought it would end this way: by her mother not coming back from one of her walks. "She'd just keep going," she said. "And maybe it would have been better for all of us if she had." Instead, the end came more dramatically. This last row of theirs happened in the store when Mother Maude and her brother were eight. Reports on what transpired vary, but Mother Maude believed this version: The night before, her mother had come in so late her father had already fallen asleep and didn't have a chance to say his piece. "He went to the Filling Station the next morning, huffing mad, and found Mama in the kitchen area around back, frying hushpuppies, surrounded by all these pots and pans. Well, Daddy must have grabbed one of them in a fit of rage. He struck Mama across the head and liked doing it so much that he did it again." The coroner's report indicated the blow wasn't what killed her, but Mother Maude suspected her father thought it had. "Must have been distraught," she said. "That's the only way to explain it." He doused the store in gasoline and set the whole thing ablaze. "I read their bodies were found mostly intact—no, they died from the smoke."

Becoming orphans proved to be as much a blessing as a curse for my aunt and uncle. The church helped in placing them with a kind-hearted childless couple in Nashville—"the perfect spot for me to end up," she said. Their lives blossomed in Music City; once out of the Neck, they thrived. My mother had a rougher transition. "I don't know if she ever told you," she said, "of what her life was like before she ran across your father." I told Mother Maude how she was always careful with the details, and Mother Maude said she didn't blame her sister. "She stayed with a family in West to finish out her senior year with her class, and after she graduated, she went wild. She got work at a lamp factory near the Choctaw reservation and took up with an Indian man—lived in sin with him until he was tired of her and put her out on the road. Oh, how far she fell! I took no pleasure in hearing of her misfortune even though she didn't want nothing to do with Johnny and me."

Mother Maude went on to tell me about the time my mother was chosen homecoming queen. "Our guardians—sweet people—drove us five hours back down to West to watch her get crowned. You should have seen your mama. Pretty doesn't do it justice for how she looked out on that football field." After the ceremony, my aunt and uncle were waiting for her on the sidelines with a bouquet of gerbera daisies. "Well," Mother Maude said, "she gave us one of Mama's silly far-off looks, the kind Mama had on her face when she'd just come back from one of her walks. DR said, 'Thank you,' like she was ask-ing a question." My mother, the way her sister told it, acted ashamed to have them in attendance. "Didn't want to know the first thing about how we were faring in Nashville or how my singing was go-ing." My mother didn't linger; she followed the homecoming court back to the dressing room in the gymnasium, promising to find her siblings once she'd finished changing back into comfortable clothes. "As she drifted away, I said to Johnny, 'There ain't nobody but you and me,' and he said, 'Sister, I guess I've known that for some time.'"

Mother Maude would always end her talks on the subject of denial—how my mother thought she could pretend what happened didn't happen. "She inherited that way of thinking from Mama and Daddy. So did Johnny. Now all of them are dead, dead, dead, and just me and you are left to carry on."

She was quiet for a minute and then looked at me, her head cocked to the side. "I think it'd do you good to see the people you came from," she said. The restaurant below had closed almost an hour ago, and the silence made her words now seem more important somehow, as if the whole world had gone quiet for this last bit of the story. "I'll show you another picture instead," she said. "I was going to wait until camp, but I don't see the harm in you getting a sneak peek." She had her gym-bag-size purse on her lap and rustled through it for several minutes until she found her leather wallet and flipped it open. "Look here," she said, and shoved a picture down on the table in front of me. "This is what Drake and I found in Manhat-tan when we went up there to see about him. Just look at him. He was talking crazy." The picture had yellowed over the years. The skin on the man's face—Johnny's face—was pulled tightly around his cheekbones, and his eyes were hollowed out. He had the faintest wisp of yellow hair above his ears, the only indicator that he might, in fact, be related to me. "His brain was all eat up with the disease. He was saying how my Drake was the love of his life and how he was sorry for me to know it. The only way to calm him down was by singing to him. He'd get real quiet then, and when I finished, I'd say, 'Now, Johnny, do you accept Jesus into your heart?'" I shut my eyes, but the tears leaked out anyway. She continued talking. Talking and talking and talking—until there was nothing, it seemed, left but the sound of her voice. "He never gave me much of an answer when the room was crowded with all his scary-looking friends, but after Drake cleared them out, I asked him again, and he nodded. He said, 'Sister, what're you going to do when it's only you?' and I told him not to worry about me. I had the Lord, and I had Drake. Then he'd get to crying again. Lord, the tears—he shed them like you are now, but it was too late for him. Yes, sir. Too late for him but not for you. He died a few days after he accepted salvation, died with the most peaceful of expressions on his face. So peaceful I got my Polaroid from my purse and took a picture of my Johnny in his sweet repose. Open your eyes, my lamb. *Look* at him. Wouldn't you say that here's a man who knew where he was going once his body was gone?"

Rick and Larry dragged me back to land by the ankles, their gloves gnawing into my skin. They dumped me into a thicket of weeds and brambles. A possum trundling past hissed as I came rolling toward it. I yelled, and the animal shuffled away, its black eyes red rimmed and depthless. Larry told me to stand. "There's no time to fool around," he said. "Your brothers need you." Rick gave me a towel to pat myself dry then handed over the new T-shirt and shorts. The clothes clung to my still-damp body, the starchy fabric making me itch. My skin felt slimy. Rick and Larry followed me back to the edge of the torchlight. Inside the circle, Rumil and Sparse and Christopher looked like they were dancing, arms lashing about wildly. But when I got closer, I saw that they weren't dancing. They were fighting. Not each other, but Dale.

"What's happening?" I asked.

"Dale," Rick whispered.

Larry clarified: "Says he's not going in the water."

The boys were taking turns running at Dale while Mother Maude stood back, pressing the glass side of the mirror to her chest. Dale was able to keep the other boys off by using his big arms to push them away. The boys were no match for him. He could swat back all night, and this seemed to be our first test: Find some way to bring this big bastard down. And he *was* a bastard. Scattered around Mother Maude were shards of glass, twinkling in the flames. No one had to tell me what had happened. This fool had punched the mirror. The knuckles on his left hand, the one he favored as he swiped at the boys, looked bloody and raw, like the top layer of skin had been scraped off. The sight of his injury stoked a growing fury in me. *Dale,* I thought. *Fuck Dale.* I wanted to give him more wounds. I was suddenly running into the circle, and without any plan or foresight, I leaped into the melee, catching him by surprise. He swung. His fist caught my ear, sending me down fast. But with his attention diverted, the others saw their chance and pounced, all together this time. Christopher managed to wrestle him into an awkward headlock. He used the full weight of his body to stymie Dale long enough for Sparse and Rumil to tear off his shirt and then snatch down his jean shorts.

"Bring him to the water," Larry was shouting. "Hurry!"

But the boys, even working together, couldn't hold Dale for long. The four of them rolled onto the ground. They twisted and turned in the mess of shirts and pants and sneakers. Somehow Dale managed to free himself in the chaos. Dazed, he sat up to find me standing over him, my ear leaking blood. "Amen," I said, and kicked him in the face. Hard. His head shot back, and he was down. He landed on top of the others who were still writhing in the clothes, unaware, I think, that Dale had escaped until his dead weight came slumping back down over them.

"Is he breathing?" Rumil lifted one of Dale's arms and let go, wide-eyed, as it fell listless to the dirt.

"We're not *that* lucky," Sparse said, shaking out from under Dale's shoulder.

Dale came to as we were carrying him to the lake. Rick and Larry had pitched in, and now he was easy to manage. "Please," he kept saying. "Please." Mother Maude met us at the edge of the lake, still holding the broken mirror. We laid Dale at her feet. "My lamb," she said to him. "We will drag you to salvation—kicking and screaming if need be." She stooped to kiss the red mark my foot had left on his forehead. "Because I love you—so much I do." She nodded to Rick and Larry, who, in turn, directed us to take up his legs and arms again. We worked together, different parts of the same machine. Dale didn't fight us—he didn't seem to have any fight left tonight. We swung him back and forth, our arcs modest but gaining momentum with each pass. "Okay," Larry said. "On three."

"One," Christopher screamed. "Two."

At three, we released Dale into the air. He didn't fly very far, as big as he was, and he landed with a weak splash in the shallows. As soon as we let go, we sank. A moment later Dale resurfaced and filled the night with a throaty roar. No one paid much attention to him as he sloshed back to us. We were exhausted. We panted and itched at our necks and the insides of our arms and down our legs. Mosquito bites *under* the skin. Rumil touched a raw place on my elbow. "Look at you," he said. "What is that?" Sores had begun to open up on my skin. Tiny wanton mouths gasping for air.

SEVEN

■

REORIENTATION

My drive along the Natchez Trace was unremarkable and easy. Grand walls of trees rose up to lofty heights on both sides of the road, shielding me from the outside. For all my years in Mississippi, I'd taken the Trace for granted. Only tourists went this way, or people with time to kill. I wasn't either, but here I was anyway. I drove without my GPS, without the radio on, and—of course—without my cell.

I exited the Trace for the town of Kosciusko. I would have to go the rest of the way to Camp Levi on highways and dirt roads as the Trace curved westward and missed the Neck entirely. Named for the Polish freedom fighter Tadeusz Kościuszko, Kosciusko served as the seat for Attala County. It was also where the trial had taken place. Evening's gauzy pink sky hung low overhead, casting a sepia glow on all the houses I passed, many of them built in the style of

Queen Anne Victorian. There was a quiet, sleepy sort of beauty to the neighborhoods. I had overlooked it the last time I'd been here when I'd been called to testify. It was during my second semester at the magnet school in Jackson. I was smack-dab in the middle of rehearsals for the drama club's production of *Twelfth Night*. It was an all-male, and decidedly queer, cast. I had been given the role of Orsino. When I wasn't studying calculus and learning the basics of computer programing, I was memorizing my lines: "If music be the food of love," I said in the shower to myself, in the cafeteria to the meat loaf, backstage to a boy whose love I craved, "play on. Give me excess of it; that surfeiting, the appetite may sicken, and so die." When my father called to tell me I had to go back for the trial, I was resentful and said no. Almost a full year had passed since camp. I had new attitudes and opinions, and saw no good reason for having to rehash that summer in front of a bunch of strangers. The boy I had been, the person seeking rehabilitation, embarrassed me, and I was worried my friends, anyone, really, would find out my past. Now, looking back, I see the irony of my situation. I had merely traded in one secret for another.

Like many courthouses, this one was located in the center of the square, elevated on a hill above a circuit of stores. I parked Doll in front of a drugstore and climbed a set of concrete steps sloping up the grassy hillside. Everything seemed quieter. I remembered Kosciusko as busy, a bustle in the air. Townsfolk traipsing up and down the sidewalks, calling out to one another, laughing. That day my father had parked behind one of the stores. He said, "I'm better off right here," and left me to walk to the courthouse alone to meet my legal representative. Along the way, I wondered if any of the people I passed knew the reason I was there. Somehow, someway, I feared being recognized and that word would travel back to Jackson, to my new life. But after I had said my piece, what little I could, I returned to school without a single classmate batting an eye when I told them I'd been away to a funeral—a distant cousin, I lied.

After the verdict was announced, a lawyer called to inform my father, and he eventually told me the outcome when I came home for summer vacation. At first I didn't understand him. He said, "He got accidental manslaughter since nobody could pin down what exactly happened beyond a reasonable doubt." *Manslaughter? Doubt?* I thought I had come in late to the conversation, that my father was referring to an incident in the news. "What?" I said. "Who?" And he took off his glasses, he rubbed his eyes. "Rooster," he said. "You know who I mean." Suddenly I did and I didn't want to. But he wouldn't let me off the hook; he required a response, some form of acknowledgment that I understood him. I decided to give my father Shakespeare's words instead of my own. I called up my favorite lines from *Twelfth Night*, words that didn't even belong to Orsino, but ones another boy, as Viola, had spoken to rapt audiences during our three-night run: "O time, thou must untangle this, not I. It is too hard a knot for me to untie." My father had the same confused look on his face he'd had all those years ago when he called me to his office for dancing flamboyantly in the choir. Only now I wasn't the kind of son who cared anymore how much he horrified his father or his father's God.

The double doors to the courthouse on this side of the square were locked so I, ever the optimist, walked around to try the others. No luck. I pressed my face to the glass and peered in at the varnished hardwood floors and row of doors leading to various elected officials. The town was known as the beehive of the hills, a little hub of industry and small businesses in central Mississippi. Flanking the bottom of the steps to the main entrance were these burnished bee-hives. The metal had, however, tarnished over the years and looked more like twin dollops of dog scat. Without thinking, I searched my pockets for my cell phone to take a picture of these little sculptures to send to Bevy and, perhaps, Zeus before I remembered I'd gotten rid of it. Crammed in my pocket instead was the floppy princess mask. When I returned to Doll, I tossed the mask in the glove compartment and promptly forgot about it as I drove to the Walmart Supercenter.

I used the remaining limit on my credit card to buy a high-performance LED spotlight, a flannel sleeping bag, a tent, a folding armchair, a battery-powered fan, a case of bottled water, Slim Jims, two bags of trail mix, half a dozen cans of Vienna sausages and black beans, and a pack of cherry-flavored chewable melatonin tablets. I brought the food and supplies to checkout line five and placed them one at a time onto the conveyor belt. The cashier—a young boy with dirty fingernails—looked up, and said, "Whoa! You look like you're getting ready for a camping trip." And I said, trying to be funny, "Or the apocalypse." Something in my voice, a strain to it that even I heard, startled the boy. He smiled at me without making eye contact, the kind of response you give to people when you think they're nuts and want to hurry them along without any trouble. I couldn't blame him—my behavior in the past few days didn't exactly illustrate someone with stellar mental health.

I took Highway 19 toward West, which cut directly through the Neck. The gravel road that led into the campsite was easy to miss. But I spotted the no trespassing sign that looked familiar riddled with buckshot and nailed to a skinny pine just before a turnoff. I took my chances that this was the right way. Night had already fallen, so I pulled off onto a grassy shoulder about a mile and a half from where I expected to find the cabins and the Sweat Shack and the lake. I wanted the first time I saw Camp Levi again to be in daylight, preferably the morning, a more hopeful time of day. That night, I locked myself in Doll and shuffled over the console to the backseat. I riffled through the plastic bags until I found the packet of melatonin and ate two pills and tried to sleep. Doll's backseat wasn't as uncomfortable as I'd assumed it would be. Sooner or later, I figured, I would spend my nights outside in the tent roughing it, but for now this would do nicely. I rolled up the sleeping bag for a pillow and shut my eyes. My time in cities had made me accustomed to distant night noises—police sirens, car horns, rowdy undergrads roaming the sidewalks. The silence of the country seemed louder now, dense and heavy. I had trouble sleeping under the weight of it, spending most of the night somewhere between sleep and wakefulness. I dreamed myself back into the courtroom. I was on the stand. Lawyers indistinguishable in their expensive suits peppering me with questions, each a variation of *What happened?* I could remember now, I told them. No more *can'ts*. I spoke about the first night, our long walk to the lake. I told them about the sores on our skin, the chants. My voice kept moving without me, telling them more than I had ever before remembered: the microlessons on manhood, the games we played, the long days of misery. My voice, at last, obliged the court.

Morning came, and I postponed going into the campgrounds, my nerves getting to me. I turned Doll around and drove into West, a much smaller town than Kosciusko, with no square and a

scattering of rundown buildings that faced the railroad and the Big
Black River. One of those buildings, I was happy to learn, was the
public library. Cutouts of drums and guitars and fiddles decorated
the big glass windows that faced the street. STEP TO THE BEAT AND
READ! hung above the front double doors in red letters.

I hadn't read for pleasure in years and was vaguely excited by the
possibilities. I scanned the titles on the shelf of new releases for several
minutes before I heard a cheery voice from the second floor. "I got
more titles in the other day. They're in the back, but I haven't cata-
logued them yet. I can show them to you, and if you're interested, I
can put your name down on the list." A woman came clomping down
a spiral staircase connecting the floor. She seemed almost to relish the
noise she made, as if purposely bucking the librarian stereotype.

I told her I would need to apply for a library card before I could
put my name down for any books. She removed a pair of baby-blue
glasses and placed them on the top of her head. She sniffed. I wasn't
aware of my stink until now. I wore the same soiled shorts and polo
I'd put on before I left Memphis. "Where you living?" she asked,
giving the impression that she was trying to determine if I was a
homeless person who'd come inside to enjoy the free air-conditioning.
I decided in that moment to never come back here, and so I told her
the truth. "The Neck," I said. "Or thereabouts."

She laughed. "Thought the only things that lived out there were
possums and ghosts." She told me I would need proof of physical
residence—a billing statement or some other official mail I'd received in the past two weeks—if I wanted to take out a card today.
"You're more than welcome to read books here until you can get
documentation," she added. I told her I'd wanted to take a book or
two back with me. "There's not much to do in the Neck but read."

The woman snapped her fingers, an idea occurring to her, and told me to follow her. "Come on," she said, and led me to the other side of the L-shaped room, to a shelf of books called trade-ins. "These are old paperbacks and not in regular circulation. People usually bring books to swap out for these, but since you're new, you can take a few with you to start you off." The paperbacks were mostly westerns and romances, and the woman informed me that the ones with the heart-shaped stickers on the cover were the ones that didn't have any dirty scenes. "Those are the only ones I can allow myself to read," she explained, "because I'm not big enough of a person to skip over the sexy parts like some people claim to do." She laughed again and told me her name was Brenda. "I got to go check in some books from the book drop, but do holler if you need anything."

After she left, I searched the titles. I'd read romances during the summer when I was home from school, the "sexy parts" my only access to pornography until I owned a computer of my own. Brenda soon returned with a question: "Hey, you aren't one of them boys from Hollywood, are you?" This time I laughed. I told her my mother's people used to live around the Neck. "So this is kind of a homecoming then?" she said, and I told her it was something like that. I figured this would satisfy her, but it didn't, and I should have known it wouldn't have. Brenda had more to say, mostly about the movie, as if she'd been waiting to get this off her chest. "Those people came by here about two years ago, scouting the area, wanting to film that trash on location." She was happy to see them move along to Georgia instead. "We here in West didn't want another Kosciusko on our hands." When she realized I didn't know what she was talking about, she continued. "Oh, honey, Dennis Hopper went to Kosciusko to make a movie once upon a time." According to Brenda, people in that town thought they were about to hit pay dirt like Canton had when *A Time to Kill* was shot there. Hopper's movie, however, turned out to be an embarrassment. "Went straight to video," she said. "*Lured Innocence*—name speaks for itself. The newspaper in Holmes County called it soft-core cinema, and everybody in West laughed our butts off." She clicked her tongue.

I confessed to never hearing of that movie until now. "And I'm a film studies major," I said. "But not contemporary film." She told me it was just as well I hadn't known of it. "The less people who know it," she said, "the better. I get so tired of how they make us look in movies—people from the outside coming down here and making us look like a bunch of undereducated hicks. Like we don't have the Internet and don't know how the world works nowadays." She told me how one of the people from the film crew for *Proud Flesh* had come into the library to ask if she knew any grocery stores in the area that sold quinoa. "I had to pause to think a minute—not because I didn't know what quinoa was, but because I was wondering if the fancy Kroger in Madison was too far away to send him. Well, he went on to give me a lesson in quinoa, and I had to stop him right there. I said, 'I know, sir, what quinoa is. Hell, I don't eat it myself, but I certainly know what it is, and if I wanted a mouthful of beach sand, then I'd take my happy ass to the Gulf Coast, where I could have my fill for free. That's better than any quinoa I ever tasted.'" She paused to take a breath, and then her eyes got big. "Didn't you say your mother was from around here? Did she go to the academy?"

I nodded.

"What year was she?"

"Nineteen sixty-eight."

She jumped, her sandals making another loud thwack as she

came back down. "I was nineteen seventy—who *was* your mama?" I told her, and she squealed. "Debra Rose!" She told me she didn't know her personally, but she certainly knew of her. "Everybody did, honey—she was so popular. It was a plain tragedy what her daddy did." She appeared shocked to hear of her passing. "Well, you could have knocked me over with a feather." She asked again what had brought me back here, and this time I was more honest and told her I was curious about the Neck, that my mother had told me some wild stories, and then, of course, there was the movie. "Honey, that movie is only half of it. Ever since that crazy camp mess happened ten years ago, stories about the place being haunted have continued. Teenagers will go out there during Halloween looking for trouble." In recent years, she told me, people have claimed to have seen strange people lurking out there. "But I don't want to worry you." She squeezed my arm and then, as if by reflex, wiped her hand on her oversize blouse. "Most of the sightings happened right after Katrina, when all sorts of people migrated up from the coast. Sheriff told me he thought a few of them hung around for a spell and then moved on. But that don't stop kids from letting their imaginations get the better of them. And now with this movie about a boogeyman killing people, I'm sure we're in for one stupid Halloween season."

I asked her if people still knew about Horace Dodd and the gas station fire, and she shook her head, and said, "Don't nobody talk about the old stories. A few years back, the mayor put together some of them in a little book for tourists." She said she would show it to me if I'd give her a minute to go hunt it up. Before I could answer, she ran off to the circulation desk to look up a book number and then dashed around the stacks until she found it. "This here," she said, coming back. "The mayor, you know, used to be your mama's friend and so she heard all these tall tales from her. I like to take a look at it every now and then, but it was never very popular—just a novelty item we keep for posterity's sake." She handed me a small saddle-stapled booklet, the covers laminated. "Local color," she said, as I turned the book over. It had illustrations and was forty-five pages long. The woman who wrote it—Sally Jo Levy—moved to Texas, Brenda told me, not long after she self-published the book. Her husband got a better-paying job in Dallas. "But she was a good mayor," Brenda said. "Really steeped in all the lore about the Neck. Good thing she left, because she was the type of person who would have jumped at the chance to have that movie shot in these parts." She took the book from me and opened to the title page and then handed it back over. "Look who she dedicated the book to." Under the title, *The History of the Neck*, was the inscription "To D.R." I handed the book back and felt dizzy, like one of my spells was coming on.

"I hope I didn't upset you?"

I told her I just needed some lunch and grabbed a few of the romances off the shelf. We walked back toward the circulation desk. She began to run the spines of the trade-in paperbacks across the magnet block on the counter so they wouldn't set off the alarms when I exited. She must have put together more pieces of my story when she paused before running the last book. "Your mama's sister was your aunt," she said. "That singer—what did you say your name was?" I told her, but the story of the camp and my family and all that came after was too tangled for her to make much sense of it right away. Instead, she did that southerner's sleight-of-hand trick in conversations when talk had drifted into uncertainty: She changed the subject. She told me how the movie producers were, on the whole,

disappointed by what they found at the Neck. "Said it wasn't cine-
matic enough—and they were, I hear, gravely disappointed to find
that the old polluted pond had been drained." A few years after the
camp, she said, the Fishery and Wildlife Commission designated it a
public health risk. "All the fish in it were long dead." When she set
Sally Jo Levy's book on her side of the counter, I told her that the
mayor's book had reminded me of another one. "A memoir," I said.
"*The Summer I First Believed*." Brenda was familiar with it. "Made a
big stir when it first came out, but not nearly as big as the movie will,
I suspect." I asked her if I could see it, maybe look at it before I left.
She hunted up the call number on the computer database and wrote it
down on a used notecard. Before she handed the card over I asked if
she would help me find it. "I'm not used to the Dewey decimal system," I said. "All the libraries up north are Library of Congress." As I
expected, her hospitality blinded her to my true intentions. She told
me to wait right where I was and scooted around the corner, out of
sight, to fetch the book I had no intention of looking at. I didn't have
long to do what followed: I reached over the counter and swiped *The
History of the Neck*, ran its cornered spine across the magnet block,
and was out the door, rushing to Doll before Brenda returned.

In the acknowledgments section of *The History of the Neck*, Sally
Jo Levy thanked my mother in more depth. "For my last year of
high school," she wrote, "I got a sister. And though it was a dark
time for my sweet Debra Rose, we told these stories, mostly wild
fantasies, and somehow we muddled through by making the world
better than it was. These tales have stayed with me, and now I'm
happy to share them with all who travel through our troubled

weeds." She didn't have an author photo and listed very little else about her biography. "Sally Jo Levy," the book said, "has served several terms as the mayor of West." Published five years after my mother's death, the book included illustrations done by Sally Jo. The women of the woods were given pioneer garb, long dresses and lanterns and hard expressions. The moonshiners wore flannel shirts and overalls, and were posed behind various contraptions that constituted a makeshift distillery. The time period blurred to sometime after the Civil War and before the First World War. As I read Sally Jo's account, it echoed what my mother and aunt had told me about the Neck. For the story of the lost mother, Sally Jo's drawing of the woman's face was wide and smooth, and took up most of the page. Her hair streamed across the page. She resembled my mother, this was true, but the depiction was supposed to be, I was sure of it, my grandmother. It had to do with the eyes, the mystery in them that Mother Maude had spoken of. I knew so many stories about the Neck, and not a one of them was completely true. Each one represented, instead, a single person's attempt at truth. My own story wasn't any different.

I spent the better part of the afternoon sitting by the dry lake bed under a nice shade tree, thumbing through the book. After coming back from the library, I'd parked Doll at the very end of the gravel road in front of the cabins. Before sitting down to read, I walked around what was left of the property. The Sleeping Cabin had caved in on itself and wasn't much more than piles of splintery wood. The Chapel Cabin still stood, but I didn't trust the structure enough to venture inside. Nature had reclaimed the farmhouse. Clots of sumac and bristly vines threaded in and out of the walls. A thin tree had broken through the floorboards of the back porch and was inching toward the roof. The lake had changed since I last saw it, too. As in the movie, the water had been drained from it, leaving behind a concave bowl full of cattails and clover. When I finished the book, I stared into the brush-choked bowl of the lake bed, listening to the wind. I set the book down in the grass and walked to the lake bed. I stepped in, sinking down to my knees in weeds. I combed through it, careful where I put my feet. Snakes or other hidden critters wouldn't take kindly to my disturbing them. I made it to the middle of the lake, the spot I'd waded to during the first night. A stick snapped from somewhere back on the shore. But when I looked, nothing. My mind conjured up the boogeyman, how could it not: all incarnations of him—my grandfather, the killer in *Proud Flesh*, the recent sightings by teenagers Brenda had mentioned.

What was remarkable about the Neck was how unconcerned it seemed with its own history, with the tellings and retellings swirling around it. The land continued to grow, ferociously so, feeding on the remnants of the camp, the house. Sooner or later, any sign of human involvement would be devoured. A blessing.

I hiked to the other side and climbed out. Here stood two granite headstones. Mother Maude had been laid to rest beside her brother. If there had been a funeral for her, my father never told me, just as he had never told me he had inherited the camp from her. Not that my knowing of her funeral would have mattered—I wouldn't have come. During my Internet searches about the movie, I had discovered some small write-ups about what happened to her after she fled on the day of the accident. She'd relocated in secret to California, living on the lam for the rest of her life. Something cancerous had killed her, and here she was, her body beside her brother's, both slowly moldering into the Neck, which I guess, for them, was a happy ending.

When I returned to Doll, the trunk was popped up. As I got closer, I saw the doors had been flung open, too, like Doll's carpet was about to be vacuumed. I eased up beside one of the rear doors. A thin boy was inside, rummaging through grocery sacks, the supplies I'd purchased at Walmart. He wore the princess mask I'd stuffed in the glove compartment. He rapped to himself or was speaking in tongues—I couldn't tell which. I let him finish riffling and climb on out, not saying a word to him. In one hand, he toted the spotlight, and in the other, my box of beef jerky. "Look at this shit, Bubba!" he said, as he straightened himself up, not yet recognizing I wasn't the person he thought I was. He stopped moving when he realized. After a brief silence, he removed the mask. He looked nineteen, maybe twenty. His hair was orangey blond, the color dark hair turns when you douse it in hydrogen peroxide. "Oh," he said, stepping sideways, as if he were considering a speedy getaway into the woods. "We saw the car, and we . . ." He looked down at his dirty high-top tennis shoes. Several bands of duct tape were wound around the toes of them.

"Rooster."

He'd slunk in behind me. I jerked around, already shouting. Ten years had done little to wrinkle his face. His teeth, however, were a different matter. A row of yellow and black bone flashed from his lips as he tried to speak, to explain to me why I shouldn't be screaming. When that didn't work, Father Drake took one big step forward, enough to close the gap between us, and placed a hand over my wailing mouth.

EIGHT

▪

TREATMENT

They never told us the mix of possible pollutants and sewage runoff and microscopic parasites in Lake John that made our skin rebel against us. We had our own name for it: *the itch*. But our language for it didn't cover all the aftereffects. The day after our first dip into the lake, Sparse and Christopher reported experiencing a burning sensation in their skin. Like a sunburn, Christopher said, only deeper. Discolorations streaked across Sparse's back and belly and thighs, and he worried that he might get keloids. For me, sores had cropped up on my fair skin soon after I'd gotten out, scabbing over by morning. The itchiest parts were along my scrotum and the rim of my anus. An ecosystem of welts had developed down there, and it only made me upset to inspect the damage, so I didn't.

We'd slept on bunk beds in the Sleeping Cabin, still wearing our yellow T-shirts and khakis. The cabin had no windows, and we'd left the door open in hopes of circulating cooler night air inside, but it didn't work. When Rick and Larry fetched us in the morning, we awoke covered in a skein of our own sweat, our clothes sticking to our wrecked flesh. Getting out of bed required a great delicacy of movement. So did walking, which was more of a waddle for most of us.

There would be no showers at Camp Levi. Only the slightest attention would be given to our hygiene because we were "roughing it" in the Neck, just as the brochures had described. Fresh water, crisp and clear and cold, had been trucked in from somewhere nearby and poured into a metal basin, which was now docked on one of the picnic tables, waiting for us. We took turns brushing our teeth and washing our damp faces. We used the toiletries they'd set out beside the basin: individual plastic toothbrushes in clear wrapping, travel-size toothpaste tubes, unscented soap bars. Rick and Larry kept our items separate. After I used my toothbrush and soap, I handed them over to Larry, who placed them in a lunch box with my initials Magic Markered on the front. For peeing, Larry told us, we were encouraged to stand behind certain girthy trees lining the perimeter of the main grounds. He pointed to the ones he meant. "Don't cluster. Only one per tree," he added, "and no funny business, no lingering." If we needed a toilet for more "pressing concerns," there was the blue-tinted portable restroom shoved out of the way beside the Sleeping Cabin. It was locked, and Rick carried the key, a gleaming speck of metal around his neck.

After we finished our morning ablutions, we gathered on the hard benches of the picnic table, and Rick and Larry dashed inside the Chapel Cabin to get our breakfast. It was then, and only then, I realized that Dale wasn't among us. He'd not been with us all morning—not when we'd awoken, not when we'd brushed our teeth, not when we'd peed and shat in various locales around the campsite. He had certainly been with us the night before. After the lake, he'd stopped his crying and didn't make a sound. He crashed on the only bed in the Sleeping Cabin that didn't have a top bunk. He wrapped himself in the thin blanket on the mattress like a burrito, even though the cabin was sweltering.

Rumil must have sensed my question because he said, "I heard them come for him early, before sunrise." His neck was coated in slashes, as if he'd been strangled.

Christopher leaned forward. "Did he leave? For good?"

"The Sweat Shack, honey." Sparse pulled from his pocket a shard of the broken mirror from last night and examined his face, the rawness around his lips, the scabbiness in the creases of his nose and above his left eyebrow. "I look a mess," he announced. Rumil said they must treat Lake John with a chemical. Sparse, licking his inflamed lips, said, "It's how they'll keep us horny queens from fucking each other. They want to make it so we don't even want to touch ourselves when we go to take a piss." Sparse was correct about the last part. I had held my bladder for that very reason.

Christopher patted his puffy face. "Is this legal?"

No one answered. I believed nobody cared one way or the other about the legality of our situation. Our parents cared less about the means so long as the ends were delivered. Last night we'd come together in our violence, agreeing—without verbally acknowledging it—to see this process out. As I saw it, our orientation by the lake was nothing less than a forging of a holy covenant with the Lord. Now my groin ached so badly I sat with my legs spread out, as if I were airing myself out. *Good,* I thought. *Pain was progress.*

The counselors returned with Styrofoam plates of eggs, passing them out quickly and hurrying back inside. No time for small talk.

Christopher said, "I thought they said he wasn't getting sent there this time."

"Ah," Sparse said. "He didn't get sent for what he did at dinner, but for what he did in the circle." He waved the glass at us. "That probably signed his ticket."

At the edge of the pasture, the woods were alive with bird cackles and shivering trees as warm southerly winds rustled through their branches. From our table, the Sweat Shack was visible. I imagined Dale in there, his tall body hunched inside. The idea, I was beginning to understand, was for the sinful camper to sit in almost complete darkness, cocooned in thick ovenlike heat, and contemplate his sins. In essence, *sweat* them out.

"Mother Maude was with Rick and Larry when they came for him," Rumil said. "She saw me awake and came over."

Sparse said, "And?"

"She just put her hand on my forehead like this." He placed the back of his hand over his brows. "And she said, 'Peace, peace.'"

Sparse pushed his plate away. He'd barely touched his eggs. "Damn," he said. "They're good."

After breakfast, we went into the Chapel Cabin. Like the other buildings, there wasn't any electricity, but this cabin had more windows than the one we slept in, so it was almost cheery looking in the morning sunshine. On the walls hung posters with inspirational quotes from the Bible, encouraging us to be Christian soldiers. On a table in the back, there were several iceboxes, with the word MEALS scrawled across the lids. The four of us sat cross-legged on a tan horsehair rug that smelled of sawdust while Rick and Larry loomed over us. Our first microlesson, they told us, would focus on a series of responsible and irresponsible behaviors when interacting with other men. "For instance," Larry said. "It is responsible to stand about two feet from a fellow brother in Christ when conversing with him." Any closer, however, was irresponsible. Such closeness for boys like us could lead to inappropriate thoughts. Inappropriate thoughts, sooner or later, led to actions. "Men," Larry went on to say, "are physical creatures—our desires begin and end in the flesh. We must stifle the stimulus to protect the core. Remember David? Remember how he ran buck naked from the temptress's house?"

Standing back, Rick suddenly looked quizzical and interrupted. "You mean Joseph, brother." This would be his only notable contribution to the microlesson.

"Exactly!" Larry cried. "Exactly right."

Both counselors were young and attractive. Their athletic bodies were obscured on purpose, I figured, in their oversize yellow T-shirts and baggy khaki shorts, their hems hanging, like ours did, well below their kneecaps. Though Larry spoke of the importance of space being put between our bodies and the bodies of other men, neither counselor seemed to be all that aware that we were huddled awfully close to one another on the rug.

As the lesson continued, my attention wavered. Larry's talk about the power of the flesh made me hyperaware of it around me, Rumil's knee in particular. He brushed his against mine. The first time I thought was an accident; he was just getting situated, settled. But then it happened again. Because of our sitting position, our long shorts were pushed up past our knees, exposing us to skin-to-skin contact. My insides were in an uproar when we brushed knees a third time. At the very moment Larry bemoaned the weakness of the flesh, here I was succumbing to it. Rumil's knee tapped against mine again, and this time a sore on his leg aligned perfectly with a sore on mine. Like this, we held position; we pressed them together, a quick kiss of wounds. A sharp searing pain radiated from my groin as my penis thickened. Woozy, I leaned over.

"You all right?" Rick asked. Larry was holding him in a hug and he was observing me over Larry's shoulder. They'd been demonstrating how to embrace another man if one absolutely must. He released Larry and kneeled down in front of me, placing a hand on the back of my head. "What's the matter?"

"I just . . ." I knew that if I confessed to this knee action I'd be sent to the Sweat Shack, and a part of me wanted the punishment, it was true, but fear of the unknown kept me silent. I was, in my heart, a coward. "Bathroom," I said, swallowing everything else. Rumil had removed his knee and was sitting away from me, his face blank, innocent. Larry took off his key necklace and handed it over. When I stood, I quickly learned another benefit of our baggy shorts: The excess fabric hid my hard-on and allowed me to shuffle out of the Chapel Cabin without embarrassment. Once I was outside, walking about, my penis softened and the pain subsided. The portable restroom reminded me of the ones I'd seen at the Neshoba County Fair. I took this opportunity to pee, finally, heartened that the peeing didn't hurt as much as the hard-on had. When I was finished, I went back outside and darted around the cabin. In the distance, Mother Maude was standing beside the Sweat Shack with her back to me, her great mass of hair covering most of her broad shoulders. When I peered back around, she was stooping toward the little door in front of the Sweat Shack. Dale was crawling out on his hands and knees. After he was back on his feet, Mother Maude gave him a little applause and hugged him. Then, with her arm around his shoulder, she led him to the washbasin on the picnic table. He was given the same toiletries as us—toothbrush, bar of soap—and then Mother Maude guided him into the Sleeping Cabin.

I headed back to the microlesson. Rumil smirked at me when I reentered. I handed the key back to Larry, apologizing to him for taking so long. I decided to sit on the other side of the rug from Rumil for the remainder of the lesson, beside the dough-faced and harmless Christopher.

"You okay?" he asked me.

The question baffled me with its simplicity.

"Of course not," I said. "And that's good."

Dale rejoined us at lunch.

He lumbered over to our table and shoved in between Sparse and Rumil. There was barely any room, but neither of them complained. Dale didn't say a word about what'd transpired the night before. He ate his meal quietly, keeping his eyes trained on his food. For lunch, they'd served us ham-and-cheese sandwiches and more salt-and-vinegar potato chips. As with the other meals, Sparse ate very little, and when Christopher asked if he was done, Sparse shoveled his leftovers onto Christopher's plate. Dale's skin looked as ravaged as ours, but with one noticeable difference: The red mark on his forehead had turned purple and green, vaguely in the shape of California. He stopped chewing when he caught me staring at what my foot had done. "What?" he said, and I started and looked down at my own plate.

The rest of the afternoon was spent with Mother Maude in the

Chapel Cabin doing an activity that would come to be known as testimonials. For this activity, folding chairs were arranged in a circle. Mother Maude was already seated when we came in, smiling at us. Once we were seated, she explained how we would spend the next few hours. "The key to healing," she told us, "is knowing our stories front ways and back—being able to articulate them to God in prayer. It shows him we are serious." This gathering would be a kind of workshop for our stories, she explained, a time to confess and pick apart the events that had led us to this camp. "But first," she said, holding up a manila folder, "I want to show you how your story could end, how it most certainly *will* end, should you carry on down the path you are on." She opened the folder and held up a picture. "This is DeWayne—I met him hours before I took this picture of his body." The picture showed an emaciated face, the eyes staring listlessly at a spot just above our heads. She passed the picture to Christopher, who was sitting beside her. "I want y'all to look at these men." She passed out more, naming each one as she handed them out. "This here is Micah, and this is Darnel. This is Howard, and Carl, and John, and Edmund, and Garth." All of these pictures were taken, she told us, at the moment right after their souls had left them. They were men she'd ministered to in New York City in the early 1990s, men who'd had the plague. "Same as my Johnny," she said. "Look here." She held up the picture I'd recognized from that night with her in Hawshaw. This time I saw the resemblance in his lifeless face. Johnny *did* look like me. We shared the same cheekbones and nose. I panicked, briefly, that someone else would notice. No one did. Most of the other boys didn't stare at the pictures of the men for long—a fast look then they passed them on. "I want you to know the truth, and this is the truth about sin, the only truth that matters."

Christopher started crying, and when Mother Maude asked if anyone would like to go first in explaining how they arrived at Camp Levi, he raised his hand. "Started in youth group," he said, and Sparse whispered, "Don't it always?" Christopher continued. "Last year," he said, "our church got a new youth leader. He was still in college." According to Christopher, the new youth leader played the guitar. He also possessed a pair of blue-green eyes and the cleanest pair of New Balances he'd ever laid eyes on. "The *N*s on them were so bright," he said. "They glimmered." Mother Maude interjected here, telling him in her gentle singsong voice to get back to the point of his testimony, so he did. He told us how he'd just turned fifteen and was the oldest boy at his church. The youth leader asked him to help out with Wednesday night devotionals. They would meet about an hour before the other teenagers arrived. At first they spent most of their time arguing over the music. The youth leader preferred praise music while Christopher insisted on traditional hymns. "I thought we hated each other," Christopher told us, but then one Wednesday night after devotionals, the youth leader asked him over to his house to listen to some new CDs. "When I got there, he put on a DC Talk album—the one with the 'Jesus Freak' song on it." Christopher didn't like this music very much and told the youth leader he wasn't sure how they'd ever use any of this for their Wednesday night devotionals. "Normally, we played songs that everybody could sing along with—that's why I liked the hymns more than praise music. You could sing along to them, and the lyrics were more intricate. The other was too stripped down." Mother Maude took this opportunity to say she, too, didn't understand musical trends in Christian music anymore. "There's something, I don't know, too worldly about it." Christopher agreed and said that the youth leader wanted to show him how the music sounded on his guitar. "Of course he did," Mother Maude said, then gave us all a knowing look. Christopher remembered how fast it happened: the guitar, the youth leader's low voice. "I felt overwhelmed," he said. He was crying again.

Mother Maude touched his shoulder. "Of course you were."

"After it happened, he wouldn't even look at me."

"Shame," she said, "is powerful."

Sparse raised his hand, and Mother Maude nodded for him to speak. "Wait a minute," he said. "You didn't tell us how you got here—you just told us how you got your cherry popped."

Dale burst out laughing, triggering laughter from Rumil and Sparse. Mother Maude stood, frowning at them, and they got silent. "Now listen," she said. "You haven't heard the rest of it. Please, Christopher—tell it all." He hesitated, and Mother Maude told him that he would have to be clear about it down to the last detail before he brought it before the Lord.

"When it was over," Christopher said, "I was guilty, too. So I told."

Still standing, Mother Maude said, "Who did you tell?"

"My parents—they—they were horrified."

Sparse sat up in his seat, visibly shocked by something. "You told?" He looked at Rumil, who seemed to be signaling him to calm down. "He told? What a fucking moron!"

Dale was laughing again, but none of us joined in. Mother Maude walked outside and returned with the counselors trailing behind her.

"Robert," she said. "You need some time, my lamb, to think

about today, to think about Christopher's testimony and how it might be similar to yours."

Sparse was looking at his feet when he said, "Shut up, Dale!" But Dale kept on laughing to himself. Larry got beside Sparse's chair. "Don't fight us now—we love you." And Sparse didn't. He gave a little shrug to Rumil and followed the two men out. Sparse was absent for dinner—pimento cheese sandwiches, more chips—and didn't return until we were all in our bunk beds. There was only one place they could have sent him: the Sweat Shack. He came traipsing into the Sleeping Cabin, not bothering to be quiet, since he probably figured we were all awake. We were. He climbed up onto his bunk, the one above Rumil's bed.

"How was it?" Rumil asked in the darkness. Sparse turned onto his side, the squeaking metal bed frame the only answer he gave.

We would spend the first two weeks with Mother Maude and the second two with Father Drake. That was the plan. They wanted to emulate childhood development as they understood it. Campers would bond with the mother and then the father. It's important, I think, to mention that neither of them held degrees in psychology. They were running this camp on instinct and prayer. In any event, we didn't see much of Father Drake for the first fourteen days. He kept to his side of the lake, and Mother Maude held testimonials on most days in the afternoon, then we'd eat dinner with Rick and Larry, and after dinner, we'd journal in our sin diaries for several hours until bedtime.

At the second testimonial, Sparse went, but not before listening to Mother Maude recount her brother's many backslides. "Poor man," she told us. "He couldn't help himself. Every time I thought he'd gotten better, there he'd go again, fooling around with somebody he shouldn't." She used this anecdote to pivot to us. She asked us how many times we had tried to turn from wickedness. For the longest time, nobody spoke, and the only sound in the Chapel Cabin came from Rick and Larry, who were stationed at the back table preparing our dinner—spreading thick gobs of pimento cheese on white bread. The silence was not bothersome to Mother Maude. She sat in her folding chair, her hands neatly folded in her lap. She was a woman who knew how to wait for things. Finally, Sparse raised a hand, and Mother Maude nodded for him to speak. "Mama and Pop blamed Disney movies," he said. Christopher and Rumil laughed at this until Mother Maude gave them a horrified stare that immediately hushed them. Sparse continued, his voice thin. "Not all Disney movies. *The Jungle Book*, *The Aristocats*, *Lady and the Tramp*. They was fine. It was the princess movies they didn't want me seeing. Claimed it gave me these mannerisms." He folded his wrists in an exaggerated way to show us what he meant. My dancing in choir came back to me suddenly, the memory roaring back so strongly that I felt my ears prickle into a blush. I shook it away and listened to Sparse go on with his testimony: "Mama and Pop are both in the army, and they kept telling me I needed to toughen up. I wasn't strong enough. Not by half if I wanted to make it as a black man. But I kept messing up, doing things I had no idea were wrong, but then I messed up really bad when I was eight. That's when they started with the therapy."

Mother Maude asked him what happened when he was eight, and he said, "*Sleeping Beauty*." His parents strictly forbade him from seeing these movies, but one day at school, the teacher showed the class this one. Sparse described to us how he had sat with the rest of the third grade in the dim classroom that smelled of chalk and forgot all about his parents' objections and raptly watched the images flashing on the TV screen. *Sleeping Beauty*, he explained, was no ordinary cartoon: the pageantry, the opulent scenes flush with vibrant, heart-pumping color. "Later I'd learn Disney had insisted on the filmmakers using individually hand-inked cells for each shot and filmed the picture in Technirama widescreen."

Sparse could have continued talking about the movie, but Mother Maude jumped in and asked him to get back to his relationship with his parents and how this movie interfered with his development. "Well," Sparse said. "All I could think about after seeing the movie was the kissing scene." He was referring to the moment in the movie when Prince Phillip, having vanquished Maleficent, storms the castle and climbs the tower steps to the sleeping Aurora, the moment when he touches his lips to hers, breaking the curse. "Must have been no more than a second, that kiss. A half second maybe." For Sparse, that's all it took to set his imagination on fire. The rest of the day—during lunchtime and math and social studies—the act of kissing occupied his thoughts: what it must feel like, taste like, to have another's wet mouth pressed against your own. "Even then I knew the kind of mouth I wanted, but I didn't dwell on that part." The weekend came along, and he went to the park to play while his parents slept in. Because they were military, they had moved around several times in Sparse's childhood. He didn't know the boys in his neighborhood all that well; this was a suburb of Little Rock, and most of the other children were white and regarded Sparse with contempt and suspicion. So when he found one of them in the park, alone and bored, Sparse suggested a game they could play.

"We didn't know each other, so it was easy for me to just try something with him, something that had been tumbling around in my head since seeing the movie." The way he told it, he was reclined on a seesaw, lying stock-still, and the other boy pretended to be the prince and tried different things to wake Sparse up. That morning, a jogger passed by at the exact wrong moment. She was a friend of the other boy's mom and shrieked when she recognized him leaning over a black boy, kissing him on the lips. She broke them up, snatching the white boy by the arm and dragging him home with her. It didn't take long for the news to travel back to Sparse's parents, who were horrified, but not, Sparse told us, all that surprised. "I think I just confirmed what they had been suspecting for some time." First, they went through their church in Little Rock to send him to a program in Memphis. "I did their workbooks and talked to people and still felt the same—nothing changed." A few years later, when he was a little older, they sent him to a rehabilitation clinic in Florida for an eating disorder. "There I got the name Sparse from a white girl who threw up her meals." Mother Maude asked him why she named him that, and he said, "Because no matter how much I eat I still look barely there, she told me. Sparsely drawn." He choked up a little when he talked about the girl and his name. All his bravado and sassiness had been, in the telling of his story, peeled away. Sitting nearby, Rumil leaned over to touch Sparse's hand, and then several things happened at once. Mother Maude stood. Rick and Larry paused in their sandwich making. And Sparse, very gently, nudged Rumil's hand away. Only then did the rest of us understand the error.

Rumil understood most of all. "I didn't mean—" But then he stopped himself. "I'm sorry," he told us finally. Mother Maude said,

"I know you are," and gestured for him to rise. Rick and Larry had already stepped outside and were waiting for him to follow them. After Rumil had left us, Mother Maude asked Sparse if there was anything else he wanted to add. Sparse thought about it, and said, "Last year we moved to Biloxi, and when I turned sixteen, Mama said I was big enough to make up my own mind about my future. I could choose to come to this camp, or I could choose to hit the road and never see them again." He said this matter-of-factly, not stifling back tears as he had before, and Mother Maude wanted to know if he thought he made the right choice. Sparse laughed, not with happiness but with a kind of bitter resignation, the same sort of laugh we'd heard earlier from Dale. "I don't know," he said. "I don't guess I had much of one."

Rumil stayed in the Sweat Shack through dinner and on into evening while we journaled outside at the picnic tables. We scribbled down our testimonies, the wheres and hows of our lives. I was jealous that Rumil and Christopher already knew what to describe, had already confessed so much already with Mother Maude. My problem was knowing where to begin. I started copying out my mother's stories of the Neck, but then I remembered Mother Maude's version, so I wrote what she'd told me when we were alone. But that didn't seem right, either. Frustrated, I sat back on the bench and rubbed my eye sockets. Christopher and Sparse were writing so furiously that I suspected they were only pretending, scratching incoherent marks into the lines of their pages. Dale appeared to be drawing, making dramatic swooping gestures on his page.

The Sweat Shack loomed in the distance. A little bump of a building. Suzette and I had seen the old *Invasion of the Body Snatchers* in Greenwood once, and I had this idea that there was something supernatural about the shack. We'd crawl in, and alien vines would swarm us, cover our bodies, suck out our nutrients, and refashion another version of us. I imagined, as we were peacefully writing in our notebooks, aglow with torchlight, that Rumil was being repurposed. He'd come back without any emotion, like in that movie—but no, not without *any* emotion, that's not quite right. He'd come back with all the right emotions. I was troubling through these possibilities when Dale spoke, causing me to jump. "I have a grandmother," he said, and the oddness of this declaration overshadowed my reaction. Sparse put his pen down and looked at him. "Big fucking deal—we all got grandmas." We weren't supposed to talk during our journaling, but no one was around to supervise us. Mother Maude and Father Drake were across the lake holed up in the RV. Rick and Larry had taken the truck into town for more supplies.

"No," Dale said. "I mean I got a grandma who lives in Orlando, close to Disney World."

Sparse cocked his head. "You been?"

Dale told him how he'd been a couple of times. His description sounded more like science fiction than any movie I'd ever seen. Elevators that dropped thirteen flights. Mechanical bears that sang country music. A humongous spaceship that took you back in time to the dawn of civilization.

"My parents wouldn't take me there if you paid them," Sparse said. "But sounds like you got to do everything."

Dale smiled, the grin contorting his face as he remembered something. "Oh, yeah. We did everything all day long."

Sparse ruined it, however, with a non sequitur. "Let me ask you, Dale," he said. "Now that we are friends. Which one would you rather fuck—Rick or Larry?" Dale's smile vanished. "Now I," Sparse continued, "am partial to a man with a bandanna, but then Rick has those lips." He puckered at Dale, and Dale pushed away from the table. He relocated to the other one and returned to his notebook, doodling and sketching, as if he'd never opened his mouth. Sparse kept going. "But maybe, Dale, you like a man with a sad story, maybe you've seen Rick's wrists and that does it for you." Christopher threw his notebook at Sparse, and Sparse easily swatted it away. "You should be ashamed of yourself," Christopher said. Earlier that morning, during our microlesson with Rick and Larry, the counselors had compared our brains to computers, and now I spoke up and used their exact terminology against Sparse. "Garbage in, garbage out—didn't you hear what they said? Don't you listen?" Ignoring me, Christopher slid out of the picnic table and retrieved his book, but he didn't return to our table. Instead, he sat with Dale.

Sparse went back to his own notebook, bearing down so hard on the page that the tip of his pen broke open, splattering ink everywhere. "Fuck," he said, sighing, slamming the book closed. The ink bled on the table, on the bench, on his T-shirt and khakis. Dark blue smudges, the color of nighttime. For a few minutes, Sparse remained quiet. Then he reopened his notebook and started to read. Reading his story to himself over and over, I hoped, getting it down just right, so he wouldn't be doomed to repeat it.

Before dinner on the next day, Rick and Larry took us to the abandoned house. The rooms were arranged one after the other like train cars. The first room was crammed with furniture: two tables, chairs, a wooden cabinet that Larry told us was an old-timey icebox. From the ceiling dangled sticky paper to catch flies. The counselors wouldn't let us tarry. They took us on to the second room, which was more of the same, along with a headboard turned sideways and leaning against the wall. It wasn't until we were in the back room that I remembered this house had been the site of my mother's childhood. The realization hit me when I noticed these little dolls, caked in dirt and missing limbs and clothing, stashed in the corner. "Those," I said, and Christopher heard me. "I wouldn't touch them," he told me. "I have a feeling they might be a trap." Ever since Rumil got sent to the Sweat Shack for touching Sparse, we had been on guard for other actions unbecoming to boys that might get us sent away. Like Sparse, Rumil had returned not long after we had settled down for bed in our bunks. This time nobody had asked him how it was. Half of us already knew, and the other half, Christopher and I, were hoping we didn't have to find out.

In the back room of the house, we found various used gym equipment. Dumbbells and a weight bench and plastic mats like the kind I used to nap on in kindergarten. Rick and Larry provided us with a list of activities—arm curls, bench presses, crunches, squats—to be accomplished before bed. The exercise, they informed us, would awaken our muscles and allow our bodies to produce more testosterone. Christopher and I halfheartedly bench-pressed, spotting for each other even though we only used the bar. Rumil was a natural with the dumbbells, using the fifteen-pound weights in lifts designed to strengthen his biceps and triceps. Sparse went through an ab workout on one of the mats, and Dale, the only one of us at home in this makeshift gym, took on squats. After some time had passed, Rick and Larry made us move on to something else. Our bodies had begun to heal from the sores, but the twisting and turning had torn open some of them. A sour smell developed in the room, the commingling of our body funk that seemed to bother only Rick. He wore his shirt over his nose until our stink became too much for him and he rushed outside to puke. Larry told us to rotate to different activities in five minutes and then left us to see about the other counselor.

At testimonials that day, Rumil had confessed to having sex with another boy at his school, a senior who was the varsity quarterback. Rumil's sport was soccer, and the team had recruited him in ninth grade because they needed a kicker. A janitor had caught them in the locker room, and the parents of the quarterback had paid Rumil's parents to send him to a private school in another town. He gave the impression in testimonial that this was the end of it, but now in the weight room with the counselors gone he became more candid. "My parents, his parents—they thought separating us would work," he said. He had moved to the weight bench and was using dumbbells to do butterflies. "But he couldn't stay away." According to Rumil, the quarterback would drive over to Rumil's house while his parents were still at work. "We ordered dirty movies on the satellite, and I thought my parents wouldn't mind about it because it was man-and-woman porn, but watching it got us all started again." He grunted as he brought the weights together above his chest. He described the things he and the quarterback would do to each other, and the rest of us, one by one, stopped our exercises and listened. Dale had a queasy look on his face, as if he were about to run out of the room to barf as Rick had. Very politely, he asked Rumil if he would please stop talking.

Rumil dropped the weights to the floor, making a loud racket. "You want to come spot me then?" Dale agreed, and we did the rest of our exercises in silence.

Later that night, I overheard the rest of Rumil's story. We were in our bunks, and I think Christopher and Dale were already asleep. Rumil was whispering to Sparse, who lay in the bunk above him, the part of his story when his parents confronted him about the movies he'd rented. "I knew they would show up on the bill, I knew it," he said. "But I just didn't care." He then told Sparse that he was adopted. "They got me from the Philippines, so I know what they think."

"What they think?"

Rumil made these choking noises, the sound people make when they're letting themselves cry and not worrying about how it makes their face look. "They think, they think I'm defective. They wished they'd been given somebody else."

I leaned up from my pillow. "They tell you that?" I whisper-shouted across to his bunk.

"Don't have to—I ain't stupid."

They stopped talking, and I couldn't help but feel excluded. I began to hate them, these boys—not as a group but individually and in different moments. First, I hated Sparse. I hated him because Rumil had chosen him to confide in. I wasn't sure why. He looked sickly. A waif. But he was funny, and his personality gave him points, perhaps. Even his eating disorder made him, somehow, seem trendy. He lorded his thinness around as if it were something to be proud of, a condition that took discipline. During one of our testimonials, he claimed that food became a problem after he came back from his treatment in Memphis. "Everybody was telling me what I should do, how I should feel, and all I had control over was the food I put into my mouth."

In the weight room one day, Christopher admitted that he wished he could learn to control himself like Sparse had. We were alone again, so Sparse took the liberty of pinching one of Christopher's pudgy pecs. "Cindy Crawford says nothing tastes as good as skinny feels," he said. "Something to consider, baby." When Rumil laughed at Sparse's joke, my hatred for Sparse shifted to him. Sparse glanced at me suddenly. "Cheer up," he said. "You starting to look as sad as old Dale did his first day." Dale paused from his set of push-ups to tell us all to go to hell.

"Too late," Sparse said.

At our next testimonial, late into our first week at camp, I told them about my own personal history of sin—my troubled relationship with my father, how he had caught me in the church. I wanted to shock them, especially Rumil and Sparse, so I was very specific about my abominable behavior, mentioning the candle and the dirty thoughts that'd been running through my head at the time. Christopher seemed the most shocked. "How far was it?" he asked, and I told them. Outside, Rick and Larry were trimming around the cabins with gas-powered weed eaters. The smell of freshly cut grass seeped in, making my eyes water.

"He's lying," Christopher said. "He's just trying to be cute."

I made a show of clenching and unclenching my fists. I wanted to do to his pudgy face exactly what I'd done to Dale's. My hate swirled, but I remained seated, gripping the bottom of my chair, holding myself in place.

"Nothing cute," I said. "Nothing cute about it."

Sparse had a question for me. "What did you say your father calls you?" I told him my nickname, and he said, "No, you don't look like a Rooster." He paused, possibly considering his next words very carefully. "You shouldn't let people call you something you're not."

"But I want to be," I said. "I want to be Rooster—I *will* be Rooster."

The other boys remained silent, uncomfortably so. It occurred to me that they weren't reacting to what I said but to how I said it, to the desperation in my voice.

But Mother Maude was pleased with my fervor. "Amen," she said. "Now *that* is a testimony."

The same routine continued the next week: microlessons with Rick and Larry in the morning, testimonials with Mother Maude in the afternoon, and evenings spent writing in our sin diaries or doing exercises in the gym at the abandoned house. Our bodies were healing up and getting stronger. Christopher had changed the most, losing his baby face. His shorts were so loose Rick had to give him a cord to tie through the belt loops to hold them up. At testimonials, we plunged deeper into our histories. Mother Maude was adamant that all of us were products of our ancestors' misdeeds. I led the way, recounting for them what Mother Maude had told me, and she seemed pleased at my memory. I changed it just enough so that the other campers wouldn't be able to connect me with her, but the gist of it was the same: my whorish grandmother, my murderous grandfather. When the other boys claimed ignorance of their family history, Mother Maude supplied them with questionnaires their parents had filled out, charting their darkest deeds for us to read and contemplate. My father's was fairly uninteresting. Especially when compared to what I knew of my mother's side of the family. He spoke of his drinking in high school, various indiscretions with girls. Nothing much to account for. "Ah," Mother Maude said, after I told her I thought my mother's side was the more sinful. "Look again. What does he say about his parents?" I flipped through the pages and saw what she'd meant. It was a yes or no question about divorce. He'd circled yes. His parents had not stayed together, and divorce, Mother Maude said, was like a tumor in the family tree, one that could, in the right circumstances, turn malignant for later generations. "So my life," I said, "is like a perfect storm of sin." She told me that was exactly right.

But other campers' families were harder to trace. Sparse's family didn't have any divorce, but his grandfather had suffered, the questionnaire said, from "emotional disturbances" that caused him to beat his wife and children. Christopher had an aunt who'd been in and out of rehab for an addiction to painkillers. Rumil, however, didn't know much about his blood relatives beyond the country they lived in. "But there's the clue," Mother Maude told him. "Is the Philippines a Christian country? Don't they worship Allah and Muhammad?" Rumil said he didn't know, but apparently his parents did. In the questionnaire, they'd listed all the possible reasons a Filipino boy would end up a homosexual.

The only person who didn't contribute to testimonials was Dale. While the rest of us talked about ourselves and our families, Dale stayed mum. Midway through the second week, Mother Maude had begun to devote much of her attention to drawing him out. We'd spend most of the afternoon in tense silence as Mother Maude waited, never losing her cool, for Dale to respond to one of her questions. *What led you here? Why do you think you are afflicted?* Each time Dale responded the same. "I don't know," he said. "I can't say." One day she made him bring his notebook to the Chapel Cabin and read from it. Dale told her that was impossible, and she said, in her musical voice, "Why, Dale, I know you can read." But it wasn't that, and he opened his book to show her. He'd not been writing but drawing. The sketch was of a young woman with a prominent nose and sad eyes. Her hair was short, asymmetrical. "Is that supposed to be your sister?" she asked him, and Dale shrugged.

Frustrated, Sparse spoke up next. "He told me he had people in Orlando."

Dale shut his notepad and clutched it tightly in his hand. The only thing that kept him from throwing it at Sparse, I guessed, was his not wanting to spend a night in the Sweat Shack.

Mother Maude seized on this tidbit of information. "Is that where Laura lives now?"

"Who's Laura?" Christopher asked. "He says he has a grandma in Florida."

Mother Maude asked Dale if he would let her see his notebook. He scrutinized us, all gathered around him, and then he glanced over to Rick and Larry, who were watching this interaction with great interest. Shaking his head, he handed the book over. Mother Maude thanked him and began to unfold the pages, inspecting them, before finding one she liked. "This here," she said, holding the book up so we could see for ourselves. "This here is his sister, Laura." The sketch was done with pen, but there was shading on the cheeks and jawline. Dale was skilled.

Mother Maude asked him if he wanted to tell us more about Laura, but when he didn't say anything, she took it upon herself to give us his story. "Dale's family probably lives the closest to camp— what is it? Twenty miles away?" Dale had gone very still, but if his nonresponsiveness bothered Mother Maude, she didn't let on. "They have a big horse farm. Well, when Dale was a boy, he caught his sister—" Dale jumped up, as he had on the first night. Rick and Larry were quick. They got on either side of him and, using gentle force, pushed him back down to his seat. They remained beside him while Mother Maude finished the story. "He found them in the hammock. His sister with another girl. Being innocent, being not yet eight, he didn't know what he was looking at, so he went to ask his mother about it. He tattled on his sister, but he didn't mean to, I am sure, and maybe he feels some guilt over it." Here she looked at Dale when she spoke. "But he shouldn't. No, sir. What he did was alert his parents to the rot." As Mother Maude continued, Dale got to crying again. Mother Maude told us how his sister had run away from home when her parents tried to get her help, how she spent the rest of her teenage years with a liberal grandmother and was now working at Disney. "Did he tell y'all what his sister does at Disney? She cleans the toilets at the most magical place on earth. Can you imagine?" We couldn't. "His parents were always worried about him, fearful her sodomy had infected him. So when his mother came in on him—"

"I was jerking off!" he said. "That's all! For fuck's sake, I told Mama I was thinking about a woman, too! And I was!"

Mother Maude was shaking her head. She lifted her hand, giving a signal to Rick and Larry, who began to usher Dale out. As with the first night by the lake, he fought. He was on the floor, grasping at our chairs, trying to untangle himself from their grasp. We rushed out of the way. Mother Maude appeared to be the only calm one. "Like I told you, my lamb. We will drag you kicking and screaming to salvation if need be." And that's exactly what Rick and Larry had to do to get him out of the room.

On Mother Maude's last night, she took us back to Lake John. A storm cloud had blown up earlier in the day. One that promised rain and made the dark come sooner. She didn't have a mirror with her. "Tonight," she said, "I will be the mirror." She climbed atop a small embankment overlooking the water. The torches were not lined up in a circle as before but as two lines running parallel from the water. A kind of landing strip. Looking at us, she spoke our names. "I see Christopher, I see Rumil. I see Robert, I see Will." With a heavy voice, she added, "And I see Dale, sweet Dale." He stood beside me, silent. In the days after his second night in the Sweat Shack, he had only gone further into himself. He didn't talk at testimonials. He only went through the motions during our exercises. And, what's more, he no longer drew in his notebook. After Mother Maude said our names, she motioned for us to move closer. "You boys have been honest with me," she told us. "As honest as you have probably been with anyone else in your lives. And now I want to be honest with you." She ran her hands through her hair and pulled her wig off. Her head was as bare as a stone. "You see, when I was in New York," she told us, "and surrounded by all that death, it affected me more than I knew." She had stunned us to full attention. "It started to fall out not long after Johnny died. A few strands here, a clump there. Doctors called it alopecia—sounds like a foreign country to me, sounds like someplace Rumil's people would be from." She laughed but only a little. "But I know it to be the unmistakable hand of God." No *amen*s from Rick and Larry tonight; they stood by the water, heads bowed.

"Can I touch it?" It was like someone else had spoken, had mimed my voice. "I'm sorry," I said. "I didn't mean—"

"No, no," she said. "Come forward."

I skidded up the embankment, and once I reached her level, she knelt. Carefully, I placed my hand on her skull. Her bare scalp was coarse and patchy, especially around the ears. Her skin smelled of baby powder. Up close, without all her hair, she looked smaller, frailer. But more beautiful, too.

"I am nothing," I said. My hands moved to her temples, where her pulse thumped against my fingers. "I am no one. God, rend my flesh. Burn me anew."

She looked up at me. "Peace, son. Peace." I slung off my clothes and raced toward Lake John. A crackle of thunder rippled above; I threw myself headfirst into the water. When I surfaced, I saw the other boys on shore were copying me, clamoring to touch Mother Maude's bald head, even Dale. It was a good-bye, and as with most good-byes, it was tinged with sorrow and relief. All at once, the other boys came splashing into the lake. Dale swam out farther than the rest, his legs kicking hard behind him. It rained, and the feel of pure water on my skin was a revelation. I stood in the waist-high water and soaked it in. At first I didn't hear the shouts over the pounding water clogging my ears. It was Christopher, and he was saying something about Dale, telling them to hurry. Rick and Larry had already dashed in. The other boys had stopped swimming and faced the other side of the lake, where a dark figure was undulating toward us. Shirtless, Father Drake was wading through the water toward us, as methodical as a shark. He carried Dale around the chest as if he were a piece of luggage, and he came by me with such a force of waves that I was knocked over. When I got back to land, dripping and itchy, Dale was on his knees, coughing up water, and Father Drake towered over him, screaming. "Think you can just get away from me that easy, huh?" There was such joy in his voice. "And miss all the fun I got planned?"

Christopher, Rumil, and Sparse were grouped together by the last two torches at the edge of the water, and Christopher was telling them what he'd seen. "He just went under and I knew, I knew, I knew." He was shaking so bad that I slapped him. "Knew what?" I said. "Knew what, goddamnit?" Christopher touched his face, stymied. Sparse stepped between us and used both hands to push me back so hard that I went tumbling and cartwheeled into the lake. "Dale," Sparse hissed, as I stumbled back to my feet. "He tried to drown himself, you damn fool. Don't you understand anything?"

The next morning began our third week at Camp Levi. The end of June. Heat followed us everywhere. It pushed against our chests during sleep, haunted us throughout the day even in the shade. At breakfast I could hardly choke down the food—Cheerios in reconstituted powdered milk. My skin had been peppered with a new batch of sores from last night's swim, and a new alliance had coalesced in the meantime. Christopher and Sparse and Rumil. They had bonded in their hatred of me and their newfound pity for Dale.

They showed their dislike by ignoring me. I almost relished the ostracism. I suspected true rehabilitation required it. None of them, not even Christopher, was fully committed to the process. I recognized their weakness now and pitied them for it. All morning they kept talking around me, to one another, meaningless talk, while they slurped cereal from their plastic bowls like greedy savages. Christopher asked about Mother Maude. "What happened to her?" Dale surprised everyone by jumping into the conversation, very briefly, to inform us that he'd seen her drifting away quietly. "After she saw I was all right, she put her wig back on," he said, "and started walking around the lake." His voice, as he spoke softly and calmly, took us all aback. Christopher admitted that he was going to miss her, and Sparse snorted. "I can't say the woman will ever make my pen-pal list," he said. Rumil, shifting topics, wondered about Father Drake. "You think he'll make us tell him all that stuff we told her?"

Not long after Rumil's question left his mouth, Father Drake's voice, as if answering him, bellowed through the trees like the roar of a locomotive. We heard him long before we saw him. "You boys get enough beauty rest?" he yelled. He capered down the clearing at a fast clip. A thick white layer of sunblock coated his nose. A Mississippi State baseball cap sat on his head, the long bill pushed low to hide his eyes. Like us, he'd taken swims in Lake John and had the welts along his arms and legs to show for it. If it bothered him, he didn't let on. Once he got close enough, he leaped onto our table, kicking over our cereal bowls. Mine and Sparse's were mostly full, and lumpy milk sloshed into our laps. Father Drake found this hilarious. He laughed so hard it sounded like a cough. He referenced the clipboard in his hand as he spoke, giving the impression he was reading from a script. "Once upon a time, my children," he said, "I used to chew tobacco. Big wads of Red Man if you can believe it. But now I get my kicks by chewing on weak sissy ass. I chew and chew, and I spit it out." He swatted the top of Dale's head with the clipboard. "You understand me, mermaid? You get to leave this camp one way, and that's through *moi*."

Rick and Larry bounded out of the Chapel Cabin at a brisk jog. Larry was clutching a foam football, and when Father Drake nodded, he pitched it over. "The microlesson for today will be a little different," Father Drake told us. "A little more intensive than what I suspect you're probably used to." He explained that we would spend the morning in a rousing game of Smear the Queer. "I wanna see what I'm dealing with. I wanna see what kind of stuff you're made of." Because I had never spent much time on playgrounds, the game was new to me. The rules, though, were fairly straightforward: After we scrambled for the ball, the boy who secured it became the target. He'd run from one end zone to the other—in our case, from the Sweat Shack to the abandoned house—dodging tackles. Each time he touched either spot, he scored a point. The only way he gave up the ball was if it was taken from him. "Now, we are not hooligans," Father Drake said, pacing back and forth across the tabletop. "So there are certain prohibitions: no knuckle sandwiches, no kicking, no elbowing, and no girly antics, either, meaning no scratching or biting. This ain't *Dynasty*. You're men. Use your shoulders, use your bodies. Okay?" We nodded, not knowing what else to do. He added that the boy who racked up the most points would have a special responsibility later tonight. "But more on that later. For now, let's see what happens." He dropped the ball on the table, and it bounced once, twice, then flipped into a roll, finding its way to Rumil. Father Drake grinned. "Let's go."

The game started slowly. Rumil was sprinting to the Sweat Shack before it occurred to us that we needed to catch him. "Move, you bastards!" Father Drake said, and we were off. Sparse had no muscle, but he was fast, spiriting ahead. Dale was the slowest, but he would be the most dangerous, I suspected. Sparse got to Rumil first, looping an arm around his waist only to be shrugged off like an old coat. Sparse tripped on his own legs and got a mouthful of grass for the effort. Rumil stretched out his arm with the ball and touched the side of the Sweat Shack. "One point for Rumil," Larry announced, and Christopher cheered, which infuriated Father Drake. "Why you stopping, fatty?" Father Drake screamed. "Get him!" Father Drake had remained standing on the picnic table to watch us better. Rumil dodged and weaved on his path to the abandoned house. He easily missed Sparse and Christopher; neither seemed to be trying very hard. Then he outstepped a heaving Dale and came stomping by me. I lowered my shoulder and swung out my arm, clotheslining him in the middle. He hiccupped as the air pushed through his gullet. He flipped back onto the ground, which was soft and muddy from last night's rain. He was back on his feet in no time. But the ball was mine. I ran to the abandoned house and slapped the railing on the front porch. "One point!" Larry yelled. "For Rooster!" I turned back toward the Sweat Shack to find Sparse and Christopher much more interested in the notion of bringing me down. They rushed me, Christopher's head battle-ramming me in the gut. My body was tossed, scraping away grass as I went tumbling across the slick mud. Now Christopher had his hands on the ball, but he didn't keep it very long as Dale, while not fast, was faster than he was. He gave the one true tackle of the game, using his shoulder to bring Christopher down fast and efficiently. It was almost artful. Once Dale had the ball firmly tucked under his arm, there was no chance for the rest of us. He blocked and faked; he sidestepped and charged. He broke through every attempt we made, going back and forth from the Sweat Shack to the abandoned house at a slow, deliberate speed. "One point for Dale! Two points for Dale!" Larry's voice became a refrain to our game. "Three points for Dale!"

As the game progressed, we got more and more ragged and dirty. Our yellow T-shirts and khakis hadn't been washed or changed since our first night by the lake. The fabric was easy to tear once snagged in a fist. Though Dale would clearly win the game, it became a point of pride for us to throw ourselves against the great bulwark of his body as he crashed through the clearing. Father Drake egged us on. I ran at Dale three times before my nose got bloody enough for me to notice and three more times before a ringing sprang into my ears. Fluid leaked from the nastier sores on my arms and legs; it felt like my insides were escaping. Still, I raged on. So did the others. We were no longer driven by our hatred of Dale. He didn't even matter. As we bashed ourselves against him, we were only damaging our own bodies, a kind of self-hate that was somehow honorable. I wanted to keep going. I wanted to sling my limbs and organs against his until all my clothes had been torn away, all my flesh and meat, too, until there was nothing left of me to give.

By point twenty, Dale threw the ball down and sat on the edge of the abandoned house's porch, huffing. He said he was done. "If that ain't winning," he said, "then I don't know what is." Father Drake jumped down from the picnic table and came running over. "My

God, my God," he was saying. "You sure do like pounding them boys, don't you, big fella?" He waved over Rick, who presented Dale with a bottle of water. Dale poured most of it on his face, his tongue wagging out of his mouth like a dog's. Sparse was spitting blood, and Christopher was hacking into the crook of his arm. Rumil stared longingly at the water Dale was lapping up, and I was still prone in the mud from Dale's last run-through. Father Drake hooted. "Y'all got your asses whooped." When Christopher finished coughing, Father Drake said, "You, boy—here." Christopher was too slow for him, so Father Drake slapped the clipboard against his own hip. "Hurry, son. Get the lead out." As Christopher neared him, he unfolded his right arm and showed Christopher something, and Christopher, squeaking, took a step back. Father Drake's face puckered. "I knew you didn't have the stomach for it." He whistled for Larry, telling him to take the fat one to the Sweat Shack. Christopher didn't move and watched, stunned by the quick turn of events, as Larry nodded and went over to the front of the Sweat Shack to jimmy open the door. Father Drake pushed at Christopher's shoulder. "Go on," he said, and Christopher snapped out of his daze. "Yes, sir," he said.

The door to the Sweat Shack was about a foot high and made of a thick wood that had been painted and repainted so many times I could no longer guess the kind of tree it had been. It swung open into pitch-black. Rumil, Sparse, and I moved around to the front to watch, as if this were a public execution. Before Christopher went in, Sparse told him to shut his eyes. "Pretend," he said, "like you are taking a nap." Christopher wasn't upset but seemed mystified by his own rotten luck. Larry, who was standing beside the little opening to the Sweat Shack, told him to go in feet first. "And stay lying down on the ground," he added. "You'll only knock yourself out if you try to stand." After deliberating over how to manage it, Christopher finally got on his back and crab-walked inside. Larry shut the door behind him, and Rumil jumped when the latch caught. That was that.

Father Drake was leaning against the house, watching me with the same pained expression he used back at the apartment in Hawshaw. Like he didn't know what to do with me. He said, "Rooster—you come." Now he showed me his arm. A fat gray tick had nestled in the seam where his forearm met his bicep. "Pull it out," he said. "Go on." When I hesitated, he grunted. "Don't make me try to fit two of you in there." I pinched the bug and pulled on it. It dislodged the way an eraser top twisted out of a pencil. Father Drake bent his arm to staunch the blood, and I held the tick between my fingers not knowing what to do with it. The insect was still alive and convulsing, so I flicked it to the grass. For this, Father Drake took off his cap and whacked me across the face. "You got to burn them," he said. He squatted down and fingered around in the grass until he found it. "They're too hard to be squished, and if you don't kill them, they are likely to go looking for you again." He wrapped it in a piece of tissue paper he'd pulled from his pocket, then from the same pocket he retrieved a lighter. "Once it gets a taste for you, it'll never stop until it can get another." He let the ball of paper burn in the grass for about a minute, then he stomped it out with the heel of his sneaker.

The others had gathered around me. Rumil and Sparse. Rick and Larry. Even Dale had wandered over. Father Drake seemed pleased to be holding court and smiled like he was meeting us for the first time. "Well, now," he said. "Who's hungry?"

For the afternoon, instead of testimonials, Father Drake put us to work. As Rick and Larry supervised us, we carried the old furniture out of the abandoned house and piled it in the middle of the clearing. Father Drake took an ax to the bulkier pieces, breaking them down. Rumil and Sparse hung together, lifting together, moving in a synchronized silence that excluded Dale and me. Dale didn't need any help. He toted the heavier pieces just fine all by himself—the wooden icebox, an old curio—while I struggled, grasping and pulling, to move anything. I was in the middle of dragging out a desk when it got stuck in the front doorway. Rumil and Sparse were outside milling about the growing pile, pretending not to notice, and I was too proud to ask for help. Dale appeared behind the desk from somewhere in the house and heaved the back of it out in one push. He was carrying two drawers, and it wasn't clear to me if he was being helpful or just wanted the piece of furniture out of his way. After he slung the drawers onto the pile, he returned, shoving me aside. He dragged the desk off the porch and across the clearing, leaving muddy ruts in his wake. I got behind the desk and tried to help, but he barked at me to get back. Father Drake had paused in arranging the pile, and Rumil and Sparse moved away from Dale as he marched by. After Dale positioned the desk by the edge of the pile, Father Drake handed him the ax. Dale gripped the handle like a bat and swung. Shards of wood exploded from the desk. He swung again, and again, his grunts turning to screams. It didn't take Dale long to smash the desk down into manageable pieces. "Lord," Father Drake said. "I could power a city grid with that kind of rage."

Dale dropped the ax and sank to his knees to catch his breath. Meanwhile, I took the broken pieces and tossed them onto the pile.

We finished at sundown. After the pile was arranged to Father Drake's liking, he doused the furniture in kerosene. He motioned for us to sit on the ground in front of it, and once we were down, he explained that the purpose of tonight was to symbolize our turning away from the past. We had spent two weeks acknowledging it, he told us, and asking for forgiveness, and now was the time to repent. "How many of you have ever heard of the refiner's fire?" he asked. I raised my hand, but Father Drake ignored it. "In Malachi, chapter three: 'Behold, I send my messenger, and he will prepare the way before me . . . He will sit as a refiner and purifier of silver, and he will purify the sons of Levi and refine them like gold and silver, and they will bring offerings in righteousness to the Lord.'" He repeated the phrase "offerings in righteousness." Rick and Larry had appeared. Larry carried our notebooks; Rick, a fire extinguisher. "Now, Dale," Father Drake went on, "has proved today that he is ready for the purifying heat of the Lord by his awesome display of strength earlier today, so he will start us off." He asked Dale to come to the front, where Larry handed him two notebooks—his and Christopher's. "Since Christopher cannot do it himself," Father Drake said, "you will absolve him of his past." He pulled out the lighter, the same one he'd used to burn the tick. Father Drake flicked it on. "Now, the refiner's fire," he told us, "is different from other fires. A forest fire destroys; a campfire gives warmth. A refiner's fire, however, is localized, directed. It burns away our impurities." Dale held both books over the flame, and the flames grew around the books, licking up the pages. "It purifies us." Before the flames reached his fingers, Dale threw the books into the pile of furniture, and the fire caught, turning the pile into a pyre. Black smoke whooshed off the flames, causing us to cough. Father Drake told us to get close, then closer, until we stood at the very edge of the fire, the heat singeing our eyebrows and cheeks. For an instant, I imagined him coming behind us and pushing, sending us headfirst into the flames. Instead, he made us stand there until our foul bodies were coated in an extra layer of soot. Then he told us to imagine that who we were, everything that made up our identity—he said "identity" as if it were a disease—was bound up in the pages of our notebooks. "Now," he said, "throw your offerings into the mouth of God." I chucked mine and didn't see where it landed in the fire, for the smoke had become too much for me. I stumbled back, coughing. Rumil had already heaved his in, too, and stumbled back out of the way of the smoke. Only Sparse remained at the edge, gripping his book, shaking as if he were cold. "It's not real. It's just a symbol," Rumil said to Sparse's back, until Father Drake told him to shut his mouth, threatening him with the Sweat Shack. Sparse might have stayed there all night in front of the fire, refusing to destroy his notebook, while the top layer of his flesh burned away. But Dale stepped in. He seized the book out of Sparse's hand and flicked it in as if it were just another piece of trash, then he pushed Sparse away from the fire. "It ain't worth it, Robert," he said, and Sparse corrected him, his voice thick from emotion. "That's not my name, Dale." Dale shrugged. "Whatever, but it still ain't worth all that."

Christopher came back later that night.

We had been in the Sleeping Cabin, quietly dozing, or so I thought, when he charged in. To my surprise, the other boys began talking to him as if they had been waiting up for his return. Christopher said the bugs were the worst of it. "Creepy-crawling all around me." Rumil asked him how the heat affected him, and Christopher said it was not bad in there at first, almost cool, but when we started the fire, he thought he was going to cook like a turkey. "I could smell myself roasting," he said. "And that stunk, but nothing compared to the funk in here." He was right. The Sleeping Cabin smelled worse than the inside of a gym bag. Christopher said he spent most of his time in the dark thinking. Rumil laughed, and said, "What about?" and Christopher told us he was picturing ways to kill Father Drake. "First, I thought about what would happen if I ran him over with a lawnmower," and Rumil said that was too messy. "I know, I know, so then I thought about drowning the bastard in the lake—all of us ganging up on him and forcing his head under." Sparse said that Christopher didn't sound like himself. "And that," Sparse added, "is a good thing." Christopher said, "I finally thought about poison—something neat and efficient."

Christopher's list of ways to do in Father Drake sparked a lively debate among the boys. While they were plotting murder, I seethed. I was about to speak up, tell them to hush, when Dale, who'd also been quiet during the conversation, jumped in to share his two cents. "What we need is a plan."

Sparse said, "You mean make it look like an accident?"

"No, I mean Orlando."

Christopher and Rumil spoke at the same time. *"Orlando?"*

Dale reminded them about his grandmother in Florida. She was a liberal, he added. That's where his sister went when their parents threatened to send her away. "They don't know I'm here. They'd help us. Take us in."

Sparse was unconvinced: "And how, pray," he asked, "do you expect us to get to Florida?"

Now Dale was laughing—that same bitter chuckle he'd had during testimonials. "I doubt we could steal the keys. But my dad taught me how to work on cars. Small engines mostly, and it ain't nothing to hot-wire something." He told them they could all live there until they turned eighteen and were legal. He told them about Disney World, and how much they would like it.

I stayed very still in my bed, my silence slowly making me feel uncomfortable. Like an intruder. I feigned sleep, but they knew that I was wide awake. Though nobody said it, I could feel them all coming to the same silent conclusion: That if they escaped, I wouldn't be going with them.

Christopher sounded like himself again when he asked, "But what will we *do* in Florida?"

"Whatever we want," Dale said. "Every day. All day long."

Days blended together in a haze of activities designed to toughen us up. Father Drake took us on long hikes through the Neck, forcing us to use our senses of direction (or lack thereof) to find our way back to camp. He joked about our finding the lost whorehouse during our excursions. "We find those women," he said, "and I might let them teach y'all a thing or two." We played more Smear the Queer. Now, once I got the ball the boys would let me have it, tackling me hard, but not hard enough for me to drop it and force one of them to become the target. "Get up," Father Drake yelled. "You ain't done yet!" And he was right; I wasn't. I kept running back and forth from the Sweat Shack to the abandoned house until my legs were numb, until the tackles felt more like hugs.

My time for the Sweat Shack came during one of those rounds of Smear the Queer. Sparse had the football, and everybody else was running him down. Dale had gotten faster, and in a burst of speed, he clipped Sparse with the side of his arm. Sparse flipped, the football knocked out of his hand. I scooped up the ball and pivoted on my right foot, about to make a run for the abandoned house, but Rumil was waiting for me. His shoulder hit me in the ribs, and I was down, flat on my back. I tried to get back up but was too dizzy, so I lay back down in the cool grass. The ball had hit the ground beside me, and nobody wanted to touch it. Clearly, Christopher, Rumil, and Sparse wanted me to get my hands on the ball and keep going. A sore on the back of my neck had been ripped back open during the fall, and I felt the warm blood leaking down my shirt onto the grass. Father Drake was yelling something about taking too long for a break, and I could hear him approaching. I should have gotten up, I told myself to get up, but my body was unwilling. Above me, Rumil stood wiping his grimy face with his equally grimy shirt, showing me a flash of his belly. A tuft of hair was gathered below his navel then trailed down below the waistband of his khakis.

Rumil noticed my looking and covered himself. "Just get up," he said, but before I could, Father Drake was on me, shouting that he had caught me. "Yes, sir!" he was saying. "I saw you. I saw it myself, I did, I did." He grabbed me by the arm and hoisted me to my feet, keeping his fingers hooked in the fat of my neck as he pulled me along toward the Sweat Shack. Behind us, Rick and Larry were telling the other boys to hustle, and the game was restarted in my absence. I tried to justify my staring. I had looked, that was true, but not sexually. At least I didn't think so. But maybe that's just what sinners say to justify their abominations to an angry God. Along the way, Father Drake mumbled under his breath, more to himself, it seemed, than to me. "Yes, I saw him looking," he said. "Just like Johnny. Looking like Johnny. Looking just like Johnny."

We rounded the Sweat Shack and he pushed me to the ground and pinned my head against the wall. His hand pressed into my chest like he intended to crack my breastbone in two. He threw off his cap and told me to look him in the eyes. I did. "You hear me now," he said, almost out of breath. "Don't go thinking you're special. Nope. Johnny was just like you. So well-meaning, but deep down he was a snake in the grass always waiting to strike—when Maudie wasn't around, when it was just us. He'd come for me. And when she was around, he'd look at me just like you was looking at that Oriental boy, waiting, biding his time." Father Drake wheezed as he spoke, his breath hitting me in hot, wet waves of air. He scooted closer and pressed a knee between my crotch, my poor wrecked crotch, causing me to cry out, but he covered my mouth with his hand to blunt the noise. Little sores were dotted along his forehead, bird tracks on sand. He moved his hand from my mouth to my throat, pulling my face into his. I had no time to brace for it, his wide mouth on mine, a moist sponge pressing onto my lips. I screamed, but that only made it worse. My mouth opened, and I took more of him inside me—his tongue, his teeth. When I gagged, he pulled away and fell down beside me as if he'd been injured. "Be still," he managed to say, as he propped himself up against the Sweat Shack. "Don't move." And I didn't. I couldn't. Because I had passed out.

W hen I came to, we were still behind the Sweat Shack, the shouts and grunts of boys knocking the hell out of one another ringing through the air. Father Drake had his hat back on, shielding most of his face. There was a new dampness between my legs. I had peed myself, which I'd not done since I was a young boy. "You trying to stall, Rooster?" he asked, more curious than angry. I wondered if I'd dreamed it. My mind, my sick and troubled mind, conjuring the whole scenario. "I'm sorry," I said. "I think I went out or something." I was thankful that my khaki shorts were so soiled with mud and soot that the piss stain didn't show up as much. I stood and followed him to the little door of the Sweat Shack. Unlike Christopher, I went in headfirst, and once I'd crawled inside, Father Drake shut me in.

My eyes remained closed until I felt the prickle of something wriggle across my hand. They flashed open to a darkness deeper than black, like a great yawning void. Not a speck of light shone through the roof, and yet the temperature kept rising as the afternoon persisted. Soon, I dripped, my sweat pooling around my belly. In the heat, my wounds seemed to expand and ooze. I imagined poison, my body expelling all those toxins I'd absorbed in Lake John. I turned on my back, and more critters scuttled by my ears. I held out my hand in front of my face: nothing. The hours lingered. I forced myself to be as still as possible. Never itching my sores.

Never adjusting my pants. Never flicking away whatever insect twitched on my skin. My body retreated from me, and I felt *away*. Asleep, awake—I didn't know anymore. Suzette came to mind. I'd not seen her in two years, not since she had gone away. I conjured a life for her in Memphis. The one I thought she was living this very instant. She has gone with friends to see a matinee, *I Want to Live!* or *Born Yesterday*, and when the movie's over, she tells her friends good-bye, all of them beautiful and eccentric like she is, and she goes for a walk along the river. She's cut her hair short, above the ears, and she wears a jaunty dark hat and a peacoat, a subtle allusion to Judy Garland's later years. Once she's by the water, she thinks. In particular, about the day she threw that strange boy out of the restaurant. She wonders where he is and imagines a thousand possibilities, all of them ungenerous, so she tries again, and this time she dreams him into a school like hers. She dreams him with people who are funny and kind. She dreams him into a happy life, and then she flings this dream into the Mississippi River, hoping it floats on down to him, wherever he is, and then she goes home.

Rick came for me sometime after midnight. He took me to the picnic tables and let me splash myself off with the water in the metal basin. He asked if I was hungry, and I shook my head. "Just tired," I told him, and he said everybody was tired. "But this is the last week—I bet you're excited to get back home." His yellow shirt and khakis were almost as dirty as mine, and his beard had grown wild and unkempt. I remembered what Sparse had said about his wrists and looked. He made no effort to hide them from me when he noticed me staring at them. Each one had a silver scar embedded lengthwise in the flesh. We stood there, and he waited for me to figure out what I wanted to ask him. "What are you gonna write about us?" I said, and he turned and dunked his hands in the basin and splashed them around. "I thought I knew," he said. "But now I don't know. I see you boys trying so hard, and—" He stopped just short of saying something he would possibly regret. His doubt frightened me, and I listed off all the things I could tell him to give him heart. "I feel it working," I said, even though I knew I was lying, and what's more, he probably knew it, too. "I feel myself changing." I laughed. "I doubt my daddy will even know who I am." He flicked the wet from his hands, and he again wanted to know if I was hungry, and I told him that he had already asked me that. "Just want to be sure," he said, and then he walked me to the steps of the Sleeping Cabin.

I didn't see Dale standing in the dark doorway of the Sleeping Cabin until Rick had gone back to the tent he shared with Larry. He walked out and sat on the bottom step, resting his oversize head against the railing. From a distance, a rumbling. The Illinois Central shuttling through West, its heavy rattle echoing off the Big Black River, a sound just faraway enough to be lonesome. "I've heard that train at the start of each week, and I guess that's my last one." He was barefoot and shoved one of his toes into the dirt at the bottom of the stairs. "I thought they would have kept you longer."

"Me, too."

"Were you scared?"

I told him how I thought I might have fallen asleep, and I had a nice dream.

Dale shook his head. "Don't tell the others that. Sparse bet Rumil you'd come back saying how you going in there was for your own good."

"They seem to have me all figured out."

Dale pulled his toes out of the dirt and stood. "While you were gone, we did some talking." He swallowed then continued. "We don't have long before our parents get here." I figured it up in my head: Today was Wednesday, and that meant three more days until I saw my father again. "We decided we ain't sticking around for the festivities." He took a step toward me, and in one quick motion, he had my shirt balled up in his fist. "Now they didn't want me to tell you this, but I'm telling because I think somewhere in there is a boy who has his right mind, who knows this place is fucked up." I told him that if he didn't let me go I would scream and wake up Rick and Larry. "They'll put you back in the Sweat Shack, Dale." He released me then smiled. "They can do what they want to me. That's the big joke, ain't it? I'm not gay. My sister is, and my parents think I am prone to it because of her, because my mama caught me jerking it in my bedroom."

"Sorry, Dale, but I'm tired." I stepped around him, but he moved in front of me, blocking my way inside the Sleeping Cabin.

"You don't have to stay here," he said. "We're going to slip out tomorrow night." He proceeded to tell me the plan as if I might agree to tag along if I understood the feasibility of it. "At night," he told me, "when everybody is sleeping, I go walking around the camp exploring." He talked fast, becoming more animated than I'd ever seen him. During his walks at night, he told me, he ventured to the other side of the lake where Mother Maude and Father Drake slept in the RV. "Only *she* sleeps in there—he passes out in a tent nearby." He noticed one night earlier this week that there were bags of fireworks left outside, the ones they were planning to use for the big finale on our last night at the camp. "Roman candles, sparklers, bottle rockets. Everything you can imagine." The plan hadn't come to him yet, but he stole some firecrackers. "I hid them here." He went under the crawl space of the stairs and pulled out a wad of firecrackers. "I got matches, too." I told him that I didn't understand what fireworks had to do with our getting away. "A distraction, fool," he said. He believed that in the cover of night they could sneak over to the other side of the lake and set off the firecrackers. "Mother Maude will come running outside to see what the fuss is about, and then we'll all storm into the RV. I'll connect some wires, and we'll be on the road and in Alabama by sunrise. And at Disney by nightfall."

I looked at him. "Dale," I said, careful not to anger or agitate him any more than he already was. "Then what? Your grandma can't take in five teenage boys. Our parents wouldn't let us go. They—"

"They've already let us go." He had the tone of a quarterback giving his team a pep talk at halftime. "And it ain't about what happens after, neither. It's about what we do now." He seemed to be holding back tears, and I found it hard to look him in the face. "The point is that they can't do this to us, and you don't have to come, but I think you should. I think you want to."

I told him it was a pretty good idea. "But I've made a deal to see this through. I *want* to see this through."

I tried to move around him again, but he put a hand on my shoulder, more gently than before. "But you'll let us go? Let us do what we're going to do?"

I said, "Of course," and he let me pass.

———————

An hour later, when I was sure everyone was sound asleep, including Dale, I slipped out of the Sleeping Cabin. My decision to tell on them was an easy one. I had made several bad choices, I knew, that had led me to camp. If I stood by and let them go through with this cockamamie plan, I would have made another one. I would have effectively failed the summer. I understood this decision was perhaps my last chance to prove, once and for all, my commitment to the process. I darted through the clearing, zigzagging around the Sweat Shack and through the woods. My eyes were used to the dark, and I sprinted through the trees unafraid. I veered right at Lake John and followed the edge of it around to the other side. The RV was parked on a little patch of ryegrass. Closer to the water, Father Drake's tent was pitched beside a grave.

Now that I was there, I didn't know how to proceed. I tiptoed around an extinguished campfire and examined the tent. It was one of the fancier ones, tall and long, with a zipper on the inside that cocooned Father Drake from the elements. Nowhere to knock, obviously, and this fact puzzled me. I considered going to Mother Maude's RV and waking her, but it was Father Drake's week, and I didn't want to break the rules. He would act fast. As if I might find a door on the other side, I walked around the tent. I sat down beside the gravestone of the uncle I never knew. It provided nice support for my back, and I stayed like this, dozing, until I heard movement from inside the tent. The plastic house shook, and then the front unzipped. Out walked Father Drake. He strolled up to the lake to piss, and when he came back, he was about to reenter the tent when he paused. "Who's there?" he said, and I told him. He came around to the foot of the grave. "You," he said, and before I could explain, he rushed me.

He clutched a wad of my hair and pulled me toward the tent and pushed me inside. "I knew you would come," he said. "I knew you would come to me one night. You are doing something right out of Johnny's playbook, coming to me." And then his hands were ripping at the holes in my shirt, trying to tear it off. "Stop!" I said, and slapped him away. I tried to tell him that I needed to speak with him about something important, but he wouldn't listen. I scrambled away and crawled back out into the night, but he got me by the ankles before I could stand and dragged me back in. Inside the tent were several books and wads of trash. I threw everything I could grab at him, but he laughed when anything hit him. We wrestled like Jacob and the angel. Spending half the day in the Sweat Shack had worn me out, and I didn't have much fight in me to begin with. Soon he was on top of me. His legs had my arms pinned by my waist. With one hand, he covered my mouth; with the other, he reached under the folds of his rumpled sleeping bag and found a buck knife still sheathed in a leather case. "When Johnny'd come to me, I'd be weak and give in. And he held it over my head, didn't he?" He put his forehead right up to mine and whisper-screamed, "Didn't he?" Keeping one hand gripped over my face, he worried the knife out of its case with the other, using his thumb to unbutton the leather strap from the handle, then he flung the full sheath off in one quick swipe. The blade had been blackened on purpose to prevent rust. "Oh, God," Father Drake was saying. "He would hang it over my head—threaten to tell Maudie if I didn't give him more, and then when he finally did tell her, he was all crazy and it didn't matter." He removed his hand from my mouth and waved the knife over my face. When he saw me the first day as I came walking up to the RV with Mother Maude, he thought he was seeing a ghost, he said. "But you're real and twice as crafty as ole Johnny ever was." He put the blunt side of the blade up to my face. "I could cut your face off, I could make you different, then you'd not mess with me." He raised the knife and then brought it down, slicing through the plastic flooring of the tent an inch or so from my face.

He wept into my neck, and while he went silent, I told him how I didn't want to be like Johnny. He became very still. "We have to stop them," I said. "They have to stay, so they can become better." His head leaned up, and he stared at something on my face and didn't seem to hear me. "We're almost finished with camp," I said. "We've come too far." His fingers rubbed the wet of his tears from my face. "What are you talking about?" he said, and I tried again, this time talking more slowly, telling him exactly what Dale had told me, their whole plan for escape to Orlando. But he wouldn't listen. He tried kissing me but missed my face when I squiggled out of his arms and rolled over. Now Father Drake was moving fast and erratic. He stood and unbuttoned his pants. "No," I said, and told him I was going to be sick. "This is what you want," he said. "This is exactly what you came for," and his penis flopped out, half-hard and shiny, the base of it ringed in sores from the lake. He took a step toward me, and I gagged, the bile rising to my lips. I had not eaten much today, so only a little vomit came out, but enough to shock Father Drake back to his senses. He kicked my shoulder. "Outside," he said. "This is where I sleep." I rolled out and dry heaved for several minutes.

"You better hope the camp is working," Father Drake said from inside the tent, "because you'd make one lousy faggot."

"I'm telling the truth," I said. "About Dale and them."

"Get on back to your cabin."

I remembered the proof. "Firecrackers," I said. "Dale put them under the stairs—if you don't believe me, go and look." I felt as if I were trying to save something that nobody cared about saving. I approached his tent. "We were both tested tonight," I told him. "We were both tested and didn't neither one of us fail. You didn't do anything," I knew I was stepping into a lie, but I was desperate. "You didn't do a thing to be ashamed of." He was putting his knife back in its case. "The way I see it, you got two choices, Rooster. You can go back to your cabin, or I can put you up in the Sweat Shack for a night. What'll it be?" I nodded, and he said he suspected I meant the former. I nodded again, and he said he thought so.

The interaction with Father Drake remained tangled up in my head as I made my way back to the Sleeping Cabin. I would need years to fully unwind it all, to understand how lucky I was to get away relatively unscathed. But I'm not trying to excuse my betrayal of the other boys or my stupidity in tattling on them despite all the evidence in the world, namely Father Drake's ruthlessness, that doing so was a bad idea. I can't defend it. I only want to explain, if I can, how my mind worked back then. I owed it to the camp, to my father, to God, but mostly I owed it to myself, to the man I was determined to become. I eased into the Sleeping Cabin, careful not to wake anyone. I rolled into my bottom bunk and wrapped my fetid covers around my legs. I had no sense of the danger I'd set in motion. I could only think of myself. Father Drake had offered himself to me, and I had been repulsed. In the wee hours of the morning, before I went to sleep, my last thoughts were hopeful ones: The treatment at camp had worked. It had, it had, it *had*.

W e awoke to gunfire. *Pow, pow, pow.* Someone shooting a semiautomatic rifle under our feet. *Pow, pow, pow.* We rushed outside, barefoot and sleepy eyed. It was still early, the sun not finished with burning away the last traces of night sky. *Pow, pow, pow.* Rick and Larry's tent beside the Chapel Cabin rattled and swished as the two counselors awoke to the noise and clamored outside to face the commotion. *Pow, pow, pow.* Father Drake sat on top of the picnic table, legs dangling off the edge. He was calmly slicing an apple with his black-bladed knife. *Pow, pow, pow.* The firecrackers finished, but the silence left over was worse than any racket. Rumil, Christopher, and Sparse gazed at Father Drake, at the counselors, at themselves, trying to figure out what these theatrics meant. A cloud of burned gunpowder billowed from under the stairs. Dale eyed the smoke, then Father Drake, and then his eyes, at last, landed on me. I couldn't meet them; still, he stared at me when he told the other boys to hurry back inside and put on their shoes. But they were too late. Father Drake had moved from the picnic table to stand between the entrance of the Sleeping Cabin and us.

"Orlando?" Father Drake chucked the apple core under the Sleeping Cabin. A piece of the fruit remained speared on the tip of his knife, which he carried in front of him like a torch. "Florida? Disney World?" He brought the knife to his mouth and sucked off the last bit of apple. He spoke with his mouth full, chewing. "Now I don't blame you for picking Orlando as your destination. Everybody knows there's no better place in this world for the homosexual than central Florida." We stood in front of him like we were in a lineup and he was selecting the suspected perpetrator. He hollered a

301

question to Larry over our heads. "What do you think of Disney World?" Larry said he didn't know enough about the amusement park to have an opinion. Father Drake asked Rick, and Rick just shook his head. "They don't teach y'all about amusement parks in seminary?" Father Drake laughed before either man could answer. "I told these boys," he said, speaking to the counselors as if we weren't around. "I told them the only way out of this camp was through me, and did they believe it?" He smiled at Dale. "Didn't I tell you that, mermaid?"

Dale kept his eyes on me. "Rooster," he whispered. "Will." Not angry but sad. The other campers played catch-up, putting it together all at once. "Dale?" Sparse rolled his eyes. "Please tell me you didn't—"

But Dale told them he had. "I messed up."

Sparse used his naked foot and kicked dirt in my direction. "You bitch."

Father Drake shook his knife at us to get our attention. "Yoo-hoo, boys," he said. "I think we need to talk about the matter of punishment." As he spoke, Dale took two steps backward toward the woods and the lake. The others looked too scared to move, and I was too exhausted from going to bed so late last night to care much about how Father Drake punished us. I wanted to crumple on the grass and nap until the afternoon. I almost thought of volunteering for the Sweat Shack. There, at least, I could sleep. "I hold no hard feelings," he was saying. "None at all, my children. But to make it right, we need an offering." The word "offering" pricked up my ears. A trap, I felt, was slowly closing in on us. "You see, when Rooster came to me last night and told me of your plan, I was mighty mad about it."

He pulled me over and made me stand beside him. "It seems our Rooster is more of a rat." He put his arm around me. With the other hand, he pointed the knife at them and talked faster. "Yes, I was going to make you bastards guzzle down gallons of Lake John so it could do to your insides what it has done to your outsides." He squeezed my shoulder. "I was going to put you all in the Sweat Shack, one at a time on an hourly rotation. When I got through with you, your parents wouldn't have much to take home this Sunday." Rumil and Christopher and Sparse listened intently, their mouths a little open, almost as if Father Drake were putting them in a trance. "But then I got to thinking about the ingenuity to think up such a plan and the willingness to take action. I got to thinking that real men, if that's what you're to be, must have guts." He paused. "Real men don't go tattling." At nearly the same time, the campers' heads moved from Father Drake to me, and Father Drake explained to them that the activity today would be a mix of reward and punishment. Reward for them and punishment for me. "A revised game of Smear the Queer. The rules will be suspended for, say, twenty minutes. In that time, there will be no balls, no points. Only you and the target." Father Drake mock-frowned at me. "The more you punish him, the less I will punish you." He asked Larry the time, and he said it was a quarter after seven. "Good," Father Drake said. "You can tell them when they can stop."

Father Drake shoved me into the middle of their line. "Go," he yelled. "Now!" I fell against Christopher and slid down. Once I was on the ground, he spat on me, a big loogie that landed on my forehead and in my eyes. Rumil and Sparse were circling me, getting ready to pounce. I remembered from our first night by the lake that neither of them were good at making the first move, which bought me a little time. While Father Drake and the counselors paid close attention to us, Dale was slowly distancing himself from the fray. It was as if he couldn't make up his mind which way to escape. I wanted to tell him to just run for it. Just go and don't look back. I knew what would happen next to me: Sooner or later one of them would draw the first blood and then the other two would be emboldened enough to join in.

I jumped to my feet and ran. I decided to run the opposite way from where Dale was going. The stickers in the grass needled my feet, but that just made me lift them faster off the ground. Rick and Larry had climbed to the top of the steps of the Chapel Cabin. They looked to be holding hands. As I passed through the cabins, headed toward the Sweat Shack and the abandoned house, Rick said, "You got fifteen minutes!" I dashed around the pile of burned furniture, and the other boys, gaining on me, were shouting, their words coming out garbled as if they were speaking underwater. "Just . . . let us . . . don't fight . . ."

I looked behind me to see, much to my surprise, that Christopher was in the lead, but Sparse and Rumil weren't far behind. They were only jogging while Christopher, red faced and huffing, was clearly giving it his all. I bounded into the woods and my pace slowed down considerably. Jagged sticks and broken pinecones and hard acorns. A floor riddled with traps hidden in the brush. I made it to the other side of the lake and looked around for a place to hide. I figured I would have a better chance to outlast the clock if I was hiding and saving my energy. On this side of the lake, few options presented themselves to me. The tent was too obvious. And Mother Maude was in the RV.

"Mother Maude!" I said to no one, realizing she was possibly my salvation. If I only explained to her what Father Drake was making us do, she would understand; she would stop this madness. I had about a minute before they'd come flying out of the trees. I beat on the side of the RV, slapping my hand on the door that led to the living quarters in the back. The blinds were drawn, and I panicked. She wasn't in there. I kept beating on the door, losing hope. Christopher limped out of the trees, coughing. He carried a thick tree limb that he'd picked up along the way. Soon, Sparse and Rumil appeared. The door to the RV swung open, and Mother Maude emerged, her head wrapped in a scarf. I grabbed her arm and she wrapped herself around me, held me tight. I tried to explain, but my words came out muffled against her bosom. "I know, my lamb, but this is the only way." I struggled, but she clung to me until Christopher was close enough, then she released, and he swung the branch. The stick landed against my kidneys, and I was thrown to my knees. Mother Maude moved out of the way to let me fall. Father Drake and the counselors had made it over and were hanging back by the tent, watching. Christopher swung again, and I turned in time for him to miss and strike the ground, breaking the limb in two. Sparse and Rumil were on either side of him, blocking me against the RV. I rolled over, flinging myself under the vehicle.

"How much time?" I screamed, and Larry screamed back, "Three minutes." I was not far enough in the center of the undercarriage, and Christopher was able to snag my ankle. Rumil caught the other one, and they pulled me out. They kicked and hit and clawed. Like me, they were worn-out; otherwise they would have killed me. Behind them, behind Mother Maude and Father Drake and the counselors, Dale trotted out of the woods. "Time," I called again, and Rick said, "One minute." I didn't think Dale would make it in time, but he picked up his legs when he heard the clock, turning his slow gait into a hustle. "Here, Dale," Sparse called, and he and Christopher hoisted me up. "You still got time to get a lick in." They moved me closer and locked me in their arms. Dale wasn't even looking in front of him. As he ran, he watched the ground. Father Drake waved him on. They were standing behind us, and Dale would reach us, and the adults would get front-row viewing to my clobbering. Rick yelled, "Time! Time's up!" Father Drake said he didn't give a damn what the clock said and hollered for Dale to make it count.

The other boys started chanting his name. "Dale, Dale, Dale!" He buffaloed toward me, big Dale, and I anticipated the feel of his body crashing into mine, the total obliteration of mine. If I were him, I would want nothing more than to make me into a grease stain. When he got about a yard away from me, I shut my eyes and braced for impact.

I felt the wind of Dale's giant body swoop past as he sidestepped us at the last second. He screamed and said, "Fuck you!" He powered forward, increasing his speed, taking the adults by surprise. Mother Maude screamed, and Dale barreled into them, catching Father Drake in the stomach. They rolled onto the ground and fought—or, rather, Dale threw punches and Father Drake covered himself. Mother Maude screamed for the counselors to help him, and Larry started to move, but Rick stopped him. Dale continued to hit Father Drake, not landing many of the punches, until Father Drake kneed him in the groin. He gasped and slumped off. Father Drake was spitting blood and struggling to collect himself. During the chaos of their fight, his knife had been knocked out and lay on the ground near slouching Dale. They spotted it at the same time and went scrambling for it. They both had their hands on the handle of the knife, the blade swinging between them.

"Y'all need to stop this," Mother Maude said, and it wasn't clear who she meant.

Sparse and Christopher released me, and we all dove toward Father Drake and Dale, trying to pull them apart. We became a mass of arms and legs flailing about as we had been on our first night. The knife disappeared in the press of bodies. We spilled onto the ground and rolled apart like magnets being repelled. Father Drake was facedown in the grass, not moving. Mother Maude ran to him and flipped him over and slapped his face until he seemed to be coming back to his senses. The rest of us slowly stood back up, looking sheepishly at one another.

"I hate this place," Sparse said.

"Me, too," I said.

Dale was the last of the campers to make it back to his feet. When Rumil saw him, he said, "Oh, Dale. Oh, Dale."

The knife's handle protruded from his belly. Dale glanced down at himself, and said, "I think—I think I am going to be sick." Very calmly, he wrapped his fingers around the handle and pulled the blade out in a slow suck.

I was the first to get to Dale. He was somehow still standing, blood seeping through his dirty yellow shirt. I put my hand over where I suspected the wound was and pressed down. He didn't move; he looked confused by the whole thing. "I think," he said again, "I think I am going to be sick." Blood was coming out faster now, dripping through my hand and down his legs. I removed my hand long enough to take off my shirt, wad it into a ball, and use it to staunch the flow. Behind us, meanwhile, a plan had formed without words. Rick was asking Mother Maude for the keys to the RV. Sparse, who had already jumped inside the camper to look for them, popped his head out of the door to announce they were in the ignition. I told Dale that I thought we were about to go for a ride. "We are gonna get you help," I said. "You are going to be fine." He told me it wasn't so bad. "I feel like I've been hit in the balls really hard," he managed to say, and then Christopher and Rumil were behind him, putting his large arms around their shoulders. I stayed in front, holding the blood in, and like this, we walked him to the RV and helped him up the stairs inside. Mother Maude had gone back to Father Drake, who was still prone on the ground, dazed. She was the only one who was speaking now, explaining to him what we were doing. "They are taking him to the hospital, honey. He had an accident. Do you hear me? The boys are leaving. You got to get up and help me now."

We got Dale onto the mattress in the back, then I removed my blood-soaked shirt and replaced it with a bedsheet. Dale asked me if I knew what I was doing, and I said not at all. He laughed a little and allowed me to wrap his stomach in the cotton fabric. The other boys had gathered in the back around us. "Why aren't we moving?" I asked them, and Sparse went to see. At the front, Mother Maude was at the side door of the RV, trying to get inside. Rick was in the driver's seat, telling her they had to move and that there wasn't enough room for her, but she was insisting that not all of us had to go. "I know what you're doing," she told us. "I know what you will say!" Larry blocked her entry but was hesitating. "Maybe we should—" But whatever else he was going to say was drowned out by the turn of the engine. Sparse took this as his cue and shoved Rick aside. "Get back, bitch!" he yelled and forced her away from the clear, then he shut and locked it. In another minute, Rick had us turned around and pointed down the dirt road.

The four of us settled around Dale on the bed. The bleeding had slowed, and when my arm got tired from keeping the sheet wrapped around him, Christopher took over, then Sparse. We tried to keep him talking, and it seemed to work for a little while. He told us to make sure when we get to the hospital to call his sister. "Not my parents," he said, and then he told us the phone number. He made us repeat it until we had it memorized.

Rick and Larry had decided to drive to the emergency room in Kosciusko twenty minutes away. They figured it was the closest. Rick was speeding, taking crazy turns, sending Mother Maude's collection of wigs and clothes flying out of the closet. "Jesus, that woman!" Sparse said. "The only taste she has is in her mouth." We held on to Dale to keep him as still as possible. I was sitting on the bed against the back wall, close to Dale's head, which I eventually placed in my lap. It was as heavy as I expected it to be, and the weight of it pressed into my groin, aggravating the sores. His eyes were open and he was talking, talking more than he ever had in the past three weeks, telling us about a roller coaster at Disney World. "A runaway train," he said. "That's what riding in this thing feels like." I tilted my head back and listened to him, we all did, knowing that as long as he kept on talking he would be okay. Christopher said that's what these paramedics did in this episode of *Rescue 911* he remembered watching, but then Sparse gave him a look, and he didn't make any more comments. I shut my eyes, and there was just Dale's voice. In my memory, the drive to the hospital took much longer than twenty minutes, but I'm sure this is wrong. Dale was chattering about how his parents would feel so guilty now that they would have to let him go and live with his grandmother and sister. "Or maybe they will let Laura come back to visit." He told us he was going to milk his injury for everything it was worth. "*Every* day," he said. "All day long."

When I opened my eyes, we were at the hospital, and everything had changed. Nurses in green scrubs and plastic gloves were inside the RV shouting questions at us. "Who's hurt? Who's hurt?" For them, it was hard to tell. We were coated in weeks-old dirt and grime, in clothes they would have to cut off, in skin they would have to disinfect. Dale's blood was on all of us, too. He lay at the center of the bed wrapped in the sheets, pale and stiff like a piece of furniture. The other boys were talking at once, not making any sense, and one by one, the nurses were hurrying them out of the RV. Dale's eyes looked up from my lap, glazed over and lifeless. The nurses came for us last. They needed to separate us, they said. They needed to get us help. I gripped Dale's big, ugly, awful head and wouldn't let go of him. "Please," one nurse pleaded, an older woman. Her name tag said Bernice. "Please," she said again, and they were pulling us apart anyway. And I screamed for them to *close his eyes*, but words were lost to me. As they carried Dale away, Bernice held me down, my puny nothing body convulsing in her arms, wild.

There are limits to my story. My recollections can send me in only a few directions—but no matter which way I go, I always inevitably return to the camp. I know of events that occurred in the Neck while Rick and Larry hurried us to the hospital. I don't exactly know how long it took me to untangle all of these knots of information—the bit I gleaned from what my father told me and from what I overheard at the trial during my one and only day in the courtroom. More still from what I read in Rick's memoir and the subsequent writings about it and the movie on the Internet. All of it coalescing to become the story I tell myself: After Father Drake regained full consciousness, he and Mother Maude squabbled over what to do next. Mother Maude wanted to follow us to the hospital, and Father Drake didn't. During their bickering, he must have revealed something that shocked his wife. I don't know this for sure, of course, but I certainly have my suspicions. Regardless of what he said to her, Mother Maude walked back through the woods to the cabins and the fire pit and the Sweat Shack. She found Rick and Larry's midsize sedan parked on the side of the road. The keys were in the ignition.

She drove Rick and Larry's car as far as Oklahoma and then disappeared from the authorities, telling those she met her name was Rosie. Here, her story becomes murkier. I know she died in a small house in San Bernardino. I've heard tell she was active in a small community church near her neighborhood, and the congregation reported her to be a reliable member, one who pitched in during fund-raisers for mission trips and inner-city-youth projects. And sometimes, on Christmas or Easter, she would be convinced to sing. "But we hated to ask her," the preacher of the church said in an interview. "Because the poor thing could hardly make it all the way through a song without crying." I don't know if she ever felt remorse for that summer, and I don't know if remorse would have made any difference to me or the others.

Father Drake never heard her leave that day at camp. He had gone inside his tent to nap. Like the campers, he had gotten very little sleep the night before. He had no way of knowing, I am sure, that he and Mother Maude would never, as far as I know, see each other again. He would be in prison when she died. That evening, a policeman came and found him still inside his tent, unmoving until the officer kicked Father Drake's foot. The policeman reported he must have been having some kind of dream. He jumped awake as if he'd been electrocuted. He apologized and said he thought the officer was the boogeyman coming to get him.

I have no way of knowing how much my testimony hurt or helped him at the trial. Even today, when I think of the knife and the fight, I cannot say if Drake stabbed Dale or if the knife got knocked in there by accident. While this may mean the difference in a court of law between murder and manslaughter, or between malice and accidental, the difference means very little to me. Father Drake, I know, didn't kill Dale all by himself. He had help from Mother Maude and from our parents who sent us there, who believed we needed radical treatment to better fit their ideas of who we should be. He had help from the counselors who stood by. He had help from me, too, who'd betrayed Dale in service of a lie that I knew to be a lie even if I had said and thought otherwise at the time.

After I gave my piddly, incoherent testimony at the trial, I had to sit in the courtroom with my legal representative until the court was adjourned. There weren't many people in attendance. None of the parents attended. Like I had been, the other boys would be ushered in by their legal representatives to give their spiels. Our parents allowed even this begrudgingly. Even Dale's didn't want charges to be pressed and wanted the whole business with the camp to go away. I often wondered if this lack of support on their part didn't play some role in Father Drake's lax sentencing, too. Everyone, it seemed, agreed Dale's death was a terrible accident, but they saw no need in

lingering over what happened. It would be better, my legal representative told me after the judge called a recess, if all parties involved
found some way to move on and forget about it. And I agreed with
him. Wholeheartedly. I wanted nothing more than to get back to my
new friends and my new life in Jackson.

As I exited the courtroom, I spotted two women in the very back
row. They were dressed as if they were going to church. It was an old
woman, maybe seventy, and her granddaughter. The granddaughter,
who I would come to realize was Dale's sister, Laura, wore a navy-
blue pantsuit with a button of the rainbow flag pinned to her lapel, so
tiny I almost missed it. They remained seated with their arms linked,
their eyes following. Once I was outside and alone, I ran. The day
was bright and warm. The more space I put between the courtroom
and me, between Dale's family and me, the easier it was to pretend I
hadn't seen them. To believe they weren't his grandmother and sister,
but just an old woman and a girl, nobody's anything.

Father Drake was sentenced to ten years of prison for accidental
manslaughter and the willful endangerment of a minor, and got
out for good behavior in three. Of course he would go back to the
Neck once he was released. I should have known, but I assumed he
was still in prison. He, for one, didn't look surprised to see me back at
camp. He seemed resigned. As if he believed all along I'd return, once
and for all, to complete my rehabilitation.

NINE

.

REHABILITATION

B y the time I finished my screaming, they held all the power. Father Drake had removed his hand from my mouth and stepped around me to stand beside the boy and the car. The boy, shaking, pulled a pistol from the back of his jeans, which he now was aiming directly at my skull. I managed a lie about having people in town who were waiting on me. Father Drake shook his head at this and said, "I speck Cake here will have his feelings hurt if you don't stay for lunch." He reached inside the driver's side and pulled out the keys from the ignition. "Plus, now that you are here, I want to discuss a little business matter with you." He leaned back against Doll's hood and shut his eyes. "I was awful shocked to find out Maudie deeded this land over to your daddy—she did it somehow before she died. Only reason I could reckon was to protect it from being taken by the law."

Cake dropped the gun long enough to wipe sweat from his face and swat at a horsefly lobbing around his blistered ear. Then he repositioned himself in his former stance with the gun, his torso hunched over one of Doll's open car doors. He sighed, apparently bored or frustrated by this reunion between Father Drake and me.

"Seeing as I'm her husband," Father Drake continued, "I thought it only right to seek my claim to the property. Looked up your daddy, and when I came calling, he wouldn't even let me through the front door—said the land was *your* inheritance." He spat, and said, "Now you think Maudie would have wanted that?" When I didn't answer, he spoke to Cake, asking him if he'd found enough food in my car to scrape together a meal for three people.

Cake loosened his grip on the pistol. "There's beans and shit. We can figure something out."

Father Drake, gazing over at his companion, appeared suddenly puzzled. He seized the mask still perched atop Cake's head. "What the hell?" He stuck his thumbs through the empty eye sockets. "What sort of foolishness you call this?" He slung the mask at me, and on reflex, I caught and pocketed it.

Cake shifted his fingers around the gun, revealing there wasn't any trigger. Only a metal rim, smooth and polished. The more I looked, the more I understood. The metal was too shiny for gunmetal, and it looked, in fact, more like plastic. I understood, and my body responded, exploding into a sprint. Yelping, Cake threw himself back into the car as I charged toward him and Father Drake. I darted by and skidded onto the gravel road. For his part, Father Drake remained where he was. He didn't chase after me or even holler for me to stop.

I kept on running as if they were right on my heels, my thighs burning as I flung my legs into longer and longer strides. A half mile down the road, I cut left into the tree line. My path became crazed in the clot of trees and brush. My only goal was to put as much distance between Father Drake and me as I could. I pushed deeper into the Neck, slowing down to a jog. It was cooler in the trees, less sunlight seeping through the limbs. Gnats and mosquitoes swarmed my face, blurring my eyesight. Swatting them away only slowed me down, so I pulled out the princess mask and placed it over my face for protection from the insects—the mask also served to muffle the sobs shaking loose from my chest.

The trees were so tightly packed I felt like I'd stumbled into a maze. My jogging became a brisk walk. I was exhausted, hungry, and lost. I had no way of knowing if I had backtracked closer to camp or moved deeper into the woods, into the wide stretch of the Neck where people wandered in and were never heard from again. Some of them, of course, probably wanted to get lost, but I wasn't sure if that was necessarily my goal. Finally, I stopped moving. Every direction looked the same: trees. Vines and weeds burst from the ground and twisted around and in between low-hanging branches, blocking most pathways. Too tired to fight my way through, I selected a shaded thicket underneath a warped pine that arched over the ground like a lamppost. I sat down. I had gone into the woods to elude capture, but now that seemed rash. Father Drake hadn't seemed too keen on chasing me down. Neither had the boy. I felt foolish. My neck and back ached; I itched and was in need of a warm shower, a new set of clothes. I had come full circle, it seemed, returned to the similar predicaments of my younger self at camp. Oddly enough, I didn't despair over this. For despair took energy I didn't have. I didn't mean to fall asleep. But I did, and the only time I realized I'd nodded off was when I woke up—very suddenly, with a jolt—to the sound of voices in the distance.

Evening in the Neck: The sky hung close to the earth, tacked above me by stars, its billowing darkness bleeding into the shadow below, crowding out anything discernible in the woods except noise. Crickets, frogs. And the voices of women—their laughter strange and tinny, like a recording of laughter from long ago. To my right, in the distance, the faintest glimmering of light. The yellow-red tongue of flames. I moved toward the light, my feet crashing through the brush. I made enough noise to announce my presence before I arrived. The chatter went silent. Their hideaway was a little opening in the trees, a meadow of monkey grass and ragweed and clover. In the center, a campfire popped and crackled, illuminating the wall of trees rising up on all sides, sealing in the two women like a house without a roof save for night sky. I wedged myself through. They stood, not alarmed, but on guard, reasonably suspicious.

They wore camouflage and matching trucker hats with their hair tucked through the backs in sloppy fat ponytails. The woman on the right was huskier than the one on the left, but both were broad shouldered and, there was no other word for it, *brawny*. The women were gripping metal rods with chunks of meat and vegetables speared onto them. The huskier one said, "Mister, you got a face underneath that mask of yours?"

"Oh, gosh—sorry." I had forgotten I was still wearing it. It occurred to me how frightening I must have looked, especially given the circumstances of the movie, as I had clawed my way out of the darkness into their campfire wearing this princess mask. I took it off and apologized again. "I didn't mean to startle."

The littler one said, "You can't scare us now. We know trouble when we see it." She sat back down and returned her kebab to the fire. The huskier one remained standing a minute longer, inspecting me. "You look rough, son," she said. "Here." She came around the fire to hand me an open mason jar half-filled with a cloudy liquid. "Take a nip." She returned to her post beside the other woman and I sampled the product. The liquor burned going down, but its aftertaste was sweet and left a pleasant tickle in my chest. "Why don't you take a seat," the littler one said.

I sat on my knees facing them, the fire bubbling between us. Neither woman asked for the jar back, and I took more swigs of the moonshine. Because I was drinking on an empty stomach, the alcohol worked fast on me, turning my joints to jelly and making my body limber enough for me to lean back on my elbows. When they finished roasting the kebabs, the littler woman scooted over and handed me hers. They shared the other one, blowing on the steaming meat and vegetables before using their mouths to pick it clean from the skewer. I followed their lead, chewing off a piece of meat first. "Is this venison?" I asked, and the huskier woman snorted. "Naw, honey," she said. "That's the best cut of flap steak money can buy at the Piggly Wiggly in Durant."

"I thought y'all might be hunters," I said.

The littler one said the only thing legal to hunt in the summer was wild pigs. "And they've been mostly rooted out nowadays."

"We're what you might call wildlife enthusiasts," the huskier one added, her mouth full of onion.

The explanation for their presence in the woods didn't square. I was drunk enough to press my luck. "You ever hear stories about the Neck?" I told them my mother used to tell me some, most of which I later found out were either wildly exaggerated or misconstrued. "She lied," I said. "But she lied beautifully."

"We heard a few of them," said the littler one. "One in particular about this camp where boys were sent to get fixed." She summarized the plot of *Proud Flesh*: "This boogeyman stalked the woods, a leftover from the camp, killing people left and right—heard it was a big mess."

The fire had weakened, and we could better inspect each other.

"I'm not the boogeyman," I said. "If that's what you think." I asked them if they knew about my mother's stories. "Did y'all hear about the moonshiners?" I shook my empty mason jar at them. "Or the women in the woods, moving from place to place so nobody would ever find them?"

"Nobody, that is, until the boogeyman came looking for them," the littler one said. Their faces went flat at the same time, and then the huskier one lurched forward suddenly, yelling, "Boo!" And I fell over, landing on my side to the sound of their cawing laughter. "Well, baby," the littler one said to the other, "I guess he done caught us. We *are* women and we *are* in the woods." They laughed some more until I righted myself back up.

"What are y'all doing out here then?"

The huskier one said, "Complicated. You?"

I held up the mask and shook it at them. "Same." The littler one asked me my name, and I said, "People here know me as Rooster." A look passed between them, the kind exchanged between two knowing parents about their child. "That may be what people call you," the huskier one said. "But who do you answer to? I mean, what do you want to be called?"

"Will," I said. "Plain and simple."

The littler one repeated my name, elongating the vowel sound. "*Wheel*," she said, giggling. "Like the tire?" The huskier undid the flap of the leather satchel beside her and pulled out another jar of moonshine and three mugs, each a different shape and size. She passed them around and then poured us each a swallow. "I'd like to make a toast," she said. "To my sweet love here and to our new friend Will, plain and simple." She paused as if something had just occurred to her. "To love," she said, "to love, plain and simple. I am plain and my sweetheart's simple."

We all roared with laughter now, our voices causing a ruckus of noise behind the trees. I stood. The ground tilted, and I stumbled down again. "Probably just a deer," the huskier one said, and the littler one came over to help me up. "Oh, honey, you *are* just a mess." She said they had an extra sleeping bag if I wanted it, and I tried to tell them that this felt like one of my spells. "I panic some-times," I said. "And the world goes weird." Two realizations came to me after I spoke: I'd not suffered one of these attacks since Mem-phis, and this one felt different. Not weaker but fading more quickly.

"*Shh*," the littler one said. "Ain't nothing wrong with you but a little too much hooch." With her help, I managed to sit back down on my perch in front of the fire, and then she returned to hers. I told them some people could be looking for me. "Might be dangerous." Neither seemed too concerned. They told me not to worry about it, either. Strangely enough, I wasn't. They'd been coming to these woods for years now, they said, and didn't nobody bother them unless they chose to be bothered. "Like by me?" I said, but they didn't answer, maybe because the answer was obvious. My face was slick with sweat, but I felt so cold inside, deathly cold. All the moonshine in the world couldn't remedy it. Only thing to do was remove it. Get it out. "You remember that camp you were talking about?" I said. "The one for the boys? Well, I was sent to it. My father sent me. About ten years ago. He loved me and thought he was doing the right thing. But it wasn't and a boy—he died, just like you said." The words came easy. I didn't feel better after saying them, exactly, but I didn't feel worse, either. My head cleared. At my feet was the princess mask. I picked it up—"His name was Dale," I was saying—and threw it into the fire.

That night I used their extra sleeping bag. I made myself a pallet on my side of the fire and went to sleep with the flames raging a few feet away from me, the two women talking and talking. The fire drowned out most of what they said. I heard only the shapes of their words, as if they spoke in a very old and forgotten language. With my belly full of moonshine and grilled meat and vegetables, I slept soundly, more deeply than I had in weeks, only waking once. It was very late, and the fire had been stomped out recently, with curls of smoke still crawling in the air. I leaned up, expecting to find the women tucked away in their own sleeping bags. Only they weren't. They were at the edge of the trees. They moved slowly, arms around each other's waists, turning round and round in a small circle. My eyesight blurred into double vision. The image of them echoed into several repeated images. There were many women in the dark now, multiplied over and over, dancing to music that must have existed only in their own heads.

The next morning the women were gone.

Beside the foot of the sleeping bag, I found the gifts they had left: another jar of cloudy moonshine, a magnetic compass the size of a fifty-cent piece, and a note written on a crumpled paper bag tucked under the jar of moonshine that said, in careful block lettering, to follow "due west" if I wanted to find my way out. Patches of morning sky were visible through the trees, pale blue and powdery. I held the compass in front of me and shifted my body until the little arrow closed over the W, then I walked. Several times I had to go southwest or even northwest for several feet until I discovered a passage through the bundle of trees. A half hour later, I staggered out of the woods in front of the gravel road leading to camp. When I reached my car, I remembered Father Drake had taken the keys, so I passed Doll by and went directly to the Chapel Cabin, where I suspected the two slept.

Father Drake was sitting on the Chapel Cabin's bottom step as if he'd been waiting for me to arrive. He was stock-still, and I suspected he'd been on that step all night. His eyes looked glassy, and he didn't seem to notice me there until I was a foot away from him. He blinked then, extending his arm and unfolding his fist in one almost graceful movement. He dangled my set of keys in front of him. "Cake said you'd be back before sunup—he didn't think you had the gumption to spend the whole night out in them woods." He was barefoot and wearing cutoffs that showed off a pair of old-man legs littered with bug bites and scabs. "You must of forgotten them stories the women in your family liked to tell." I snatched for the keys, and like a taunting child, he pulled them out of my reach in plenty of time for me to miss them. He reiterated his one stipulation from the day before: "You'll speak with your daddy for me?"

"You should move on," I said. "Try to get some help." I added that this was no way to live. "I can get you some help," I said finally. "Take you to a hospital or a shelter or something." Then I immediately regretted the offer; the thought of sharing a car with him for any length of time was unbearable.

"Help?" The word hiccupped from his mouth. His head dropped, and he began to laugh, all raspy. "You just can't *help* yourself, can you? Always the superior one. Thinking you know better. That's why them boys was so ready to beat the shit out of you. All I needed to do was to give them permission."

At camp, Father Drake had shared precious little about himself. Fragments I would have to put together later to form the story about his love for the uncle I never met. My resemblance to this uncle was enough to make me a target for his rage, and Dale became the poor boy unlucky enough to get caught in the crossfire. But Father Drake and I are not enemies, I know this now; he is not the villain of my story. I understand the rage that lives in him lives in me, too. We are made brothers by it. We grew up being told our love was filthy and wrong. And later we were drawn back to the camp, still fascinated by this place and its failed promise to restore us into the Almighty's fold. He was, and is and perhaps always will be, the distorted reflection of my own worst desire, which turned out not to be my attraction to the same gender but my longing to obliterate myself completely and remake something new and wholesome in its place.

But it would take time, many months after this interchange, for me to articulate these thoughts to myself. In this moment, with his ugly maw so close to mine, I only wanted to unleash ten years' worth of anger onto this man. So I flew at him, tackling his body off the steps. We slammed into the ground and rolled. He curled his body into a ball, the way an armadillo might, holding my set of keys close to his chest, clearly thinking that's what I wanted. Only when I threw my first punch did it occur to him that my goal was more basic. He twisted onto his stomach, his back taking the brunt of the beating. My knuckles rang with pain, digging deeper and deeper into his spine with each lick. "Cake!" he cried. "You, boy!" We were both weeping now. Spit drooled from my lips onto the back of his head. My punches devolved into slaps. Soon after, it was over and I lay on top of him, winded.

"Keep going, you bastard," he said. "Kill me."

I rolled off onto my back beside him. A bank of clouds the color of smoke slugged eastward.

"No," I said.

"Why not?"

I told him why, and he whirled around to look at me.

"What did you say to me?"

I sat up and said it again, then once more for good measure, screaming it. "I forgive you, you motherfucker!"

His old self, war ready and fast, returned. He was on me and had taken my shirt collar in his fist before I could move away. "What gives you the right to forgive me?" he asked. But this burst of strength was short-lived. He was an old man now, someone who'd had a remarkably hard life, and it was easy for me to hold him in my arms and let that old rage of his flare one final time then die out. Afterward, I stood, half carrying him to his feet with me. I told him how I might not have the right, but I was forgiving him all the same because I was tired of hating him. He pushed me back, and we lumbered away from each other.

He threw the keys at my stomach. "Just leave us alone."

Cake stood in the doorway, shirtless and rubbing his eyes with one hand, the toy pistol held down at his waist with the other. He climbed down the first step, paused, and observed the two of us as if we were figments of his imagination. He shook his head, still waking himself up. His skin was as pale as bone; the only coloring on him was the trail of pink pimples lining his collarbone and chest.

"Hey, Cake," I said, and his mouth screwed up with confusion. He pointed the gun at me halfheartedly. "I can take you somewhere— if you don't want to stay." He put the gun down, looked at Father Drake, and shook his head again, this time indicating no. "Cake's happy just where he is," Father Drake was saying. "Same as me. We're done with the world telling us it ain't got no place for us. Well, we ain't got no place for it. Do we, Cake?" Cake didn't answer and drifted back into the darkness of the Chapel Cabin.

Before I left, I mentioned to Father Drake about Larry's plan for the campgrounds, speaking louder so Cake could hear me, too. "This place is going to change," I said. "Maybe for the better, maybe for the worse, but it's changing."

Father Drake told me I came back to the camp for a reason, and telling him about that wasn't it. "But I think I know why." He limped up to the top stair of the Chapel Cabin. "Why don't you just stay here with us, Rooster, boy!—come inside the Chapel Cabin, and we'll love on you and keep you safe." He held out his arms. "We can all just be here at camp and let the world burn."

I told him over my shoulder as I walked away that I'd already spent far too much of my life at camp. "It's everywhere else I got to work on figuring out." But I wasn't saying this aloud for his benefit.

The drive to Bucksnort took up the rest of the morning. I parked Doll, all dusty and corroded, down the road from my father's double-wide. I walked the rest of the way because I needed another few minutes to collect myself before I stood on his doorstep. Never mind I'd had three hours on the road to mull over what to say to him. I expected resistance on his part. I expected him to take off his glasses and rub his eyes at my request. "I just don't know," he would say, I figured. I planned out my response accordingly. I would have to explain to him, at long last and with no evasions, the terrible legacy of Camp Levi. I would be clear about our roles in the debacle, his as well as mine. I would be firm in telling him how this plan for the other camp, if carried out correctly, represented a chance for us to achieve some measure of redemption. The dramatic language was intentional. Words like "legacy" and "redemption" would appeal, I hoped, to his love of rhetoric. I expected the conversation to be tense, for there to be a rough back-and-forth, but ultimately I expected him to relent. I didn't expect, however, what I discovered at his home when I arrived.

Zeus would later disagree with me on this point. He would believe, or claim to believe, that I had somehow orchestrated this reunion that followed for—in his words—"maximum dramatics." He would point out that I must have known Bevy would be worried to the point of hysteria when I stopped taking their calls. He would say that I had called their bluff and that they had folded. After scouring the Internet and engaging in mild forms of electronic stalking, Bevy tracked down my father's address. When Bevy called him, the search for me officially began. Believing they could do more, Bevy and Zeus bought plane tickets to Jackson, and after they'd touched down, they rented a car and drove into the heart of the Mississippi Delta, a place neither of them had ever been before. They made it to my father's the day before while I was wandering, lost, in the Neck. Since then, they had already contacted the local police and were waiting to hear back from them. Bevy, in keeping with her general distrust of the law, wanted to go looking for me herself, but Zeus had convinced her to wait to hear back from the police, then they would make plans accordingly. At lunch, they had all gathered in the living room to discuss strategy. As I was walking up the front lawn toward the door, a deputy had called my father to tell him the latest on my whereabouts. He took the call in his daughter's bedroom, and his wife decided to make lunch for everyone— ham-and-cheese sandwiches. She and their daughter stepped into the kitchen, leaving Bevy and Zeus on the couch to wonder in whispers if I was even still alive. "Surely he wouldn't?" Bevy asked Zeus, and Zeus said, "No, not intentionally anyway." Which, they later reported to me, didn't make them feel any better.

I was climbing up the concrete steps that led to the double-wide's front door, finding it wide open. For this reason, I didn't knock. Zeus would suggest later that I wanted to surprise them all at one time. The truth was, I was afraid to knock. Afraid they'd take too long to open up and I would chicken out like before. I pulled on the screen door, and it squeaked open, but nobody heard. I knew they were home; three cars were in the driveway, one of them belonging to Zeus and Bevy, though I didn't know that yet. Instead, I assumed they had visitors, and I was crashing into the middle of something. I stepped into a little foyer with a mirror to greet me. With my tousled hair and dirty clothes, I looked as if I had just survived a hurricane, but it was too late to worry about that now, I told myself. I was walking into the living room, my mind racing with what I should say first. I was walking into the place where, days ago, I had seen my father singing alongside his new family. I decided now to lead with an apology—*Sorry to bother, I don't mean to intrude, but.* I entered the living room in the middle of two people deep in conversation. I blinked and looked again. At first, I regarded them as hallucinations until they slowly became aware of my presence. They were still in the clothes they'd worn to bed the night before, warmups and oversize T-shirts, when they went to sleep on twin air mattresses in the dining room of my father's house.

Bevy glanced over at me first. "Holy shit," she said dully. "Holy shit, holy shit."

I was just as baffled. "The fuck is going on?" I said.

Zeus stood, more angry than surprised. "You tell us, bastard. Why you stop answering the phone, huh?" He poked at my shoulder, and we continued to argue like this while my father's wife and daughter were returning from the kitchen with food.

My father's wife was carrying a tray of sandwiches into the living room when she found Zeus and me still arguing over who was more at fault. I had lost my temper. "You were the one," I reminded him, "who went silent on me first!" The tray crashed onto the carpet, and our quarrel stalled. My father's wife called out to him. "Frank! You better get on out here."

"That's Lila," Zeus said.

"Who?"

He pointed to my father's wife. "Your stepmom."

Behind her, their daughter appeared. "What's that smell?" she said, for she would tell me later, along with everyone else, that I stunk. When she realized the smell belonged to a person, to me, this strange-looking man with bits of grass and pine straw in his hair, she stopped asking that question and replaced it with another one: "Who is *that*?" Everybody ignored her. Bevy sank back down on the sofa, her jaw locked shut for once, her eyes wide and unblinking. Zeus took a step closer to me and slapped dirt off my shoulder. And Lila kept calling for her absent husband. Meanwhile, I stood at the center of them gazing down at the girl, my sister. "Her name," Zeus said, enjoying himself, "is Cecily."

My father wasn't paying attention to the commotion in his living room because he was, he'd tell me later, busy talking on the phone with the sheriff, trying to understand the latest on my whereabouts. They had found nothing yet, the sheriff told him, adding that he should "hold tight." He burst out of his daughter's room, his face flushed.

When she saw our father emerge, Cecily chanted her questions at him. "Who is this, Daddy? Daddy, please! Who is that?" I inched backward toward the door. Here he was, my father. In his late fifties, in a green polo shirt. "Who is it?" he said, repeating his daughter's question back to her. Then he rushed me. As in the sanctuary when he came barreling toward me years ago, I had few precious seconds to brace myself for however his feelings would break over my body. He pulled me to him and shoved his face into my neck, into my prickly under beard. "I'd have known this boy anywhere!" he said. "Anywhere." Still holding me in his arms, he lifted me off my feet and turned us around so that he faced his daughter. He spoke to her over my shoulder. "Sugar pie," he said at last. "This here's your brother, and his name is Will."

TEN

∎

RELEASE

Around the one-year anniversary of the release of *Proud Flesh,*
Sparse gives an interview in an entertainment magazine. In it,
the reporter asks him about his movie's much-debated ending. "People are mixed," the reporter says. "Some think it's a political statement
and others bark about it being an exploitation of what actually happened and a few claim it's actually a failure of imagination. What do
you say?" In the article, the reporter writes that Sparse's face "curled
into a smile" at the question. "Obviously," she writes, "this is not the
first time he's been asked this, and each time he has given variations of
the same answer. Now he smiles and shrugs." Sparse replies, "Why
can't it be all three? I did the ending I wanted, and people are welcome
to respond to it however they wish—that's none of my business." Not
long after I returned from Mississippi, Sparse admitted to being sent
to the camp that the movie was based on. When the reporter reminds
him of his time at Camp Levi, Sparse references the book. "*The Summer I First Believed* is not a bad book; it's just Rick's version. I wanted

to retell it, I wanted to twist it to my own devices, to my own understanding of truth, and this is what I came up with." The interview concludes with the reporter asking if he had any thoughts about how the camp he'd gone to was redone into a retreat for gay teens. Here, he is his clearest and most resolute. "No."

I stumble across the article while at work at the library and photocopy it and take it home for Zeus to read. At first, he can only laugh. "You do know," he says, "that you could have probably found this online and saved yourself the trouble." I maintain that it wasn't any trouble—none at all. Ever since I started my job at the library, I have begun to treat old-fashioned ways of consuming text with more respect. Zeus thinks I'm slowly becoming more and more twee. "If you start smoking a pipe," he told me once, "adios!" Over dinner, Zeus reads the article, and we spend the rest of the evening discussing the subject of endings. Now we both are writing—his process is slow, a paragraph or a sentence a day, while mine pours out pages at a time. It's as if I were trying to finish it, my reckoning with that summer, before I lose the nerve. At night, before bed, we sometimes share what we've worked on. When the writing's good, we make love to celebrate, and when the words force a painful memory to surface, we hold each other and whisper the hurt away. More often than not, our work is neither, and we bicker over how to go about fixing things, but even then, our disagreements lead us, more often than not, back to having sex.

Tonight he tells me how queer endings are remarkably easy to fuck up. "But neither of us died, so I guess we've already crossed the biggest hurdle." We're in bed, naked, our legs locked together under the sheets. I tell him I should end my story here, in this very moment, and he bristles. "That makes me want to throw up in my mouth a little," he says. "Too much cheese." This has become his favorite critique of my work. "You don't want the ending to be *too* happy," he says.

I don't tell him my fear that our relationship is doomed. Six months after we returned from Mississippi, Zeus and I moved in together. "Not as fast as lesbians," Bevy remarked to me in private. "But close." In the months following my impromptu road trip, I ditched my dissertation and suspended graduate school and soon got a job as a clerk at one of the branch libraries in the city. Between our incomes, Zeus and I were able to afford a nicer living arrangement than both of us could have had on our own. I left my run-down garret and my noisy neighbors, Elementary Ed and her Great Dane, for two bedrooms, two bathrooms, a living room, a full kitchen, and—perhaps most important—a boyfriend who knows how to tell a story and, as a plus, can coax me into telling my own. The apartment's downtown, within walking distance to the hospital where Zeus works. It's the first time either of us have lived with such nice amenities—a dishwasher we revere and a garbage disposal we've yet to fully figure out though we have our theories.

Lately, I've been worrying we would run out of stories to tell each other at night and that our love, if that's what this is, would wither. So far, we've not been faced with this problem. Each time I suspect he's told me every possible fragment from his life, he will surprise me with another family story of some distant aunt or cousin back in Puerto Rico. Similarly, I've found that with him I am able to retrieve new memories that have lain dormant inside me for years until he poses some innocuous question that breaks the memory loose from my mouth.

I confessed to Bevy my fear once. By then she had passed the bar exam and felt herself entitled to give all kinds of advice, legal or otherwise. She told me that she was shocked to hear me talk this way. "You mean you're actually afraid that you and Zeus will run out of things to say to each other?" She snorted. "Oh, baby, welcome to relationships—you're so *normal* now."

After mulling over possible endings, Zeus tells me I should end with the new camp. "It's the most obvious, but also—possibly—the most satisfying." But the reasons for not ending there seem glaringly apparent to me. "For one," I told him, "I didn't go to the orientation." None of the original campers from Camp Levi attended. Larry invited us, but we had, individually, declined. I think we liked the idea of the new camp, but we didn't necessarily want to have to be there again, in the heat of the summer, at a place that we'd all, in some way or another, put behind us. I'd not spoken to Rumil or Christopher since Memphis, and I imagined it would always be awkward between us. "That doesn't matter," Zeus says. "You can focus on your father's deal he made you agree to before he signed the deed over—or you could talk about Father Drake and what happened to him."

The first thing Zeus was referring to was my father's request that I call him at least once a month and visit a minimum of twice a year. My father wanted me to give him my word that I would let him be a part of my life, and I gave it, thinking our habit of silence would be harder to break than he realized. But so far, he has been consistent, almost annoyingly so. If we're ever approaching a month when he's not heard from me, he will call, and call, and call until I answer. He says, "I was just making sure you were still enjoying that fine piece of property I gave you," and I apologize, and then we talk. Sometimes we talk about nothing in particular, the little happenings in our lives: my new job, Cecily's first day of kindergarten. Sometimes we reminisce about our hardest moments together and acknowledge to each other all those old feelings that needed acknowledging. It is taxing, and afterward, I feel exhausted, as if I'd just completed a long session of cardio at the gym, my heart thundering in my chest.

Zeus also mentioned I should end with Father Drake. Because the police had been looking for me, they eventually checked the campsite at the Neck before word traveled that I had shown up at my father's, and they found him and Cake there instead. The police were suspicious of Father Drake and took him and the boy into custody for questioning. Cake's family was notified, and an aunt and uncle in Little Rock agreed to take him in, and he stayed with them for a month before having an argument with the uncle that sent him back on the road. Father Drake was held overnight in a jail cell and released the next day, with the sheriff of Attala County forbidding him to return to the camp. As far as anyone knows, he didn't.

At the new camp this summer, however, the boys and girls described seeing strange things in the woods. Larry believed it was the influence of the movie playing with their perceptions. After camp had concluded, he called to give me a full report, telling me the sightings were nothing to worry about. Overall, the two weeks went very smoothly, he told me, and I agreed to renew his lease on the land for another year but not before having him delve into more detail about what the campers had seen. Some reported seeing a man, he said. He would come just to the edge of the trees, and like a spooked animal, he'd run off if one of the campers spotted him. But that wasn't the only kind of sighting in the Neck. Other campers claimed to see various kinds of people in the woods, the most popular description being a pair of women. They didn't run from the campers but waved at them as they passed through. "But that's just stories, stuff they told at the campfire," Larry told me. "You know as well as I do that nothing can live in the Neck."

We're still lying in bed, Zeus and I. He's tweaking my nipple and tells me I should make sure to credit him now for the ending. "In the acknowledgments," he says. He has been working on his own memoir for several years but hasn't finished because, as he's told me, he hasn't completed becoming the person he wants to be. "I'm still moving," he says. "But I haven't settled." I tell him that sounds like a cop-out. For this, he tweaks my nipple harder and I yelp. He says, "Okay then—how about this: I'm not ready to write my ending yet—once you write it, then you have to start thinking about putting it out in the world for other people to read." I say that doesn't make any sense, and he says that he wants me to be his only audience. "For now," he says. He hasn't been home in nearly five years, not since he began transitioning, and he tells me this has something to do with his hesitation. He surprises me by summoning my mother. She didn't, he believes, tell me those stories for my benefit, at least not entirely. "She told them," he says, "because she longed for it—your mother loved the Neck despite everything and knew she couldn't go back." Before I can argue, he says to me, "But you can't go back, it's yours, and you love it, too." Then he corrects himself. "Well, maybe not love, but you *understand* it."

"Do I, though?"

He doesn't say anything. Partly because this is a question we will need to ponder for many more nights, maybe years, before an answer can be decided upon. There's a comfort in this. He returns his head to my chest, and I ask if he wants to hear my idea for an ending. He says, "Shoot." I begin to tell him about the afternoon at my father's house, the day I returned. After our emotions calmed down, Lila had suggested we barbecue ribs. "I was there," Zeus says, interrupting me. "I remember." But he doesn't really mind hearing this again. He has taken great pleasure in retelling this story himself to some of our friends: how he and Bevy decided to come save me from Mississippi and then ended up staying there for a reunion celebration. While my father grilled under the shade of the trailer's awning, the rest of us sat outside on the deck. Cecily had taken a particular interest in me and had decided to ask me all the questions nobody had answered for her during all the excitement: "Where did you go? Why did you go there? Who did you see?" I tried to be as honest as I could with a four-year-old, and Zeus and Bevy often interjected to ask me to elaborate on, things they had never heard until now.

When I told them about seeing the two women in the woods, Lila shot up from her seat to say she had just remembered something. She went inside the trailer and came back out seconds later with a wooden box I hadn't seen in years. "I wanted your daddy to mail this to you, but he was worried it'd get too banged up in transit." Inside, there were all the old familiars—the tiara, the sash—but also wedged in there was my notebook, the one I'd written in shortly after my mother died. Cecily came over and peeked in. She took out the tiara and examined it. A few more rhinestones had fallen out, but it still sparkled. Cecily had very serious eyes, the same eyes as my father, and when she stared at me without blinking, I discovered that I would do whatever she asked of me. "Lean," she said, and when I did, she placed the tiara on my head. She pushed the combs deep into my scalp. Cecily plucked the book from the wooden box and got into my lap. "Now," she said, flipping through the pages. "What is this?"

"Words," I told her.

She rolled her eyes. "Read," she commanded.

And so I did. I read her all those pretty lies my mother had told me, and Zeus and Bevy scooted closer to hear them. When my father got the ribs started on the grill, he joined us on the deck. He told us dinner would be ready shortly. Then he asked if I wanted to take a shower. "No offense, son," he said. "But you smell ripe."

Cecily howled with laughter.

"Hmm," Zeus said, examining the crown. "Your hair's so tangled you'll probably have to cut that thing out of your head to get it out."

"Or," my father said, as he went over to kiss his wife, "he can just leave it in. I'm sure his mama wouldn't have minded."

D o you remember him saying that?" I ask Zeus, but he's snoring now. Gently I slide from our bed and tiptoe into the next room, our second bedroom that we use as an office. I sit down in front of our desktop and go online. This has become a ritual of mine. Come in here alone, in the dark, and look her up on the Internet. As with most everyone, she was easy to find. Tonight, like always, I compose her an e-mail. Many times I have intended on sending one to her, but I've never quite worked up the courage. All my talk of endings tonight with Zeus, however, has me convinced that I might follow through with it this time. In the e-mail, I write how I have been working through the details of that summer. I tell her how her brother was the main reason for my survival, and how, until very recently, I hadn't lived the sort of life worth saving. Once I finish the e-mail, I'm confident I won't hit delete, not this time—but then I read it over. On second thought, I doubt these are the right words to send, so I hit backspace and try again. I begin the new e-mail by telling her how I remember seeing her and her grandmother in the courtroom that day. I write how sorry I am for not contacting her sooner, but I was afraid, a coward, and I am trying to be braver now. I try and try and try every day, all day long.

ACKNOWLEDGMENTS

■

First, I want to thank my family in Mississippi. I never take their love and support for granted.

No book is ever written alone, and this one exists because of a series of talented and bighearted teachers who helped me along the way. I am a product of several public universities, and I want to give my professors their due because, Lord knows, most of them were probably woefully underpaid for the amount of time this young and overeager and (possibly) high-strung writer spent in their company, mostly during office hours: Andrea Mooney (who introduced me to Eudora Welty's work by telling me how I reminded her of Sister from "Why I Live at the P.O.") and Billy Wilson at Holmes Community College in Goodman, Mississippi; Carolyn Elkins, Bill Spencer, Susan Allen Ford, John Ford, John Pursley III, Dorothy Shawhan (who was the first novelist I ever met in person), Bill Hays, Beverly Moon, Marilyn Shultz, and everybody else in the land of the Fighting Okra at Delta State University; Rich Lyons (mentor-at-large), Michael Kardos (who lured me from poetry to prose), Catherine Pierce (the person I pretend to be when I'm leading workshops and get nervous), Becky Hagenston (whose stories are better than anything I will ever write, period), and all the wonderful people at Mississippi State University in Starkvegas; Michelle Herman (Goddess Divine), Lee (and Cathy!) Martin, Kathy Fagan, Erin McGraw, Andrew Hudgins, and Lee K. Abbott at Ohio State

University—many of them are now my colleagues at OSU and their influence has made me a better human; Jonis Agee (who said, "Yes, you will write a novel," and put my book in the right hands), Tim Schaffert, Stacey Waite, Amelia Montes, Joy Castro, Jennine Crucet, Chigozie Obioma, Melissa Homestead, Marco Abel, Grace Bauer, Ted Kooser, Kwame Dawes, and the rest of the distinguished and generous faculty in the Department of English at the University of Nebraska at Lincoln. Higher education gave me courage and set me free. These people are my heroes, and I love them.

I also have several dear hearts to thank (in no particular order) who gave me encouragement and feedback and love when I needed it the most: Asha Falcon, Kathleen Blackburn, Shelley Wong, Christie Collins, David Johnson, Silas Hansen, Dillion and Jacquie Dunlop (thanks for listening to me that one night), Leslie Adams, Brad Vice, Dan White, Abigail Voller, Jessica Mann, Raul (and Mix!) Palma, Lauren Galietti, Doug Lane, Marianne Kunkel, Amina Gautier, Sarah Fawn Montgomery, Robert Lipscomb (who always sees the potential in my drafts, no matter how horrid they happen to be), Jamie Brunton, Katie McWain, Stevie Seibert Desjarlais, Jordan Farmer, James Crews, Sam and Nancy Zafris, Erin Busbea (the best damn librarian in the world, possibly the universe), Hattie-Frank Maloney (I remembered!), Garrard Conley (his book cleared the path for mine), John Rechy, Claire Vaye Watkins, Brett Beach, Molly Patterson, Preston Witt, Elise Randall, Annie McGreevy, Ashley Cavada, Rebe Huntman, Ann Glaviano, Gabe Urza, Ali Salerno, Derek Palacio, Jill Patterson, Christopher Coake, Linda Garcia Merchant, Dave Madden, Geeta Kothari, Ellen Graham Weeren, Jill McCorkle, Marcus Jackson, Lina Ferreira, Gale Massey, Rebecca Makkai, Steve Yarbrough, Randall Kenan, Garth Greenwell, Belinda Acosta, Maria Nazzos, the wonderful writers and readers at the Sewanee Writers' Conference, the good people at the *Kenyon Review* for inviting me around and letting me sit at the cool table, Justin Taylor, Matthew Frank Dadonna (who took a chance on a book and an idea), and—last but certainly not least—Joshua D. Kertzer (who took a chance on me).

Noah Ballard is the best agent a boy like me could ever want or need in this life. He's the Mickey to my Rocky, the Rhoda to my Mary, the Lady to my Tramp. Many thanks, too, to Curtis Brown, Ltd., for all their support.

Kathleen (or "Kate the Great" as she is known around my house) Napolitano is steadfast and true, a fearless and kind editor—this book is a testament to her patience and keen insight. I won the lottery when she became my editor.

Thank you to Rebecca Strobel for keeping us all on track and focused during the process of bringing this book to life. She's the bee's knees. Thank you to Aileen Boyle and Kayleigh George, who gave me invaluable counsel and advice. Thank you to Hailey Hershberger and Gwyneth Stansfield, who helped me spread the good word. And many, many thanks to David Hough and Joel Breuklander, for saving my ass, time and time again.

I want to add my appreciation to everyone else at Blue Rider, especially David Rosenthal, for treating me so kindly during this wild rodeo. As Minnie Pearl once said, "I'm just so proud to be here."

My acknowledgments could go on and on and take up more pages than the novel itself. If I have forgotten anyone (and it's likely I have) then please use my carelessness to your advantage and guilt me into buying you a drink. Nowadays, we could all use one.